WRAITH LORD

BY C. T. PHIPPS

CHAPTER ONE

When I dreamed, I dreamed of the days when I was still human. That was two and a half centuries in the past, a different age, and things had been simpler then. Terrible but simpler. The King Below had invaded the Southern Kingdoms with his armies of Shadowkind for the fourth and penultimate time.

Villages were put to the sword, citizens were carried off by the hundreds, and terrifying creatures roamed the land killing with impunity. The roads were crowded with refugees, bandits, deserters, and farm animals.

In many places, those seeking relief from their fellow man were enslaved or turned away. The only hope for these unfortunates was the collected armies of the Anessian Empire and its allies. These forces were a motley collection of conscripts and levies collected by ruthless nobles who hated each other more than they did the King Below's horrors.

In my dream, I rode on the back of a brown Imperial warhorse, I kept pace with a luxuriously saddled chestnut G'Tay mare. I, Jacob Riverson, rode beside Jassamine, the first great love of my life, across a muddy back road in the Gael Lowlands.

We were near the front of the war, Winterholme and the now-destroyed nations of Chodar and Ren having fallen in the past year. Despite this, I treasured the opportunity to spend time with my lover. We rarely got to see one another in those days, with my recent promotion to Knight Commander and her rising status in the Imperial Court.

Jassamine had been a beautiful woman in her late twenties with olive skin and twisted hair she had pulled up in the manner that befit the Imperial patrician class. She wore a purple toga with a heavy gray hooded cloak. Gold necklaces and jewelry adorned her fingers and throat. A ghostwood staff was attached to her saddle for ease of drawing against potential foes. Desperate men might see her as an easy mark, but such fools would find themselves swiftly overwhelmed by one of the Mysterium's master mages.

The farmland we were passing through was uninhabited, and had been for weeks, tools abandoned on the ground and crops left to rot. Crows were pecking out the eyes or hanged corpses that had been left to decay long after they should have been cut down for burial. There was no sign these men had been hanged for a crime, and I couldn't help but imagine they were people mistaken for looters by whatever locals remained.

"In the next few months, the people are going to look at this corn and maize's decaying remains and wish they had harvested it. People are already slitting each other's throat in Kerifas and Castule for bowls of stew," Jassamine said, shaking her head. "The smart men are cooking the dead and selling the meat as such."

"Farms don't magically harvest themselves," I said, gesturing around us. "It takes hundreds of strong backs to plow, reap, and grind this much produce."

"I forgot you used to be one of these people," Jasmine said, grinning.

"I still am," I said, smiling. "I am a shit-stained peasant from hair to toenail."

Jassamine just laughed.

I was mildly offended, despite the fact she was right to laugh at the idea. I was a Knight Commander of the Shadowguard now, having risen rapidly through the ranks since the war began. I wore a fine black cloak over enchanted scale-mail with numerous runes woven into the plates. My swords alone were worth the price of a small farm, but with them I could kill the King Below's strongest monsters. In the past year alone, I had paid the empire's investment back many times over.

"Some nobility is inherited and some nobility is earned," Jassamine said, looking to the horizon. "I think you have more than proven that you deserve the latter."

"I have no interest in the pomp and ceremony of the aristocrat's life. I came to the capital to help people and that's what we're doing.

After this war, I don't intend to sit upon a throne overlooking a bunch of peasants as they break their backs so I can take their next meal."

"Even for me?" Jassamine asked.

I looked at her. "I'm not sure what you mean."

Jassamine shook her head. "Come, let us continue our survey. We can get some press gangs together to harvest this territory's crops along with the other villages we've scouted. With the excess food, we can save a few thousand lives this winter."

"We should consider preserving it for the army," I said, not happy to say it. "Every soldier who eats is another to fight the King Below's madness. It won't do any good to feed those who don't fight if they're just going to become fodder for the undead."

"That is remarkably cold-blooded of you."

"Another fact of being born a peasant. You know how the world really works." Truth be told, I'd been making a lot of hard decisions lately.

And they were getting easier.

There was a rustling in the corn around us and I glanced at Jassamine. I'd known there were people moving around through the corn out of sight, perhaps even considering robbing us, but I had hoped they'd be smarter than that.

Apparently not.

A group of almost a dozen of the local farmers moved out, more than I'd expected, armed with makeshift weapons. Men, women, and children who looked haunted in a way even worse than most refugees I'd encountered. Their clothing was ragged and patched but not so much I believed they came from much further than the nearest village. Something had happened to them, though, because I could sense the desperation in their eyes.

Their leader, a tall elderly woman with white hair and a mole on her cheek, pointed at me with a long fingernail. "You two folk will be emptying your purses and leaving your goods on the ground. We'll also be taking your horses. Everything."

I looked at her, blinking. "Why?"

"I think they're threatening us," Jassamine said. Without drawing attention to herself, she used her right hand to make the mystical sign of the Adaras.

"Oh?" I said to the old woman, feigning indifference.

"Fuck talking! They're responsible for this! Them and all of their kind!" One of the would-be-bandits lifted a crossbow and pulled the trigger. The bolt sailed through the air only to smack against the newly erected magical barrier around us. The bolt fell to the ground, plopping into a muddy puddle beside us.

That caused three of the peasants to flee outright.

"Cowards!" the crossbowman shouted.

I stared at his weapon, concentrated, and snapped my fingers. The weapon burst into flames, causing him to jump backwards. Almost all the remaining peasants scattered at that. One young woman, braver than the rest, tried to stab me in the back with a pitchfork. The barrier, which covered us on all sides, caused the old, rusty prongs to break. I had to admire her courage and made a mental note to see if she wanted a job in the Imperial Legion.

"Of all the people in the world to rob, it'd have to be two wizards," the old woman muttered, clearly resigned to whatever happened.

The crossbowman drew his dagger, not yet realizing the fight was over.

Jassamine made several gestures with her hand. The crossbowman then put the knife to his neck and she prepared to make him slit his own throat.

"Stop," I said. "There's no need to shed blood."

Jassamine gave a half-amused laugh. "I believe you are the only one who believes that, Jacob."

"We can't stop you; get it done," the old woman said. "Just know it was my idea and my grandchildren are not responsible for this."

Jassamine sniffed the air. "That doesn't mean much in cases of banditry and treason."

"Treason?" I asked.

"Just adding a bit of spice," Jassamine said. "Of course, I don't think these are common bandits."

"Strong words from a woman who never worked a day in her life," the old woman said.

"I could speak of the horrors and abuses I've endured as a half-caste woman of Natariss, but I have little care to explain myself to those who would rob me," Jassamine said, glaring down at the woman. "Instead, I must ask you where you got your demon brand?"

The old woman pulled back in horror, covering the black mole on her right hand. The other two reacted as well, covering their neck and oft-hand respectively.

I almost cut them down where they stood.

Demon marks were one of the "gifts" the King Below bestowed upon his followers. They were a means for his agents to identify one another in foreign lands, but had lately been more often bestowed upon those forced to participate in his rituals at sword-point. Because armies could not tell who sincerely followed the Trickster and who had been coerced, most simply put them all to the sword. I encouraged it, in fact.

"It wasn't our choice!" the young woman behind me hissed. "It showed up a month ago, killing every man and woman who stood against it. We tried to flee but it corralled us back here, killing others. It makes us...do things. Give it sacrifices. It's why we wanted your horses and gold—we can't live like this anymore."

As much as I hated those who willingly betrayed the path, under duress or not, I couldn't help but ask, "What is 'it'?"

"A Nuckelavee," the old woman said.

I cursed under my breath. Nuckelavee were powerful mid-tier demons in the service of the King Below. One this far south meant that the enemy's forces were already starting to corrupt the local populations. It meant that we had to move fast if we weren't going to have to destroy everything between us and Winterholme. The Dark Lords and their servants were masters of breaking human will.

Jassamine took her staff and pulled it free, raising it to the sky and bathing the entire area in a brief flash of light. The three villagers stopped dead in their tracks and stared with an empty expression on their faces.

"Tell us—everything."

They did. It was not a terribly complex story. The Nuckelavee had arrived within the past month with its lesser demons and ghosts. It had killed everyone who resisted and forced the rest to participate in worship of the King Below. That was the nature of demons.

Demons did not leave you a choice save death or pain, knowing most people were not strong enough to resist either. They then set their new worshipers on one another, letting them degrade themselves until there was nothing left of the people they once were. Fighting them was why we fought this war. To bring an end to the King Below's evil.

"We need to destroy this creature," Jassamine said, looking down at the three peasants. "If what we're hearing is true, we can turn this around. The King Below sending its demons so far abroad means the Nuckelavee is isolated and vulnerable."

I agreed but had other concerns. "What will happen to them?"

Jassamine stared down at them. "They've forsaken the Path, the Lawgiver, and their faith. The Grand Temple would have them all burned as heretics. I think that is an appalling waste of life and think they should be enslaved instead."

I lowered my voice, disgusted with her suggestion. "Slavery is one of the great evils of the world. It is no better than burning, worse even."

I had grown up in the Borderlands, in what was now the Riverfords, where slavery had never been an accepted practice. My first exposure to it had been slave hunters attacking farms to drag off men, women, and children to become the property of someone else. Even there, it had been a criminal practice performed by ruffians and those blinded by greed.

Only when I'd reached the empire had I seen places where citizens treated slavery as perfectly natural. I had even met slaves who found the idea of freedom as alien as a fish might find a world without water. The very concept frightened them.

That had been horrifying in an entirely different way.

"I agree but they have been marked," Jassamine said. "Would you have each of them cleansed by holy rites?"

The cleansings were expensive, sacred rites, reserved only for the corrupted children of the nobility or priests.

"Better than living with the taint. Better than death. Better than a slave."

Jassamine seemed to consider my words. "You are a great progressive, Jacob Riverson, as well as very foolish. Every slave chooses life over death. Otherwise, they would find a way out. Still, I shall propose a cleansing for the villagers. We'll see if it is a trial run. Those who involved themselves in the human sacrifices will have to be killed, though."

I wasn't sure I disagreed with her but that was going to get ugly fast. Groups had a way of normalizing monstrous behavior. I'd seen the gentlest of souls cheer as criminals were fed to monsters in the Great Games. "See if you can get the emperor or the Prince to change the punishment for heresy from burning to hanging. There's no need to be sadistic about such things."

Jassamine smiled. "My soft-hearted rogue."

"There's nothing soft hearted about me. I just blame the King Below for this, rather than his victims."

"Is it not better to punish ten innocent men than let one guilty man go free?"

"Don't quote the Codex at me. Come, let us kill this thing," I said, kicking my horse into a trot toward where the villagers had said the monster rested.

I knew how to do this. Killing was easier than politics.

It took half an hour of moving past abandoned farm houses and empty buildings until Jassamine and I rode into the middle of the empty town square. There, the Lawgiver's temple had been burned to the ground. The place was deathly cold with little patches of snow on the rooftops and street, despite it being the middle of autumn. Most of the buildings were abandoned and I wondered if that was because the inhabitants moved out further away or the Nucklavee had killed them.

Jassamine lifted her staff and then spoke. "Servant of the Darkness, creature of the World Below, in the name of the emperor and the Lawgiver, I command you to come forth! Know your evils will no longer be tolerated for we have come like the morning sun to banish the darkness."

Her words bound the demon by a powerful geas, compelling it to reveal itself. In front of the church, a miasma of green fog swirled together into the centaur-like form of the Nuckelavee. They could appear in many shapes and sizes, most horse-related, but this one had the lower body of a horse and the chest of a man with a head possessing two giant horns that jutted out from the sides. Its skin was gray and its eyes a sickly yellow with a thin layer of ice covering it entirely. Its right arm was a spear made of bone, jutting from one forearm. I was in the presence of pure evil.

It wasn't alone. Dozens of dead villagers, their skin translucent, their necks broken, and bodies bloated from the manner of their deaths, rose from the ground around us—those who had willingly sold themselves to the King Below and taken the Unspeakable Oath only to find that nothing but death and damnation awaited them.

As if reading my mind, the creature laughed. "You will find there is no such thing as pure evil, King Below to Come and Bride of the Lawgiver. Good and evil are but labels we ascribe to what we love and hate. My master has chosen to embody evil for the love of his brother. Yet the Lawgiver is unworthy of such devotion and has made a mockery of everything good."

"I command you to stay and fight," Jassamine said, continuing her spell. "You will be undone this evening, condemned to be less than a spirit's shadow in the World Below."

"Death's sweet sorrow is no punishment for one who has endured the horrors of becoming a demon," the creature said. "It is a fate both of you will suffer. Yet, as one ascends to the light they will lose everything warm inside them even as the one who descends below shall gain love in ice."

"Enough!" I shouted, drawing my sword and charging.

The Nuckelavee fired a bolt of black lightning from its spear. I knocked it away with a spell. Jassamine drained away its barrier right before I struck the creature through its neck with my blessed blade, killing it in one blow.

It was an all-too-easy victory. Then I saw the creature was smiling. Staring into my eyes, a sword jutting from the top of its head, the creature said, "You will become as me."

I noticed my hands were covered in demonsteel gauntlets, forged in the fires of the World Below. My clothes had been replaced with black sackcloth, like the robes of a Dark Lord. I let go of my blade and the Nuckelavee's body fell to the ground before vanishing. Gone was the village. Instead, in its place was an ashen battlefield where I saw all my comrades-in-arms spread across the ground. They bore the marks of torture from where they'd been executed by the Grand Temple.

Turning to Jassamine, I saw she had been replaced by a burning angel, surrounded by the corpses of the villagers. She was naked in a nimbus of fire, a look of righteous bliss on her face even as dead children surrounded her.

"No..." I whispered. "This is not real."

"It is, my love," Jassamine said, her voice the voice of the Lawgiver. "You have become what you despise."

I reached up to my face and found I no longer had one.

Somehow, I still screamed.

CHAPTER TWO

I awoke, my eyelids flying open.

I was in a bed many times the size of a normal one, enough for a half-dozen people, the candles to its sides extinguished. The room was massive but unadorned with only simple wooden furniture and a witchfire hearth to fill it. A set of glass-and-iron doors led to a balcony in front of the bed, open to the freezing cold outside. It was midnight with not a single bit of light to illuminate us, but I could see as if in daylight. I also felt not a single stirring of chill against my body. Indeed, the cold made me stronger. It was the benefit of being a Wraith Knight.

Raising my hands up, I looked at them. They were olive, hardened by years of labor, and beautiful. Reaching up to touch my face, I felt the angular contours of my skin. It was my face, but not my original one. My old body was lying in some unmarked grave, somewhere, unmourned along with thousands of others forgotten in the aftermath of the Fourth Great Shadow War's final battle. I was a ghost now, just one as solid as a man. No, not a ghost, a god. The new King Below. Yet I felt anything but divine.

I felt a stirring beside me and I looked down at the beautiful forms lying beside me. To my right was Regina ni Whitetremor, a platinum-haired woman with skin the color of marble. She was elfblooded and surpassingly beautiful, her face marred only by a broken nose and a scar on her right lip. The rest of her body was well muscled and similarly marked, the signs of a warrior's life. This just increased her attractiveness to me as I'd never found myself drawn to the dainty willows of the nobility's courts.

Regina was naked under the black silk sheets conjured by magic, sleeping the peace of the righteous. I struggled with how she was able to do so, lying with a monster. She was a Shadowguard, too, one sworn to fight the King Below and his minions. I'd managed to win her heart, but I worried I was dragging her down to my level.

"Mmm," a voice muttered beside me.

My attention turned over to her opposite in appearance and temperament. Lying on my left was Serah Brightwaters, a woman with chocolate-brown skin and black curly hair falling down her back. Serah was a sorceress, like Jassamine, but one who had always been drawn to the dark and macabre. Regina's lover, she had joined our cause to seek the King Below's power, only to become our bride in the end. Serah was a plain woman without her glamours to cover them up, but her fierceness was what made me love her.

Polygamy was not uncommon in the Southern Kingdoms or Shadowlands amongst the rich. Men took multiple brides to sire heirs and women took second husbands for amusement after marrying first husbands to seal alliances. The Path did not recognize marriages between the same sex, but I had lived too long not to realize the same love existed between my brides as their love did with me. It made my situation all the more confusing. I had only ever wanted to love one in my life.

And now she was my enemy.

I slipped slowly down between them, waking neither up before stepping my feet onto the cold, hard stone. Taking a deep breath, I walked to the balcony and placed my hands on the snowy bannister. Before me was the city of Everfrost. It was a land of steam, smoke, iron, and gears existing at the top of the world. Gigantic pipes pumped massive amounts of water into rune-covered turbines as a million citizens worked feverishly to build the devices I'd instructed them to construct. The citizens were building railroads, power lines, telegraph poles, and sewer systems throughout my territories. They were preparing for a coming invasion of the Southern Kingdoms. An invasion that would, hopefully, never come.

"You can't fool them forever," the Trickster said, behind me. He took the form of a foppish, angular-faced man, wearing an elaborate ruffled coat and ascot of my era's nobility. He looked like me, now, beautiful but false. "They will figure out you have no interest in waging war against the Southern Kingdoms. You gave them their freedom, but they don't want a king of peace. They want a god of war."

"Silence, spirit, you are dead," I said, shaking my head. "Worse than dead. You destroyed yourself utterly and do not even possess a soul."

"I gave you my divinity," the Trickster said, shrugging. "So I am inside you now. Though, truly, I have to ask which is worse—talking to me or talking to yourself?"

"The latter. I am not afraid of you." I stared down at the massive statue they were constructing of me in full demonsteel armor. It was an extravagant waste of resources, yet the trappings of power were also the source of it. If I did not give the Shadowkind races a constant reminder of my presence in pageantry, I would have to give it in blood.

"Then hear my counsel that building a nation is not a matter of giving them clocks, food, and parties. I spent centuries making the Shadowkind hate each other only slightly less than the Lightborn species. They are bound together only by fear of you and promises of conquests abroad."

"You were a poor ruler."

"Yet I still ruled longer than any mortal monarch." The Trickster rolled his eyes. "If you do not give them blood, they will take it from you."

"I have greater faith in people than you," I said, lying. "Peace is addictive. Those who desire war are most often those who have nothing to lose or everything to gain. Those who have something to protect are more likely to use caution. It may take centuries but I intend to reverse the damage you have done to them."

"Because choosing to mold them into something you like is so very different from my molding them into something I liked." The Trickster conjured a glass of wine and sat down on the balcony's railing.

I wished the Trickster would stop haunting me. The King Below had kept me for centuries as his slave and he still bedeviled me despite being a ghost. The Nine Heroes had killed the King Below six years ago, but while it had freed me from his control, it hadn't removed his ghost from my mind. It was strange since my assumption of the

King Below's power should have meant the Trickster, the God of Evil's favorite avatar, was no more. He, obviously, disagreed.

"I am merely offering them a choice," I said, sighing. "I believe people will choose progress over ignorance, prosperity over poverty."

The Trickster smiled. "Yet the Southern Kingdoms are ruled by tyrants they voluntarily placed into power."

I had no rebuttal for that.

"The Nine Heroes will bring war to this place," the Trickster said. "As soon as they have finished murdering everyone who disagrees with them, they will come here, and tear down all of your works. They will exterminate those races you seek to save. Jassamine promised you as much in your last battle."

"I know."

"Jacob, who are you talking to?" Regina's voice spoke.

The Trickster vanished.

Frustrating creature.

"Myself," I answered.

"You know they say people who talk to themselves are crazy," Regina said, approaching the balcony.

Regina had slipped on a white cotton robe and a pair of wooden sandals. Like me, she showed no sign of the cold. I had bestowed a portion of my divine essence upon her with our marriage and it was having an effect on her. The Shadowkind were already calling her the Unicorn Queen and Goddess of Starlight. Titles I felt fit her well.

"I've declared myself the new King Below," I said, shaking my head. "If that isn't crazy, I don't know what is."

Regina shrugged and leaned over the railing. "You're a god now, Jacob. I've seen the miracles you perform. That you have inherited the mantle of an evil one is no different from a tyrant passing his crown to a just man."

"*Am* I a just man?"

"Of course."

I knew better. "The locals may call me a god, Regina, but I think otherwise. All I gained from seizing the King Below's title is the ability to conjure a body at will and a boost to my magical reserves. I'm not that much different than the Wraith Knight I was before, a wizard and a warrior who just happens to dead."

Regina leaned over and placed her hand on my shoulder before giving me a light peck on the cheek. "You don't feel dead to me."

I smirked. "Because that would make you a necrophiliac?"

Regina snorted and gave me a light punch to the shoulder. "I'm not one of those empty-headed lasses who swoon over books of romantic ghosts and strigoi carrying them off. I fell in love with you because you were, are, a builder and a soldier."

I took deep breath and sighed. My breath created so steam because it carried no warmth. "Perhaps you're right. What's the situation with the army?"

I had made Regina Supreme Military Commander of the Iron Order. Not only because she was more than capable, but because I was more comfortable designing magitech devices and managing logistics than leading armies. Once, I had been capable and willing to make decisions even lord marshals would balk at, but those days were long past. War was a young man's game, and Regina was full of a righteous confidence she could whip the divided Shadowkind's armies into a single unified force.

She'd exceeded all expectations.

"We've won our fortieth battle against the rebels and I don't foresee them being able to put up resistance for much longer. Discipline is still problematic but not overly so. I've had to hang several hundred rapists and looters but they're starting to get the message," Regina said, putting her hands on the railing. "In some ways, it's a good thing they're used to autocratic rule by an immortal god king. They're used to obeying orders that make no sense to them."

"Instead of four Dark Lords, they answer to a Bright Lady."

"A queen of starlight married to a king and queen of shadows." Regina smiled at that title. "We've managed to bring most of the Shadowkind in the North under our rule. Giving them back their free will has made it a costly conflict but I'm surprised to say many seem to welcome the new laws."

"Surprised?"

"Well, they were races created by the God of Evil to be, well, evil."

I frowned. "You shouldn't let them hear you say that."

"They take pride in being evil. It means something different to them." Regina looked over at me. "Also, could you put on a pair of pants? You're kind of distracting."

I looked down at my nakedness then over at Regina's arousing form. I felt the blood rushing to my lower regions. "Perhaps I could distract you in other ways."

"You are insatiable. I approve." Regina wrapped her arms around my neck, a hungry look in her eye. Then said look softened, becoming wistful. "When I lost my family, I thought would never be happy again. I would wake up crying, dreaming of Gewain, Ketra, and the others I lost. You and Serah have filled a void I never thought would be full again. I would thank the Lawgiver, but…"

"I understand, I do."

"I shall thank the universe instead."

"There are better gods out there than he. We shall find them."

"Or be them."

Both of us were great believers in the Path, but the Lawgiver was responsible for Jassamine and the Nine Heroes'—no, Usurpers'—tyranny. The Lawgiver was the hidden hand behind their rise to power. While he had taught of concepts like justice, mercy, and tolerance—he'd never practiced them. Where did that leave his followers who believed in such over him?

Abandoned, the Trickster said. *But perhaps that's what why the universe has given us a God of Evil who is good.*

"I would be lost without you," I said, placing my left hand on her cheek. I wanted to take her again against the bannister. Regina gave me a smile and I knew such an advance would be welcome. Moving my hands to her robe, I heard a throat clear.

Dammit.

"Yes?" I asked, turning around to look at Serah.

My other wife's hair was hanging wildly around her neck and she had managed to conjure up a plain black dress around herself that I wondered about the nature of—was it an illusion or real? Serah's ability with sorcery was such she could make illusions so real that, if she conjured a bridge, you could walk over it.

"Am I interrupting something?" Serah asked.

"Would you care to join in?" Regina flashed a wicked grin.

"I fear that business will take me away from such," Serah said, chuckling. "I also do not possess your same level of insatiability. Twice a night is more than my fill."

"A pity," Regina said. "Insatiability should be the mark of all witches."

"Regina is exhausting even to gods," I said, smiling at her and remembering the night before. "One of the many qualities I admire about her."

"And about me, husband? What do you admire?" Serah asked, raising an eyebrow.

"Your absolute indomitable will and ravenous lust for power."

Regina rolled her eyes.

Serah, instead, just nodded, satisfied with my answer.

"We have much to plan today," Serah said, holding out her hand and summoning her demonsteel staff. It was topped with a black diamond the size of a man's fist, which I'd retrieved on a visit to the now-empty World Below. I called it the Heart of Midnight and it was the most powerful wizard's staff ever created. "You mentioned that we've managed to finally assimilate the remaining dissidents?"

"If you mean I've finally killed all the bastards, blackguards, psychopaths, and warlords that won't toe the line, yes," Regina said, chuckling. "I joined the Shadowguard to kill the Shadowkind. Now I'm leading them and still killing more than I ever did with them."

I grimaced.

So did Serah, surprisingly.

"I'm just asking what the shape of the army is," Serah said.

"Stronger than it's ever been, and I don't mean under us," Regina answered, closing her robe tight and tying a knot with her cloth belt. "The machines Jacob has designed are amazing, as good or better as anything the empire has. A few more months of training and their discipline will be up to snuff too."

"Good," Serah said, her voice lowering.

The black diamond on her staff twinkled, signaling she was channeling a large amount of magic.

Serah's power had reached the point where she could wield it unconsciously.

"What are you thinking?" I asked, disturbed.

"I believe it is time we discuss invading the Southern Kingdoms."

CHAPTER THREE

When are we invading the Southern Kingdoms? That was a question I had hoped not to hear. I'd witnessed the kind of chaos, destruction, and madness brought about by a King Below leading his armies to the Southern Kingdoms. Even knowing the Southern Kingdoms were now synonymous with the empire that occupied them, I was hesitant to repeat the evils of my predecessor. I did not want to become a murderer of innocents, and they were the always the first to die in war.

You are already a murderer of innocents, the Trickster whispered. *You just have to accept that it is the price of change.*

I almost said 'never' aloud. "It is not the right time."

Serah was not easily dissuaded. "If not now, when? Each day the Nine Usurpers tighten their grip over the South and eliminate their enemies. They burn books, kill sorcerers, persecute the non-human, and convert more to their cause."

I grimaced. "They have taken the reforms I made with Jassamine centuries ago and turned the Grand Temple into a kind of....holy cause."

I tried not to think about all the people Jassamine and I had killed in our attempts to reform society. We had been able to do so because of the desperation of the circumstances but they had just led to greater evils. Well, not all was evil; we had ended slavery. Unfortunately, those very reforms had strengthened the power of the Imperial throne to the point it had been able to seize power across the entirety of the South.

"The Nine Usurpers' supporters call it the Second Reformation." Serah sniffed the air. "The empress has called for unity and any who disagree with her new laws are sent to die in her labor camps or to be burned at the stake. If we do not act now, there will be no one to ally with."

"The people cry out for salvation."

I think they both overestimated how many people would ally with the King Below and his wives. We were, after all, heads of an army of monsters and the figures mothers used to scare their children at night. "Serah, Regina—"

"We need to begin making preparations now, while we are at our strongest and they are still consolidating power," Serah said. "The longer the Anessian Empire occupies its territories, the more legitimate its authority becomes. Not all people hate the Nine Heroes' rule. Draconian as their laws may be, they are universally applied and fair. The empire's rule brings riches to its loyalists."

Much to my surprise, Regina came to my rescue. "Jacob has brought us this far, Serah. They are not the Nine Usurpers anymore but the Seven. Two of them have already fallen and gone to meet their maker. We but need to focus on destroying the remainder to achieve victory."

That had been my original plan.

Things had changed.

"If that is our goal, then we have made little progress to it building roads and grain silos for goblins," Serah said, using a slur about our Formor allies. "We have gained great power and should use it."

"You would have us tear down our homelands to get at seven people?" Regina asked.

"Eight," Serah corrected. "Jassamine, too, must die. Nine if we have to overthrow the Lawgiver."

I tried not to snort at her idea of overthrowing the God of Gods. Mind you, Jassamine was the Lawgiver's right hand.

The Lawgiver is no more or less a god than you, the Trickster said. *Older, yes, but not more powerful. In the end, whether you can defeat my brother or not depends on whether you step off the path he has cleared for you.*

I ignored the Trickster's statement. "It will not be as easy as that, Regina. If we kill them, the empire will not magically fall. I have viewed the Southern Kingdoms through the divination stones. They have recruited many lackies from the worst of humanity. If we strike down the Nine, or Eight, then a power vacuum could appear that could place someone even worse on top."

Jassamine and the Lawgiver were the evil heart of all this. If they survived, she would just choose new champions. But you couldn't kill a god. The Trickster's continued existence in my head was proof of that.

"Then what is your plan, Oh Dark Lord of Dark Lords?" Serah asked, surprising me with her viciousness. She was angry about something and I didn't know what. Serah had been one of the least hawkish individuals in my inner circle.

Regina turned, now looking concerned. "As much as I am wondering where this newfound viciousness is coming from, Serah, I have to wonder as well. Jacob, I have been giving you time to formulate a strategy while you build up our forces but if not war or assassination then…what?"

What, indeed.

I looked away, ashamed. "There is no plan."

You could have heard snow fall.

"What?" Regina finally said.

"I knew it." Serah cursed, clutching her staff. "You've been vacillating for over a year now."

"I was focused on other things," I said, undaunted. "I had many plans at the beginning while trying to forge this land into something that might grow stronger and purer but the hypocrisy is not lost on me. If I bring war to the lands of my birth, how am I different from them?"

I clenched a fist, feeling a metal gauntlet slowly form from the shadows around my hand. Seconds later, I was once more wearing my demonsteel armor and hooded cloak. It was protection against my true self: the ghost who pretended to be a man.

"Have the courage to look us in the eye, husband," Serah said.

"My eyes rotted away long ago."

Serah narrowed her gaze.

The truth was I was sick of war and didn't want to start yet another one with the entirety of the Southern Kingdoms. Even if we would win, which was a great *if*, it would be a conflict that would last decades and kill hundreds of thousands. I had already spilled more blood than any man in history through my use of the Terrible

Weapons during the Fourth Great Shadow War. I didn't want any more blood on my hands and was hoping, against hope, something would allow us to find a peaceful solution for all this.

Or a way to victory that did not require setting the continent on fire.

Peasant women hope a handsome prince will sweep them off their feet and men desire to discover a genie that grants wishes. Neither of these are things you should count on, the Trickster taunted. *Especially when my brother is involved.*

"People die in war." Regina said, putting her hands on her hips. "Did you not make me a promise that you would hold the Usurpers down as I cut off their heads off?"

"You were considerably more graphic," I said, remembering what she'd described as wanting to do to the Nine Heroes' teats and balls. "I have not forgotten, though. I am…simply torn."

"About *what*?" Regina asked, as if it was the clearest thing in the world to lay waste to a land I had once protected.

"Do you still harbor affection for that madwoman?" Serah asked. "Is the specter of Jassamine binding you from acting with the courage we fell in love with?"

I clenched my jaw, offended at the very suggestion. "Hate is all that dwells in my heart for her."

"Then why?" Serah said, reaching up to my hood and removing my helmet. It revealed only shadows and cold.

"I have said my words and you have chosen not to hear them. I see in you both power beyond belief. You are the greatest mage in an age, Serah. You have absorbed centuries of learning in our time here and you, Regina, have taken an insurmountable task to heart. Yet I ask if you truly are ready to burn and ravage your kinfolk in the name of building a better world."

I referred, of course, to humanity when speaking of their kinfolk. Serah had already proven capable of killing her family and Regina's own family had been slain by the Usurpers. It might not have been the best choice of words.

Regina looked away. "My kin are dead, Jacob. All at the hands of this scum. Evil thrives when swords are sheathed in the name of mercy."

"The kingdoms are already burned and ravaged," Serah said,

turning around. "You just refuse to put a stop to it. I will form my own force to invade them if you won't. I expected better of you."

"He will do better," Regina said, looking at me. "After he thinks on it. In the meantime, I'm going to the baths and am going to drink myself silly before breakfast because, as a god, I can do that and be right as rain before the water cools. Care to join me, Serah?"

"As I said, nay," Serah said, dropping my helmet on the ground and striding to her dresser. "I have other matters to attend."

I reached down and placed my helmet on my head. "I will find a solution to this problem that does not require invasion."

"Let us hope the frozen wastes of the World Below do not catch fire before," Regina said, going to put on her armor.

Knowing I'd been dismissed, I took my leave. The fish-like Formor guards at the door stood at attention when I passed but I gave a half-hearted wave to relax. I was uncomfortable with the prestige of monarchy, let alone godhood, and half-wished I could go back to my status as Lord Commander of the Shadowguard, but those days were past. My old comrades would hunt me down to the ends of the World Between if permitted by their empress.

I needed something to calm my nerves. In the old days, I would have gathered a group of my Shadowguard brothers and sisters to get utterly pissed on alcohol. Sadly, that was forbidden now. I could not taste the fruit of the grape or honey or hops anymore, so drinking was out of the question.

Sex was out of the question, with neither Regina or Serah likely to want my presence, and I wasn't the kind of man to seek their attendants. All that was left was the forge to work at and even that was not much of a respite anymore. No, I was a monster who needed to be alone with his thoughts and there were very few places the King Below could go to hide from his responsibilities.

Not that I wouldn't try.

Casting a spell of obscurement over myself, I walked through the halls of the tower without drawing attention to myself. I could not deal with my worshipers, subjects, or scattered few friends right now. Instead, I just focused on my surroundings and looked for some place to be alone with my thoughts. The Tower of Everfrost was one of the largest buildings in the world: surely it had some place I could go to to think?

I wouldn't count on it, the Trickster said. *It was as much my tomb as my palace.*

Wandering out into the halls outside my bedchamber, I took in the sights of the tower. The hallway walls and floors were made of thick black metal, illuminated by green glowstones, with white-and-black banners glorifying the new regime everywhere. The halls were crowded with workers of a dozen races hammering and sawing away on new additions to the tower, despite the fact I could conjure almost anything I wanted within its eldritch walls.

This was to give the population something to do and take their minds of the fact they were now subjects to a foreign-born ghost. Others were supplicants who had come to pay homage to new King Below or hold audience with one of the many bureaucrats I'd spent much of the past few years appointing. They were the most frightening since I could hear their prayers to me, many of which were sincere.

I couldn't help but be overwhelmed it all. Thousands depended on me and millions more worshiped me as a god, which I found to be insane. Even worse, they were the heathens and monsters I had been raised to believe were the enemy of all that was good and pure in the world. My life felt like a dream some days, and not always was it a pleasant one.

"Praise be to the Black Sun!" a black-robed Bauchan priestess spoke to a gathered crowd at the end of the hall I currently walked down. She had silver-white hair tied in a topknot and wore a medallion bearing my sigil around her neck. Bauchan were a gray-skinned angular-faced race with coal-black eyes, more resembling elves than either their Formor or human parents. The Bauchan were surpassingly beautiful to most species and possessed of great magical power.

This one was named Nyht and that she was a true believer in my divinity. I had made it a point to memorize the name of each of my clergy, if not my worshipers. "He is the guidance in the winter, the gift that protects us from the cold, and the blade in the night that slays our enemies."

"Created by the old King Below, we have long suffered in toil and damnation, but the new lord promises rebirth and redemption!" Nyht said, holding her hands in the air. "Where once we have known starvation and poverty, we shall know bounty. Where once we have known suffering and persecution, we shall know glory! From the ashes of the dead god has been reborn his successor!"

I grimaced. I hadn't exactly done all that much for them.

"He has done nothing!" an angry Formor among the crowd gathered around her spoke. "We have killed many of our brothers and sisters but when shall we lead our armies south?"

Nyht had an answer for him and I wondered if he was a plant. "Brother, I speak to you that the time of the Endless Night is coming! Revenge will be yours and your ancestors! For millennia, we have been hunted as vermin. Driven to the dark corners of the World Between, lest we be exterminated."

"We will exterminate them!" the man in the crowd shouted.

"Yes," Nyht cried out. "For centuries, we have known nothing but defeat, but the Black Sun shall fly over all nations and bring them under our sway."

That got the crowd truly excited.

"Such is what happens when you do not write your own religious texts," I said, shaking my head. "If I refuse the mantle of kingship, then the mantle will conjure its own monarch. Dammit, I need to figure out something to tell them. Set down some rules and let them know…" What? I knew less than anyone what I was going to do.

I decided to risk a divination in hopes of gaining some insight into my situation. I had never been a fan of divination since it was tricky business. Self-fulfilling prophecies and the desires of the seeker tended to influence the revelations. The future was composed of a million separate destinies that could be altered by foreknowledge or simple will. Closing my eyes, I tried to see if peace was an option or if there was a way I could avoid the coming war.

What I saw was death. Death on an unimaginable scale. If I did not attack the Southern Kingdoms, then they would attack en masse and drown the Northern Wastelands in the blood of their own dead. Whole villages and cities were massacred from the eldest Formor to the youngest cub. Where the city of Everfrost stood outside of the tower became nothing more than a graveyard of frozen bodies with all the hopes and dreams I'd had for the Shadowkind left to rot in the garbage pit of history.

I shifted my vision, seeing what would happen if we attacked first instead. What followed was equally horrible its own way, a century of war with millions of dead on both sides as whole cities were caught up in a conflict that neither side was strong enough to triumph over. In some realities, the Nine Heroes killed us. In other realities, we killed the Nine Heroes. In some realities, Regina killed the Lawgiver only for their battle to leave the world an uninhabitable ball of ice.

I tried to adjust the terms of my vision several times but it all came back to numbers and logistics. The Lightborn races would not bow to the King Below. The Formor would not kneel to the Lawgiver. The Lightborn races had a decided military and infrastructural advantage that could only be compensated against through horror and genocide. Peace was the only option, but our enemies did not want peace. The Lawgiver, Nine Heroes, and Jassamine all believed the destruction of the Shadowkind was righteous.

It was insoluble.

"Fuck." I stared at my hands, ones that held the fate of the Three Worlds.

I had no idea what I was going to do.

That was when I heard a voice behind me. "Milord, we have a problem."

CHAPTER FOUR

I turned around, expecting to see Regina or Serah behind me. Instead, I saw a woman with long, silky hair and pearl-white skin, angular-shaped eyes, and sharp features. She was dressed in a sparkling white dress covered in teardrop-shaped diamonds conjured by magic. Both her earrings and bracelets glowed with supernatural energy, providing her with protection spells as well as constant contact with her spies around the Iron Order's territories. An amulet around her neck sported a black sun, moon, and star in one symbol.

"Midori," I said, speaking to my chamberlain. "How pleasant to see you."

Midori Silverstone was a woman of mixed G'Tay and Gaelish blood who had once been the heiress of a prominent merchant house as well as a priestess of the Great Mother. Serah and she had been friends, which resulted in me lending aid to recover her when Midori had run afoul of the Temple Archons.

The Great Mother was considered an aberration now, only to be worshiped in relationship to the Lawgiver. Those who worshiped her exclusively or even as the Lawgiver's equal were considered heretics now, blasphemers equal to those who worshiped the Gods Between or the King Below. What I'd found had been done to her in the Grand Temples' dungeons had chilled my blood, and I was far from squeamish. It amazed me she'd managed to rebuild herself.

"I wish to have your attention, milord," Midori said.

"Did Serah send you to convince me to go to war?"

"I doubt I could do so where your wives could not. Besides, this may surprise you, but I find your lack of bloodthirst endearing," Midori said.

"Thank you." My people had worshiped the Great Mother to the exclusion of all the other gods. I had no idea what the Great Mother's opinion, if any, was on her husband's actions. Indeed, of all the Gods Above, she remained the most mysterious. "What is it you want?"

"Your opinion, milord." Midori produced a small crystal from her pocket and held it in front of me. It conjured an image of a short red-haired woman with elfblooded features and conspicuous freckles. She was dressed in a rich moonsilver chainmail coat with a fur-lined leather cloak, absent of any markings or signs of nobility. The woman was riding on back of a Lesser Yellow Dragon across the Devil's Sea. She would reach the edge of the newly expanded borders of the Iron Order soon.

I then saw a dozen dragons following her. Great Blacks. The Great Blacks were some of the most powerful dragons in the world and even one of them could destroy a Great Yellow Dragon easily. Whoever had chosen them for the chase, though, had done so poorly because they were not fast creatures. They did, however, have stamina and would catch the Yellows when they tired.

"That *is* unusual," I said, taking the crystal. "That is a force one would bring to assault a city."

"A large city," Midori said. "Even more so, these are all Shadowguard Elite."

If there had been any heat left in my blood, it would have gone cold. "So, my old comrades have become hatchetmen for the empress."

"Yes," Midori said. "They have turned from eliminating the followers of the old King Below to destroying those considered heretics to the empress'sreforms. Their support has much strengthened her position."

I focused on the girl instead of thinking about how far my order had fallen. I, after all, wasn't one to talk about treason against its principles. "This reminds me of how I met Regina. She was being chased by the Shadowguards' dragons when I first met her. Who is this woman?"

"I do not know," Midori said. "I have the faces of ten thousand men and women stored in my crystals but she is not one of them. I do know that one of the dragon riders is Fel Hellsword."

I stared at Midori. "The Chief of the Mysterium?"

"And the Shadowguard," Midori said.

Fel Hellsword was one of the Nine Heroes, the most powerful of them after the empress in fact, and widely considered to be a key part of the reason the empire had managed to maintain its control over its newly conquered territories.

Hellsword was a Natariss archmage of incredible power, a master swordsman, and a spymaster without compare. Most of my information had come from Serah but everything she told me suggested he was possibly the most dangerous of the Nine. This was an almost-too-golden opportunity.

"It could be a trap," I muttered, contemplating possible reasons for why he would endanger himself by approaching our borders.

"If it is, it is a poorly planned one." Midori gave a slight smile. "Presenting Serah and Regina his head would be a most satisfying apology."

I couldn't help but chuckle. It would be a nice way to get back in their good graces. "Better than sweets or flowers."

"I doubt either woman cares for such."

"Everyone loves sweets."

Midori smiled and took back the crystal. "The girl is unimportant, whoever she is. This is an opportunity that cannot be missed. Can I prepare your forces?"

"Inform Serah and Regina of this opportunity. They will want to be a part of this."

"Yes, milord."

"I will gather our forces," I said, nodding, and heading to the dragon pens.

"Do we have enough to defeat him?"

Defeating a group of twelve Great Blacks would take a fantastic amount of power and we were still building the Iron Order's military forces to a level that could compete with the empire's own. Still, the problem wasn't whether I possessed enough power to defeat the dragon squadron, it was mobilizing and moving my forces fast enough to intercept them.

"Yes. We can get there if we respond quickly. One of the benefits of a…recent creation."

Midori nodded. "The Night Bridge."

Dragon riders, report to the pens for a mission. We ride to battle, I said, projecting my thoughts to Regina's finest troops. I then sent similar instructions to the hundreds of workers needed to equip and prepare a suitable strike force for engaging Hellsword's force.

Walking down to a nearby door, I opened it up to reveal a massive spiraling set of stairs that led down to the lower levels of the castle. The Dragon Pens were something Regina insisted we always have direct access to.

"You should let this one go," the Trickster said, appearing beside me, dressed like one of my priests. He had a hood over his head and his hands pressed together as if in prayer. "You're a great warrior and a wizard but capable of fighting that many dragons? You'd kill one of the Great Blacks, maybe mortally injure another, before the third killed you. That would be a terrible ending to your story."

"I'm not you, I don't fight alone. I also don't hide behind my armies."

"And if Regina or Serah were to die in this battle, would you finally want to battle my brother? Would the death of one of your lady loves inspire you to vengeance?"

"Vengeance solves nothing."

"I've found it makes you feel better, much better in fact."

"They are both great warriors. I have accepted that we all risk our lives when we go into battle. Never send someone into battle without awareness of the potential for loss."

"You'd murder the world," the Trickster said, his voice mocking. "That is the real reason you don't lead your armies to attack the South. It's not because of any moral reservations against sacking the land. You're just afraid of losing what you've earned. Your little kingdom plus its queens of night and day."

"Silence."

The Trickster stopped. "You can't hide from the truth and the truth is you want a war to fight. You just don't think you'll win."

"Begone!" I shouted, turning around to face him.

The Trickster wasn't there.

I was alone.

"I am going mad," I muttered, more convinced than ever that the Trickster had somehow deceived me into taking his power. I was becoming more like him every day. A fate infinitely worse than death.

Continuing down the steps for several more minutes in silence, I emerged in the Dragon Pens. They were a massive colliseum-sized circular arena with stalls as big as houses for each of the two dozen or so creatures we kept in the castle. A long, smooth tunnel with a tower-sized hole gave the beasts an exit when they wanted to fly. The pens were treated by over two hundred workers and all were scurrying about, equipping the beasts for battle. Sixteen Great Reds and eight High Blues were present in a circle with their ornate enchanted plate mail around them. Their dragon riders wore helmets shaped in the manner of a dragon's head. They were all gathered around the Night Bridge with their lances, swords, and fire-cannons.

The Night Bridge was a pair of rune-covered rings that spun together and were attached to several cables that ran throughout the tower down to the Great Abyss below it. They channeled power from the World Below's ambient magic and ley stones spread throughout the city. The Night Bridge was magic well beyond my ability to create and never would have been possible if not for Serah lending her own magical expertise for it. As powerful as becoming a "god" had made me, I was nowhere near omnipotent. The Night Bridge, though, could send everyone here across the continent in an instant. Perhaps once or twice a month. It was not equal to the late Tharadon the Inventor's mirror but it was close.

"You move quickly," I said, looking to see if Serah and Regina had arrived.

"We have to if we're going to get anything done," Regina said, stepping through the crowd of knights. "You better hope this is worth my giving up my bath."

It had been a year since House Roger's attempt on her life in the bath and the resulting deaths of two of Regina's attendants. For the longest time, she'd insisted instead on showers and magic to clean herself. The fact she'd returned to her favorite hobby, one beloved by Imperials everywhere, was a good sign. One I almost hated interrupting her for.

Almost.

"It will mean the death of one of our foes," I said, smiling. "Hellsword."

Regina smiled back.

Serah did not.

I took a moment to look over my wives. Regina was wearing a suit of shining star metal that I'd spent the better part of a month crafting. It was practical, rather than flattering, but still worked as both a work of art as well as protection for someone on the battlefield. At her side was the sword *Starlight* in a dragon-bone ivory sheath with a long white cape. An engraved helmet covered the top and sides of her head but left her mouth and chin exposed. Her hair was tied into a braid behind her neck, secured for combat. While Regina preferred to be attired by her attendants, I knew she must have covered herself with magic this time.

"Are you sure it's him?" Serah said, stepping forth in luxurious black-and-white robes with a demonsteel ring of thorns amulet around her neck to match a similar ring where her white-gold wedding band should be. She was holding her staff close to her and I could tell the revelation of our attacker's identity was troubling to her.

"Midori has never been known to lie," I said, still surprised there was anyone honest in our ranks. "Nor has she ever been wrong."

"Then we can put aside your own untruths and take a moment to work together to get that bastard and cut his balls off," Regina said, clenching a mailed fist. "Afterward, we will have words."

It seemed she was angrier than I'd expected over my unwillingness to go to war. Then again, her family had been exterminated by the Nine Heroes while mine had merely fallen prey to the ravages of time. If I had someone to blame for their loss, wouldn't I pursue it with no end of fury? I would tear the world apart before I let anyone stop me, spouse or no.

"Your language has changed a great deal since coming up here," I said, shaking my head. "I approve."

"I have always had more of a low sensibility," Regina said. "It was my uncle who beat the High Imperial way of speaking into me. I tend to average out with an Easternary accent as a general rule. Is your mount ready, yet, Jacob?"

"Smoke comes on her own time but she has never missed a battle before."

As if on cue, Smoke emerged from a separate tunnel that appeared when it wanted to. Her head was almost my size in height and twice again as wide, long with a massive mouth of teeth like steak knives. Smoke was one of the twelve Demon Dragons, those members of their race possessed by fallen angels who'd offered their services to the King Below in exchange for freedom from the Lawgiver's edicts. She was also a Grand Red, a dragon whose size and power were greater than any other. The Great Reds beside us looked almost like adolescents compared to her. It was a pity she was the last of her kind for the other Demon Dragons had all been hunted to extinction by the Shadowguard.

I'd killed one myself.

"I hope this fight will contain the opportunity for dining on elves and their kin," Smoke said cheerfully, little bursts of flame accompanying each word. "I do so love their taste."

Regina glared at her.

"Oh not you!" Smoke said, waving a set of claws in front of her. "Well, maybe after you're dead."

"Did Midori give you an explanation?"

"On the walk down, yes," Serah said, shaking her head. "We should try to take Hellsword alive."

"Like hell we should," Regina cursed. "He's a fucking monster, cursed from birth and should be sent to his god with all due haste."

"His god? I thought you still followed the Path?" Serah said, walking up to the Night Bridge.

"I follow the Path, not the Lawgiver."

"We don't have much of a distinct advantage over the attacking force," I said, shaking my head. "If we managed to engage them on the coast, assuming that's where her quarry takes them to begin with, it will be an intense fight. I don't know much about Hellsword's abilities, either, only that he's formidable."

"He steals the souls of the living to feed his magic," Serah said, lifting her staff to start the process of teleportation. "His sword, *Plaguebringer*, is a former Wraith Knight's. He's 'cleansed' it with light magic while practicing all the foulest necromancies the Path supposedly forbids."

"Charming."

"He's also my ex-lover," Serah said, lifting her staff to increase the power being fed it. "Just so you know."

I did a double take. "What?"

"Another reason to kill him," Regina said, narrowing her gaze. "We should try to keep the woman they're pursuing alive. She might be trying to seek refuge with us."

"Protecting the innocent is not our mandate," Serah said. "But we can try not to target her deliberately. Who may I ask is in charge of the attack?"

I grimaced. That was another point of contention in our marriage. In addition to giving up a third of my power to both, I'd also made them co-rulers of the Iron Order. This was something that had gone over poorly with the Shadowkind since they were used to a single autocratic leader.

It was a testament to Regina and Serah's ability to lead they'd managed to gain the respect of the old King Below's followers so quickly. Still, there could be only one commander in battle and I was, ostensibly, the ruler of all Shadowkind.

"Regina is a superior tactician and dragon rider," I said, not afraid to admit the truth. "She should handle the commands. I'll just throw what spells I can at Hellsword."

"Thank you," Regina said. "I'll take care of the Great Blacks. You try to engage Hellsword directly. I've seen you kill demons and demigods in battle. I can think of no one better to engage him personally."

"Just make sure I have space to do it," I said. "Once they see me, it'll be a scramble to try and take down the new King Below."

"And if you should fall in battle, sir?" A female dragon rider asked.

"Then Regina and Serah will continue the fight," I said. "If they fall, Midori is in charge followed by the Speaker of the Winter Council. The Iron Order's chain of command is long and strong."

"We will also beat you with said chain if you keep asking stupid questions like that," Serah replied, finishing a mystical with her staff. "I will lend my spells to you from a safe distance. I have no desire to get up close with a horde of foul-breathed reptiles."

"Says the small squishy thing," Smoke muttered.

Serah shot Smoke a dirty look. "The Night Bridge is almost fully charged. I recommend you all get mounted and prepare for battle. Surprise will be your chief advantage and you will need every edge you can get. The empire has ten thousand dragons. We have less than eight hundred and mostly smaller breeds."

"Understood," I said, turning around and conjuring an armored saddle as well as harness for Smoke.

Regina walked over and then gave me a hug before kissing the side of my helmet. "Don't get yourself killed, husband. I don't want you to die while I'm pissed off at you. Not unless I'm the one killing you."

I smiled. "I love you too."

Serah looked between us "We should always be at war. It's the only time we're ever at peace."

Chapter Five

A s I mounted Smoke's back, I couldn't help but look at the people around me and wonder if I was failing at being their monarch let alone god. No, I didn't need to wonder. I knew I was.

I'd had the benefit and misfortune to grow up on the edge of so-called civilization in a community of pacifists. They'd been stupidly idealistic and refused to defend themselves against those who sought their harvests, but they'd been passionate in their beliefs. Now, centuries later, I still admired their powerful disdain for the elite of society, but I had abandoned their philosophy of nonviolence. How much effort had it taken to convince me to go after Hellsword's group? A couple of confusing visions and the disdain of my wives? Perhaps the Trickster was right and I just was doing what I wanted.

Or maybe there was no way out but forward.

"You're brooding again," Regina said, bringing her mount up beside Smoke. Regina's dragon was named Blaze and was one of Smoke's many animal-brained children, products of her mating with similarly dumb dragons for pleasure.

"I'm what now?" I asked, seeing the Shadow Bridge starting to spin its rings. Our teleportation was only a few minutes away now.

"I can always tell when you're lost in self-recrimination," Regina said, shaking her head. "I know you think we're angry at you and you're damned right we are, but you surprised us. That's all. Admittedly, not so much as finding out Serah used to fuck Hellsword."

"This isn't the time, Regina."

"It's time when I damn well say it is," Regina said, hefting her lightning lance up. It was an immense spear of steel and silver that caused the air around it to crackle with every movement. "Besides, we both might be dead after this."

"Such is the case with every battle." I had to admire her spirit, though. She reminded me of the Shadowguard of old—strong, passionate, and fully aware they might not make it through the next battle.

"Best to live like every day is your last, then. Honestly, one of us should be staying behind to rule in case this turns out to be a disaster."

"I would be a poor god and king if I did not take as many risks as the men under my command."

"I could point out the many flaws with that argument but as I find it admirable, I shall not."

I chuckled then spoke seriously. "I do not want another war, Regina, but I will defend this land if I can. I also know the Nine Heroes deserve to be brought to justice. I just wonder if I only begin conflicts but never finish them. War has an addictive quality to it, one that can consume your entire life. I would not damn you the way I have damned myself."

"What does damnation mean to the King of the World Below?"

She had a point. "The World Below emptied when I ascended. So I have no idea."

It was a hard thing to accept that you were responsible for the thousand hells' damned being freed but such was the case. I'd let loose every one of the damned to flee to newer dimensions, whether they were good, bad, or indifferent. They had been tortured and mutilated for eternity, so I felt they'd all served their sentence. It bothered me that plenty had chosen to stay behind, preferring slavery to the God of Evil than an uncertain future in a newer realm. Then again, I was still pretending to be alive myself.

"Leave it the theologians," Regina said.

"I'll have to hire some."

The power of the Night Bridge was growing in front of us. The circles were spinning faster and faster with a white light growing within the center. It was powerful, indistinct, raw magic that was barely controllable. I had used the Night Bridge less than a dozen times since creating it and was certain it worked but that didn't mean it wasn't dangerous.

"I'm sorry for deceiving you," I finally said.

"I will forgive you, eventually, if only because life is too short to hold grudges. Which cuts to the heart, really." Regina's expression turned serious. "I won't lie to you, Jacob, I suffer for the Nine's existence. For the betrayal of the Lawgiver, empress, and my people. I dream nightly of the screams of my family, friends, and homeland as well as the piles of burnt corpses they made of them."

I grimaced at her description. Regina had lived an adventurous life before I'd met her, being both a Shadowguard and a member of a now-extinct Great House. The Whitetremors were royalty, rather than nobility, with descent from the emperor I'd once served. Empress Morwen had slaughtered them with the same feeling one might give swatting an insect. Similar purges happened every year the Nine remained in power, a reminder that my inaction had a price.

Regina continued. "You were not born to the purple so you cannot know what it is like to have been instilled from an early age that you were destined for greatness, only to have those illusions cruelly stripped away by all-too-banal cruelty. *I want revenge*, I want to see them die screaming, and I want to lay waste to their works as if I was a god—a status you have given me."

"Regina—"

"Do not interrupt for this next part is important. *Despite this, I will not lower myself to their level*," Regina said, taking a deep breath. "I numb myself to the pain with drink, your and Serah's love, plus whatever other pleasures I can enjoy. I cope with my loss of faith with the dream that there is something worth worshiping above the Lawgiver. Yet, regardless of my pain, I would set aside my desire for retribution."

I blinked. "What?"

"Peace is a finer thing than the satisfaction I get from wetting my blade with the blood of monsters," Regina said, clutching her hands tightly. "But do you really think sheathing my sword is an option?"

I stared at her and realized she'd given this matter as much thought as I had. Which made my next words all the more painful. "No, it is not. To set down our weapons is to invite attack." It was the hardest thing I'd ever said.

"Then what choice is there?"

I was silent. I could tell her I had come to that conclusion myself, that I knew there was no other war than to find a third option but that wasn't possible now. We had but a few seconds left and not even the gods knew what would happen during the next battle. I just prayed, to the universe itself, that there were other options to pursue. I didn't want to lose Regina or Serah to war the way I lost Jassamine. "Victory, I suppose."

"You *suppose.*"

"Not a very kingly response, is it?"

"No, not really."

Smoke snorted and rumbled beneath me. "You humans. You speak of ethics, morals, and philosophy as if they were things that exist outside your head. The Lawgiver and King Below never gave half a thought to such things."

"Which is why they're assholes we want to kill," Regina said.

"That's true," Smoke admitted. "I'm just saying life is nothing but mating, eating, and sleep."

"There is wisdom in that I suppose," Regina said, smiling. "Another reason I always liked dragons. They are less complicated than people."

"Smarter too," Smoke said.

I was about to respond when a brilliant white light exploded from the Night Bridge, engulfing us all. We emerged seconds later in a light snow near the coast, storm clouds above our heads, and the winds howling around us. The enemy's dragons were all about us and didn't have time to react before we made our attack.

Poets and balladeers had spoken of war since the first songs were set down on lutes, but they rarely managed to capture the frenzied madness conflict actually entailed. We vanished from their current position and re-appeared seventy feet in the air, right above the enemy forces. Dragons did not fly like birds, instead propelling themselves forth with a kind of telekinesis, but it was still shocking to see them immediately zoom into one another with claws, teeth, and flame.

The teleportation had not been without flaws, either, as one of the Great Reds had physically merged with one of the Blacks, killing both instantly, I watched out of the corner in my eye both dragon riders fall to the ground below, perishing without any sort of glorious end. That was another truth of war that storytelling often ignored: death in war was frequently absurd.

It's hard to put into words what battle was like for those who had never experienced it, harder still to describe the exhilarating but terrifying experience of combat on dragonback. Magical spells flew through from the air from both sides, the Shadowguard elite recovering quickly even as Regina's plan left many dragons impaled or wounded in the opening battle.

Dragons were not soft creatures, though, Great Blacks especially, and the opening salvo did not kill many. Smoke, herself, breathed out a salvo of fiery red flames that washed over an entire Great Black yet the creature passed through it like it was only a minor inconvenience. Our opponents were well protected by magic and it soon became a series of individual duels that looked like a flock of giant-tailed crows flapping against one another.

"Curse, strike the one to your North Upward degrees! Payne, aim for the rider! Serah, we need the barrier spells around them weakened!" I could hear Regina's commands, projected through a spell around her helmet to everyone else's, but she did not try to control every detail either. Instead, she left me with but a single command, and that was to do what I did best. "Jacob, kill."

"With pleasure," I spoke, summoning forth a storm of black lightning from my fingertips that wrapped around one of the closest dragons like a trout in a fishing net. It wasn't enough to kill it but it stunned the creature long enough for me to leap onto its thrashing neck, bury a gauntlet underneath one of its scales and hold on long enough to draw my sword.

Chill's Fury glowed as it was drawn, a weapon forged by the old King Below for the late Kurag Shadowweaver. It was a curved sword with teeth and terrible runes of power that sucked the life out of every being it killed. I jammed the weapon hard into the side of the dragon and drank deeply of its life force, using that to empower another spell of black lightning that caused the creature to thrash wildly.

Somehow, I managed to hold on.

"Profane creature, I strike at thee in the name of the King Above!" I heard the Shadowguardsman speak at the base of the creature's neck.

It was a white-cloaked man with long red hair and angular features, clearly elf-blooded, with golden eyes I could see through the acute vision of the dead. His armor was gilded and covered with blood runes, magic that required the sacrifice of the living to perform. It was possible he was Fel Hellsword. I'd never actually seen the man so I had to guess. The figure aimed his blade right at me and the terrible flame shot forth at my face.

I summoned a ward just in time to prevent the flame from striking me in the face. While my barriers were powerful, I was nearly knocked away by the force of its power. It wasn't the magic of humans but Nephyr, those possessed by the Lawgiver's messengers. In my living days, like blood runes, such magic had been forbidden.

"The Lawgiver is no god worth worshiping!" I shouted, leaping forth from my position at the Nephyr, burying my blade into the human-spirit hybrid's chest. The momentum of my attack carried us both off the creature's back and to the side into a free fall.

I looked into the face of my opponent as we fell, the nineteen-year-old man's features contorting and twisting into a hideous scaled green creature with reptilian eyes. The Nephyr's face then faded away as *Chill's Fury* disintegrated the spirit inside him, leaving only the man breathing his last.

Looking into my eyes, the Shadowguard's eyes lost their anger. "Thank you."

We were about to strike the ground as a set of clawed talons grabbed my shoulders and pulled me upward, the corpse impaled on my blade falling to the rocky coast below. Seconds later, the headless corpse of the Great Black he'd been riding fell past me, the two landing in the black waters of the sea.

I looked up to see who had caught me, only to see Regina riding on Blaze rather than Smoke. Above her head, I saw the battle was not going well. The person I'd mistaken for Fel Hellsword was dead, but another similar in appearance destroyed a Great Black with a spell that caused its body to explode outward like a poorly made barrel.

Other Great Blacks and Reds were destroyed but the numbers weren't favoring us. The elite Shadowguard soldiers were firing powerful spells of light magic, far more than a normal human being or elf could conjure. That was when I realized a fact that made our situation infinitely direr: they were *all* possessed by messengers.

"Dammit," I said, climbing up the side of Blaze as Regina pivoted her dragon up toward the new figure.

"I'm not sure that qualifies when you're the King Below," Regina said. "You know, I never expected to be killing messengers as my religious vocation."

"Now's not the time for jokes!"

"It's always the time for jokes!" Regina shouted. "Get rid of the next one's barrier and put one up around us."

"What?"

"Now!"

Regina thrust Blaze forward at a Great Black standing in the way of the man I believed, now, to be Fel Hellsword. Casting rapidly, I found myself facing a powerful and intricate barrier spell that protected against everything from magic to explosives. I could have spent hours unweaving it, but, instead, just threw everything I had against it to annul trying to raise one around us both.

I wasn't fast enough.

"*Y'aghul al'mathan!*" the figure on the dragon, a crimson-haired woman with deformed avian hands and features shouted.

It was, roughly translated from the old Terralan Tongue, an invocation to the Lawgiver that called for his retribution against the unrighteous. The actual words mattered little compared to the spell behind it, a mental command that invoked the Ultimate Holy Retribution spell. It was capable of killing the strongest demons that only archmages and great wizards were said to know. I struggled to finish the barrier but the Ultimate Holy Retribution passed through it like light through glass only to strike Regina in the chest.

And wash over her like raindrops.

"Retribution!" Regina shouted, lowering her lance and spearing the Great Black and its rider with a single lance thrust.

Both fell to the ground, the lance inside them exploding halfway down.

"That's three for me! How many for you, Jacob?" Regina called.

"One."

"Shameful! I'll give you half!" Regina then pivoted Blaze to the right, barely avoiding a spell of concentrated light as hot as the sun.

Fel Hellsword had noticed us.

"I need that barrier spell now!" Regina shouted orders to the remainder of our group. There only a few dragonriders left, tearing apart messenger-possessed Shadowguard and devouring them to absorb their power.

I finished my spell and gave every little bit of energy I had into it. What followed were a torrent of a dozen spells shot forth in rapid succession, faster than any human being could cast them, each slamming into the barrier with the force of an elemental-powered locomotive. Somehow, they managed to hold their own against it as we came closer to our quarry, soon only a hundred feet away.

"You cannot win this day, Black Sun and Starlight Maid!" Fel Hellsword's High Imperial-accented voice echoed through the battlefield, using titles far more respectful than I expected. "I fight so this world may have a future beyond the next age!"

A group of four Great Black Dragons came up behind us, riderless but glowing with a control spell visible to the eyes of a wraith. That was when the sky cracked open and a thousand black crow-shaped imps poured out from a gate to the World Below, swarming our foes. Serah had brought us allies from the World Below.

"I guess your demons were sick of being bored, Jacob!" Regina said, closing the ranks to a few dozen feet. "Time to die, Hellsword!"

Regina drew her blade, *Starlight*, from its sheath and the glowing blade of living light caused the very air to crackle.

I saw Hellsword then, my vision capturing his full likeness better than any human's could at that distance. He was a chalky-skinned human with hair like dull straw. He was delicate looking with a red splotchy birthmark over his right eye. The Usurper was wearing form-fitting ancient Terralan armor of indescribable beauty. It was absolutely covered in blood runes, more than a hundred, and enhanced his aura to such a degree I could feel it even at this distance. In Hellsword's left hand was *Plaguebringer*, the sister blade to *Chill's Fury*, a weapon that wailed with the spirits of a thousand imprisoned souls. I could defeat him alone, perhaps, but with Regina at my side? He didn't stand a chance.

"Give my regards to Serah!" Hellsword then said, smiling. "She's much improved."

He lifted *Plaguebringer* into the air and then aimed it to side, conjuring another rift in the sky before flying through it.

"No!" Regina shouted, trying to move Blaze fast enough to follow.

But it was gone before we reached its side.

Hellsword had escaped.

Chapter Six

"Shit-eating whoresons!" Regina shouted, turning around Blaze and doing a circle about the area where Hellsword's portal had appeared. "What was that!?"

"The stories about him binding souls to empower his spells are true," I said, disturbed at the implications of that.

Necromancy was nothing new to me, let alone the world, but I'd never heard of someone who had been able to successfully bind more than a few souls to themselves. Even a few imprisoned ones were great sources of power to those who knew how to feed upon them as magical reservoirs. Hellsword had bound an entire city to him. Enough to open the kind of portals I'd needed an entire city's worth of machinery to create. The pain he was causing those spirits had to be immense.

I was still more powerful than him, such as one might want to measure a god versus a mortal, but the ability to deploy power on the world was not a one-to-one affair. I could draw on great power, power which would change the laws of reality, but the consequences to the people of this world—as well as myself—were things I'd need omniscience to predict. That hadn't come with my ascension to the King Below's throne. Hence, I relied on the same (im)mortal sorcery I'd used in both life as well as undeath. It usually didn't fail me. Usually.

"Can you open it behind him? Follow him!?" Regina shouted, shaking with rage. "We can't just let him get away."

I closed my eyes, taking a deep breath. "We don't have the Night Bridge here and it'll be a days-long journey back to the Eyes of the World on dragonback. That portal he summoned could have gone anywhere, too. Hells, the ancient sidhe moongates led to other worlds and times."

"Then it was for nothing," Regina said, shaking her head. "Alayx, Vain, Bloodsplatter, Dwain, and Kull."

I took those to be the names of the dragon riders who'd fallen in battle. It was, in military terms, a pyrrhic victory. Even if we'd managed to kill thirteen of the empire's finest warriors and their dragons, they could afford to soak up the losses of such far better than we could. With Hellsword's death, Regina might have been able to justify the loss as in a good cause. Without it? It was just the death of five good soldiers.

Such was war.

"I'm sorry," I whispered, removing a glove and placing my hand on her shoulder.

"They trusted me to lead them to victory," Regina muttered. "I should have made their deaths count."

"War is not so easily measured," I said softly. "It is made of a thousand failures, mistakes, and misjudgments wrapped up in pretty banners to disguise how so much of it is pointless."

Regina stared forward, silent for a moment. She then said, "We should rejoin the others."

"You are a good commander, Regina, and I—"

"Please, Jacob, just leave it alone for a bit."

I didn't say anything else.

Blaze settled down with the remaining riders of our group: Serah, Curse, Payne, Archus, Regina, and myself. Smoke was standing amongst them, unconcerned with my survival one way or the other, but two of the Great Blacks were gravely wounded by their struggle. With alchemy, magic, and time they would heal, but that would be a long time coming.

Months.

Serah was, thankfully, already lending what little aid she could to the dragons by clouding their minds before starting the healing process. Magical healing had many benefits, but pain was its price.

The area around us was rocky and not too far from the shores that the Devil's Sea crashed into. Bits and pieces of grass grew all around and there was a forest to the north. The Northern Wasteland was somewhat misnamed and had much habitable land inside it. We weren't that far from Caer Callig, a former fortress of the Shadowguard. Several dragon corpses were nearby and I spotted the remains of the fallen Lesser Yellow nearby. It wasn't dead, but soon would be, and I had little hope the rider had survived her treacherous journey.

Regina slid off the side of her saddle. "I'm sorry, my friends, Hellsword escaped."

"No war is measured in victories alone," Serah said, lifting her staff above the arm of a handsome sidhe man. "Sometimes even the greatest generals must acknowledge the bitter sting of defeat."

The sidhe, the self-titled Curse, had brown skin and long silvery black hair that hung down to his waist. Curse had traded his ornate elvish armor for the more modest attire of a dragon rider, but he was still someone who looked more like an artist's romantic conception of a warrior than one. Either way, he was still one of the deadliest killers in the North.

"We bloodied him and made him retreat," Curse said, clenching his teeth as I heard a broken arm set before beginning to heal under Serah's care. "To do that to the people who killed the old King Below will win you many accolades."

"I'm not interested in accolades," Regina said, gritting her teeth. "Only the destruction of my enemies."

"You sound more like a proper Formor every day," Payne said, her voice raspy and cold from where her throat had been deformed by acid. The Bauchan wore a veil to hide the injury and was, otherwise, one of the more beautiful members of an already-attractive race. She had her red hair tied in a topknot and I wondered how she managed to hide such a thing underneath a dragon rider's helmet.

They had been two of my earliest supporters and while I hesitated to call the couple friends, I couldn't help but think the world would be diminished by their loss. I somehow doubted Hellsword felt anywhere close to the amount of emotional strife Regina was feeling right now over the loss of her soldiers.

"I'm sorry," Serah said, surprising me. "I should have anticipated that he'd grown strong enough to open portals at will."

"Archus, I'd like you to go investigate the Lesser Yellow," Regina said to a particularly large and brutish Formor warrior. "See if she's still alive and if not, if there's anything useful we might get from her. Don't harm or frighten her if you don't have to."

Archus was over six feet in height, gray skinned, and had a

scaly noseless face with extra-large shark-like teeth. Formor were as hideous as Bauchan were beautiful, but had no consciousness of this fact, considering other species' ideal of attractiveness to be hideous beyond belief. I didn't know the dragon rider well, but he'd apparently been a warchief of the Dragonbinder clan before deciding there was more glory as one of Regina's lieutenants.

"As you wish, God Queen," Archus said, walking off.

"I might be better for meeting this girl," Curse said. "I am less likely to terrify, at least."

"My orders stand," Regina said, glaring.

Curse shrugged. "As you wish, my Queen."

We were an odd collection of individuals and I couldn't help but wonder what life would be like for us if we were able to live in peace. I would never recover the honor I'd lost during the Fourth Great Shadow War and my subsequent enslavement but that didn't keep me from trying. Regina wanted, desperately, to be the hero of a story where the Nine were the villains. Serah was determined to be the most powerful sorceress who ever lived and now that she was close to achieving it, had no idea what she would do with the rest of her life. Curse and Payne were a sidhe and Bachaun couple, something only slightly less likely than the stars falling from the sky. I couldn't help but wonder if the Northern Wastelands had become an island for misfits and the lost. If so, it was better company than I deserved.

Regina turned to Serah, bringing up a topic I had all but forgotten. "You mentioned Hellsword was your lover. I've known you since we were newly women and this is the first I've heard of it."

"I don't like talking about that time of my life," Serah said, her voice quivering just the slightest bit. "I also knew the Usurpers were not something you'd like to know I had an association with."

Regina crossed her arms. "It seems today is a day for lies and deception."

Serah looked away, stricken.

"I, for one, am not so much a hypocrite as to complain about your past lovers trying to kill us."

Serah smiled then pushed it away. "I'm afraid my association with Hellsword is a long and complicated story. It does, however, deserve to be shared. Are either of you familiar with the Oghma?"

I was.

So, too, was Regina. "My information may be out of date but in my time that was the name of the secret society of high lords and great wizards, wasn't it? The ones devoted to preventing the King Below from conquering the world."

"Indeed. I know precious little more, though, even given my encounters with a few members."

Most scholars thought the Oghma were myths, stories of ancient heroes and legends that had no relevance to the modern day. They'd been instrumental in the protection of humanity during the Second and Third War but had been conspicuous by their absence during the Fourth War.

I knew they were real, though, because I'd killed both Tharadon the Black and Co'Fannon the Forgemaster to seize their knowledge as part of my efforts against the King Below's forces. Both had been reputed members of the Oghma and there had been references to the organization in their notes. If they were real, though, it actually gave me some hope the Nine Heroes might be overthrown—the Oghma were a force for good in a world too often absent of such things.

"Yes," Serah said, sighing. "It was an organization founded by Ethinu the Wise and other luminaries during the First War. The Oghma was broken before the Fourth War by the Prophecy of Morrigan the Lesser."

I grimaced. "I *hate* prophecies."

Curse suddenly looked interested. "The blood of Ethinu and her kin runs through my veins and I've never heard of any such prophecy."

"Few have," Serah said. "I have never read it, but the Oghma kept it within its ranks and only a select few were allowed to read it. Details Hellsword allowed to slip were that it spoke of the rise of a new King Below, stronger than the last, and the end of the world."

Everyone looked at me.

"Well, we know the prophecy is wrong now." Curse snorted. "The only way he might destroy the world is by accident."

"Perhaps the prophecy meant Regina," Payne suggested.

"That might work," Curse said, smiling. "Albeit, one might wonder if her poor taste in lovers is mentioned."

Neither Regina nor Serah looked amused.

"Where I'm from, subjects are supposed to treat their kings with less insolence," I said, shaking my head. We were surrounded by the blood of our fellows and he was making light of this.

"Weren't you from a village in the middle of nowhere?" a dragon rider I didn't recognize asked.

I glared at her. "I was speaking rhetorically."

Curse said, "You'd receive less insolence if you acted more like a proper...mmmph."

Curse's mouth disappeared. Instead, a thin layer of fatty flesh covered its location, conjured by magic.

Serah was holding her two left front fingers together, showing where the spell originated. "Your mouth will return when you remember to show respect."

Curse stared, then shrugged before nodding.

"Please go on," I said to Serah. "I'd very much like to know more about this group and how it relates to Hellsword." It wasn't every day you found out you were fated to destroy the world. I would have been worried if I believed in predestination.

"The Oghma reformed in secret," Serah said, looking down. Her voice changed and I was surprised at the genuine shame of it. She was not a woman who reacted with guilt, to anything. "They regarded the dangers threatening the world to be too severe to deal with in public and, instead, that it would be better to manipulate events from behind the scene. Hellsword recruited me, and, together, we became members. He was my mentor, friend, and, yes, lover."

Regina's eyes widened. "Hellsword is a member of an ancient society of heroes and archmages?"

"And so is Serah," I said, stunned at the implications. "That explains much."

Regina shot me a dirty look. "*In what world* does this explain much?"

"Serah has always been an exceptional mage," I said, shrugging. "One far and above the ability of most. Besides, magicians interfere in politics. It's what they do. When I was training in light magic at the Grand Temple, there were hundreds of fraternities, sororities, and cabals to join. Jassamine outlawed most of them with the help of Prince Alfreid, but this did little to bring them to heel."

I had felt isolated as a student at the Grand Temple, the son of Borderland peasants living and working amongst the children of Imperial nobility thanks to a famous uncle, but it was almost nothing to the loneliness being a god king brought. I had always wondered why so many kings and queens were shameless bastards but the nature of the crown was an evil thing. If not for Serah and Regina, I probably would have gone mad.

Says the man who talks to a dead god living in the back of his head, the Trickster said.

"I liked it better when I thought you were gone forever," I muttered.

That was when Serah destroyed my trust in her. "Jassamine is also a member of the Oghma. Ethinu trained her, just as she trained Hellsword."

That was like a punch in the ribs. "What?"

Jassamine had been my reason for living during the third decade of my life and the thought of her had been the first thing in my mind when I emerged from the King Below's slavery. I would, and had, done anything for her. However, the gentle woman of my memories had been an illusion covering a fanatic willing to kill children to achieve her ends. I had shredded my honor by that point but there were some lines I wouldn't cross and she merrily leaped across them. It stunned me, the monumental level of the betrayal, that Serah had known vital information about our enemy, about her, and kept it from me.

"Why?" I asked.

Perhaps because she didn't want you turning on her as you did your previous lover? the Trickster suggested. *You do so love to put your lovers on pedestals. I think you'd be happier if you assumed everyone was a vile scheming wretch like me. Then you might not be constantly disappointed.*

Be quiet! I shouted in my mind.

The Trickster, remarkably, fell silent.

Regina clenched a fist, looking ready to explode. "You have been lying to us."

"As if you did not keep secrets!" Serah said, suddenly shouting. "You had no intention of waging war on the continent!"

"Do not compare this!" Regina snapped.

"How is this worse!?" Serah retorted.

"One is conspiring with the enemy!" Regina shouted, ignoring the uncomfortable looks of our soldiers. "How could you conceal this from us!? Hellsword was one of the conspirators behind my family's death! If she's part of some..." She shook her head. "Magical conspiracy then that might explain how the Usurpers gained such quick control over the southern continent! You know the names of our enemies! Hell, you might—"

"I might what!?" Serah shouted back, trembling with a mix of outrage and offense. "Be one of them?"

"Please!" Payne screamed, causing all three of us to pause. She was holding her husband by the shoulders as he pried at the fatty tissue around his mouth. "You are monarchs and gods; act like it."

I gritted my teeth, trying to gain control over my emotions. I was a ghost and what I felt was an echo of what a living man might yet what I experienced now was a mixture of white hot rage and betrayal. I wanted to smash the rocks around us or freeze the oceans or something. Instead, much to my surprise, I forced my emotions down and decided to give Serah a chance to explain. No one was more surprised than I by this turn of events, but I trusted my wife. I wanted to hear her reasons.

"Kindly explain," I said, clenching my fists and looking down at the gravelly shoreline beneath me. We were close to the sea and the cold sea air burned against my lungs. "Have you been in contact with them this entire time?"

"No, never," Serah said, taking a deep breath. "Not until yesterday did I have any contact with Fel."

"Yesterday," I said, remembering how she'd been unusually nice to us that evening. Serah was no stranger to decadence but that evening she'd encouraged us to indulge in drink, food, sex, and revelry. "That's why you brought up the issue of the invasion. You wanted to eliminate the ties to your past." It was monstrously manipulative and it bothered me that I was, on some level, impressed.

"I hoped the Oghma would never come up again," Serah said, her voice soft. "Understand, when Fel found me, I was half-mad due to my shadow powers. My family's money protected me but a succession of tutors taught me nothing but a bare minimum of sorcery. He was the first teacher to teach me how to embrace my powers and rejoice in what I was. I was also suffering unrequited love for you, Regina, and he was there to fill the void. You preferred a succession of whores, knights, and your own cousin to me."

"I wonder if that was not the better choice," Regina said, her voice cold.

Serah looked as if Regina had struck her. "Understand I have never put much stock in prophecies, but I rejoiced in the power of the Oghma. The chance to manipulate kings, queens, and lords like game pieces. It was they who made me and my brother our uncle's greatest advisors—and prevented me from being arrested for possessing night magic. Then I met you, Jacob, traveling with Regina, and saw an opportunity. I'm sorry to say I didn't realize who you were until much later."

"Who I was?" I asked.

"A hero."

I snorted. "That's either grossly inappropriate flattery or simply poor observation. What did Hellsword contact you about?"

"Yes, Serah, tell us what you hid from us," Regina said, her voice still low and angry. Serah's explanation was not being received by her the way it was by me. Then again, Regina trusted far easier but felt betrayal far keener. I do not think she would hate the Anessian Empire so greatly if she had not once been its most loyal citizen.

"Fel asked me to not intervene in an attack that would take him near our territory. Which I did not, I point out." Serah looked more offended by her ignorance than the fact that she'd alienated us. "I do not know who this woman is, why she was being targeted, or what her role in all this is. My loyalty is to you, though, and I arranged for Midori to find out about her arrival."

"Through the most duplicitous means possible," I said, amazed at her cheek.

"It's what makes me good at what I do," Serah said, straightening her back. "You could not count the number of plots I have thwarted behind your back. Assassination attempts, sabotage, propaganda, and the arming of our enemies. Only the massacre at the baths escaped through mine and Midori's network, and it was I who helped you bring your revenge down on House Rogers."

"Which does not make up for the ones you've initiated this day," Regina said, quickly changing the subject. The destruction of House Rogers was not a subject any of us wanted to discuss ever again. "I trusted you with all my secrets and you didn't think to share one of your own, knowing what the Usurpers mean to me."

Serah didn't apologize. Regina would have forgiven her, in time, if she apologized. But Serah was a proud woman. I did not think she would do it. Regina was a raging storm, but Serah was the mountain it beat against.

I did not know how to fix this.

Damn.

That was when Archus returned from his mission to check the woman Hellsword had been chasing. "My lords, the female is still alive!"

"Thank the universe for distractions," I said, turning around to investigate.

Regina, meanwhile, just shot Serah a glare. "This is not over. Also, give Curse his fucking mouth back. Her spouse might need it some night."

Serah reluctantly waved her hand and Curse's mouth reappeared.

"Thank you!" Payne said, waving.

"You're welcome." Regina then turned to walk beside me toward a figure that would change our destinies.

CHAPTER SEVEN

It was about an acre and a half of walking toward the Lesser Yellow Dragon and the woman I'd seen in Midori's vision had, apparently, broken her leg. Regina and I both followed Archus while Serah chose to stay behind, perhaps realizing that now was not the best time to be around her bride.

"Can you believe her?" Regina said, gritting her teeth. "Of all the double-crossing, backstabbing, Natariss-like....argh!"

"You're degenerating into anger-ish again."

"As well I should!" Regina snapped back. "I knew Serah had other lovers, but one of the fucking Usurpers? And what's this about the Oghma? Was she *spying* on us the entire time? Then she has the audacity to get mad at you for your secrets...and don't think I've forgotten about that. I'm still mad at you, just significantly less."

"Marriage," Archus grunted. "This is why I don't believe in it."

Regina's glare looked like it could cause him to explode.

"Sorry, your godship," Archus said, scrunching down as if he could feel her glare. "I won't speak again."

"Don't worry about it," Regina said, sighing. "What do you think of all this, Jacob?"

I wasn't sure how to answer but I decided to try anyway. "Truth be told, I am rather difficult to shock. Jassamine was a woman of countless secrets. That Serah kept the fact she was involved with both the Usurpers and an organization our enemies belong to secret irritates me, but I knew Serah was..."

"What?"

I chose my next words carefully. "Who she was, when I married her."

I had been attracted to her *precisely because* of the fact she was manipulative, power hungry, and secretive. It wasn't the healthiest attitude to possess but, the simple fact was, I enjoyed having someone at my side who was as interested in power as Serah. Part of the reason I was so hesitant about attacking the South wasn't just because I didn't want to subject them to the horrors of war. It was because I *liked* the idea of hammering the northern and southern continents in one gigantic empire.

I'd been spit on, derided, and loathed my entire life as the bastard son of a mixed-race fisherman and a seamstress. I'd witnessed unimaginable atrocities, horrors, and purges both during the war as well as before it. People, both noble and peasant, had shown themselves utterly unworthy of any sympathy. Crushing them all underneath a demonsteel boot had a certain appeal. Which is why I had to resist it.

Hehehehe, the Trickster chuckled in the back of my mind. *You won't be able to.*

I gritted my teeth at the Trickster's words.

"Perhaps I did too," Regina said, frowning. "But it was because of the lies, manipulations, and deceit that ended my first relationship with Serah. I decided we were better as friends—and now I wonder if she was ever that either."

"Serah would burn the world down for us. You know this." I felt, curiously, like I was seventeen again and still living in my father's house. I'd had to play diplomat between my sisters, Chastity and Virtue, like this all the time. I missed them.

Regina sighed. "Perhaps she would burn the world for us. Perhaps I'd would like her to consider whether I'd want her to first."

I wasn't happy with the way this conversation was turning even as I knew it was inevitable. A single relationship was a difficult thing to manage and two was almost impossible.

"Do you remember when she didn't want to have a marriage ceremony?" Regina asked, throwing her hands out. "She said that it was a useless concept. Useless! As if it wasn't the greatest sign of a commitment one could make. She said none of us worshiped the Lawgiver anymore and we were gods anyway so—"

"I was there," I said, knowing this could lead nowhere good. "We should change the subject. Give ourselves some time to look at things objectively. We've just started the war we were discussing earlier."

"All right," Regina said, lowering her hands. "Do you have any suspicions as to who this woman could be?"

"Not a clue," I said, pausing. "It could be a trap, though."

"What?"

"Hellsword may have arranged this chase so he could push an agent of his into our ranks. He, after all, informed his ex-lover of events with the full knowledge she would pass the information onto us. It's also possible the Nephyr and Great Dragons were part of an ambush designed to draw me, you, or Serah out, knowing that we all lead from the front. I find that less likely but still possible."

"You have a devious mind," Regina said. "Much more so than your appearance suggests."

"My spiky black armor does suggest a certain honesty."

"We shall have to get it redesigned when I'm crowned empress and restored the Whitetremor lineage to the Gryphon Throne. We can have something bright and shiny made with wingtips. I love wingtips."

"You really want that?"

"Wingtips? I admit, I prefer unicorns as a heraldic animal, but—"

"The Imperial throne."

"Oh." Regina shrugged. "I guess. Someone must rule the empire after Empress Morwen is drawn, quartered, and fed to wild dogs. My family has as much title to it as anyone."

Regina was only distantly in line for the throne via blood but every candidate between her and it were loyal to Empress Morwen. Morwen, herself, was only the empire's ruler by marriage but had managed to secure the allegiance of those beneath her through her heroism on the battlefield and copious bribes.

Ironically, it had been the destruction of the storied and well loved Whitetremor lineage that had intimidated the Anessian nobility into completely submitting. After all, if Empress Morwen could destroy them she could destroy anyone. The price had merely been creating an enemy of one of the most determined and capable women in the world.

"You'll have double title to it because you've killed everyone else," Archus said. "Ma'am."

"I suggest we consider finding an appropriate candidate to assume the throne in your stead. A puppet or, at least, compromise candidate who will be friendly to our cause. It will be easier than convincing the majority of the Imperial populace to follow the King Below and his wife."

"They will follow us because we are in the right." Regina's tone brooked no argument.

"I...see."

We were about halfway to the woman and I got a closer look at her with my dead eyesight. She was slight of frame and more delicate looking than a woman who rode across the Devil's Sea on dragonback should be. Yet, despite that, there was something greatly familiar about the woman. As if she resembled someone I knew.

The woman did not appear to be afraid, even as she'd cast some sort of relaxation spell to help her horribly wounded dragon. The beast was sleeping calmly despite its grave injuries. I did not think it would live through the night, though I'd try to save it. I did note, however, the woman hadn't cast any similar spells on herself. She was enduring a broken leg through pure will.

Impressive.

I continued talking as we walked, trying to figure out how we could convince the Imperials to believe we weren't monsters out to kill them all. "We must persuade them of our point of view. If the rest of the world rallies behind the Lawgiver's armies then we can only destroy the world rather than rule it. We must undercut their support and I believe we can do that by spreading our message."

"We have a message?" Regina asked, chuckling.

"The absence thereof is what I'm getting at, yes."

"I suppose 'obey or die' is rather crude," Regina deadpanned.

"I never know when you're joking."

"I aspire to virtue and settle for triumph." Regina placed a hand over her heart. "Let's put that in our holy book, as soon as we write it. Seriously, though, I want to liberate the people of the empire and bring justice to them, not cause them suffering."

I wondered how many would care once we started laying siege to their cities. "I suppose every holy book should have a collection of pithy sayings."

"The holy book is actually a good idea. If people read it, they can know what we stand for and that we're trying to help people.

It would also provide the Shadowkind with direction. Not that they need it, they're adults after all, but we are in charge and they need to know our values. We should also make festival days, lots of them," Regina said, treating the suggestion far more seriously than I expected. "Everyone loves a party."

"I like her religion already," Archus said.

I was thinking of a rebuttal to that when we arrived at the side of the Yellow Dragon. The young woman was a couple of years younger than Regina, older than I'd initially expected, but otherwise much like the image I'd seen of her earlier. The girl's sword hilt took me by surprise, though, since it bore the unicorn symbol of House Whitetremor. I'd grown accustomed to the image of the foul beasts, as Regina loved to cover just about everything in her section of the tower with its image.

Regina, meanwhile, stared down at the girl as if she'd seen a ghost. No, wait, she saw ghosts as a regular part of being married to a necromancer and the God of Death. This was far, far different, closer to seeing something that rocked her to the very core of her being. The woman on the ground, meanwhile, had a similar look of shock. Regina fell to her knees and embraced her, giving the woman kisses on the cheek before squeezing her eyes so hard that I thought tears of joy would spontaneously emerge.

"Cousin!" the woman shouted.

"Sister!" Regina replied.

"I really hope one of those is just a term of endearment," Archus muttered, "but you never know with nobles."

I made a slashing gesture across my throat.

"Do you want me to kill her or are you telling me to be silent?" Archus asked, confused.

I pressed my hand to my face in frustration. "The latter."

"Oh, sorry."

And you wonder why I abused their race for ages, the Trickster muttered. *Never forget the first rule about mortals: they are deeply stupid.*

"I take it you know this woman?" I asked Regina, standing over the pair as they continued to embrace.

Regina opened her eyes, now actually crying. "This is my cousin, Ketra, sister of Gewain. I was raised with her from the time my parents were killed."

I found myself speechless. The death of Regina's family had weighed upon her like a millstone around her neck, crushing her with guilt and anguish. I'd heard much about both Ketra and Gewain, the latter being Regina's first love despite being cousins, and I felt I knew them.

Clearly not.

"If I may," I said, gesturing to her leg.

"Uhm, if you may," Ketra said, looking at me for perhaps the first time. I had to be a terrifying figure given the fact I was wearing the attire of a Wraith Knight. It was the same armor I'd worn while being mind-controlled into being one of the old King Below's generals. As such, I entered the popular consciousness as an everlasting symbol of evil. Then again, it might be she just thought it strange to be meeting her cousin's husband under such odd circumstances.

Regina removed a dagger from her side and gave it to Ketra to bite down upon the hilt of. The young woman did so and I cast a spell of healing. Ketra screamed through the knife, biting down hard. Dark magic did not heal painlessly, any more than Light, but it was effective.

Ketra took out the dagger, spitting. "Thank you. I've been using every bit of energy I've had to keep Shooting Star moving ahead of those monsters chasing me. I fear he's about to die of exhaustion."

"You are trained as a temple mage?" I asked. I found it confusing a woman who knew enough light magic to keep a dragon speeding along didn't know enough to properly set a bone, exhausted or not. I'd learned that in my first month studying to be a Temple Knight.

Ketra snorted. "As if I would lower myself to study with those superstitious religious fanatics and fools. They believe in nonsense like invisible sky kings and horrible demon kings who live in the earth plotting the end of the world. It's foolishness like that which they exploit to keep the ignorant masses oppressed."

Regina and I looked at her before looking at each other then back at her.

"I see," I said, unsure how to react to this woman's blatant disregard for reality.

"I believe in the Formor, of course, and the opposing religions the Grand Temple oppresses," Ketra said, putting her hand over her heart. "That is part of the reason I am here."

Regina shook her head, raising her gloved hand. "Please, before you continue, you have to explain to me how you survived. Jon Bloodthorn razed Whitehall to the ground. I saw the bodies, thousands of them, in a hundred stacked pyres."

Regina's voice shook a bit.

Ketra placed her hand on Regina's, her accent slipping from High Imperial to something closer to Regina's own. "'Twas terrible, that night. Fire and blood and death with not a hope of protecting the people who've looked to our family for centuries. Gewain led me, Rebecca, and the children of the hold to the city's sewer system, but there were soldiers waiting for us there too."

"Rebecca and Gewain are alive?" Regina asked, hope springing into her voice.

"Gewain is alive," Ketra said. "But missing an arm. Infection came in and I stupidly never studied healing."

"Rebecca?" Regina asked.

Ketra's voice hardened. "One of the empress's thugs stabbed her in the chest before I burned off his face."

According to Regina, her youngest cousin would have been eleven this spring.

It wasn't even surprising.

No one was safe during sackings.

"Where have you been?" Regina asked.

"Gael, then Winterholme," Ketra said. "I have been fighting with the Resistance against the Imperial occupation wherever I can. There's always a demand for a battlemage and I've tried to make them bleed whenever possible. They call me Rainfire."

I'd heard that name in reports from Serah's spies in the South. Rainfire was a bringer of terror who conducted many strikes against the Imperials and their nobility, some of which had involved innocents being killed. But who knew if that were true and if it even mattered. One man's brigand was another man's champion. Civilians died in war and it was the rare commander who was able to get through one without oceans of blood on his hands, which was precisely why I didn't want to start a new one.

"I have much more to ask you," Regina said, before looking up to me. "Also, my husband to introduce you to—"

I interrupted her. "Forgive me, Regina, for ruining a moment you have been too long denied, but I must ask something myself. Why was Hellsword chasing you?"

Ketra blinked then nodded. "Oh, that. I suppose it's a secret I can share with my kin. I am seeking the King of the Northern Wasteland. The warlord claiming to be a god and his she-devil brides."

"His what?" Regina said, blinking.

I tried not to chuckle. "Why?"

"The Jarls of Winterholme want to ask for his aid," Ketra said, her voice low. "The entirety of their peoples are being exterminated."

Regina stared.

So did I. "I think we need to talk someplace more private."

CHAPTER EIGHT

It was several hours later before I could revisit Ketra's statement in any depth. Regina and she had much to catch upon and there were still many other affairs to deal with, not the least being retrieving the bodies of our fellows and arranging for their transport back to Everfrost. We ended up transporting Shooting Star and other wounded over to the nearby Caer Callig.

Caer Callig was a twelve-tower castle constructed in the side of a cliff-face overlooking the Devil's Sea. It had long since fallen into disrepair, if one was being generous enough not to say ruin, and was a far cry from its glory days during the Third War when a thousand Shadowguardsman attended its walls. The fortress was now inhabited by a full complement of two hundred Formor warriors and twice as many workers.

The base commander had taken to using massive freeman Trow to carve out the stone and haul it around. Ending slavery of the horned race had resulted in me gaining a substantial number of enthusiastic stonemasons and carters that, apparently, nearly all Trow were. Really, I'd thought the whole trolls and bridges thing had been a myth.

Either way, we'd found a warm welcome even if the sounds of ongoing construction were not conducive to casual conversation. In the end, it was well past noon by the time I managed to separate Ketra from her sister and the three of us sat down in the northernmost tower away from the goings-on below. Serah had tried to sit down with us, but it had ended up in a shouting match between her and Regina that I'd, rather cravenly, decided to be elsewhere during.

The chamber we sat in was an old brown-stone chamber with a single window that didn't have any glass in it. The tower's lightning-rune-powered generators hadn't arrived from Everfrost yet, so the chamber was warmed by old-fashioned logs in the hearth beside us. It would be sunset in a few hours and we'd need candles as well since Ketra, unlike the Formor and gods, couldn't see in the dark.

Sitting down at a round wooden table with my cohorts, I took a sip of a weak beer from a tin stein. I'd changed out of my demonsteel armor to a plain black doublet, pants, and vest. "All right, please explain to me what you mean about the treaty. I want to be absolutely clear about this."

Ketra had a glass of expensive wine in front of her, drawn from the castle's cellars. "Again?"

"Again," I said.

Ketra sighed. "The nobles of Winterholme are trying to form an alliance to extirpate the empire from their lands. Half of them have been fighting their own private wars against the empire's presence only to be destroyed every time they met their foe in open engagements. Even working together, they've had minimal success and the reprisals have been horrible. Their seers have been talking about a new King Below rising in the North and everyone heard about your killing Jon Bloodthorn in Lakeland. They're willing to swear allegiance to you if you drive the empire's forces out."

"You'll forgive me if I remain skeptical," I said, taking a sip from my stein. The beer was tasteless like all food and drink to me but it helped maintain the illusion of being human. "The Winterholme have ever been the first to be invaded by the King Below's forces and have suffered the most from the Formor's depredations."

"They're also, traditionally, the people who ally first with the King Below," Regina said, taking a long drink from a stein twice as large as mine, full of a heavy intoxicating brew that would kill a normal human. "The wild men who live in the northern continent are all descendants of those Winterholme who chose to worship the old King Below rather than suffer under him. There have always been rumors about their nobility too: secret rites, cults, and unnatural practices. It's why no one ever really trusted them in dealings."

I wanted to point out that that was because Imperials tended to be racist shits, but I doubted that would go over well with my audience. "Please go on."

"I doubt they would be turning to you if they had much of a choice," Ketra admitted. "The empire has gone mad, though. Tens of thousands of people have been uprooted from their homes around the Imperial city to be resettled in Winterholme and other lands. Freemen land is confiscated on a daily basis then given to the Usurper's supporters. Forests are being eradicated league-by-league and mountains reduced to pebbles for their minerals. Massive work gangs are laboring everywhere with conscripts from every village. The slightest offense brings terrible sentences, and that's including the people who simply disappear never to be seen again."

All in all, it didn't sound that terribly different from business as usual in the empire under a new monarchy. "Are they preparing for war against the North?"

"That's the strange thing—no, they're not," Ketra said, leaning back in her chair. "The empire is stretched to the limit as is with its current occupations and that's with punishing levies as well as mass conscription. The vast majority of resources are going to other projects. Grandiose temples, magical devices of enormous size, railroads, dams, factories, and crystal hothouses."

"Crystal hothouses?" I asked.

"Like a greenhouse but the size of a colliseum," Ketra said. "It's beggared the empire and they've been confiscating the property of nonhumans to compensate as well as those of non-Imperial descent."

Regina took a long drink from her stein and laughed. "Your strategy of waiting and doing nothing may have actually been wise, Jacob. It sounds like the Usurpers will defeat themselves through incompetence. I just hope we're able to get them first before the mob storms their homes and executes them."

I was less pleased. "There's just one problem with that, Regina."

"Oh?"

"Incompetence and tyranny have long been bedfellows, but the Nine Usurpers answer to Jassamine and she has been many things, but never stupid. Nor was my impression of the Usurpers as less than capable. If they're doing something seemingly stupid then it's probably for a very good reason."

"I don't care about their reasons," Ketra said, gritting her teeth. "I joined the Army of Free Peasants to kill as many of their supporters as possible and I'm not done yet. I'll help any group that wants to kill Imperials and you seem to be one of them."

"Ketra....we're Imperials," Regina said, sounding genuinely troubled.

"Not anymore," Ketra said, slamming her fist down on the table. It was a dramatic gesture lost on Regina and I. "I'd summon a volcano like old Valance the Red and sink the Imperial city if I could. Not one of them spoke up against the horror brought down on us."

"Maybe they did and were silenced," I said.

Ketra's look didn't waver in its intensity. "Whatever the case, they want to meet with you. I don't believe for a second you're actually Jacob Riverson reborn, some mythical hero out of the stories, but my sister loves you so I don't care one way or the other. The Jarls are willing to send their representatives to meet with you in the port city of Kerifas. It's under the cruel dictatorship of Queen Morwen's son, Marcus, with the support of the Usurpers Thermic Redhand and Fel Hellsword. If you can take that city, the rest of the country will fall in line behind you."

I doubted it would be that easy. "All right. I shall consider your proposal."

"They are awaiting your answer," Ketra said. "You must move quickly."

"We agree," Regina said, shooting me a question look. "Don't we?"

Truth be told, her offer was barely registering with me despite its fortuitousness. It was incomprehensibly unlikely that, of all the billion or so inhabitants of the World Between, Regina's beloved cousin would end up at our doorstep. I had subtly probed Ketra's mind, tested a fragment of her hair, and even listened in to the details of her conversations with Regina to determine everything she said seemed to be true.

Accepting that, yes, this wasn't a trick by the Usurpers or Jassamine to destroy us, I still had difficulty with everything else she was saying. The timing was just too perfect. A young woman being delivered on our doorstep, long-lost relative or not, carrying an offer of alliance against our enemies when we needed it most. It was a miracle and I did not believe in miracles.

The Lawgiver often granted the prayers of his subjects, the Trickster said. *No rhyme or reason to it, really, but did so with the whims of a proper god. You should try it sometime.*

I'll pass, I said, still turning over Ketra's words in my head. *I'll grant all my worshipers' prayers or none of them.*

Then you'll never grant any of them.

The only way I could make sense of this, disregarding the ludicrous idea of destiny, was that there was simply something abnormally exceptional about the Whitetremor bloodline. This did not sit well with me, either, since I had long since rejected the idea the nobility were anything more than people whose ancestors had been in the right place at the right time. Yet, the evidence was before me, that the Whitetremors had produced not only Regina but two infamous revolutionaries rocking the empire.

"All right, yes, we agree. If the people of Winterholme wish our assistance then it would be morally repugnant to deny them it," I said, staring down at the table. "This is a very different set of circumstances to an unprovoked invasion."

"Is it really?" Regina asked.

I wasn't sure, no. "Yes. The righteous must ever be ready to strike at evil but equally so to sheathe one's sword lest the innocent be slain. Warmaster Kalian used to make up things like that and pretend they were in the Codex."

"Oh, that's definitely going in the holy book then," Regina said.

"Eh?" Ketra asked.

"Long story," I said.

"Jacob and I are gods. So is Serah but I loathe her right now," Regina said. "Worship us, puny mortal." She then took another long slog of the Formor brew.

"And people wonder why I'm an atheist," Ketra said, taking another sip of her wine. "So are you two divine majesties thinking about having kids?"

Regina almost choked then put down her drink and shook her head. "Not...now."

"No," I said, my voice soft.

Ketra blinked, realizing she'd unwittingly stumbled on a sore subject. "I see."

We'd tried for the first year of our marriage, flush in our

newfound love and heedless of how dangerous it was to bring a child into the world with the blood of two gods. One of which was a physical ghost. I'd met several children of physical ghosts in my career and they'd been universally 'troubled.' Yet, conception had not occurred.

Serah, despite having no interest in children herself, had spent many hours poring over tomes and potions in her lab trying to fix the problem. She took away valuable time from her efforts studying the King Below's sorcery and building her spy network to help us. It had gotten to the point Regina and I had to physically sit her down to prevent her from invading the World Above to get a sample of the Great Mother's menstrual fluid. I didn't want to know how that would have worked.

"That's unfortunate," Ketra said, shrugging. "I know Regina wants children. Personally, I can't stand them. We need to figure out a way to grow them in tubes and get rid of the whole pregnancy and child-rearing process. It's an unfair burden on my sex and does no one any good."

I stared at her. "You went to Hildenstadt University, didn't you?"

"How did you know?"

"Some things never change," I said, remembering that horrible place from my youth. Warmaster Kalian had recommended I study magic there, but I'd chosen the Grand Temple instead. Last I'd heard, all the professors had been arrested for heresy and the facility shut down. "I will meet with your friends in Kerifas. I'll need to check out the city's defenses before I consider any actual plan of attack, though."

Ketra nodded. "The Jarls will want to make arrangements with you beyond this as well. The legions are scattered through the countryside, though, and should be easy pickings once you liberate the city."

I sighed purely for effect. I didn't need to breathe, after all. "It's not going to be that simple. As soon as we take over Kerifas, the legions are going to want to rally together into a single formidable force that we'll need to defeat in battle. We'll be at war with the entirety of the continent then and the one thing that might be able to rally support for the Usurpers after all their atrocities would be an invasion by the new King Below."

Regina wasn't happy with my summation. "We should still strike. War is inevitable. This way, we choose our battlefield."

Ketra finished her glass of wine and poured herself another. It was her sixth. "Not to interrupt, but speaking of invasions by the King Below, why are you impersonating the God of Evil and his bride? You'd think you'd choose something a little more heroic-seeming if you were serious about winning support for your cause. It's not exactly inspiring to see your black-armored troops and black sun banners."

She should have seen what they'd replaced. Instead, I said, "What is a hero to one culture is a villain to another."

Ketra raised an eyebrow, giving me a 'what kind of fool do you take me for' look. "No need to be condescending."

"I'm not. The Formor have a very different opinion of the King Below and we must maintain appearances. Even if it makes us look like villains."

"How is Gewain?" Regina surprised me by asking.

"You mean aside from having lost his arm?" Ketra asked.

"Yes." Regina's eyes narrowed. Already, her joy was dimming at her cousin's return. "I mean aside from that."

"He is well," Ketra said, frowning. "They have clockwork arms in Lakeland and we acquired one recently. A good thing, too, since they haven't produced any in years. Accadia was badly ravaged after their ill-conceived attempt at rebellion. Jon Bloodthorn's death caused the empire's forces to make an example of the region."

My guts twisted. "I see."

"It didn't work out too well for them," Ketra said, chuckling. "It turns out if you keep kicking someone, they start to kick back."

"Gewain..." Regina reminded her. "Please. I wish to know more."

"Oh," Ketra said. "Sorry. My brother has been doing his best to move from place to place, trying to persuade people to rebel against the empire. I've been traveling beside him, mostly, but we're not always in agreement as to what we should do. The Army of Free Peasants is more an idea than an organization, anyway."

"Is he happy?" Regina asked.

I tried not to be uncomfortable as Regina asked about the man she wanted to marry before me.

Tried and failed.

"Yes, he's found a lover named Rose who shares his passion for revolution," Ketra said. "The cause is his life, Regina. I'm sure he'll be happy that you've found someone."

"Someones," Regina corrected.

Ketra blinked. "Yeah, two spouses. That's…something I never expected from you."

"It suits me," Regina said. "For now."

Serah, Regina, and I would really have to sit down to settle this.

"Will Gewain be meeting with us?" I asked, deciding to turn the conversation to more pleasant topics.

Like war.

"Yes," Ketra said, nodding. "Though we need to move quickly. The crackdowns in the city are getting worse and worse. Prince Alfreid is just a puppet and powerless to control either Redhand or Hellsword. Whereas Hellsword seems to be interested in ruling, Redhand is just a monster. There are burnings in the streets, mass arrests, and some even are talking about a purge of the Nonhuman Quarter."

"Nonhuman Quarter?" I asked.

"What they now call the Fire Districts. It's not just the Fir Bolg who live in them now, but anyone who isn't human or elf. The sidhe get a pass, it seems, and so do elfblooded. Everyone else who isn't one hundred percent human is getting resettled."

I stared. "I see. The empress is trying to divide and conquer the races of the southern continent. To give the human and elven citizens a scapegoat while enriching their spent coffers."

You give them too much credit, the Trickster mocked in my head. *They are just prejudiced themselves.*

"When do you want to arrange the meeting?" Ketra said. "They're waiting for my signal. It should be soon because someone betrayed my journey to Hellsword."

I frowned. "Tomorrow. We'll journey there tonight."

Ketra nodded. "Thank you. You won't regret this."

I already did. "In the meantime, I must make preparations."

"Like what?" Regina asked.

"I want to read that damn prophecy of the Oghma," I said, getting up. "If you'll excuse me, Gina, I must go speak with Serah."

I needed her to set up a communication with this secret society.

Hellsword with them or not.

Chapter Nine

I stepped out of the room where Ketra and Regina were still talking, only to find that Serah was already waiting for me on the other side.

Serah had changed into a simple but attractive black robe that I assumed was either an illusion or something she packed in her dragon's saddlebags. Her hair was flowing downwards and the scar on her face from an ill-fated servant's dagger was prominent. She was clutching her staff tightly, and I had to wonder how long she'd been standing outside the door.

"Ah," I said, trying not to look uncomfortable. "I was looking for you."

"A proper Dark Lord should not go looking for someone, Jacob, they should summon them."

"I find men who summon their wives often find themselves in unhappy marriages."

Serah tried not to smile. "It is more than mere hyperbole. You are a wise, protective, and merciful monarch."

"I had a thousand Formor hanged last year. That's including the one's Regina killed with my blessing."

"Terror is a weapon you use most effectively. It is one of your better qualities."

"I see." I tried to figure out if she was trying to compliment me and failing badly or if this was just a difference in our values.

In my day, armies engaged in rape and pillaging because their blood was hot from the drug of battle. They were poor, scared, and emaciated people who did terrible things because someone handed them an ax or spear before telling them to kill. In this day, armies were well fed and highly disciplined men and women who would kill every tenth child in a village because they were ordered to do so. I wasn't sure which was worse.

Serah sighed. "How is Regina?"

"Ecstatic that her sister has made a miraculous return from the dead. It *is* Ketra, correct?" I wanted to double-check my findings with the only mage on our side I knew to be wiser and more powerful than me.

Serah nodded. "It is, most sincerely, Ketra Whitetremor. The Blue Rose of the Empire."

I raised an eyebrow. "Really, that's what they called her?"

Ketra was many things but not one I'd call a great beauty. Cute rather than gorgeous in the way most elfblooded were. Her youthful features and mannerisms contrasted greatly with the fact that I knew Rainfire to be responsible for dozens of deaths.

"The Duchy of Whitehall was a land renowned for its ballads, plays, universities, and sculptures. Artists tend to praise individuals who throw money their way."

"Or condemn those they're paid to defame. I see your point."

"She was often compared to her ugly mannish cousin."

I snorted in disbelief. "Who is the blind, deaf, and dumb fool who said that?"

"One who I imagine has not your appreciation for women who cuss like a Riverforder and drink like a quarrywoman."

"And kisses like a goddess."

Serah looked down. "I regret losing her respect."

"Regina will forgive you," I reassured her. "She loves you."

Serah looked unhappy, an all-too-frequent look for her these days. "When I was sixteen, I fell in love for the first time with a friend of my family, Karl ap Eldrath, who was third in line for any inheritance. I lost my virginity to him, painfully, but pledged my eternal devotion to him and he did the same to me. When a young nobleman's daughter became pregnant by a singer, her father hastily offered her to Karl as an opportunity to improve his fortunes. He took it."

I frowned. "His caddish behavior—"

Serah continued. "Fel Hellsword killed him as a romantic dinner date's climax. He turned Karl into a mouse and fed the rake to a cat. You have to work extra hard to keep them from reverting past death."

I stared at her, unsure what to say. This was a revelation to me like so much of her past with Hellsword.

"That was one of the incidents that inspired me to turn against my former teacher."

"You made the right decision."

"I made a rational one. The right decision would have been to do so the first time I saw him do evil. I wanted to learn from the best in the world, though, which caused me to turn off my conscience for a time." Serah put her staff to one side and crossed her arms beneath her breasts. "Too long, I think. I am not a great believer in love. I betrayed my first love, I betrayed Fel, and now I have betrayed both you as well as Regina this day. She is not wrong not to trust me, for I am untrustworthy."

I placed my hand to the side of her face and looked into the eye. "You are my bride and I will give you the world if you but ask. I would die for you, again, and this time forever. Love is something you should believe in because, with the betrayal of the Lawgiver, it is the only light in this dark empty void we call a universe."

"It is an illusion. I know it is because I am the mistress of them." Serah then grabbed hold of me and kissed me passionately before biting my lip. "Perhaps it is a good illusion, though."

I was startled by her sudden display of passion but not displeased. "Perhaps. I am not going to judge you, though, Serah, and would forgive you anything. So will Regina, in time."

I heard the door creak behind me and turned to see Regina staring at the two of us. There was a foul expression on her face as she stared daggers at Serah.

Then slammed the door.

"Yes, I'm feeling the love and forgiveness," Serah deadpanned. "It's rolling over me like the tides. Ooooh."

I sighed and shook my head, gesturing down the hall. "You are too hard on yourself."

"Am I? Do you love me, Jacob?"

"Of course."

"I am not just a substitute for Jassamine, who shares my skin color and love of sorcery?"

"No," I said, growling. "Don't even—"

"Would you choose me over Regina?"

"What?" That left me short. I struggled for an answer but my feelings on the matter were clear. "I—"

Serah snorted. "It's all right, Jacob. I would choose her too. It's just that I know she would choose you."

I tried to figure out what to say. "Women will always remain a mystery to me."

"It is not women who are mysterious, but simply Regina and I. We are unique among our sex, like all women. Men too." Serah picked up the Heart of Midnight and walked down the hall. "I am sorry to bring my turmoil to you, Jacob. I count you as my closest friend even if we sometimes feel like more like that than man and wife. What can I do for you?"

I ignored her slight to our marriage and walked beside her. "We're attacking Kerifas, probably in the coming week." I explained to her Ketra's statements and gave her a brief rundown on our military and strategic situation.

Serah frowned deeper, which was impressive since she'd already looked sullen. "I have very little information on Kerifas at this present. Midori's spies have been having difficulty sending information and the city is warded against scrying. Everything I've read tells me it is the center for the empire's power in the region as well as a hotbed of tensions. It is likely to explode into violence even if we don't attack it but if we do, holding the city will be difficult without burning it to the ground."

"Ah, just when I thought things were going to be easy."

"You should stop thinking that. It's never right."

"The Jarls and earl's offer is too good an opportunity to pass up, though."

"You should send a proxy. This reeks of a trap."

I shook my head. "I need to show them I'm not the old King Below."

"That may not be who they're looking for. The prophecy warned them against the new one."

"Then that's their problem." I paused, knowing there was more to it than that. "I also have to kill Redhand and Hellsword."

Serah was silent. "Yes, you do."

"Is that a problem?"

"How would you feel if I said you had to kill Jassamine?"

"That you were stating the obvious."

Serah smiled. "I thought I loved Hellsword but after all the black magic, murder, and experiments we performed for the so-called greater good, I realized I loved Regina more. By that time, though, she'd moved on. Now my homeland is reduced to rubble and he's trying to manipulate our past relationship to kill Regina's sister. Would have done so if I'd agreed to let him murder her. You will not kill Fel Hellsword, Jacob, because I'm going to."

How did I get married to such formidable women?

Fortune favored me there, it seemed.

And cursed me because I would have to ask for a favor now. "I wish to meet with the Oghma."

We reached the end of the hallway where Serah stopped, holding her staff close. "That is an *extraordinarily* bad idea. The Oghma was founded for the purposes of fighting the King Below and you're going to walk into the dragon's den?"

"I...saw things in the future," I said, still remembering the terrible visions of the world destroyed and Regina killing the Lawgiver. "I need to consult with the prophecy you mentioned to see if it really does refer to me."

"Prophecies have a way of making themselves come true," Serah said, shaking her head. "Destiny is a force that exists only in the abstract. People born poor are likely to remain so. People born rich are likely to be entitled. Circumstances push us in certain directions and divination just collates that knowledge."

"I need to know, Serah."

Serah looked at me, unhappy. "All right. I will take you to meet with their leader."

"Thank you."

"The Oghma does not meet through normal methods. It summons its members through the call of its leader, Ethinu," Serah said, lifting up her palm and the ring on it. "This is my means of contacting her. She lives in a castle of glass in the Astral Plane."

"Impressive. How long until we can meet with her if you do so now?"

Serah extended her finger and a glowing rift in the fabric of reality appeared in the center of the hall, this one leading to a misty green haze beyond. "Now. Don't ask me why it's easier to tear a hole in dimensions than teleport around the World Between."

"I've stopped asking questions about why magic works. I just study how it does."

"A wise decision."

I stared at the rift and took a second to catch my breath. This was a large decision to take on at the drop of a hat, but time was not on our side. If we were going to press our advantage into Winterholme, then we needed to do so now before the opportunity passed us by. But I needed to know just what I was up against too.

"What do I need to know about this woman?"

"Ethinu is an ancient elf, older than perhaps any other in the world. She is one of the original high lords and a sorceress without peer. She appears young and beautiful, but do not be fooled, because she is a woman who casually destroys kingdoms. Ethinu is greatly confident that everything she does is in the name of the greater good but….be warned, her ideas of that will not be easy to understand. Also, she is the former lover of the Lawgiver."

I soaked up that last fact. "Great."

"And the Trickster."

I did a double-take then chortled. "Now I *want* to meet her."

No, you really don't, the Trickster said. *Believe me.*

"Don't let her manipulate you. For the longest time I believed I was serving a greater cause as an agent of the Oghma. It took Regina's and your arrival to make me realize all I was doing was making the world worse."

I thought about Serah's ill-fated uncle and his attempts to foster a rebellion against the empire in the former Lakeland territories. He had been a cowardly sort of fellow with only the petty ambitions of a traitor. I couldn't help but wonder if another hand had been guiding him to the destination that had gotten him and his nephew killed. If the Oghma were truly playing at the games of kings then they could have done worse than arranging such a thing. "You're coming with me, correct?"

"I wouldn't dream of leaving you alone with Ethinu. If she turns against us we'll have a long fight ahead against the Oghma but we can win if we engage them one by one. It will be a long and hard battle, though," Serah said, walking to the edge of the rift and stopping. A strange look passed across her face and, for a moment, I wondered what she was thinking.

"Is something wrong?"

"Just contemplating something," Serah said. "Have you ever considered just...leaving?"

"And go where?" I said, avoiding her question.

"Away from this. All of this...responsibility and conflict. The three of us and perhaps a few other friends with whatever mementos we wish to take with us."

I was surprised by her words for she, of all of us, had been the most power hungry. "There's no place the Lawgiver wouldn't find us. He is capable of viewing all nations in the World Between simultaneously."

"There are other worlds, Jacob. We could go through a moongate to some other planet and start anew. Find some world where humans live and rule them—or just live together in peace."

I paused, thinking about that. "Sometimes I think about that. Other times I think about the fact it is good to be the king. I grew up as nothing more than an inconvenient extra mouth to feed by my father and an embarrassment by my sisters. But—"

"But what?"

"It would not be honorable."

"Honorable."

"Strange how a concept popularized by the nobility and scorned by peasants has become so important to me." I paused. "Earlier today, you were fine with going to war. Eager even. Why the sudden reversal?"

"I have never had so much to lose before. Regina lost everyone and everything at Whitehall. I lost my brother. Regina will never stop seeking revenge and all I can think of is what life would be like without the two of you. Now she has her cousins back and it's possible she might heal. We could let this go. Strange, but I can't help but think you're actually more important than being Queen of the Shadows."

I put my arm around hers. "We will talk about this at length. I promise. But first, we need answers. Answers only your former employer can provide."

"All right."

Serah held me and together we walked through the rift.

Chapter Ten

Ihad seen many wondrous things on my journeys. I was almost three hundred years old and while I had spent the majority of that time as a mind-controlled slave, I had witnessed many things both beautiful and strange. The crystal palace of Ethinu was not the greatest of them, but it was an impressive spectacle. The palace was formed, as the name attested, of living crystal that had a brilliant inner luminescence that my attire contrasted to strongly. Everything was made in shades of white, light, or brilliance without actual colors.

The chamber we were in was thirteen stories tall with free-floating display cases, bookshelves, and furniture, as if gravity was not something expected of the residents. A seventy-foot-long iris-shaped window was present to our side, showing the vast endless blue-silver void of the astral plane along with the thousands of pale-white stars within.

I stood awed.

I'd never felt smaller looking out into the blue vastness and wondering if there was another world out there with another Jacob Riverson, Regina Whitetremor, or Serah Brightwaters. A world where I was dust and bones so there had never been anyone to save Regina on the Storm Giant Mountains or Serah from the sacking of Lakeland. A place where they had not been there to save me from the despair I'd felt following my freedom from the old King Below's service. Alternate timelines, places, and people that showed what might have been or could be.

Yes, there are, the Trickster said. *You are not unique.*

As Serah says, we are all unique.

How would you know?

I chided myself for once again paying attention to the madman inside my head, god or not, and looked to Serah. She was looking wobbly, motion sick really, and I extended my hand over to her. Serah took it, surprising me, since she had always disdained help. "Thank you, Jacob. This is not a place for those of flesh and blood."

I blinked at her observation for I felt surprisingly good. Better, indeed, than I had felt in a long time. I could taste the world on my tongue, the air on my face, and countless things around me with senses I didn't even know I had. I felt, for lack of a better word, more real. Some philosophers had speculated there was a universe of true forms where ideas had a perfect semblance. I'd always found that to be nonsense but, again, it seemed today was a day for opening up my mind.

You are a god, the Trickster said. *This is the realm of ideas. The backstage of the universe. Where else would a god be able to manifest fully?*

"I wonder why Ethinu chooses to live in such a place," I said, looking up to the room's ceiling. "Extra living space aside."

"It is said after the First Humans left for the higher planes, the Lawgiver stayed behind and created the elves. Ethinu was one of these elves who wandered the universes, seeding countless planets with life and teaching them the way until the Lawgiver settled on this planet with the rest of the sidhe."

"And they were all but eradicated in a pointless war with the Formor," I said, finishing that thought. "I suppose I'd want to live in another reality too."

"The sidhe are not gone yet, Jacob."

"Their time has passed. Not because they choose to live but because they choose to not. The sidhe do not dream of a better tomorrow but ruminate over past glories and lost wonders. I am dead, Serah, but they are the ones who act as ghosts."

Serah took my hand. "You feel real enough to me. You are alive, Jacob, no matter the form of it, and where there is life there is hope."

"That hardly sounds like the professional cynic I've always taken you to be."

"Perhaps you are a bad influence."

I chuckled. "I admit I have had bad experiences with the sidhe in the past. The high lords I've met have all been arrogant and condescending at their most polite. I do not expect this meeting to go well."

"Do you truly think the prophecy will allow you to avert your fate?"

"I don't believe in destiny or fate. There is but one ending that is predetermined for all beings, god or mortal, and that is death."

"And *I'm* the cynic?"

"I consider that rather optimistic actually. It means everything until that point is our own responsibility." I walked around the room, looking at the strange objects and items around me. "Does she know we're here?"

"Undoubtedly. That doesn't mean she'll see us. Ethinu and I are not equals in the Oghma, assuming they still consider me after marrying the heir to their greatest enemy. She makes kings wait on their knees to visit her, just a few of the petty mind-games she likes to play."

"I see," I said. "Maybe we should start smashing things and see if she comes then."

Now it was Serah's turn to laugh. "I would pay good money to see that."

I looked at a nearby statue of an elf maiden reaching to the sun, about two feet in height, freestanding in the air, and casually knocked it over.

"Jacob!" Serah said.

"This is a place of the mind," I said, watching the statue disintegrate and reform. "None of it's real."

Serah frowned, seemingly considering that fact for the first time. "True. I remember how impressed I was when I first came here. However, it's like my illusions, nothing but mummer's tricks and flash powder."

"You were with Hellsword when you first came here?" I tried not to sound jealous.

I failed.

Serah frowned then shook her head. "You wish to know about my relationship to another man?"

"No," I said. "And yes. Such is the province of human emotion. We often want what's worst for us. I trust you and do not—"

"You shouldn't," Serah said. "I've said I'm untrustworthy and I meant it. I cannot control my feelings towards you and Regina. It makes me act…unwisely. Hellsword is taking advantage of our past to manipulate me. Do not trust my decisions as long as he involved in events."

"Serah—"

"Fel came to me at my most vulnerable. He proclaimed that it was not I who should be afraid of them but other people. He was ruthless, amoral, and hedonistic. He broke down my resistance to using my powers for my own benefit, using methods that were… unkind. In the end, once I unleashed them, I relished them and relished him. I found I preferred to be evil than good as the latter had made me nothing but miserable my entire life."

"I know that feeling."

"Do you? I find that hard to believe."

I had spilled far too much blood to judge her for her past actions. She could admit to any number of crimes but nothing she did could match what I'd done as a slave of the King Below. There was only one crime I was not guilty of and I held fast to that. "You speak of admiration but say you won't hesitate to kill him. What changed between you?"

Serah looked at me. "I…fell in love with Regina, admiring her often simple-minded worldview of light and dark. In the end, I don't think I realized I had changed until after our marriage and that I cared whether this world lived or died. It separated me forever from my previous lover because he believed in nothing."

"If Hellsword was so nihilistic, why did he join the Nine Heroes?" I asked, confused by her description.

"I don't know. It's out of character. That bothers me."

"It bothers you he believes in a cause?"

"It makes me question what makes one of the evillest men I've ever known decide to become a hero."

"Perhaps the fact that he's a monster impressed by them should cause you to think about their cause more negatively."

"Perhaps."

Shaking my head, I turned around and searched for an exit. Any exit. There was no point in searching this place, since it might be miles long and full of infinite halls, and it didn't seem like there was much in the way of physics limiting a world built on thought. It felt good, however, and I found myself departing into a gigantic circular chamber surrounded with ionic columns and a balcony overlooking it. A mural of the Lawgiver's All-Seeing Eye was in the center of the floor.

Serah followed me, continuing to talk even when it should have been clear it was a better idea to let the matter drop. "The Lawgiver, Jassamine, and the Nine will not leave you alone. Therefore, you should strike first and annihilate them. If not, then you should leave and go far-far away from them. You cannot do as you've done and just try to live in peace. They will not leave you be."

"And if our conflict destroys the world?" I asked, thinking about my vision of the future.

"What do you think? Truly?"

"I care about that less than I care about you and Regina surviving." It was a grim admission.

"I find that frightening. Do not live for others, Jacob. Live for me and Regina and our family to be. We will be here forever at your side if you want."

"Nothing is forever." I wasn't here to debate philosophy but get answers. Ethinu's absence was starting to bother me. What was she waiting for? I decided to risk asking Serah more about the Oghma. "You mentioned Jassamine's relationship to Hellsword, which means you knew she was alive the entire time we were getting to know each other. When I was falling in love with you and mourning her death."

"I knew she betrayed you long before you remembered she was a child-killing psychopath."

"And yet you didn't tell me."

"No."

"How much do you know you haven't been telling me?"

"Much."

I took a deep breath, trying not to become furious. "Can you promise me that you will stop lying to me? Hiding things from me?"

"Would you believe me if I did?"

"Yes."

"Then that is your mistake. I am sorry, Jacob. I am what I am."

I turned around to face her. "Then perhaps Regina is—"

Serah pointed over her shoulder. "There's a monster slithering down the balcony."

"Gods dammit."

The sight filled me with a terror that chilled me through my soul. It had an expansive serpent's body entirely covered with feathers made of star metal. Six wings came out at various points, and two of them from the side of its head and folded over its eyes. It was repeatedly speaking a holy invocation the word ringing in my ears like a deafening temple bell.

A glowing nimbus of light radiated from it, pure light magic, draining away my powers as if I were a strigoi in sunlight being forced back to its tomb. I recognized the creature for what it was due to my studies of the Codex. I knew of grand priests who, flush with the hubris of the self-righteous, used forbidden texts to summon such creatures. They were the highest messengers, created as weapons for the Lawgiver, and could flatten cities with their power or deliver judgement on whole armies.

And Ethinu had sent one to kill me.

Drawing *Chill's Fury*, I drew comfort from the weapon's power even as I knew this would be a fight I would probably not win. God or not, there were simply some things beyond the power of a man to triumph over.

"Get behind me or flee!" I shouted, hoping to at least die in the good cause of defending someone I loved.

"Nay!" Serah shouted, raising a barrier above us both, just in time for a golden torrent of flame to fly from her fingers. I felt every bit of her magic pour into our attacker and almost crumble, but, somehow, the barrier stood. "You split your power with me when all others would have ruled. There is a reason I love you more than the world."

Oh spare me, you two, the Trickster muttered. *You were just about to start fighting!*

Clearly you know nothing about marriage! I lifted my left hand and conjured my demonsteel armor around me. From my gauntlet poured forth a storm of frost colder than the World Below's most savage blizzards.

The Seraph reared back, injured by the attack, perhaps not least because I had spent months refining every inch of my armor to magnify and strengthen my connection to my still ill-understood new powers. It did not react poorly, though, raising its four wings and delivering a bolt of brilliant golden lightning from each of them toward me. The first two struck the same spot and shattered a tiny hole in Serah's barrier before the next two bolts passed through. I cut the first bolt in half, only to be struck square in the chest by the fourth.

The pain was indescribable, equivalent to being burned alive and if I'd been a normal man then I would have mercifully died from it but, instead, I lived on. I fell to one knee, my connection to the universe disrupted and my physical body passing away to become my ghostly self once more. Despite that, I staggered forward and slashed into its chest with *Chill's Fury.*

The demonsteel blade was covered in flaming ichor from where it struck home. *Chill's Fury's* black magic warred against the Seraph's holy essence and I felt the weapon quiver in my hand. For a moment, I thought the blade would explode, only for the true names of Serah and Regina on its side to glow brilliantly alongside the runes for Hope and Redemption.

The holy nimbus around the Seraph vanished.

And my strength returned to full.

"Unclean!" the Seraph shouted in a voice sounding like a thousand chanters speaking in unison. "You have made me unclean!"

"Death cleans us all," I said, pulling my blade out from between the star-metal feathers and striking again with more force.

Serah, meanwhile, conjured a host of horrors that would have given me nightmares if I was still the kind of man to dream about monsters. Hideous creatures made from eyeballs, cannibal slime, tentacled abominations, and more assaulted the Seraph. They were all illusions but, in the astral plane, were as real as anything else. The Seraph destroyed them one after another but could not penetrate her barriers even as she finished her menagerie with a perfect replica of Regina. That joined me in slicing away the creature, whose wounds were growing worse all the time.

We were close to killing the creature, against all possible odds, when it released a powerful wave of concussive force that threw me backwards and knocked Serah to the ground. The wounded Seraph fled through a nearby doorway and I was about to pursue when I heard a powerful female voice shout, "Enough!"

That was when I felt the strongest presence I'd ever felt from a magic-user in my life.

Divine or mortal.

Ethinu had arrived.

CHAPTER ELEVEN

I looked up to the expansive balcony from that the voice came, forcing down any sense of unease I felt from her power. I hadn't expected to be able to defeat the Seraph and, honestly, I wouldn't have been able to if not for Serah. But with her at my side, I had a far better chance of protecting myself than if I had gone after Ethinu alone. Besides, I wasn't here to do her harm, Jassamine's mentor or not, but to look at Morrigan's prophecy.

Still, I would be cautious.

Your lack of self-confidence is appalling, the Trickster grunted. *A god should, if nothing else, be confident in his sovereignty.*

Says the god killed by mortals, I replied.

Touché.

Standing above us, clothed in radiant azure robes, was perhaps the most beautiful woman I'd ever seen. I say this not to disdain either of my wives, but as a warning about Ethinu's character. All sorcerers and sorceresses were vain things, myself included, adjusting their appearance to either reflect wisdom or beauty but elves were the most obsessive about it.

There was a quality about the sidhe that I'd always found vaguely disconcerting. They had the appearance of young men and women, even the eldest appearing to be in their late twenties at best, but their eyes always carried a far older look. Not the romantic agelessness spoken of by poets or the wisdom of sages but the ugly eyes of crones and bitter old men. Ethinu dwarfed them all with the kind of attention to detail she'd taken in giving herself unnatural beauty.

This woman had altered her face with magic both biomancy and illusion, I could tell at a glance, to be perfectly symmetrical with long, flowing flame-like hair that moved as if there was a light breeze flowing. Her skin was so porcelain as to look like marble and her height was at least a head taller than other elves, let alone that of regular human women who rarely reached six feet outside of Winterholme.

Her body was a pleasant hour-glass shape that her ostensibly modest robes seemed to cling to in a disconcertingly provocative way. Even her eyes were different, being slightly larger than average, as if she were a portrait an artist was trying to make more soulful. But those very eyes were every bit as bitter and contemptuous as any other elf's.

Worse, I recognized her.

"Mighty Ethinu the Blue, Great Wizard and High Lady of the Oghma, I present myself and my lover, the new King Below, unto you." Serah curtsied. "We come beseeching an audience from you so that we might avail ourselves of your tremendous wisdom gleaned through the sum of countless ages."

I glared at her at the use of the word lover instead of husband. "You'll forgive me if I am less courteous after your attempts to murder us."

"What is the normal response to trespassers where you hail from?" Ethinu said in a voice that I found to be refreshingly unpleasant. It seemed the one element of her body she hadn't altered with magic and thus the most real. "And please, dispense with the false courtesies, Serah, or we'll be exchanging titles for hours. I've already heard the ludicrous new religion you've crafted around yourselves: Serah the Black, Mistress of the Night, the Black Sun...horrible joke that...the Hero Reborn, the Starlight Maiden, the Unicorn Queen, the Bloody Unicorn. Ugh."

"The Black Rose of the Eternal Isles, the Befouler of the Eternal, the Fire that Dances on the Graves of the Innocent," I said, repeating some of the titles I'd heard about Ethinu in my mortal days. "The Demon Counselor, Poison Tongue, the Bitch of Belenus."

Serah shot me a look of absolute horror. Apparently,she had expected me to react with a trifle more respect to the Oghma's leader despite her attempting to kill us.

"I take it we've met before?" Ethinu asked, not showing the least bit of reaction. "I don't recall. "Were you someone unimportant then? Yes, undoubtedly you were. I remember interesting people and the vast majority of them spend their lives very uninterestingly."

"You were Fredericka Fireblossom then," I said, recalling my many visits to the Eternal Isles during the war. It had been an earthly paradise of endless gardens, parties, music, and art with a populace utterly devoid of joy. "The chief counselor and closest friend to High Queen Fand. You were the one to convince her not to send magicians to back us up during the siege of Hammerhold and caused an additional ten thousand deaths both in and outside of the city."

"Ah, yes," Ethinu said, wrinkling her nose in distaste. "I do recall that period of my life. Fand was a deeply stupid girl, but useful for the few centuries she ruled until I had her strangled in her birthing bed so I could raise her daughter."

Serah's eyes widened at that.

I just kept my eyes level with her. "Charming."

Ethinu showed no sign of shame. "You'd have preferred to let her husband rule? It was the perfect excuse for having him eliminated, as everyone assumed he'd had his wife murdered. The man spent centuries buggering human boys and having them killed when they reached adulthood."

The sad fact was that I didn't doubt her statement in the slightest. Madness was a common affliction of the elven nobility. The only reason their peasants didn't revolt was because they had so few remnants of their glory days left. "Which you, notably, did nothing about until a new heir was born. When I oversaw the Shadowguard, I had child rapists buried alive."

"Which somehow gives you the moral high ground," Ethinu said, tapping her left palm lightly with her right hand three times. "You must be so pleased with yourself."

"I sense this conversation will be a duel of barely concealed sarcasm," Serah said.

"You're wrong," Ethinu said. "I have no intention of concealing mine."

Point to her. "We need to speak regarding the Black Sun prophecy."

Ethinu looked down with disgust at Serah, which increased my dislike of the archmage. "I see your bride has been free with the Oghma's secrets."

"Far less so than I would have liked," I replied dryly. "She is also, of the two of us, the only one who has slightest respect for you or your position. I thought I was going to be a wise and ancient magician, but now the plot thins. Jassamine spoke often of Fredericka Fireblossom and her spider-like ways, manipulating the war to drag on in places where she could derive the most political gain. If she is typical of your unseen hand, it is infinitely less subtle than I expected."

Serah looked like she was going to die of embarrassment and horror both. Putting her hand on her face, she whispered, "Jacob—"

"Jassamine studied under me to learn how to lie, cheat, and control the minds of men as well as women. She was Emperor Edorta's mistress, you know, before becoming his son's. Often she would talk of how slavishly devoted you were, turning down hordes of willing maids and their mothers out of sincere devotion to a woman who would use any weapon in her arsenal to further her agenda. Men gave their lives and lands for her favor, even knowing they were nothing but a means to an end—including you."

I crossed my arms. I knew how this game was played and was not so easily rattled as she might think. "You think I did not know this? I, who murdered men for her and did his own unpleasant things to rise to the status of Knight Paramount? I knew what kind of person she was. I just assumed I held a place in her heart regardless."

Ethinu narrowed her eyes. "Which made you a fool."

"Says the woman who fucked the Lawgiver."

Ethinu smiled. "I like him, Serah. Perhaps this one might actually have some merit."

Serah sighed and felt her head as if possessing now a monstrous headache. "If I believed in the gods, I would be praying to them to kill me now."

"We enjoy your suffering too much." I said.

"I have long suspected that," Serah said.

Ethinu raised her arms and slowly levitated over the balcony bannister before moving down beside us. Ethinu used no staff, unlike most magicians, but I saw her hands were covered in almost invisible white rings made of moonlight. I suspected she had many other enhancers hidden on her persona, rendering the lack of a staff moot. Besides, she had the most powerful aura of any wizard I'd ever encountered.

If her aura is real, the Trickster said. *Do not confuse chicanery with power. All too many high lords are frauds. After all, they are like kings and what makes a monarch is tinsel and lies.*

You forgot swords, I said.

My, you are witty today.

"I have ever felt that those individuals who wither amongst the slightest bit of scrutiny are the least important to the grand scheme of things. Peace-makers, conciliators, and diplomats do not make the world go round. They merely provide administration for those who carve it up between them."

"You and the Lawgiver must have gotten along famously."

"We did, for a time. Then his arrogance and desire to control everything drove me away," Ethinu said. "Do you possess a similar urge? Is that why you parade around as a god? You are not the new King Below. You've seized his power but divided it with your concubines like strong wine mixed with water."

"*Concubines*? You shallow, glamour-covered, tart-dressed shitstain," Serah growled, shocking me. "As if you have done anything but the most basic witchery in a centuries! Where were you at Accadia? Where were you at Whitehall? What battles did you fight against the old King Below or against the Nine Usurpers? How dare you mock Regina and Jacob's accomplishments."

Ethinu blinked, taken aback by Serah's sudden outburst. "And you, Jacob Riverson? How do you defend yourself?"

"I wasn't aware I had to defend myself," I said, shrugging. "I am aware I nearly died facing the Seraph back there and am far weaker than the Lawgiver and Trickster. A god is not measured by his power alone."

Ethinu gave me a quizzical look, genuinely intrigued. "Oh? Then what is a god measured by?"

"The love of his worshipers and how much he can help them."

Ethinu looked torn between laughing in my face and becoming ill. "I take back any praise I have given you. Clearly you have only gotten as far as you have because of Serah."

"I never denied it."

"I do," Serah said, her fury radiating outward. I half expected her to start slinging spells. "Ethinu is afraid and seeks to demoralize us with words. I am not twelve, however, and do not fear the nattering of a pointy-eared hag. Show us the damn prophecy."

Ethinu smiled and waved her right hand, conjuring a black leatherbound book with a golden seal upon it. In the center of the book was the Black Sun symbol I'd created for my standard. I had dreamed of it during my recovery from battling Jassamine and chosen it as a more suitable icon than the old King Below's skull and sword. Reluctantly, I took the book and began looking through it. Serah read over my shoulder and the two of us were silent for the next hour. Ethinu, mercifully, kept her commentary to a minimum and allowed us the peace of study.

I wish she hadn't.

The Prophecy of the Black Sun by Morrigan the Lesser was shockingly free of vagueness, symbolism, or metaphor. I had always thought a proper prophecy should work as poetry as well as foretelling but this one was more like a report. The details were not always precise, but they depicted a shockingly accurate record of the past few centuries.

There were the names, dates, and parties involved in a hundred or more notable events. I read of dynasties falling, kingdoms splitting, natural disasters, and a number of peculiar events that did not seem of much note like births or marriages. These latter additions became noteworthy when I realized they were a genealogy for tracking the birth of the Nine Heroes, Jassamine, myself, Serah, Regina, and several people I hadn't met yet.

The book, perversely, had several letters shoved inside it, along with scribbled-in annotations as if it weren't an immensely important relic but a wizard's cookbook. The Oghma had sought to change the prophecy at numerous points. However, history had a strange way of rebounding itself despite numerous examples of destiny being thwarted in the past.

Specific kings might die or children be smothered in their cradles only for someone nearly identical to assume their place. Many times, the self-fulfilling prophecy was in effect and it was believed Morrigan was deliberately manipulating her peers to bring about the destiny foretold. One note in the margins indicated the Oghma subjected her to torture and psychic probes to determine if this were true. In the margins, it said she'd taken her life after one particularly invasive session had removed her sanity permanently.

Charming.

In the end, the Lawgiver was presented with the prophecy during my era and had decided to weather it rather than thwart it. The King Above took the sole surviving arch-messenger, G'zaralle, and placed her spirit within a little girl as to birth her as a weapon. Such had been born Jassamine according to the prophecy. He'd then attempted to kill his own brother, the King Below, and enlist the Nine Heroes who were fated to destroy him. I was but a footnote in history as the prophecy ended peculiarly.

The Black Sun will be crowned in Everfrost and will raise vast armies in the aftermath of the Fifth Great Shadow War. They will conquer their foes and lay waste to the Nine Heroes. The world will suffer the Lawgiver will lead his armies to silence the Triumvirate before their power eclipses his own.

The Terrible Weapons will shatter the crust, creating vast volcanic eruptions of the like not seen since Valance the Red's revenge, and fill the sky with ash. An ice age will exterminate all but a handful of Shadowkind and Lightborn races.

The Lawgiver and Triumvirate will fall.

I stared at the document's end then shook my head. "You mean the past two thousand years of history has been the result of this *rubbish?*"

"I am a trifle more credulous," Serah said. "Have you not seen... things...in the future?"

I had seen the end. Yes. I, however, did not believe the book's prophecies were anything more than the manipulations of a particularly gifted oracle and the machinations of a cabal with far too much time on their hands as well as far too much power.

There were many places where it seemed they'd interpreted events to fit the idea they couldn't thwart the prophecy. Places where things could have gone differently but they'd chosen to continue propping it up like some sort of master plan rather than the ramblings of a mad oracle.

I shook my head. "I am not going to live my life dancing on the strings of a long-dead sorceress."

"Then I suggest you do as the Lawgiver should have done," Ethinu said. "Avert the prophecy. The destruction of everything suits neither of us. He has decided to ride it out. Jassamine will take its place with his most fanatical followers preserved in great temples under the ground through the worst of the disaster."

That made a disturbing amount of sense of the Nine Usurper's recent actions. "And how do you think I should avert this? I am less than impressed with your efforts so far. I think I would do better to try and avert it my own way and pay less attention to your mad oracle."

"Make peace with the Lawgiver, submit to him if you have to, and get your associates to do the same. Allow him to remake the Southern Kingdoms as he sees fit and in a few centuries we can forget this entire ordeal. Prophecies can be thwarted, even those spoken by Morrigan the Lesser; one simply needs power."

"You advise me to surrender to him completely."

"Yes."

"He and his minions have shown no interest in peace."

"They might if you are willing to die for it."

"Is that what you ask of me?"

"Yes." Ethinu nodded. "If you are the hero you claim, then you would be willing to take whatever terms he offers."

I contemplated it for all of a second. "I'm afraid I must decline."

Serah, however, looked less troubled. "There is no future for you or Regina in this prophecy, Jacob. Let us leave together."

"Peace is not made with friends," Ethinu said, her voice now sounding desperate. "It is not done so you can feel good about the dead being unavenged; it is so future generations need not be. The Lawgiver will bring about Morrigan's prophecy because he believes a new world can be built from the ashes."

I stared at her, knowing what she said was true. "Madness."

"For once, we agree," Ethinu said.

"You will stand against this evil?" Serah said, looking at me. "No matter what?"

I realized now why Serah had been asking me to flee. Why she'd urged me to attack and retreat in equal measure. She had to have known the basics of the prophecy and was struggling against its puppet strings the same way the other Oghma were. Gods, I wish she'd just come to me and talked about it. I could have reassured her my actions were not going to be affected by it. It was a mistake coming here. "I will do what I must."

Ethinu seemed to calm down, her voice icy cold. "Is that your final decision?"

"Yes."

Ethinu nodded. "Thank you, Jacob."

"For?"

"Letting me know what my next course of action must be."

That was when I felt suddenly dizzy and she conjured a staff of living light I had not seen. Serah was blasted backwards by a blast of light from it before I could react. Ethinu began speaking a series of magic words in rapid succession.

My own included.

"To save creation, I will claim the Black Sun's power for my own!" Ethinu shouted. I felt unimaginable pain, like my soul was being torn in half. Ethinu was trying to rip the godhood from my body.

And was succeeding.

CHAPTER TWELVE

It was a horrific sensation, being torn apart, piece by piece, in the astral plane. Here, it wasn't the case of being stabbed or burned, things that would kill your body. That would have been merciful. No, this was far worse. To get at the divine power the Trickster had bestowed upon me, Ethinu was opening the book that was my essence and tearing out pages one by one.

I found myself helpless against her sorcery and couldn't help but realize she'd prepared for this event well ahead of time. The entire castle was a focus for her magic and I'd stupidly missed how perfectly she'd laid her trap. Even the attack of the Seraph had been designed to exhaust my power before her initial attack. In the distance, I could hear Serah scream and strike out, but there were sounds of monsters wailing and I knew Ethinu was striking at her as well.

Never trust a sorceress, the Trickster said. *They'll always get you in the end.*

I struggled to grasp at the parts of my memory flying around me. I remembered my father's beatings, the drunken strikes against my face, and the constant resentment. Foul bastard, unwanted bastard, leech, parasite, and a hundred other words. If he had been purely hateful, I might have been able to let him go but there were long periods of good and joy too. Places where we bonded and learned to trust each other, right until he'd sold me to Warmaster Kalian.

I remembered beautiful periods of my courtship with Jassamine as we built messengers out of snow and made love in the days when we could find time away from each other's vocations. I remembered pledging my love for her and asking her to be my wife, only for her to reply soon or deflect my requests until after the war.

I remembered murdering her enemies for her in back alleys, torturing political opponents for confessions, and the bloody room where children had been massacred to provide her with power. The sight of the last had driven me to seek death on the battlefield because I hadn't the courage to drive a sword through her chest. Because my convictions hadn't been strong enough to kill the woman I loved.

I tried to find other memories that I could latch on to, hold on to, but they became like water flowing through my fingertips. I'd gone from one cause to another throughout my life. I'd been a Temple Knight, a Shadowguardsman, a Wraith Knight, and now the King Below but was I anything more than an empty vessel trying on one suit of clothes after another?

Did I have any loyalties? Any cause? Or was I just a man who stumbled through the motions of life? I wasn't even alive. I was a ghost. A ghost of a man who had been nothing but a pawn for others his entire life. Unworthy of the title of a god, king, or hero. It was better that it end here. Then I saw Regina's face and knew I could not let myself fade away.

"*No!*" I cried out into the darkness. "I am not a pawn, a knight, or even a king! I am the one who moves the pieces!"

With that I found myself once more living a moment from my past. This moment was not centuries ago but weeks. It was strange because almost all my defining choices and memories had been before I'd become a Wraith Knight.

Yet this moment was enough for me to hold on to.

It was a moment of who I was.

I found myself riding on the back of a Nuckelavee across the snow-covered ground leading up to a Formor village several hundred leagues away from Everfrost. The burned-out buildings were still smoldering despite the cold. The invaders had spared no one. The sight of men, women, and children scattered across the ground made me sick to my stomach despite how many similar massacres I'd seen. The bodies had wounds from crude Formor spears, pitchforks, and makeshift farm equipment. This was a war between villagers rather than professional warriors.

Beside me, Regina was riding on the back of a black unicorn, one of those corrupted nature spirits that had chosen to ally with the old King Below. Despite the fact that it was opposed to everything she stood for, the creature had an unnatural submissiveness around Regina and obeyed her every command with an eerie poise.

Regina was wearing a plain shirt and leather vest with linen pants, a star-metal pendant of a unicorn amulet around her neck. *Starlight* was sheathed at her side but she wasn't wearing her usual armor, because she could summon it at will and because this hadn't meant to be an investigation. Just the two of us finding some alone time in the middle of nowhere, away from the responsibilities of being whoever we were. Unfortunately, that wasn't going to happen today.

"Monstrous," Regina said, riding us through the carnage. "They killed everyone."

"Yes. We should be cautious. This kind of slaughter tends to draw Corpse-Eaters."

Corpse-Eaters were just one of the many unfortunate remnants of the old King Below. When I had ascended to the Black Throne, I had proclaimed an end to the mental slavery he had used to hold all his subjects in check. This had applied to his endless armies of the dead as well. Most had left for whatever awaited beyond the afterlife but a handful had stayed behind. Corpse-Eaters, properly called wights, wandered around feasting on the living or dead to try to regain some semblance of their previous selves.

Most didn't.

"I'll keep a look out for them," Regina said, sliding off her saddle. "We need to find out who was responsible for this and punish them."

"Aren't you cold?"

"Your spell still keeps me warm," Regina said. "Or maybe goddesses don't get cold."

"You actually believe you're one?" I asked, still surprised she was so strong in her faith we were divine.

"I believe a power higher than the Lawgiver has chosen us both to correct his misbehavior and provide the world's peoples with moral guidance. You *don't* believe you're a god?"

"Sometimes."

"I do. I was born for greatness. I just never knew how great it would be."

"I was born a peasant. The only thing I was born to do was swing a hammer or cast nets."

"The gods have a plan for us all."

"Death is the only plan I'm certain the gods had in store for us all." I also wanted nothing of the Lawgiver's plans for me.

Regina rolled her eyes and leaned down to pick up a tattered war banner attached to a broken spear. "I don't recognize this heraldry. It's very crudely done, but it doesn't remind me of any of the rebel's banners."

She picked it up and showed me an image of a crudely drawn stallion with a spear protruding from its forehead.

I looked at her, wondering if she were serious.

Regina's look to me told me she just wanted me to tell her she was wrong. I didn't. "This is the Blood Unicorn. Those who have abandoned their old clan allegiance to worship you and the Iron Order you promise to bring all Shadowkind."

Regina stared swearing like one of my sisters.

"You kiss your mother with a mouth so foul?" I asked. "However sweetly shaped."

"This is not the time for flirting!" She put her hands to her face. "This is vile. How could they have done this? In my name!?"

I surveyed the village square around us and saw an ebonwood statue had been knocked down. It was made in the image of a hideous crone with its arms outstretched and a wooden bowl built in at her feet to receive offerings. The statue had been pissed and shit upon, set on fire, and hacked with axes. It was the image of the Night Mother, the nonexistent goddess that supposedly had been the consort of the Trickster. In truth, she'd been nothing more than a creation of the Trickster to increase his devotion amongst the faithful.

"It seems these people clung to the old ways," I said, not at all surprised. "Those who follow the new are less than tolerant of such."

Many Formor considered the old King Below a monster for the ages of slavery they'd endured. Others believed it was their duty to follow him no matter what abuses he'd inflicted. They awaited his return.

Something that would never happen.

"We need to find them and punish them," Regina said. "Make an example of them as a lesson to the next thousand years of

Shadowkind we will not tolerate this sort of evil."

"You would execute a bunch of people for their devotion to us?"

"I would execute murderers!" Regina shouted. "Don't you feel anything about this?!"

I took a deep breath. "Of course, I feel for these people and so many others. You are a magnificent soldier Regina and a far greater leader than I ever was. But I have walked the roads of war far longer than you. You see the people who have done this and see monsters. Yet they saw monsters too when they came here and in the Southern Kingdoms, and both victim and killer would have been exterminated by plain-speaking peasants who help each other when short of food for the winter. You can kill the people involved in this horror but if you do, you will just leave their children bereft of mothers and fathers come the next long snowstorm, which will do nothing but compound the tragedy."

Regina stared at me then turned her head. "I hate you sometimes."

"I hate me sometimes too."

"Then what should we do?"

"I don't know. The last time I was in charge of an army, my solution would have been worse than anything you could have suggested."

"I'd like to hear about those days sometime."

I blinked. "I'd rather forget they ever happened."

Regina closed the eyes of the child and folded its hands before rising. "That's not going to happen, though, and I think you may need a confessor...or a friend."

"Maybe someday," I whispered. "Just...not now."

Regina walked over to me and took my hands. "All right." That was when she paused. "Taxes."

"Hmm?"

"We cannot slaughter every single monster in the North without emptying it. These lands have known nothing but war for millennia and that's the old King Below's fault. Forgiveness will be a long and hard process but perhaps we can usher it along by making it expensive. Any unauthorized military activity shall be fined, heavily."

"Fined."

"People will rush to avenge the fallen but no one likes paying the taxman. They will think twice is it means their killings come out of their purse."

I smirked. "That may actually work. At least, it'll give far more pause than executions."

"Thank you." Regina reached up and kissed me on the lips.

I looked down, guilty. "When you see me, Regina, I worry you see a great warrior. Jacob the legend rather than Jacob the man. I would rather swing a hammer than a blade."

"Your love of peace is what makes you a great warrior," Regina said, missing my point. "I believe there are some causes worth fighting for, though. There is true evil in this world that must be stamped out. The struggles against these are the righteous wars."

Lovely, how she justifies everything she does, the Trickster whispered. *Almost poetic.*

"I do not know if I agree." I placed my hand on her cheek and stared into her beautiful steel-gray eyes. "I would go to war with the entire world for you. Break any oath and cross any boundary. You are worth it."

"I don't want you to do any of that. I want you to be the great hero I know Jacob the man is. Together we will make this world a better place." Regina stared up into my eyes and placed her arms around my neck.

"Perhaps."

Regina sighed, aware she wasn't going to convince me tonight. "Someday we will have a large family and raise them up in the light of a new dawn. One where Formor, sidhe, human, Jotun, boggan, and every other race can live together in harmony."

"Thank you," I whispered.

The area around us filled with the sounds of inhuman guttural growls. All about us, coming from the houses and cellars, poured forth blood-strewn Corpse-Eaters. They were hairless warty things with sallow skin. Their mouths were four times the size of a normal human's with teeth three times as long and sharpened. Their hands were tipped with steel-like claws that glowed with witchfire drawn from the World Below.

A clan had taken residence here, leaving the bodies to rot for flavor, and were already moving out to deal with us. I counted two dozen emerging and wondered if there weren't twice as many around us.

Regina pulled out her sword, smiling. "This should be fun."

"Overconfidence appears to be a downside of godhood," I said, not nearly so confident we could defeat them all.

"Our destiny was not to die here."

And she was right.

We killed them all.

Filled with a righteous anger at the realization that Ethinu was trying to take away my relationship with Regina and Serah, I realized one indisputable fact: *I wanted to live.* I would not abandon my lovers, the kingdom I'd conquered, or the life I'd built. I would not abandon future generations to the tyranny of the Lawgiver or the deranged dreams of Jassamine.

No, I would *survive.*

With that, I drew back all my memories. I could feel Ethinu's shock as she felt her spell easily cast aside. I had no access to the higher levels of magic but I did not need to: I was a god and she was not. I obliterated her ever defense and grabbed her throat.

Ethinu screamed, more from shock than terror, as I forced her to the ground with my fingers squeezed tightly around her neck. Behind me, I could see Serah barely managing to hold off two more Seraphs with a third on the ground behind her.

My next words were simple. "Call off your attack on my wife or die."

Chapter Thirteen

From the expression of Ethinu's face, defeat was not a possibility she had prepared for. I had my hands wrapped around her throat and had managed to smash through all her magical defenses. Hearing the sounds of battle behind me, I had to make a decision. Did I kill her or now or seek her submission? I decided on the former. I released one hand and drew *Chill's Fury* forth to cut her throat.

"Stop!" Ethinu shouted, raising her hands in surrender.

Behind me, I felt the Seraphs vanish except for the one on the ground. It was the same one that we'd been fighting earlier, which Serah had managed to kill. I couldn't help but feel a mixed sense of guilt as well as triumph at the destruction of such a powerful creature. Guilt for the fact I'd destroyed a being that had traditionally been one of the secret protectors of humanity from supernatural evils and triumph because it was a blow against the Lawgiver.

"Are you all right, Serah?" I said, keeping my blade at the neck of the elf. If she so much as summoned a cantrip, I was ready to put an end to the monster.

Ethinu had earned it and more.

Serah leaned on her staff, taking several breaths. "I am...alive. I wouldn't have been if I'd had to do that much longer. Thank you."

"We'll work out an installment plan like boggans."

Serah gave a short chuckle. "Perhaps I'll pay in kind."

I smirked then turned back to Ethinu, all mirth leaving my body. "It now remains to be seen what is to be done with you."

"Spare her," Serah said.

I blinked, since I'd intended to kill her. Contrary to Regina's sometimes-rosier views of my nobility, I wasn't the kind of person to leave loose ends. "Excuse me?"

"Thank you, child," Ethinu said, closing her eyes.

"Shut up," Serah said. "Do not speak until you're spoken to. Believe me, I am not asking Jacob to do this out of mercy. This is a request born of practicality."

"It seems to me killing an enemy is extremely practical," I observed.

"Tempting as that may be," Serah said, shaking her head, "our situation would not be improved by her death. The Oghma would become our enemy just as they were the King Below's and believe me, you do not wish for that to be the case."

"And you think they might become our friend?"

"Perhaps," Serah said, using her staff to walk over. "The prophecy serves neither of us and you don't want to see the world destroyed any more than they do. In that respect, you are different from the Lawgiver. The only reason she chose to strike here is because Ethinu thinks he's going to win any confrontation between us. Isn't that right?"

"Oh, am I allowed to speak now?" Ethinu said, faking shock. It was amazing how quickly her insolence had returned.

"Within reason," Serah snapped.

"I am ten thousand years old and have known the Lawgiver the entire time. He created this world and many others. The Lawgiver is not a god, at least not in any supernatural sense, but he might as well be. Everything you know, every race and species, is because he and his kind wished to create the world of their fantasies. The Old Humans, what most races across the universe call gods, are immortal and all-powerful."

Serah looked down at her. "And yet the King Below, the Lawgiver's brother died."

"Did he?" Ethinu asked, looking at me intently. "I'm honestly not sure you exist."

"What?" I stared at her. "I'm fairly sure I do."

"The Trickster taking the form of Jacob Riverson and living inside him with false memories is not the strangest diversion he'd have taken. You wouldn't even be aware of your condition until he decided to snap his fingers and ceased to exist."

How stupid. The Trickster chuckled in the back of my brain.

"Other gods died too," I said, remembering details of the King

Below's past. "The Lawgiver killed the Gods Between with his brother and lover's help. As you say, they are gods only in power rather than spirit." I then realized I had very potentially damning information. The question was could I share it with her safely. In the end, I chose to be ambiguous about it. "I have also seen the Lawgiver's death. I know the circumstances of it and how to bring it about—perhaps even avoiding the fate you foresaw."

I did not mention I had seen the Lawgiver's death on the ruins of a snowy, ashen world. However, that didn't mean I was lying. Perhaps was a very broad term and Ethinu was desperate. If the prophecy of Morrigan could manipulate generations of leaders then I saw no reason not to do the same with the prophecy of Jacob Riverson.

Oh, how deliciously evil, the Trickster said. *I'm impressed. You'd risk the entirety of the world on a hunch.*

Those who are obsessed with this prophecy are the only ones driving it forward.

So you say. Yet, here you are, using it to your advantage. The irony? I wrote the prophecy and placed it in her mind.

Did you?

You'll never know.

Ethinu looked up with a mixture of suspicion and hope. "You lie."

"I swear to you it is true and offer to let you geas it from me." I would be very exact about what I said, of course.

"As if you couldn't break it!" Ethinu snapped.

"It would be sealed with my own power."

Ethinu suddenly looked thoughtful.

"Perhaps this conflict can be won then," Ethinu said. "Details, though, I need details."

"You forfeited the right to those when you tried to seize Jacob's power. However, allow me a counterproposal: the Oghma remains neutral."

"Neutral? In a war for the fate of the world?"

"Open conflict is the enemy of the World Between," Serah said, her voice almost seductive. "The Oghma have the power to destroy the northern and southern continents, which will only make whichever side so struck more willing to destroy the other. If they choose not to involve themselves that greatly restricts the amount of magic being thrown about and increases our chances of victory."

Ethinu was not convinced. "The Lawgiver will not forgive neutrality. Neutrality is the same as supporting you."

I took a deep breath. "I will assume Serah is telling the truth when she says that you were Jassamine's mentor. As such, you have undoubtedly a deep insight into her character. Do you *really* think the Jassamine we both know would ever let a woman like you live in her paradise?"

Ethinu was silent.

"I thought not."

"Allow me to my feet," Ethinu said, turning her head to one side. "You have nothing to fear from me for the remainder of your stay here."

"How terribly reassuring." Still, I stepped back and allowed her to rise.

"I cannot guarantee the Oghma will agree. We have fought against the King Below for centuries and your adoption of his name will be...problematic. However, I still wield exceptional influence and persuading someone to do nothing is easy enough with wizards. Hellsword, of course, will refuse, as he believes he can avert the prophecy by killing you. Valance the Red hasn't been seen in centuries. Jassamine, as you might guess, is less than inclined to favor any plan that doesn't result in your death."

"We're going to kill her anyway," Serah said.

"A wise choice," Ethinu said. "You might be able to break the Lawgiver's resolve if his Chosen is gone. The others: Margaret, Morgause, Nymaena, Brigit, Lugh, and the Nameless One—yes, they'll agree to stay out of your way."

"The Nameless One?" I asked.

"Men." Ethinu wrinkled her nose. "You always seem to want to make things more theatrical. He probably was named Myron or Thomas and felt neither was suitable for a proper wizard."

"I see."

Serah and Ethinu spent the next hour negotiating terms. I merely stayed back, keeping an eye out for any treason or hint of betrayal from the Blue Sorceress but saw none. Just watching the two interact left me feeling vaguely sick as they discussed the fate of kings and nations.

Serah demanded proof of Ethinu's neutrality, which amounted

to sabotaging harvests, spreading slander, assassinating the Nine Usurpers' supporters, and other acts that seemed to contradict the concept. Ethinu, by contrast, took the opportunity to demand help against various foes as well as access to the King Below's libraries. Despite how impressive Serah's negotiated terms were, all I could think was the Oghma's support was going to drastically increase the amount of chaos in the Southern Kingdoms. Ethinu would take advantage of that chaos and increase her own position. No matter who won the war between the Lawgiver and I, it was likely Ethinu would emerge better off than before.

Such is the way of the ruthless and cunning, the Trickster said. *Just look at you.*

Ignoring the Trickster, I watched as the two of them exchanged geases on one another that were backed up by Sera's power. I was sworn to a similar agreement by my own power, which I was very careful about wording. Even so, I felt ill for the fact I was manipulating the situation so. I also was worried about Serah since, unwittingly or not, I'd once again involved her in the politics of the Oghma. She'd escaped them by joining me and I'd brought her right back to involving herself in the power games of this weird cult. Worse, I'd potentially put her in the sights of a wizardess fully capable of killing us both. I had no doubt Ethinu was willing to murder anyone or anything that stood in the way of her ambitions.

"We're done," Serah said, watching Ethinu leave. She turned back to me. "Are you all right?"

"My father was a drunkard who did terrible things when he was indulging in spirits. He always felt terrible about them afterward, however, and often swore to give it up. A few times, he made game efforts at it and went weeks, even months, without it. When he did, though, he inevitably said he'd drink just a little only to return home three sheets to the wind."

"I'm not sure I get your meaning."

"I'm just wondering if we are, in our ways, more similar than I ever realized."

Serah looked at me, turning her head to one side as if trying to see something new inside me. "You are a very strange man, Jacob."

"That I am." I was unable to meet her gaze "We should depart this place."

"I agree," Serah said, conjuring yet another rift in the fabric of reality before departing.

I paused before turning around the open air behind me. I needed to leave Ethinu a message. "I know you can hear me so I'll just make this brief. I don't believe for a second you were persuaded. So, instead, I'll content myself with the fact that you will probably make another attempt on my life in the future. That's fine. However, it occurs to me you might be inclined to come after my wives or my people. That is *not* acceptable. I could rant and rave or threaten, but I know you're not going to be easily intimidated. So I'll put my the situation into perspective for you. Here, in the heart of your power, you took your best shot at me and you missed. If you harm Regina or Serah or my subjects, I will come after you. I swear I will hunt you across the multiverse. I will spend *a million years* finding you. If you die before I catch you, I will raise you from the dead so I can torture you until you swear your soul to me in order to make the pain stop. Then, once you are mine, I will *damn you* in a hell made especially for your wretched soul." I clenched my bloody fist. "May I cease to exist right now if every syllable of this is not true."

Nothing happened to me.

I lifted *Chill's Fury* and sliced it over the edge of my palm. A small sliver of blackish-brown blood fell from it onto the ground. And it began spreading a terrible blackness throughout the crystal palace. The light dimmed everywhere and it slowly began to crumble. I began to absorb the power within and redirected it. Within the next hour, the crystal palace would disintegrate into nothingness.

One of the walls beside me collapsed and I suspected Ethinu was in the hasty process of evacuating whatever valuables she had stored in her home to a new location. My curse was spreading throughout the palace now, the black magic undermining and unweaving the extensive spells Ethinu had woven into the place. Destroying her home was a small punishment to inflict upon her for trying to kill both me and my bride, but it was all I could manage now. I hope Ethinu realized I'd do a lot worse the next time.

Either way, there was no answer.

"I think we have an understanding," I said, turning around and walking through the portal away from the astral plane.

Much to my surprise, I arrived on the deck of a ship with

black sails and it was the middle of the night. There was a crew of Northerners manning it and I could see Regina at the vessel's stern. Serah was to my side.

"Why the delay?" Serah asked.

"Politics."

Serah snorted. "I heard your entire rant, Jacob. All it did was expose something I'd known about you all along."

"Which is?"

"The three of us were made for one another."

CHAPTER FOURTEEN

The ship was one I recognized as the *Ghostly Runner*, a smuggling vessel crewed by a mixture of Winterfolk and Northern wild men. There had always been a reasonable amount of trade going on between the northern and southern continents, it just had to be done by the most open minded, corrupt, or both.

The amount now fluctuated madly given the Grand Temple considered it heresy to trade with the northern continent, yet it had never been more profitable do so. The *Ghostly Runner*, led by Captain Vass, was one of the few vessels I knew that had no fear of the Grand Priestess or her witch hunters.

"How did we get here?" I asked. "The Night Bridge required months to charge."

"Another benefit of Ethinu's palace is easy teleportation throughout reality," Serah said, looking up at the starlit sky. The Peaceweavers were high above and formed a pair of crescent moons. "Time flows differently in the astral plane than in our world, though. I was protecting us from the worst of it for most of our trip, but that failed when fighting the Seraphs."

"So how long have we been gone?"

"About thirty-six hours," Serah said. "Not thirty-six years or thirty-six centuries or however long you may have been thinking."

"Another reason to never visit again."

"You don't want a crystal palace?"

"The only illusions I need are that everything will turn out all right."

Serah gave a half-smile. "I suppose we could all use some of those."

"Let's go speak with Regina," I said, starting to walk toward her, only to have my wrist grabbed by Serah.

"I'll hold off on that for a bit, if you don't mind."

"Are you sure?"

Serah's eyes met mine and I stared into her brown orbs, absorbing the depths of sadness behind them. "What I did wasn't a small betrayal, Jacob. I wanted to cover up my sins and bury them deep in the ground. I want to end that part of my life, believe me, but I am not sure I can. I carry it around like a turtle does its shell."

"We all do that. The thing is, being a spouse is about helping you carry your burdens."

"Jacob, where did you get your view of marriage? It is quite unlike anything a sane and sensible person would have."

"Nowhere. Just about every married couple I've ever met has been miserable in one form or another. However, it's taught me that the best thing anyone can be for someone else is miserable with them."

"If that's meant to cheer me up, you failed."

"Yes, well, we'll keep that out of the holy canon."

Serah turned away before shaking her head in amusement. "I knew there was a reason I loved you." Her expression turned serious in an instant. "Actions speak louder than words. If I am going to prove to Regina that I can be trusted, then I must prepare to deliver Hellsword's head on a plate. Redhand's, too."

"If you have lingering feelings for him, then you—"

"No, Jacob, please."

"Pardon?"

"Don't try and soften this." Serah's gaze narrowed as shadows seemed to creep up and down her body, a sign her magic was escaping her control. "There are some things you can' be reasonable about. There are times in one life one must make a choice and cast aside one's neutrality. Hellsword taught me to embrace every horrible thing other people said about me. He made me dirty, filthy, and vile while making me think I was powerful as well as wondrous. He has to die…and painfully."

I understood that sort of hatred, and it frightened me that I did. "I understand… more than you could possibly imagine."

Serah reached over and clutched my hand. "You need to know some basic things about them before we reach Kerifas. Important things. I'll share everything I know about both men, the Oghma, and myself. It's important I disclose all my secrets. I want Regina to know too because what you don't know might kill you. You have to convince her to listen."

I saw no reason why she would refuse.

Clearly you know nothing about your spouses, the Trickster said.

"I will," I said, ignoring him.

"Know only this: that Hellsword is one of Natrariss's degenerate magocracy's nobility and was presiding over blood orgies and human sacrifices before most men hit puberty. He recovered *Plaguebringer* from the Final Battle of the Fifth War, having defeated the Wraith Knight who wielded it. He is a poet and lecher who fancies himself a genius rather than a despoiler of men and women. He is also one of the most powerful wizards alive, having bargained or stolen knowledge from individuals far greater than himself. He hurts people to make himself feel strong and prove the weak deserve being abused because they cannot defend themselves."

I absorbed these facts as she spoke them, nodding. "He is a man without honor."

"I have never met a man with honor, Jacob. Not even you."

I tried not to be offended. "And Redhand?"

"He is the son of the Lawgiver and an immortal."

That required a second for me to absorb. "Could you repeat that?"

"In the Terralan Dominion, there was a powerful High Human Queen named Kastalas who ruled over her fellow mortals as an immortal demigod. She offered up human sacrifices by the thousands and was prone to torturing any individual who did not follow her insane whims. Somehow, the Lawgiver came to her and their encounter resulted in her becoming pregnant. At age thirteen, Redhand strangled his mother and ruled over the High Humans as God Emperor for a thousand years."

"Until Valance destroyed it."

It was a classic story. A wizard appointed by the gods used his powers to bring down terrible vengeance on a decadent and evil society. The Codex was full of such events.

"Yes."

"Which Redhand survived."

"He has been a hero under many names you may recognize. Dodos, Harmab, Thul Firehand, Beorn Grimwulf—"

My eyes widened at that last one. I had grown up with legends of that relentless berserker slaying an entire army with an enchanted sickle made from a dragon's jawbone. The other names were familiar to me too.

"Wherever there is violence, Redhand is drawn. He is hideously deformed by ever-burning wounds that never heal but cannot kill him. He was imprisoned under a mountain, forced to hold up a mountain when the Usurpers found him, and the price for his freedom was to serve them. This, above everything else, has guaranteed their victories but destroyed their reputation. He is an indiscriminate killer and the worst of them."

I could not hide how disappointed I was in her. "You should have told this to me months, if not years, ago."

"I would have had to have revealed the origin of the information. I was not ready for that."

I shook with frustration then pushed down those feelings. "You will be honest with us from now on?"

"As much as I can be."

My next words were as much those of a military commander as those of a husband. We needed every bit of information we could to stop my vision from coming true. That would require honesty, absolute honesty. "Work on that."

"I will. I will also see if I can determine any weaknesses before you face him."

"Please do."

"You are mad at me as well now."

"Yes."

Serah closed her eyes. "It is to be expected. Even you have—"

"Do not turn this into an occasion for self-pity. It does not suit you. You have lived with being hated and loathed your entire life, but should have faith in those who love you. We will forgive you, but do not try to drive us away. We deserve better."

Serah's eyes flashed and she curled her mouth into a sneer. For a second I thought I would be subject to one of her epic tongue lashings but she, instead, turned around and walked away toward the ship's cabins.

That could have gone better, the Trickster said.

"Shut up," I muttered aloud.

I turned around and took a moment to look over the smuggler's crew. They were a collection of humans, Fir Bolg, boggarts, and Bauchan. Shadowkind could find work in the Southern Kingdoms. Dirty, disgusting, or criminal work, but work nonetheless. None of them seemed to think the arrival of the King Below and a wizardess via magical rift was anything of importance, though, which said a great deal about how jaded Captain Vass's crew was.

Taking deep breath to calm myself, I decided to go speak with Regina. A part of me wanted to go find a cabin myself to sleep in but there was never any real comfort in rest. As much as I could conjure the trappings of life, I was undead and always would be. Sleep was more drifting into old memories and the darkness of oblivion rather than anything resembling true rest. After my encounter with Ethinu trying to rip away my spirit, I was wide awake and wanted to just clear my head. There wasn't much to do for that in the middle of the Devil's Sea, though.

Walking over, I tried to shove away thoughts of immortal demigods and insane wizard nobles. Instead, I just focused on the beautiful white-haired woman who was leaning over the railing and looking out into the frigid waves beyond. She had changed out of her armor into a set of leathers and furs with a hooded cloak over her head. It was normal attire for a mercenary, not the kind you would find on a royal or a queen, but none of that would disguise that she was one of the most beautiful women in the world.

That's merely love talking, the Trickster said. *Above average, yes, but far too unfeminine.*

Your definition of femininity is far different from mine.

Lowering the hood of my cloak, I put my arms on the railing and gazed out into the night. The waters were surprisingly peaceful, but there was a storm in the far distance. I couldn't help but remember the time I'd first crossed the Devil's Sea with my fellow Shadowguard, taking residence at one of the forts like Caer Callig in hopes of hunting Formor to win coup points. Now I was the Formor's leader and killing Shadowguard.

Just being around Regina, though, made things better. She was a reminder to me that there were still good things left in this world to fight for. More than that, I loved how she could drink three men under the table, hated elvish music, and treated everything like a competition even when we were just talking about what to eat. Once I had only thought I'd known what love was with Jassamine.

Now I did.

"A bit for your thoughts?" Regina said, pulling out a copper coin and handing it over.

"You'll get much more than a copper's worth." I took it and smiled before putting it away.

"G'head," Regina said. "We all need to unleash every now and then."

"Are you sure? It's heady stuff."

"I'm a big girl."

"All right. If you were given a choice between your loved ones and the world, which would you choose?"

Regina snorted. "That's a stupid question. My loved ones live on the world."

"You know what I mean."

Regina turned around and leaned against some netting. "Honestly? I don't know. I know what I'd want *you* to choose, though."

"Which is?"

"That you'd save the world. I don't want to live with the death of others on my conscience because someone loved me more."

I looked at her, uncertain how to respond.

"Hypocritical as that may be," Regina said, sighing, "I struggle with the fact that this entire war we're planning is in large part *because* of your love for me. Your desire to please me. What does the destruction of Whitehall and its people mean to you? Nothing. You walked with me in the ruins of it, looking at the horrors done there, but it is one land in a million to you."

"It is your home."

Regina started to say something, stopped, then looked to one side. "Yes, mine. I...don't want to drown the world in blood because of my pain. I can't overlook the horrors they're committing, though. It's... I don't know what the right thing to do is."

"Because of Ketra?"

"Yeah, I've been thinking about her a lot. My cousin has changed a great deal over the past three years—not all for the better."

I'd seen the fury and intensity in the young woman's eyes. Ketra was beautiful, a reflection of Regina in many ways, but there was none of my wife's restraint behind those windows to the soul. Ketra was eager to bring the horror of war down upon Winterholme, if only so she could do more damage to the empire.

"Where is she now?" I asked.

"Sleeping in the hold," Regina said, gesturing with a slight tilt of her head. "She had a very busy day."

"We all did."

Regina looked up to the stars. "All this time I thought I was Whitehall's sole survivor. I wanted to make the Usurpers pay for the death of my family. Yet, two of my family are still alive. I could have searched for them, found them, and been with them this entire time. Instead, I was playing lord marshal, trying to strike out in the same way they were."

"Does it change how you feel?"

Regina looked down. "No. Not really. Because while Ketra and Gewain managed to get away, Rebecca did not. Nor Yanna the cook, Marci the chambermaid, the groom, Anders, or a hundred other names that conjure memories for me but would be just a list to you."

"Ghosts would not prevent you from choosing a new life away from all this." Now I was playing the same role Serah had before. Strange.

"I'm unsaddled and confused by your feelings on this. Do you support war or not?"

I put my arm over her shoulder and gave her a light hug. "Would it help if I said I have no idea?"

Regina buried her head into my side. "Quite the opposite. You're supposed to give me an easy answer. That's what gods do."

"Then I will just repeat what Warmaster Kalian once told me: Our emotions are our guide because motivations do not exist in logic and numbers. We value a thing because we feel for it. We act on our desires, whether they're the smart thing or not. In the end, just do what you feel is best and you'll regret it later. But know that the greater loss would not to act at all."

"Thank you, Jacob." Regina pulled away. "That helps a little. Does it help you?"

"Not in the slightest."

Regina snorted.

"You're the reason I keep going, Regina. You and Serah, not any higher ideals. Just those I love. I suppose I feel a sense of duty and friendship to those who follow me but even that pales in comparison to the feelings I have for you."

Regina gave me a kiss on the lips then pulled away. "What would you do if I died?"

"Avenge you."

"And then?"

"Stop." That was all that needed to be said.

"Even with Serah?"

"That is assuming she would continue, which is a big assumption...but yes. I could not go on without you." I could survive Serah's death, just as she could survive mine. Neither of us could live without Regina.

I hated that fact.

Regina smiled. "Let's forget the rest of the world for a little while. Come to my cabin and we'll just be husband and wife for a time. Just the two of us."

"All right."

And for a time, our troubles vanished.

CHAPTER FIFTEEN

I could have stayed there in the captain's bed, lying next to Regina, for the rest of eternity. She was an exuberant lover and insatiable, always driven to see if she could perhaps exhaust a man who was more spirit than flesh. Often, she succeeded. This time, though, I knew it was she who needed to be exhausted as our time together was a necessary escape for her. A chance to empty the cup she'd filled with pain, sorrow, and remorse.

In the end, she lied nuzzled up against me with her eyes closed and a smile upon her face. I wanted to stay up all night next to her and just look at the Lady of Starlight, my Unicorn Queen, but I wanted to escape too.

And I fell asleep beside her.

A terrible mistake.

Sleep held no joy for me.

Only memories.

In this case, I found myself wandering the Ashlands on the back of an old broken-down horse, still a young man in my early twenties. It was dusty-gray land of dead cracked earth and fossilized trees in every direction for miles. There were mountains in the distance covered in an eternal storm, shooting out lightning every few seconds. It was neither night nor day since it seemed the two states didn't quite exist here. People called the northern continent a wasteland, but those who did so had never visited the Ashlands. They were a slice of hell in our world.

"What have I gotten myself into?" I said, shaking my head as I continued on the road to Twilight's End.

"You're going to become a Shadowguardsman," my elvish companion said from behind me. "You should be honored."

Mikael was a brown-skinned low sidhe with long blond hair tied in a ponytail, wearing a Gaelish tartan, and carrying a crossbow on his back. My banishment from the Grand Temple, voluntary or not, had been months ago and I'd welcomed any form of companionship on my long road to reaching this territory. Still, I couldn't help but be annoyed by the man's chipper attitude.

I hated elves.

"I am honored. It's why I'm making this three-month journey," I said, my throat dry. There was a strange bitterness to the air as if there was nothing in it but stale wind. It was said that not even microbes existed in the Ashland's air. The leftover magical energy from the First Great Shadow War killed everything but those who were altered to resist it.

Like the Shadowguard.

"Are you sure you don't have any Fir Bolg blood on you? After a month traveling with you, I'm sure you must. Only they can be so grim and sarcastic."

In the Imperial capital city, such a claim was a deadly insult. The Fir Bolg race was considered vermin by most Imperials. I'd been born in the Riverfords, though, where my bloodline was considered almost as foul. Even so, my father would often speak of the Stagmen with gross distaste.

"I do not have any of that honorable people's blood within me, no," I said, remembering Warmaster Kalian's words about them. They were a proud people with a glorious history. This was their world and only the Grand Temple and the empire's greed had made humans and their race enemies.

"Hmmm," Mikael huffed. "Do you know the history of this land?"

"Is this another elvish history lecture? Because I learned more than enough about it before ever meeting you. What I know if you're a race that claims to be the best at everything while never being able to prove it—yet never quite learning the lesson to treat other races with respect."

"A man who doesn't hate the Fir Bolg for being Anessia-Killers or want to exterminate the Shadowkind but who hates elves," Mikael said, shaking his head. "You are a very strange man."

"Is it so strange?"

"There are places in the empire where rich merchants pay the lowest of our kind to impregnate their daughters in hopes of siring a bastard with elven features. Places where the Lawgiver is depicted always with pointed ears and angular faces, for we were his chosen first children and humans merely his second unworthy creations. Places—"

"I have seen hundreds of farmers driven off their land so elves could create estates for themselves of illusion and magicrafted animals. I have seen sidhe lords and ladies waste ten thousand silver coins commissioning great statues and portraits during famine. I had witnessed them ride on golden white horses, immune to disease and blessed with healing magics, walk past plague houses with their nose upturned. I once saw an elvish lord cut a human girl's face up in a brothel after paying more than the building for the sheer pleasure of defacing a monkey-person. *That* is why I despise elves."

I still regretted not killing that elf.

"Oh," Mikael said. "Well, then, I suppose you have your reasons."

"Do I still have to hear the lecture?"

"I'm afraid so," Mikael said. "Last one, though, I promise."

"We're about five miles from Twilight's End."

"That would be why."

I sighed. "Fine, go ahead. You haven't been completely terrible company."

"You have blessed me," Mikael said, putting his hand over his heart. "More than you could ever know."

"I'm going to start fantasizing about a good round-eared human woman soon. You better start before I block you out completely."

"Just be certain that fantasizing is all you do. I know humans love playing with themselves almost as much as they love throwing their shit at each other."

I chuckled and dreamed of Jassamine. Her beautiful twisted black hair, her lovely chocolate skin, and the feel of her touch against my body. It was possible I'd never see her again, but I trusted her vision enough that here was where I needed to be. So much so that I'd let her frame me for her rape and let myself be sentenced to service here.

No one in the Grand Temple had believed it but the offer of gold had been enough to persuade them otherwise. I was to live and die now in the service of the hardest warriors in the world so that I might honor a hunch of my truest love.

What had I gotten myself into?

"This was once the kingdom of Tiarnanon, the land of the elves, which split the continent with the Terralan Dominion before they were wiped out. There were over a hundred million elves from here to the Devil's Sea, existing in a state of—"

"Paradise?"

"No one knows," Mikael surprised me by saying. "Those few old enough to remember it do not speak of it. It is as if the trauma has scarred their minds they could not access thoughts of said era without breaking down into quivering balls, screaming for hours. Such is the legacy of the First Great Shadow War."

"You have my attention."

"When the King Below brought his army of demons, undead, Shadowkind, it was an army in the hundreds of millions. He did not come to destroy the sidhe but to use our moongates to launch a great war across the universe. To bring the retribution of fear, death, and hate to a million races we will never meet or hear of. The high lords knew they could not win without the Lawgiver's help, but he turned his back on us."

I made a sign with my fingers against his blasphemy but did not interrupt.

Mikael continued, staring out into the darkness. "My ancestors broke themselves for humanity and the other races of this world and others. Every man, woman, and some children did their part. Untold numbers clashed and died until the high lords used such weapons as to permanently scar their land so there was nothing left behind. Nothing but ghosts and death. This." He gestured out to the darkness and despair surrounding us.

"I admire your ancestors' sacrifice," I said, surprising myself. "It was a worthy end. I apologize for my bias."

"Don't."

I blinked. "Excuse me?"

"Few elves would do the same today. You ask why the sidhe treat your race like vermin, the way your kind treats the Fir Bolg, boggans, and dryads? It is because they think they wasted their lives protecting someone other than themselves. The only survivors of our kind were those too young to fight or too old on the Blessed Isles. Those who cannot appreciate pride or sacrifice or honor. You hate the elves for what they have become...but I hate them more."

We were silent until we started up to the trail to Twilight's End. This was the one place in the Ashlands that seemed to have some sense of life. There was mutated, sickly looking wheat, a village built into the side of the mountain, and caravans of traders moving up the road to the hundreds of towers carved into the mountain.

Twilight's End was the largest castle I'd ever seen, more city than fortress, constructed with magics that would not be re-discovered for centuries. Hundreds journeyed to join the Shadowguard every year, but only a few were accepted. Those who were sent, like me, as part of the penal recruits were either enslaved or used as cannon fodder in their never-ending war against the King Below. There were even rumors that the biomancers beneath vivisected and experimented on the worst of its prisoners so they might gain insights into medicine.

Jassamine had faith I would pass and ascend to the highest ranks.

I wasn't so sure.

"Welcome to your new home," Mikael said, chuckling. It was as if our last conversation hadn't happened at all.

"It is a charming residence in a nightmarish fairytale story sort of way."

"The King Below erected Twilight's End when he destroyed the last city of this land. Those who took it back vowed to stay here and fight the hordes of ghosts, demons, and mutants he left behind. They eventually won."

"We won't have won until the King Below is dead."

"You can't kill a god."

"Watch me try." I would become the greatest Shadowguardsman who ever lived. Why? Because I was doing it for love.

Mikael paused. "Tell me, Jacob, did you do it?"

"Hmm?"

"Your crime."

"You have been with me for months and never bothered to ask before."

"I am now."

I sighed. "Yes, I did it."

Mikael stared at me. "Amazing. You are a terrible liar."

I frowned. "Why would I lie about such a horrible crime?"

"That's the question, isn't it?"

Looking up at the massive sixty-foot gates, I felt a surprising urge to be honest. "Someone told me the King Below was coming back. That a Fourth Great Shadow War was going to come and I needed to join the fight to save the world. That if I didn't participate, there would be a hundred years of darkness."

Mikael snorted. "Fine, you're a wonderful liar. What do you want to do once you join?"

I looked down at my right hand and gave it a squeeze. "I want to build things."

"Too bad you're only good at destroying."

"What?"

I turned to Mikael then and saw his face dripping blood from the hole in his throat, his eyes glazed over as in death. He was like he'd been when I'd found him on a nameless, unimportant battlefield during the Fourth Great Shadow War, stabbed by a Fomor during a battle of no particular import, having been distracted at a crucial time by a friend's death.

Above our heads, Twilight's End transformed into a refurbished palace as a vast decadent city of brothels, gambling dens, and bars was built at the floor. The city of Twilight's Rest was the reward for the Shadowguard winning the Fourth War and the defeat of the King Below. Its members were drawn not from criminals and disgraced knights seeking redemption, but the nobility's extra children now.

Around us the Ashlands changed as vast, mystical towers designed to suck the toxic magic from the ground were being erected, canals dug from the oceans hundreds of leagues away, and topsoil transported from far beyond—all to make the Ashlands bloom. It was said eighty thousand of the empress's enemies had already died in the process. Such was the King Above's vision of the future.

I awoke with the feeling of sunlight against my face, coming through the window of the captain's chambers. The *Ghostly Runner* was an expensive ship for a smuggling vessel, equipped with many luxuries absent for the common criminal. Trade was the life blood of the Iron Order and those willing to bring valuables to the North were well compensated. Perhaps too well compensated, though there was little that could be done about that.

I took deep breath and looked to the naked form of Regina at my side, thinking about what Mikael would have thought about my marriage to a woman in whom the blood of his people flowed. He probably would have laughed at me. My opinion of elves had improved markedly over the past few centuries, perhaps realizing humans had no leg to stand on when condemning another species for callousness.

They never had.

Awakening in the present, I slid out of bed. I lifted my muscular frame and took a moment to look in a nearby dressing mirror. Dressing the old-fashioned way, brushing my teeth, and using the privy, I tried to pretend I was alive, but there was no point in that. I didn't need sleep, food, water, or rest. I was a creature of magic now, god or not, and just impersonating a human being. The real Jacob Riverson had died centuries ago and was remembered as a very different person than he was. He also would have been horrified by the person he'd become.

So why wasn't I?

Walking out in the plain black attire I'd been wearing before, I decided to get some fresh sea air in order to clear my head. Opening the door and locking it behind me to preserve Regina's privacy, I saw the figure of Captain Vass with his arms crossed beside the door. He was well over six feet tall, skin the color of a shining bronze, white haired with a body so well formed it might have been two men merged together. The captain enjoyed his adornments with several gold necklaces around his neck, many rings on each finger, and a tattoo of two naked mermaids entwined in a sensual embrace.

Aside from his lewd body art, Captain Vass's chest was clean-shaven with only an ill-fitting black vest over it. Like all Fir Bolg men, he had no hair on his body and a pair of great antlers extending from the side of his head. He was wearing a pair of loose white linen pants with a pair of rune-covered hand-axes too large for most men and a pair of lightning pistols. Each would have cost more than a war horse in the Imperial capital and he'd gone to the ridiculous length of having all four gilded.

"The Gods Between bless you," Captain Vass said, speaking with a thick South Island accent. "Assuming that's not going to cause you to burst into flames, Black Sun."

"It will take more than the concerns of dead gods to worry me, pirate," I said, smirking. The Fir Bolg worshiped gods long gone, slain by the Lawgiver and Trickster. On some level, I admired their devotion while on others, I just found it silly.

"Smuggler, not pirate. I trade the goods they steal, not take them myself."

"Ah. Of course, how silly of me."

"Not that I haven't engaged in some banditry every now and then."

I rolled my eyes. "How long until we reach Kerifas? It was a ten-day journey across the sea in my era."

"We move a bit faster in my time," Captain Vass said, gesturing the horizon. One of his crew, a tiny boggan woman with braids who looked almost comical next to Captain Vass, handed him a spyglass, which he handed to me.

Walking to the edge of the ship, past a seasick Ketra vomiting over the side, I lifted the spyglass and looked to the horizon. What greeted me was the sight of six massive stone statues rising from the waters, each two hundred feet tall and made in the shape of female messengers with blindfolds over their eyes. The statues were contorting in pain and linked together with gigantic chains running through manacles around their wrists.

The Guardians of Kerifas were golems created by the Terralan Dominion, forged from mountains and enchanted to serve as protectors of the city during times of crisis. Each noon, they let out a terrifying, mournful song of despair that was meant to break the wills of the slaves that were trained and bred in the city. The Terralan were long gone, but the guardians remained.

The city was visible beyond, no longer a place where nothing but human misery was trafficked, filled with over half a million souls and endless trade from all corners of the Southern Kingdoms. The bay around the guardians was full of hundreds of vessels ranging from G'Tay junks to Imperial Man-o-War and new machines that looked like they were somehow made of floating iron. The air above the sky had hippogriffs, dragons doing their daily exercise, and other signs of a modernized city.

But I noticed something odd about the formation of the city's defenses. The dragon roosts were at strategic locations for deployment inside the city walls and all the iron ships had their immense cannons aimed at the interior. A dozen garrisons were visible but, again, far within the walls instead of alongside them.

It was a city the empire was ready to slaughter at a moment's notice.

Not defend.

"Welcome," Captain Vass said, slapping me on the shoulder with an immense hand, "to Kerifas, City of the Damned."

CHAPTER SIXTEEN

"City of the Damned, huh? Cheerful name," I said, staring out into the harbor beyond. We were only a few minutes away from arriving in Kerifas.

"What did they call it in your era?" Captain Vass asked, taking position beside me and crossing his arms.

"The City of Traitors," I said, frowning. "The city opened up its gates for the King Below at the start of the Fourth War. When we retook it during the final days, everyone wanted to raze it to the ground and put the populace to the sword."

In the end, they'd been enslaved. It had been an unfair decision, even then, because the populace had no choice in surrendering. It was either surrender, flight, or death. Kerifas was a natural landing point for the King Below during his invasions and was one of the most vulnerable points in the North.

"Let us hope they are equally treasonous today as they are in your time," Captain Vass said. "Otherwise, it will be very difficult to take the city."

I frowned. "You seem remarkably untroubled about allying yourself with my cause."

"You mean my decision to work for the Ultimate Evil?" Vass said, the corners of his mouth widening into a smile.

"Yes."

Captain Vass snorted. "The Fir Bolg were once the rulers of this continent and over the past twenty ages, have lost every one of our homelands. We live now at the sufferance of kings and queens not our own. We are blamed for disease, lice, poverty, and other misfortunes. The stupid amongst us fight with groups like the Free Army or the Golden Arrow. They kill the innocent and claim this will somehow lead to us becoming a great nation again. The smarter amongst us sacrifice their pride and dignity so we can co-exist as something akin to equals with the lowliest of men. They believe, someday, we will achieve a better life that way. I think differently. Neither side will amount to much."

"So you fight with me in hopes of a better life for your race?"

Captain Vass's smile turned sour. "No, Black Sun, I think you will kill many humans and elves. You will drench the lands in blood and grind the Anessian Empire into dust. I also think you will make me a rich man doing so. That, for me, is enough."

Lovely. "I suppose I asked."

"The man who thinks too much on his actions invites only sorrow. We are all pawns of our emotions and past. Live in the moment, enjoying what pleasures life offers, and you will not die with regrets."

"I'm dead, Vass."

"A dead man who regularly fucks two goddesses and rules a kingdom the size of a continent." Vass leered.

"Captain…"

"Is it true the silver-haired one picks out concubines for you to share from every race? I have had dryad women before and Bachaun but never both—"

Clenching my fists, my voice took on a dangerous tone. "Leave."

"As you wish, Black Sun. As you wish." Captain Vass spread out his arms as if to indicate he was joking then turned around and walked away.

That was when I heard Ketra vomit again. It was an impressive amount of noise for a woman her size.

Looking over my shoulder, I asked, "Forgive me for asking, but how is it a woman who rides dragonback is seasick?"

Ketra pulled out a wineskin and rinsed her mouth out before spitting over the side. "I'm not seasick, I'm poisoned. Those damned stag heads gave me bad food."

I crossed my arms. "I can't imagine why if you use such loving terminology."

Ketra shot me a glare. "I'm a friend to the Fir Bolg. I believe all races should be equal, titles should be abolished, and wealth as well as land evenly distributed amongst the people."

"Speaking as a peasant, I've never found my kind has wanted equality. We've just wanted to be rich and powerful ourselves."

Ketra closed her eyes and scrunched her brow as if trying to push away a headache then turned around. "You don't like me very much, do you, Ser Jacob?"

"I don't know you, Lady Ketra—"

"Just Ketra."

"I don't know, Just Ketra. You're Regina's cousin and ward-sister, so that naturally inclines me to like you. However, you have brought a large amount of complications into my life and I don't know if you realize the full consequences of your actions."

"I have seen and dealt death up close, Ser Jacob. Many nobles and their servants have died by my hands."

I grimaced. "Which doesn't increase my trust."

"The Army of Free Peasants—"

I cut her off, curious about this organization she kept mentioning. "May I ask what that is and how it came to exist?"

"Oh." Ketra blinked, surprised by my interest. "Well, after Gewain and I escaped from the Massacre of Whitehall, we were impoverished and desperate."

"I'm sorry."

"You didn't know anyone in Whitehall," Ketra said, her eyes narrowing. "Your condolences are well meaning but empty."

I nodded.

Ketra continued. "Gewain has always had a gift for oratory, though, and his writing is better still. His...uhm, companion, Rose, and he were very close and the bard suggested a war of words might be better."

"Rose is his lover?"

"You'll meet him," Ketra said, looking uncomfortable. "He is working on securing the Jarl and Earl's alliance for us in Kerifas. But yes, he is like Serah is to Regina in that way."

I raised an eyebrow. People in the future were peculiar about sex in ways I did not understand. "Go on."

"My brother wrote a book describing the atrocity. *The Massacre of Whitehall* was florid and despicably poetic for such a heinous act, but it made our homeland's destruction a rallying cry. He went from village to village, raising troopers, working with nobles, and attempting to persuade them to undermine the empress whenever possible. He had to make many promises, some of which were contradictory, but started spreading the movement. We even allied with the Golden Arrow. The Golden Arrow are—"

"I know who they are. You have made a poor choice of allies."

"The Golden Arrow fight for the freedom of the Fir Bolg."

"Tell that to the thousands of their kind whom they have murdered."

The Golden Arrow was an extremist religious sect born in Fireforge. After my death, Jassamine and then-Emperor Eric the Great had launched a war upon the Fir Bolg's homeland. The pair had conquered the kingdoms there, forced the populace to convert to the Path, and divided the Fir Bolg across the Southern Kingdoms to make sure they never recovered their previous strength. The Golden Arrow sought to retake their race's homeland, which they argued was best accomplished through the indiscriminate killing of humans. However justified their greviances were, it was hard to sympathize with them. They were child-killers and thieves.

"They've been good friends to us," Ketra said. "Kana, our contact, was there when no one else in the empire lifted a finger to help us."

"If so, it's only because they wanted something."

"Forgive me, but you're styling yourself after the God of Evil and everything Regina tells me says you're grossly misunderstood."

I paused. She had a point. "Please go on."

"We've had a lot of small victories since then but nothing that has amounted to anything. We need to—as much as I hate it—ally with the local nobility who oppose the empire. The ones who want to force them out of their territory and restore their privileges. If we can gather an alliance of all those who hate the empire together, we can defeat them and make a more equal society."

"Your solution to creating a more equal society is to ally with the traditionalists who hate the empress's reforms and religious zealots?"

"Gewain can make it work," Ketra said, looking up. "He's like Regina. He makes people believe."

I nodded. "If he's like her then I believe you. How much of your rhetoric do you believe?" It was hard to wrap my head around a woman of the Imperial royal lineage having embraced such radical views.

"All of it. I saw what unrestricted power and authority could do to my homeland. I want to make the world a better place."

I'd seen several peasant revolts and they tended to get out of control quickly. Many times, the rationing and taxes during the war had forced the commons to seek justice with torch and pitchfork. They massacred any nobles they could lay their hands on, good or bad, and they ended up with the rebels slaughtered to the man along with all their loved ones.

Always.

They would not care if Ketra was on their side, had spilled blood with them, or was a friend. In the end, they would see her as one of her class by birth and if she lasted past that somehow then it was only to see the doom of her dreams. The world was built on a pyramid of oppression, lies, and brutality. It was not ready for equality and its people did not want it. Only a bigger slice of bread and someone to blame for their troubles.

"I was a reformer once, too," I said, thinking back to my time with Jassamine. "How to do that is the question and the cost is often far—"

"Whatever arguments you are about to give me, I suspect I've already heard and with far greater eloquence."

I sighed, knowing further discussion was fruitless. "Very well."

Ketra looked up. "Tell me, do you really not think the empress and her cronies need to be stopped?"

I looked up to the seagulls flying around the mast. "I merely wish to share a piece of advice."

"Which is?"

"My uncle fought against the Fire Kings with the Fir Bolg rebellion. He overthrew them and instituted an assembly supported by the local chiefs. He was made a great hero in the name of freedom, justice, and honor. Fifty years later, the Fire Lands were destroyed and all the Fir Bolg clans were scattered and their civilization ruined. The very empire that had supported the Fire Kings' overthrow annihilated the Assembly."

"And your point?"

"Don't lose sight of the fact your enemies are people too or you may become what you fight."

Ketra looked unconcerned. She plopped herself ontop of a trio of barrels latched to the deck. "Is that what keeps you up at night? That you might end up becoming the villain rather than the hero?"

I glared at her. "I *did* become the villain."

Ketra bit her lip before giving me an appraising look. "I can see why Regina loves you."

"Sometimes I find that hard to believe."

"She feels the same."

I looked down at her. "Oh?"

"Regina has always struggled hard with being loved. Her upbringing in the Northern Wasteland with the Shadowguard was hard, and I think worse things happened there than just the death of her parents. She struggles to do good and help others as well as live up to her family legacy but I don't think she's ever felt worthy of it. That is why she wants revenge, I think. It keeps her from having to think too hard on it. Also, if she overthrows tyrants, then maybe she'll be worthy of being loved."

That was a remarkably similar feeling to how I felt. "I think you underestimate her."

"All I know is that in the past two days, the only thing she's said about you and Serah is how much she loves you both as well as how lucky she is to have found you. She often questioned why either of you would care for her. Yet, all I'm seeing is someone willing to go to war for people who he doesn't really believe in the future of. All because of my sister asking you to do so."

"Regina's is the face that will compel armies to march."

"Broken nose and all."

"It adds character."

"I envy you," Ketra said, looking over at the guardians as we passed underneath them. "Truly."

"Do you?"

"I had a fiancé before the massacre. I thought he loved me, but when Whitehall was destroyed, I found out he was the first to denounce me."

"Perhaps he feared for his life."

"Then he was a coward. Death or dishonor is a poor choice, but it's still a choice."

She had a point there. It didn't mean that mercy was not an option, though. "Regina doesn't believe in honor."

"No, she simply lives it. What do you think about honor?"

"I think honor is less important than good but it is easy to be the latter without having the courage of your convictions."

"Are you a man of honor?"

"I am a man of conviction. Honor is something determined by society. It can be taken away by others. Good cannot."

"And who determines good?"

"I do. So do you. It is the responsibility of the beings above the Gods Above, Between, and Below give us all. That each of us chooses what is good and bad from our own minds."

"*That* is going in the book," Regina said, behind me.

Regina was wearing a fur-trim white coat and a pair of thick linen pants with *Starlight* sheathed beside her, its scabbard a great deal less ornate than usual. Regina was dressing down for the occasion but little could do to disguise her impressive beauty. Or maybe, as Ketra seemed to think, I was letting my feelings for her influence my decision.

"When did you come in?" I asked.

"Enough to hear my broken nose adds character."

"Ah."

"Also that I could compel armies to march." Regina took her place by my side. "Have you seen Serah?"

"No," I said. "I've just been enjoying the company of your cousin."

"You had best keep the King Blow on a short leash," Ketra said. "The negotiations with Winterholme's nobility will be delicate."

Regina gazed down, her voice low. "Learn manners when speaking to those you ask favors."

Ketra looked stricken.

We passed through a pair of mountainous cliffs, each covered in thousands upon thousands of carved names. They were the Cliffs of Heroes, containing the names of all those who had died fighting for Kerifas against the King Below's forces. They were sacred and yet, after each war, the King Below had obliterated them only for new names to be carved in their place. Candles and offerings were at the base of the monument, many altars erected to the Lawgiver and shrines.

And yet, I couldn't help but feel a sense of emptiness and loss radiating from them.

As if the honor accorded to such a symbol no longer meant as much as it should.

The *Ghostly Runner* continued to pull past many other ships, past a giant chain attached to huge arcane mechanisms that could block off the harbor from being fled. There were many towers of watchmen rising from the harbor and cannon positions. I'd thought the empire's paranoia about the city was excessive from a distance.

Now I knew they intended to kill this city.

They were just waiting for the command.

CHAPTER SEVENTEEN

The smell of the harbor assaulted the senses and I took a moment to enjoy the scent of being amongst human civilization once more. There was the smell of rotting fish, offal thrown from buildings not connected to the town's sewer system, sweat, and a hundred other unpleasant smells which, nevertheless, felt more comforting to me than the sterile pleasantness of the Far North.

A quick look at them told me the populace was angry, resentful, and heavily armed. Surveying the docks, I saw three fights about to break out, two in progress, and a man bleeding from a stab wound in an alleyway. The humans were divided into G'Tay, Winterholme, Imperials, Gael, and Indaras. There were even a few merchant-caste Natariss wearing their queer robes, exotic body art, and shaved heads. None of them were intermixing, which was odd in a port city as established as Kerifas.

The situation got worse when Captain Vass went ashore and almost drew his sword due to the harbormaster wanting him to dock elsewhere. This was due to the best docks being humans-only territory. I was going to intervene, but the issue was swiftly resolved with an exchange of silver. Racism and xenophobia were truisms throughout the Four Continents, but there were few forces stronger than greed.

"Not a terribly cosmopolitan city, is it?" Regina said, looking it over.

"The refugee situation hasn't been helping it," Ketra said, staring outward. "Many people are being relocated and moved to different parts of the continent. It's meant to break down the national barriers and restructure things so they identify as Imperials rather than one of the twelve Southern Kingdoms."

"It was forty-eight in my day," I said, staring. "Relocation will not lead to peace, though, or a breaking down of barriers. All it means is that the people horrifically wronged by the government who believe they have lost their rightful lands are now concentrated together."

"You're right. The Golden Arrow kills a hundred Imperials a week in Fireforge," Captain Vass said, returning to the deck. "'Drive the humans from the Motherland!' 'Fireforge is for Fir Bolg!' So many stupid slogans. Never mind the Imperials have been there for two centuries and aren't leaving anytime soon."

"There are far more soldiers here than peacekeeping requires," Regina said, watching a patrol of gold-and-red-armored soldiers march by. "They're also wrongly positioned for defending the city from invasion."

"Perhaps they are preparing to invade the North," Captain Vass suggested. "If so, the empire will impress tens of thousands of workers, soldiers, and sailors like they have done in so many other lands. They may fear riots."

I have a more disturbing theory, Serah's voice said in my mind. Above our heads a raven circled before setting down beside us. It transformed into a living shadow that morphed into the beautiful form of my wife.

"Where have you been?" I asked. "Also, what's your theory?"

"I've been scouting the city for the past hour. I decided to go on ahead to make sure everything was safe." Serah kept her gaze from Regina and instead looked directly at me. "Things are not well in the city. I believe the Imperials may be planning to trigger an uprising in the city."

I stared. "What?"

Captain Vass gazed appreciatively at Serah's form before shaking his head. "I am no stranger to Imperial tyranny, but I have never thought the Nine to be insane. Killing their own people for no reason is a bit beyond them. They are fanatics and religious lunatics, a kind I know well, but even they tend to draw the line at senseless slaughter. At least of those they haven't judged infidels."

"They are smuggling weapons into the city," Serah said, frowning. "Quite a lot of them, and I've read the minds of many people. They have been spreading propaganda that the Black Sun and his queens will come and liberate this city."

I looked at Ketra. "Your doing?"

"Yes," Ketra said. "But they—"

"The Imperials know," Serah said, frowning. "I have read it in the minds of the guardsmen. They don't know much but they have been told to let it fester. I believe they are going to massacre this city, blame it on us, and use it as *casus belli*."

"Excuse me?" Vass said.

"An Old Human word from the Terralan's surviving tomes," I said. "It means a reason for provoking or causing a war."

"Why would the Imperials *need* a reason for war against us?" Regina asked, blinking. "We're the...well, the villains."

Ketra and Serah sniggered a bit at her terminology. I understood her thinking, though. We were, after all, the heads of the Shadowkind races. The Lightborn species had been trying to wipe them out and vice versa since the death of the Gods Between.

"To the majority of the world, the King Below is dead and is staying that way," Serah said. "The threat of the North is coinage with no value. There are few ways of uniting a divided set of nations than through a common threat, though. If Jacob will not invade the South then perhaps they believe they need to give him a push."

Captain Vass laughed. It was a deep, throaty belly laugh. "You're not evil enough for your enemies! Gorgeous."

"I'm glad you're amused." I looked between them. "Well, aren't they in for a surprise when I do invade. *Playing right into their hands*."

Serah looked guilty. "It seems I may not be quite as good at the games of kings as I thought I was."

"I'm a game piece in this?" Ketra asked, stunned. "They've been using our rebellion?" She looked like someone had punched her.

"In politics, you are always either player or piece," Regina echoed my thoughts. "Do we have much time until the city explodes into violence?"

"No," Serah said. "The question is now whether this meeting should still take place given we know it's just a set up for the Nine to eliminate their enemies."

"Never overestimate your enemies any more than you underestimate them," I said, rubbing my chin. "I sincerely doubt they expected the actual King Below to get involved in their plot. The assassination attempt on Ketra was also real. We're also assuming a great deal. I wouldn't be surprised if the plans of the Nine are less...evil."

"Now who's overestimating them?" Serah said, sighing. "We need to decide what our next move is."

"It seems obvious to me," Regina said. "Save the city from destruction."

Serah laughed then realized Regina was serious. "Oh Gods Below..."

"I agree with Regina. We must not allow ourselves to become the monsters they wish to turn us into."

One of the things I'd discovered about the King Below and King Above's relationship was that the former had ever been loyal to the latter. He'd served as a catspaw and lightning rod to force the various nations to unite against his evils.

People prayed harder if there was a physical embodiment of evil to contrast the Lawgiver against. I didn't know how this event related to Morrigan the Lesser's prophecy but I couldn't help but think they were better prepared for this war than I was.

Of course they are, the Trickster said. *The Lawgiver and his minions truly believe a utopia can be achieved and are willing to burn the world to ashes to do so. The sooner you accept your enemies are more ruthless than you, the better.*

And if I did, what would your solution be?

Become more ruthless, the Trickster replied. *Because you can survive being a monster. The dead tell no tales.*

I am unliving proof to the contrary.

"You still want to meet with the Jarls?" Ketra asked, her expression uneven. "Gewain is trustworthy; you must believe me."

"I do," I said, putting a comforting hand on her shoulder. "Regina could never love someone who was not good at heart."

Serah made a noncommittal noise behind me.

I shot her a glare.

"We will meet with the Jarls as well as those who want the city to spill out into violence," I said, a plan forming in my head.

"Then what?" Regina said.

"You do what you do best and take control over them," I said, pointing to the dragons flying above. "We take care of those and then kill every Imperial soldier in the city who resists. We make the streets run red with blood and we give them the war they *think* they wanted…before winning it with mercy."

This was where my plan would become a hard sell.

"You lost me at the last bit," Vass said.

Serah and Regina, though, were paying attention.

"You don't treat captured soldiers with respect because you are good but so the other side is inclined to do the same," I said, explaining basic military logic. "If we show the world we are not demons then we can break the enemy's will to fight and finally cause the Nine to fall to their doom."

"I object to any battle strategy that begins with the premise of winning through peace and love," Serah said, pausing. "But I know the alternative."

"I'm all for this plan," Regina said, patting the pommel of her sword. "I'm also not going to abandon Gewain in his hour of need. There's nothing in this city I fear."

"I'm actually terrified of dragons when they're trying to kill me," Serah said, pausing. "But I'll do anything to earn your forgiveness."

"Don't fuck up again," Regina said, her gaze hard then softening. "I've lost too many to lose you, too."

"Done," Serah replied, before walking over and kissing her.

Regina kissed back, the two holding on to one another in a passionate embrace.

Ketra grimaced while Vass grinned.

"So where are we meet to with Gewain and the nobles he's arranged for us to see?" I asked, feeling uneasy about this whole thing. If they hadn't intended for Ketra to fetch us, it meant we were a new player in their game. Hellsword and Redhand would probably accelerate their plans here, whatever they were.

Then again, dead was dead, soon or long term.

"Rose has instructions to watch the harbor for our arrival," Ketra said, sighing. "I wasn't expected to leave on a stolen dragon after all. If not we're going to meet him and the Golden Arrow leader, Kana, at the Wild Goat Inn."

"Kana Shattershield?" Vass interrupted.

"Yes," Ketra said, blinking. "Do you know her?"

Vass looked between me, Serah, and Regina. The latter two of which had finally stopped kissing.

"She is dangerous like a viper," Vass said, his voice low. "Beautiful like the fallen snow but deadly like a blizzard. Do not let honeyed words sway you to actions you...will regret."

"I have enough regret for a thousand lifetimes," I said, now understanding how he knew so much about the Golden Arrow.

"Do not forget you are a god of hope now," Regina said, walking over. "Come on, let us go speak with my cousin."

"That may be difficult," a voice spoke from the side of the docks and I worried we'd been perhaps a bit too indiscreet with our conversations.

At the side of the *Ghostly Runner* was a curious-looking pair. The first was a handsome man with the features of a High Human of old like Serah. He had a shaved head but a well-trimmed goatee, sparkling black eyes, rich-chocolate skin, and a square heroic jawline. The man was dressed in a luxurious fashion with dragonskin shoes, blue silk pants, a purple tunic of shimmer-thread covered in an illusion pattern of dragons fighting, and a wide-brimmed purple hat with a gryphon feather. Noticeably, he was unarmed, which seemed unwise in this sort of environment, especially along with his prominent display of wealth.

The second figure was a statuesque Fir Bolg woman with light-blue skin, silver-white hair, angular eyes like Midori's, and standing just over six feet in height. Because she was a woman, she lacked the horns of a Fir Bolg male, but instead had doe-like ears that were cute rather than off-putting. The woman was the very opposite of a religious fundamentalist in appearance, given her breasts were barely bound in a white wrap that left a plunging neckline down past her bellybutton before joining with a too-short leather skirt. In her right hand was a charm- and feather-covered staff with a tiny rabbit's skull on the top, marking her as a priestess of the Gods Between.

I snorted at their appearance. "Revolutions must be waged differently in this time than when I was alive. In my day, their participants went out of their way to *not* draw attention."

"They have a cloaking spell," Serah said. "But it doesn't excuse the harlot attire for the Fir Bolg."

"I like it," Regina said.

"Rose, Kana!" Ketra said, rushing up to them and giving them both a hug. For all her disapproval of the former's relationship to her brother, she still seemed to think of them with great affection. "I have much to say, both good and bad, and *what do you mean that would be difficult?*"

Captain Vass's crew lowered a gangplank for Rose and Kana to come up. Captain Vass climbed down a ladder into the cargo hold, avoiding being seen by the latter.

"I fear Lord Gewain has been taken in for questioning by the Mysterium," Rose said, frowning.

"What?" Regina said, her eyes widening. Her voice became soft and she covered her mouth. "No."

Rose lifted his hands. "It's all right. Believe me, I'm more worried than anyone, but it's all right."

"What do you mean it's all right?" Ketra said, staring.

"They do this all the time," Rose said, shaking his head. "They like putting the scare into the local but they don't suspect he's anything more than a disabled knight from the Riverlands with a lot of friends. They don't know about his role in the resistance."

Ketra looked positively panicked. Grabbing his hands, she stared up into his eyes. "The Imperials know about our plans, Rose."

Rose closed his eyes, an unreadable look crossing his face. That was when temple bells began ringing throughout the city.

"What's that?" Regina asked.

"The bells for public executions," Rose said, taking a deep breath. "They occur every few days now."

"Gewain," Regina said, starting to run down the gangplank and onto the pier.

I followed.

Chapter Eighteen

I could barely keep up with Regina as she ran down the crowded streets of Kerifas. The city was divided into numerous cordoned-off districts that were guarded heavily at every entrance by Imperial troops. Thankfully, due to the public executions, they were letting everyone through regardless of whether they had little scraps of paper I saw several citizens trying to flash. It allowed me a kind of perverse tour of the city as I jogged, giving me a sense of how Kerifas had changed over the centuries as well as how the city was being managed.

The lower districts were slums, to put it kindly, with poverty, starvation, and filth everywhere. Curiously, I hadn't seen any real sign of nonhumans amongst the destitute and couldn't help but wonder why the citizenry was uniformly human in those areas. Fir Bolg were traditionally separated from the other races, even in my time, but there should have been members of at least a dozen other species amongst them.

The more affluent ones were curious as there were many pyres spread about them. Paintings, books, compacts, makeup cases, and other vanities were gathered around the place in large piles that had been burning for a long time. Preachers of the Lawgiver in white-and-gold robes spoke to uninterested crowds about the glories of the Nine as well as the imminent end of the world. The number of nonhumans actually increased, at least, in terms of the elfblooded and a few low sidhe.

Most of the citizenry looked surprisingly fearful despite the presence of the Imperial soldiery around them, moving from building to building quickly and in carriages that had armed men on them. This time, people paid attention to Regina and me as we ran, though the few guards who called after us didn't care enough to give chase. I got the impression they were not the crème of this city's crop despite guarding the richer citizens. For all Serah's talk about the law being fair and equally applied under the Nine Usurpers, it was not the case in Kerifas, since there seemed a stark segregation of the locals.

It wasn't until we reached the area around the Palace District, the area where administration in Imperial cities was traditionally handled, that I finally caught up with Regina. She slowed down to take a breath, surveying the sight before her. I did the same, taking in the crowd. This group was being meticulously checked and being ushered through the gates one by one. Strange mechanical chariots with legs twelve feet tall were moving through the crowd, a single soldier operating them as crackling lightning moved around a wand at its base. The walls above the district were covered in soldiers, all humans of Imperial descent, each of them heavily armed with gunpowder rifles as well as blood-rune armor.

"The executions are going to be in there," Regina said, her voice low.

"Yes," I said, looking around. "Probably."

"Possibly Gewain."

"We don't know that," I said, trying to calm her.

But it was possible. Likely, even, if he'd been arrested as soon as Hellsword returned from his failed attempt to get at Ketra.

"Then what do we do?" Regina said, feeling her face. She wasn't the type of woman to cry, but I could tell she was on the verge of tears. Regina loved Gewain, close blood ties and incompatible orientation aside. I was jealous. Then again, if I found out one of my sisters was still alive after all this time, would I act any different? Did it matter either way? No, it did not. If Gewain was being held prisoner by the Imperials here then I would make an effort to save him.

"We will rescue him if we have to," I said, whispering. "I will not let your loved ones perish."

"Even though I love him...in that way?"

"Even so."

"He does not return that love, but even if he didn't, I would choose no other, Jacob. Fate has blessed me with the two loves of my life loving each other. That is more than even great romantics receive and I am not so greedy as to want another."

"Can we focus on something else?"

"Sorry."

Under other circumstances Regina would have cracked a joke about keeping a harem or bringing other partners to our bed just for fun, but now she was just silent. Regina was a prisoner of her feelings just like I was, or had been, for Jassamine.

Placing my hands on her shoulders, I whispered a concealment spell that would make us unnoticed by both the crowds and the guards around us. I wasn't as good a mage as Serah, the higher mysteries of the Craft unknown to me, but I had a lot of raw power. I doubted even Hellsword himself could see through the protection I wove around us. Better still, the spell caused people to ignore us rather than not see us. In many ways, it was superior to invisibility by far.

Regina placed her right hand on mine. "How long will this last?"

"An hour or two," I said, breathing out. "We won't be seen unless we attack or someone is actively searching for us. We can also let individuals see us if we want. That should give us an advantage should we need to perform a sneak attack."

"Thank you," Regina said.

Moments later, the rest of our group, sans Captain Vass and his crew, came rushing up behind us. The newcomer, Rose, looked positively exhausted, and I suspected he wasn't used to making speedy treks across the breadth of cities. The Fir Bolg, Kana, by contrast, looked completely fine, despite wearing a pair of uncomfortable-looking sandals. Serah, smartly, had summoned a black stallion that simply trotted behind them. I let them perceive us, not intending to deceive our allies.

"You could have waited," Rose said, panting heavily.

"No, I couldn't have," Regina replied.

"You should be careful," Kana said. "There are many spies in the city. It is said every rat in the city is one that Hellsword can see out of."

"Then he must see a lot of shit," I replied. "We're debating what can be done about Gewain."

"They won't harm him," Rose said, attempting again to reassure us. "They won't risk making a martyr of him."

"You have an unusual amount of faith in the empire's monsters," Kana said. "Gewain is my friend as well as oath-brother. I will fight with you if you choose to rescue him. I am a warrior of the seventh rank as well as a shamaness of the Lesser Gods Between. The spirits of those who live in every nook, cranny, tree, and brook. You have my support."

"Assaulting the gallows will just trigger a massive riot and crackdown," Rose said, straightening himself. "Gewain wouldn't want that, until the time is right at least. He's a hero."

"I don't care," Ketra said. "He's my brother."

"They won't kill him," Rose said, sounding as if he was trying to convince himself of the fact. "I'm sure of it."

"The city is ready to revolt and just needs the right spark," Kana said. "With your help, King and Queens Below, we shall liberate this city. All my people in the city have been waiting for your arrival."

"I'm sure," I said. I wasn't sure about the woman's motivations. She seemed too…earnest. Then again, I might have been letting my feelings regarding the Golden Arrow affect my judgement. Organizations could change a lot in two centuries—just look at the Shadowguard.

"How are they doing this?" Regina asked, staring around at the misery surrounding us. "Why do we even need to invade? You'd think they'd have risen up against the empire already."

"Appearances can be deceiving," Rose said, looking at a pair of Imperial soldiers kicking a brown-skinned boggan between them. "The Usurpers are very precise in their targeting. They have rewarded their followers lavishly in riches confiscated from those they have destroyed. Toadies have been given titles, endowments, and land. This is in addition to the fact many old rivalries have been flaring up in recent years between humans and nonhumans. Rivalries they play on to win the allegiance of those who fear civil war."

"They're playing everyone against one another," I said, frowning. "They don't have to have the love of the people as long as they're hated less than the alternatives."

"It's like the Reformation's worst excesses but only a hundred times worse," Kana said.

"That is because the same woman responsible for it is responsible for this," I muttered.

Jassamine. How deep did her madness run? Was she truly an arch-messenger reborn? Is that what drove her?

"The persecution of nonhumans is limited to Winterholme," Serah said, sounding almost offended at the suggestion it was Imperial policy.

"For now," Rose said. "The persecution of nonhumans and seizing of their property has allowed them to fund their elaborate building projects. Projects that have bankrupted the Imperial treasury but they keep managing to find more funds to work on. I would not be surprised if they broadened their persecutions to continue their public works."

Interesting.

"People think only the empress and her inner circle can lead them through this crisis," Rose said, frowning. "Are you truly the King Below?"

"You doubted I would return with him?" Ketra said. "Was that not my mission?"

"I doubted he existed." Rose frowned at her. "Only Gewain believed."

"He was right," I said. "I am he, or as close to such as exists. Regina, Serah, and I are the new Gods Below and rulers of the Iron Order."

Rose frowned. "I see."

"Powerful allies," Kana said, smiling. "I, too, believed. You should give my regards to Captain Vass."

"If he wants them," Serah said, glaring at her. I did not know what set her off against Kana but her demeanor was hostile and tense to the Fir Bolg woman.

"What kind of situation can we expect on the other side of the wall?" Regina asked, diverting us from topics of legitimacy.

"It depends if Hellsword or Redhand is conducting the executions," Rose said, shaking his head as if to clear it. "If it's Hellsword, then it will be quick. Heads will roll with a reading of their crimes. He will sometimes offer the condemned a chance to repent of their actions and if they do, they'll show up *changed* in a few days to a week."

"Changed?" I asked.

"Loyal to the empire, deliriously happy, and 'off' in some ways. Most believe the empire has taken to using Gael mind-twisting on their opponents."

I grimaced. "That kind of magic is forbidden."

"So is mass murder and slavery," Regina said, clenching her fists. "They both still happen on a regular basis."

"If it's Redhand?" Regina asked.

"Pain, torture, mutilation," Rose said, looking positively ill. He did not strike me as the kind of man normally drawn this deep into revolutions. He had to love Gewain very much to become involved in such a violent struggle. "If Hellsword desires to keep the peace in the city then Redhand loves inciting mayhem at every opportunity. It gives him more opportunities to indulge himself."

"I see," Regina said. "I'm not sure which is worse."

"Both are equally vile," Ketra said. "My brother would rather die than become one of the Anessian Empire's puppets. It's possible he was betrayed to the empire. Someone had to have let them know about my flight, too."

"Hellsword is a good spymaster," Serah said. "Don't underestimate him. We should attend this execution either way."

"And do what?" Rose asked.

"Observe," Serah said. "Get a measure of our enemy."

Regina, meanwhile, departed to order the two nearby Imperial soldiers away from the boggan they were abusing. Much to my surprise, she managed to convince them to leave peacefully.

"I hate public executions," Rose muttered. "Disgusting, barbaric practice. Everyone else in this city seems to love them, no matter the victim."

"Who are you, anyway?" I asked. "What is your connection to this Army of Free Peasants."

"I am Rosewood ap Gwynedd," the man said, taking a deep bow. "I am, with no false modesty, the greatest poet, author, playwright, and writer in the world. It is my words that give voice to the struggles of the common man against tyranny. I helped Gewain write *The Rape of Whitehall* and adapted it into the stunningly successful play that even now incites the masses against the empire. I'm also responsible for the comedy *A Tale of Twin—*"

"No modesty at all," I interrupted.

"He's actually famous," Serah said, surprising me as she brought her horse close. "At least, he was when I was still living in Lakeland."

"That was before I became a writer of propaganda and tragedy," Rose said. "The arts have not flourished under Empress Morwen. The definition of obscenity has become freakishly broad. It is part of the reason I have become a rebel."

"Part of the reason?" I asked.

"Love is worth becoming a rebel for," Rose said, speaking for the first time with conviction. "Something, I suspect, you know about." There was something about his tone that caused me to think he was hiding something. Then again, he might simply be put off by meeting a man claiming to be the God of Evil.

"I mentioned my profession," Kana said. "As for my lineage, I am of the Clan Shattershield and won the name Kana in the old ways. My old name, my slave name, does not matter anymore. I have heard much about you, Jacob Riverson, Regina Daelia Whitetremor, and Serah Brightwaters. I hope the tales are all true."

"Don't believe what you hear," I said, sighing. "I find that history is written by people like Rose."

"Oh no," Rose said, shaking his head. "I would do a much better job than those fools at Hildenstadt University."

"A pity," Kana said, staring at me intently. "Because we need heroes, and that is what the stories I've heard say you are."

"Then they are doubly wrong," I said, pausing. "There are no heroes here, except maybe Regina."

Regina glared at me. I wasn't sure for which part of my statement.

Kana's doe-eyes didn't waver in their intensity. "Then I hope you are simply a powerful ally who can help us destroy our enemies."

"That, I can promise you, is true."

Ketra looked up at the crowd. "How are we going to get past them?"

"I keep several spare copies of papers on me at all times," Rose said, pulling out a stack of them from his overlarge shirt.

"Regina and I will be fine," I said. "I can also cloak anyone else."

"You should take some anyway," Rose said. "There's

magic-suppression wards all around the city, and while I doubt they'd affect you much, you never can tell."

I agreed with our new associate and took a pair. "Let's go see if Gewain needs rescuing."

CHAPTER NINETEEN

The Kerifas Forum was built around the thirty-foot-tall wall of the Palace District's titular Governor's Palace. The district entrance was barred by a heavy iron portcullis as wooden platforms twenty feet high had been constructed all around it, ladders leading up to them. On the top of these platforms were men carrying crossbows, hundreds of them.

They weren't the city guard, though, or even Imperial soldiery. No, these individuals were wearing a special uniform of rune-covered chainmail with a tabard bearing the standard of a flaming sword. The Burning Blades were a group I'd researched in my studies of the Nine Usurpers. They were a legion of mercenaries divided into ten maniples of killers. Six thousand men and women total, a thousand of which were wizards. They were nicknamed the Empress's Rapine.

The stories I'd seen had, at first, seemed like libel and lurid tavern tales but the more I investigated, the more I'd become sickened. I was no stranger to war crimes. Bloodlust, fighting for one's life, and hatred for one's enemies could turn even the noblest peasant into a monster. In my darkest hours, I too, had done things I could never take back. But the Burning Blades made business of other men's shame. They specialized in pacifying rebellions and doing so through applied terror.

The Burning Blades' presence here made sense, though, as the crowd gathered at the foot of the platforms was not subdued. Contrary to the expectation of Rose that the crowds were here to watch an execution as entertainment, they seemed on the verge of rioting. They were two thousand citizens shouting, yelling, and shoved up against one another. I had seen the makings of uprisings before, usually during a siege or in occupied territory, but rarely in a place that was so heavily garrisoned.

The make-up of the crowd was surprising, too, with not just the very poor present but many members of the merchant class and more than a few of the city guard in uniform. The last look terrified, as if they suspected this was going to turn ugly soon. I didn't blame them. If the crowd hadn't turned violent, it was close to doing so, even with the presence of the Burning Blades. Several in the crowd were already throwing combinations of shit and bottles against the foot of the platforms.

"This is not going to end well," Rose said. "We shouldn't be here."

"Now you object?" Kana asked.

"I reserve the right to change my mind," Rose said. "Besides, if Gewain is up there—"

"We'll rescue him," Regina said.

Rose fell silent.

A swift look at the towers, windows, rooftops, and balconies surrounding the area gave me glimpses of the forces the Burning Blades had in position. They were carefully hidden, albeit only as much as one could do with hundreds of additional troops. As a show of force, they should have been visible, but their camouflage indicated the master of this encounter wanted to keep them in reserve as to surprise his enemies. It meant their commander either expected an attack or intended to assault the crowd himself.

I got a sense of what was really going on when two figures walked up the side of the platforms in front of the crowd. The first of them was a garishly dressed Imperial wearing royal purple, a golden gryphon sigil sewn onto the back of his cloak, and a small golden crown on his head. He was a handsome youth with a short, neatly trimmed goatee, curly golden hair, and boyish features. He also looked sick to his stomach. I took this to be Empress Morwen's son, Prince Alfreid, and a potential target. It was also possible he was one of the prince's doubles—more than likely, in fact, given the mood of things.

The second figure was far different, terrifying even. He was over six and a half feet tall with a body of muscle and hideously damaged skin hanging over it. From a distance, it was easy to assume he'd been burned as Serah had said, but my eyesight picked up that the source of his deformities was not fire but something much more common: blade wounds. I could only see his arms and face, but they looked like a patchwork of ten thousand healed-over wounds, which shouldn't have been possible for a man to survive. It was as if he'd been cut deeply on every part of his body and the healed-over tissue had melded into itself, making him one gigantic pile of scars. Dirty, unkempt stringy black hair fell from half his head and the other side was covered in burns from what appeared to be flaming oil. The front end of his nose was missing, apparently cut off with a blade. His crystal-blue eyes were perfect, though.

In addition to the man's gray cloak, which bore no ornamentation, he was dressed in adamant armor. Adamant was a substance found only in the World Above and impossible to work save by messengers or Great Wizards. It was effectively invulnerable to magic and even the strongest weapons were hard pressed to penetrate it. At his waist hung a two-bladed handax that was too small to be a practical weapon, yet was covered in the most advanced mystical runes I'd ever seen. There was also an aura of power, violence, and fury that radiated off of him I hadn't felt since my first encounter with the King Below during the final battle of the Fourth War.

Thermic Redhand.

Prince Alfreid spoke first, his voice barely audible over the din despite the fact he had voice-enhancement cantrips worked on him. "People of Kerifas, it is I, your prince! Troubled have these days been in recent months, but I come to you speaking words of peace—"

The crowd wasn't listening to them, as deafening boos and hisses filled the air. One man climbed onto the side of the platform, waving a bloody rag, which I took to be a shirt. A Burning Blade soldier raised his crossbow and fired a bolt through the protestor's chest. The crowd immediately balked away from the body as the prince looked shocked. The Burning Blade soldier's crossbow reloaded without him moving and he fired three more times into the spot the man had come from, killing a peasant instantly each time.

It would have sparked a riot then and there with many about to run, when a group of Burning Blade mages on the rooftops above us created towering six-foot walls of fire over all the exit points, causing screams and confusion. Several in the crowd were trampled as the prince tried to regain control, only for Thermic to push him back. I had to place my hand on Regina's shoulder to prevent her from running forward to put an end to the slaughter. We were exposed and couldn't risk starting a fight here—too many people were counting on us. Of course, if Gewain was to be executed, nothing I said or did would stop her.

I felt Redhand's gaze wash over the crowd and drained away my group's power so much that it appeared no greater than any other in the teaming mass. I had made a career of fighting beings more powerful than myself, god or not, but the magical weapons around us were all blessed. I could feel the Lawgiver's touch infusing every single bolt as well as their swords and armor. I had no idea if I could be killed or not but I had the sneaking suspicion I could be. I didn't want to think what would happen to my soul then.

Destroyed, most likely, the Trickster said. *Perhaps simply joined with mine permanently.*

It's the same to me.

That was when Redhand spoke. His voice was a diseased, raspy thing that still echoed throughout the area. "You, diseased wretches and wastes of the empire, make me sick. The Lawgiver has blessed you all with a perfect pristine world and life but you all waste it in pettiness. If any of you were worth a damn, you'd have one hand holding a bloody sword and the other raised in his praises."

"Lord Redhand, perhaps I—" Prince Alfreid started to say.

"Silence," Redhand said, raising his right fist as the limb caught fire and burned before our eyes. I see the top flesh burn and the brief twitch of agony across his face, though it was soon replaced with a kind of ecstasy. "Six years ago, I and the other Nine saved this city along with every city in this world from the horror of the King Below. We struck him down outside Everfrost and, by right of deed, rule this entire world. Winterholme's king sought to defy the empire and we crushed his armies. His line and all relations to that line were ended to the eighth degree. Five years ago, we installed Prince Alfreid so that we might show benevolence by giving you a taste of the empire's compassion. His gentleness has wrought only chaos and violence, though. So now you will know the price of defiance. The price of not knowing your place. Those who bite the hand that feeds them shall know not the muzzle but death."

A hushed whisper fell over the crowd as I wondered, along with everyone else, whether he was going to murder the entirety of the gathering then and there.

When no one responded with the force or defiance he expected, he lifted his flaming hand over his head. *"Bring the prisoners!"*

A group of half a dozen seven-foot-tall Fir Bolg prisoners were led up in chains. Each was a mountain of muscle, bare chested, and dressed only in loincloths, including two women. They'd been badly treated with some of the men having had their stag-like horns sawed off, others missing eyes, and a few mutilated in other places. The signs of scourging, branding irons, and other traditional tools of torture were all about them, and I grimaced. I was also grateful there were no one-armed elfblooded nobles amongst them.

"I know those men," Ketra whispered. "Oh, Caius, Joshua, Isaac, Zaal…"

"I'm sorry," I replied.

"Do not be sorry," Kana replied, comforting Ketra with a hand on her shoulder. "Be angry. Memorize their faces so that we may paint the walls of this hell of mortar, mud, wood, and straw red with blood and gore."

I knew the price of such thinking but kept silent.

"Let the torments begin!" Redhand shouted with the glee of a child on Victory Day.

I had never seen the efficacy of torture. I was no stranger to evil deeds in the name of a just purpose. I had murdered, stolen, blackmailed, and worse in the cause of bringing an end to my enemies. Torture's purpose eluded me, though. It did not serve as a deterrent because the threat of death and imprisonment was every bit as ineffective as pouring oil on flame. But, for Redhand, at least, I expected the point of the act was the act itself.

"Oh gods," Ketra whispered, looking up at the six in horror.

"Be silent," Regina whispered, her own hand moving downward to her weapon before removing it.

It was probably the hardest thing she'd done in my service.

"Do you think I do not know where the disease rests in this city? The source of the rot? It is you filthy Stagmen and your heathen religion, practiced in secret with obscene rituals. They drink the blood of children and plot to take over this city! They use night- and blood magic! They are the horror in the heart of this land!"

I was appalled, for multiple reasons, not the least being someone was sharing the blood libel slander propagated by madmen and fools in my time as if it was serious fact. The accusation of tremendous crimes that people believed because they wanted to think the worst of the race. Burning of Fir Bolg quarters and massacres had been driven by such accusations.

Recently, too, as a story of Regina witnessing a pogrom resonated in my head. The Fir Bolg and boggans in the crowd shouted at last, screams of lies and outrage, only for much of the mood in its ranks to shift. Much to my disgust, the crowd's mood was splitting, as there were many now looking suspiciously at the Fir Bolg amongst them.

"You ask who amongst you is responsible for the curfews, taxes, punishments, and the new laws? I say unto you that you know who is responsible! You have let savages pollute, destroy, and weaken this land! There is a weed in this city and it has been treated as a flower when all it does is choke the life from our fair metropolis." Redhand's voice rose until it became a booming crack of thunder across a hundred city blocks. "You ask when the occupation will end? It will end when you have shown the evil amongst you is cleansed!"

"Hells," Regina said. "What is he hoping to accomplish?"

"It is not to kill the city," Serah said. "Just the part of the city they want to massacre."

"Gods Between," Kana whispered. "He's trying to incite a purge."

Redhand turned his flaming hand toward the prisoners and from it shot forth a torrent of burning mystical fire. The Fir Bolg's skin melted across their bones as they were cooked inside out, somehow kept alive long enough to experience the entirety of their deaths despite the fact they should have died mercifully within seconds.

Their screams lasted for a minute.

Prince Alfreid stared in as much horror as the rest, shaking in fear.

Redhead turned to face the crowd. "I have killed these men, their families, and their relations. They were all traitors who gave succor and aid to those who murder the loyal guards who protect you. Those who enrich this city with their coin. Those who have shown themselves to love this city by attempting to end the violence by cooperating. I will not let their deaths go unavenged. Every day the violence continues, I will inflict ten times the blood lost in revenge. Those who cooperate will be rewarded with gold—not silver, but gold. They will be protected against the guards, Firefists, and the revenge of the Golden Arrow. Those who are found aiding them or even turning a blind eye will die." He paused for dramatic effect. "Go."

Ketra held her hand over her face as Rose placed his hands on her shoulders, giving her as much comfort as he could. The crowd's attitude was, much to my shock, pacified as the people were too confused and terrified to even think about rioting.

Suspicion of the Fir Bolg and other nonhumans in the crowd, suspicions of the humans by the nonhumans, despair, desperation, fear, greed at the possible benefits to them for collaboration, plus everything in between was now the dominant mood. Behind us, the walls of fire collapsed and large numbers of people did their best to file out as quickly as possible.

I exchanged a look with Regina. "Saving this city is going to be more difficult than expected."

Regina stared, then quietly mouthed, "Not really. We just have to kill the monsters responsible for this madness. Tonight."

CHAPTER TWENTY

Thermic Redhand was far from the most eloquent speaker I'd ever heard but he knew his audience. He'd done nothing to calm the tensions in the crowd, but he'd done an excellent job of redirecting them. It didn't start with the two sides turning on one another but the mood had shifted. Humans and nonhumans suspected the other side was thinking of turning on them first, and that kind of paranoia fed on itself.

By the time we were allowed out of the forum, I could hear people whispering about whether it would be a good idea to turn on the "Stagmen" and "Beastmen", as the Fir Bolg were known, to save their own skins. Redhand and the Burning Hand were too formidable to oppose in their minds.

I would have to convince them otherwise.

Storm clouds gathered on the horizon as the crowd dispersed, some moving quicker than others, and the Burning Hand departing to guard Redhand and Prince Alfreid as they departed. A light rain began to pour down as my companions put up their cloaks and began to walk toward where Rose said our meeting with the Jarls was supposed to take place.

Troubled by the scene I'd just witnessed, I gauged the reaction of my companions. Regina was more determined than ever to destroy the Nine here and liberate this city. Serah looked troubled, perhaps because she suspected how difficult uniting the city might be. Kana maintained a blank expression on her face, having been forced to watch companions of hers burned alive as a public spectacle. Ketra, I could tell, was sick to her stomach, but I wasn't sure if it was because of the violence or worry about her brother. Rose? Rose had the most curious of expressions.

Guilt.

"Well, that was disturbing," Rose finally said, covering himself with a purple parasol that looked ridiculous compared to us. He'd picked it up from a pocket-dimension-filled sack attached to his belt, hoisting it over his head to protect himself from the gentle rain above us.

"Fir Bolg are always the first to die when humans and elves need a scapegoat," Kana said, looking suspiciously to her surroundings. "I decided to join the Golden Arrow after I was stabbed, beaten, and left to die on my wedding day. My intended was not so lucky."

Regina looked over. "Why did they do that?"

"Because it was my wedding day," Kana said. "It is a human custom in Fireforge to try and make sure fewer Fir Bolg are born."

Regina opened her mouth as if to say something, then closed it, realizing there was nothing that could be said. It had been that way in my time too. Just not in Fireforge. The antipathy between Imperials and Fir Bolg dated back to the days before Anessia the Conqueror and the First War. There was no rhyme or reason to it, just the unthinking hatred of two groups of people who struck at each other blindly.

"We will someday build a nation where humans and Fir Bolg can live in peace," Ketra said, trying to speak with the same conviction she'd had earlier. It was a hollow but heartening gesture.

Kana looked back at Ketra, a sad expression on her face. "Oh, child, it is good that you think that is what my people want."

"We need to get to the Fire District," Rose said, turning around to face us and walking backward as he talked. "The Jarls are assembled there."

"Yes, it would be a shame for the rich and powerful of this nation to be caught up in any massacre Thermic has planned," Kana said. "I bet they're already complaining about the fleas and lice they're catching from my people."

"Your people are not in any danger!" Rose snapped back. It was a denial of reality given what we'd seen back there. "The Jarls and their allies have the full backing of the resistance gathered there."

"Which is hopelessly outmatched," I said.

Ketra didn't deny it. "We're hoping you can help with that."

"Of course," Regina said, answering before I could.

"Assuming the people want help," I said.

I spotted at least three individuals, planted agents I'd wager, talking about various crimes they'd heard the Fir Bolg committing. I imagined there were dozens more paid to do so spread throughout the area. I could hear their whispers and slander, as well as seeing silver change hands. If there wasn't a riot against the nonhumans in the next few days, I would eat my cloak.

That's assuming he doesn't kill them all himself, the Trickster said. *I know Redhand. He doesn't have much in the way of patience. You tend to lose that when you suffer no consequences for your actions.*

Yes, look at you, I replied.

"It depends which people you're speaking of, Jacob," Serah said. "Whenever war is fought, you must choose a side."

Or no side at all.

Still, I couldn't just abandon the Fir Bolg. I had seen what happened when they were left to the mercy of those who sought to blame them for the misdeeds of others.

So had Regina.

"My people know what to do when this sort of thing happens," Kana said, her voice darkening as she narrowed her eyes at Rose. "They will seize the gates to keep out the outsiders for as long as they can. They will kill the children and the elderly with poison, both to prevent their slaughter and to prevent the former from being taken as slaves. The Grand Temple's laws against such things have never been well enforced when my people are what is being sold. The elders will arm every man and woman who can fight to make one last stand, or, if they have no stomach for bloodshed, pass the midnight leaf in the sacred bread around the Grand Pyre in the district's center. They will sing until they all fall asleep to wake no more."

Rose paused and looked away. "It's not going to come to that. We will negotiate with the nobles, smuggle them out, and carry on making our alliance with the King Below. We can put the revolt on hold indefinitely—let tensions cool."

"Tensions will not cool while Gewain is suffering whatever tortures the Imperials have cooked up for him," Kana said, her tone vicious. "We cannot delay the revolt either."

"We cannot revolt now!" Rose said. "It would be suicide!"

"Craven!" Kana hissed.

"Kana, please, you're not helping!" Ketra said, grabbing her by the arm before the shamaness pulled free. "What are you doing?"

"I doubt our propagandist's commitment to the cause," Kana said, slamming her staff's bottom against the flagstones. "Since Gewain's capture, you have been undermining us at every opportunity. You have been defending the empire and urging caution when we need bold action! There is also the question of Ketra's mission being betrayed and several other curious issues."

Rose sputtered and raised his hands defensively. "What are you suggesting!?"

I decided to follow up on this but not here. Here, we needed unity. "Enough. There will be no purge of the Fire District."

"Oh, you can guarantee that, can you?" Kana asked, turning to me and raising an eyebrow.

"Yes," I said. "Let us each take a vow now to relay no tactical information about our plans to anyone outside our circle. I will lay a geas upon us to do so."

"Is that necessary?" Rose asked.

"Yes," I said. "Assuming there are no objections."

Everyone reluctantly agreed and I cast a minor spell that bound us all to silence before relaying my plan. "We will eliminate Hellsword and Redhand tonight. I know that is unlikely to contribute to the city's stability, but Serah, I want you to contact our people to get an occupation ready via our ships and conceal them. Before they arrive, we need a collection of knights to be smuggled into the city. We'll use them to kill the dragons in their pens and get our gryphon-riders to finish off the ones that aren't. Timing will be critical, but if we can seize the prince of the city we can force the garrison commander to surrender. If not, well, Serah and I have enough magical power between us to kill everyone in the garrison outright."

I imagined a terrifying blizzard murdering every man and woman inside the fortresses around the city, their bodies frozen in ice without even a chance to resist. It sickened me, since becoming a Wraith Knight, how beautiful I found such sights. It would not be as easy as I described it but the city's lack of defenses against external attack was a glaring weakness in an otherwise over-defended city.

"That's a very rough plan," Regina said.

"But it is *a* plan, one I'm happy to rely on my master-strategist to improve on." I glanced over at Rose, who seemed disturbed by my statement. He then scrunched his brow, as if committing it all to memory.

"All right," Rose said. "It sounds good. I think we can work with that."

"Thank you," Kana said. "My people are desperate and you are the best hope we have for victory."

I wanted to comment the Golden Arrow would have more allies if they stopped murdering innocents, but I had enough sense not to.

"I'll work out the details with Ketra and Kana," Regina said, nodding. I could already see the wheels spinning in her head. If anyone could cut the knot before us, it would be her. "Serah, can you send message to our coastal fortresses from here?"

"Yes," Serah said. "Though getting our troops here that quickly won't be easy."

"I ordered a large multi-branch force to be gathered before we departed," Regina said, smiling. "I figured we'd be invading soon enough. We just need to give the signal."

I smiled back.

"You are very well prepared," Rose said, not entirely happy.

Kana, however, was not convinced. "I'm going to need more than your word, Black Sun. The Golden Arrow has many agents both inside and outside the city in the forests beyond. I speak for them, but if you are to gain their aid and not their resistance, I will require guarantees. Agreements in writing and publicly spoken plus magically sealed compacts."

"My word is my bond," I said, putting my hand over my heart.

"As is mine," Regina said much more defensively.

"I'm afraid that is not good enough. Make your decision now," Kana said. "Do you abandon the people of this city and prove yourself to be liars or do you stand by us? Now is the time to choose what sort of friend you are to the Fir Bolg."

"No," Serah replied, surprising me. "You are in no position to negotiate."

Kana snorted at her. "Am I not? This city will not be so easily taken by whatever force you can cobble together overnight."

I was about to speak but Serah raised her hand to silence me.

I fell silent.

The entire group stopped moving. Serah looked right into Kana's eyes and the much-taller woman took a step back.

Serah's voice was calm, but there was a hint of deep anger bubbling just beneath the surface in her next words. "You have dressed like a *j'tekr* maiden for courting in hopes of drawing either Jacob's attention or Regina's, because of their false reputations. You have played on their sympathy and anger at injustice, hoping to turn them against Rose's allies at the meeting as well as predisposition them to favoring your people, but while you may trust their oaths— you will not get guarantees from me. The Golden Arrow has no choice but to support us."

Kana asked, sneering. "Do you think the Golden Arrow is yours to play with? That we have no pride, no—"

"Spare me your speeches because I am about to make one of my own. For centuries the Grand Temple has preached against the Fir Bolg's gods, stolen your children, converted your communities under pain of death, and tortured said converts because they cannot believe you voluntarily worship the Lawgiver. All because of the so-called Saint Jassamine and her desire to wipe your people off the face of the World Between. The same Jassamine who rules behind the empress. You will lend the Golden Arrow's archers, scouts, and shamans to our cause because you recognize *we don't want to annihilate you.*"

Kana stared at Serah for almost a minute, then laughed. It wasn't a pleasant laugh, but more the kind you gave before being hanged. "That might actually work as something I can bring to the Golden Arrow's elders."

"Excuse me?" I asked.

"Forgive me," Kana said. "But the elders have not been impressed by your brief tenure as Dark Lord of Dark Lords. They expected... more action. Saving this city, while not expected, would go a long way to winning them over."

"What do you mean it's not expected?" Ketra asked.

"They don't expect Kerifas Fir Bolg to survive the purge," I said. "In fact, given the amount of anger Redhand was able to drum up,

I suspect they've been deliberately targeting this area for months now in order to incite one."

"What?" Ketra asked, horrified. "Why?"

"Because that is the way the Golden Arrow works," I said. "Any survivors and those Fir Bolg in nearby communities would be outraged by the act and compelled to lend the Golden Arrow aid. They would also join up in great numbers."

Kana looked away. "The Golden Arrow favors the *R'tosh*, or country Fir Bolg, over the *Y'tang*, or Fir Bolg who live amongst humans. You are right that they consider the Fir Bolg living in the Nonhuman Quarter to be expendable. You, however, offer an opportunity to save them all."

Regina growled. "Assuming we want to deal with such untrustworthy allies."

Serah put her hand on Regina's shoulder. "A blade is a blade and so is a bow. It doesn't matter who wields it."

"Unless it's pointed at your back," Regina snapped back.

Ketra stepped away from Kana in horror.

Kana lowered her head. "Please, help them."

"I will see what I can provide you and your people in the way of protections, justice, or your own land," I said. "But I require honesty in return, not deception."

"The Golden Arrow wishes all humans driven from Fireforge forever," Kana said. "They wish their homeland back and are ready to cleanse it with blood if they have to."

"That may be difficult to provide," I said. "Given I see little justice in mass murder and deportation."

Kana's voice returned to being cold and unfeeling. "Then you will not find us trustworthy allies."

"And the regular masses of the Fir Bolg?" I asked, noticing she'd mentioned only the Golden Arrow.

"They do not fight," Kana said. "They believe in peace."

"And you don't." It was not a question.

Kana clutched her staff tight. "You wouldn't either after what I went through."

"I understand." Regina's next words had a tinge of threat. "But you will get the trust you give."

"Sometimes."

"We need to focus on the Jarls," Rose said, looking as if he were passing a stone. "Their safety could mean all of Winterholme falling if they're caught up in this."

"We're saving everyone," Regina said.

"Of course," Rose said. "I'll take you to them and then go get in touch with my contacts."

Regina nodded.

Rose is a spy, you realize, the Trickster said. *You saw how defensive he got regarding the empire.*

Possibly, I said. *It's also possible he's simply uncertain about the treason he's committing against his homeland.*

Then he's a liability and should be killed.

I forced the Trickster from my mind and gestured forward. "Let us continue this elsewhere."

"We are close anyway," Rose said, gesturing to a walled-off section of the city that was already surrounded by an angry mob.

Getting into the Fire District was going to be harder than expected.

CHAPTER TWENTY-ONE

The Fire Districts in my day were not constructed by the empire but by the Fir Bolg themselves. That ancient race of farmers, warriors, and tinkerers had always treated other races as ritually unclean. Much as they were treated. They raised their stonework walls up around their territories to keep outsiders, or *anass*, out, as much as other species grew to consider them ways of keeping Fir Bolg in. The Fire District within was, due to their heritage as masons and architects, always of the best architecture in whatever nation they were built in.

Kerifas's Fire District was not built by Fir Bolg. They were hastily constructed with cheaply made bricks, boarded-up buildings, and lots of wooden boards with barbed-metal wire. Graffiti with anti-nonhuman slogans were written on its sides, many quite colorful in their expressions of hatred. It was obvious Prince Alfreid or his masters had ordered the Fire District expanded, and recently too. They must have moved it to cover an eighth of the city. I couldn't help but wonder how many people had been turned out of their homes to do such as well as how many had been forced into locations beyond.

The crowd gathered outside the nonhuman district's crude gates was, perhaps, better referred to as a mob. There were hundreds of individuals, all angry and some sporting crude weapons. I saw a pair sporting a pole-mounted banner made from a bedsheet and sporting an anti-Fir Bolg message written in shit. There was chanting as well, though not organized to carry a single message, the general gist seemed to be, 'Go away' and 'Give back our homes.' To think, this was the crowd formed *before* Redhand's speech had been given a chance to spread amongst the citizenry.

I gave credit to the twelve or so human guards in front of the Fire District gates, who didn't back down but kept ordering the crowd to disperse.

"This isn't good," Rose muttered, staring at the gathering.

"As if anything today has been good," Kana grumbled.

"I take it the prince moved all of the city's nonhumans here?" Serah said, looking from her horse at the Fire District.

"Yes," Rose said solemnly. "Needless to say, the Fir Bolg didn't appreciate it. Everyone has been at everyone else's throats since then. That crowd is made of the city's poor who were evicted to make room for them all."

"The perfect sort to form a mob," Serah said, frowning. "At least they are consistent in their methodology. They want this city to boil over. That is why they armed the revolutionaries inside the city and have been stirring them up."

"One does not *arm* revolutionaries if you plan to put them down," I looked at Ketra then Kana. "This strikes me as the work ot two people planning opposite agendas."

"Hellsword and Redhand?" Regina asked.

"They would be the obvious candidates," I replied. "One should never attribute to genius what could better be explained by ignorance."

"Be that as it may," Rose said, sighing, "the Jarls were unhappy to be meeting with you in the Fire District to begin with. They might start to leave if this gets worse."

"Which is strange since there's no way you could have known I would be arriving this day as, even if Ketra left for Everfrost, it would have been a week's-long journey both to and back," I said.

Rose blinked. "Huh. I wonder how that happened."

"We have a traitor," Kana said.

"Or they simply learned through other means," Ketra said. "We are all committed to the struggle."

Kana snorted at the very idea.

"Your faith warms my heart," Rose said, putting his hand over his chest.

"Any idea how we're going to get past them without drawing attention?" Regina asked.

"I'll clear us a way," Serah said, moving her horse forward in front of the group.

Serah lifted her fingers and made a series of intricate arcane gestures. She had the hands of a master musician and they were well practiced. The words that flowed from her mouth, like the gestures, were merely aids to the magic that was generated in her mind, but the result was the same.

Before us, a hideous creature with the head of a lion, dragon, and a gryphon appeared plus the body of six-legged scaled beast that ended in a scorpion tail. The monster, a chimera, let loose a terrifying roar before running through the crowd. The screams and shouts of the crowd as it immediately broke away were accompanied by the complete panic that broke loose amongst the guards as well. Of the dozen or so there, only a single one chose to draw his sword and charge at the beast. Because it was an illusion that affected all the senses, the creature knocked him away with a furious swat of its tail, which left absolutely no one barring our passage. The creature vanished moments later as the panic spread elsewhere.

"*That* was your solution?" I said, appalled.

"So much for keeping a low profile," Regina said, rolling her eyes. "That was ill done, Serah."

Serah shrugged. "It worked, didn't it?"

"It will draw attention," I said, shaking my head. "The wrong kind of attention."

Serah started her horse to the Fire District. "If we're to take this city, Hellsword and Redhand are the only people who matter. Everything else is secondary and can be dealt with in good time. We must see how they react to such an incident and be sure we can lure them out to their doom."

"Unless they choose to burn down the Fire District from above with their dragons," I said, pointing out the hole in her logic.

"I have barriers capable of repelling such," Serah said.

I didn't comment that such barriers always took human sacrifices for the level and power she was describing. It was possible to pre-prepare barriers around cities, but such took months of spellcasting at low levels or potions to enhance the strength of the caster. Serah preferred blood magic, which simply would require her taking down a dozen or so of the guards around the city.

Technically, it was a good plan.

Technically.

Our group followed Serah into Fire District. The portcullis around the makeshift gate was badly assembled and would do little to keep away a determined set of attackers. The sight that greeted us on the inside was tragic. Even in my time, the Fire Districts were always surrounded by the kind of people who didn't have options of living elsewhere or hoped to profit from the services of the Fir Bolg. There were dens of filth and pornography, dreamlily dens, makeshift stills, and gambling halls that bet on the lowest forms of entertainment like animal battles. The rattiest and foulest housing had been emptied and were now packed with a new variety of inhabitants: nonhumans of every type, age, and class.

I wish I could say it was surprising to see respectable four-foot tall boggans in clothes far too nice for this environment, standing next to foul-toothed powries and emaciated dryads selling their bodies, but it wasn't. I'd already known what to expect even before entering this place and had seen similar sights during the Fourth War. Whenever things went bad, the nonhumans were relocated to the Fire Districts and their wealth confiscated. It was just the way of the world.

Indeed, by the looks of things, the new inhabitants had embraced the low entertainments of the out-turned dwellers. I saw an eight-foot-tall Jotun lying in a puddle of his own piss with a smell of whiskey so cheap it might have made good armor cleaner. There were numerous prostitutes, mostly recently converted amateurs, trying vainly to sell their bodies to people who didn't have much money themselves. A gallows was nearby, five bodies hanging from it, and I could tell the guards had not been kind in their attempts to maintain order.

There were few locals paying attention to us, which meant our cloaking spell was still functioning. Few Fir Bolg were amongst the crowds around us, which was understandable since I doubted many of the locals were too happy with them. There was no love lost between boggans and Fir Bolg on most days, with Jotuns considering both a blood enemy race. The fact they'd all been shoved together was another sign the lords of Kerifas were doing their best to provoke a riot. It was a miracle they hadn't succeeded yet.

"We can fix this," Regina said, much to my surprise.

I looked at her. "Fixing millennia of mismanagement and race hatred is not going to be easy."

"We have millennia to fix these things," Regina said, raising her hand. "I wasn't raised with the same daintiness and courtly intrigue other noblewomen were in the empire. I wasn't given concubines to teach me how to use sex from the time I bled or laid seed like my cousins."

"That's mildly insulting," Ketra muttered.

"Mildly?" Serah asked.

Regina continued, "But I know the ways of politics and war. We can conquer our enemies, divide them, marry the ones we need to our allies, seduce the ones who are drawn to power, bribe the ones who are greedy, and kill the rest. It will be hard, lonely, and bitter work but we can do this...together."

I could tell Redhand's speech had affected Regina, just in the reverse of the way it was intended. When she'd been a young woman, not even her age of majority, she'd witnessed the purge of High Hold's Fire Quarter at the hands of House Rogers. While House Rogers had since paid for its perfidies, the experience had inflamed Regina's passions against those who would hunt the Stagmen, Treekissers, giants, and Smallfolk. Regina's instructor had prevented her from trying to interfere then and she'd been trying to make up for it ever sense.

Even if it did nothing to banish the ghosts of the past.

Rose looked at Regina with a somewhat distasteful look on his face. "Changing the world is what the Nine Heroes are supposed to be doing, isn't it? I thought you would be fighting to keep it the same."

"Tyranny and oppression is nothing new," Regina said. "What made you turn against the Nine?"

Rose stared down at the impoverished masses around them. "Something stupid."

"Oh?" I asked.

Rose sighed. "I wrote a play that made fun of the queen in a single scene. They shut it down and ordered me to change it."

"Just change it?"

Rose frowned. "Yes. I was infuriated by that and did the most vicious satire I could. Pamphlets, cartoons, limericks, and more. I didn't think about all the lives being ruined. I just had my pride prickled—Gewain found me through a mutual friend and sent me to start gathering allies as well as figure out ways to undermine the empress."

"Is it working?" I asked.

"Sometimes," Kana said. "Other times, it just gets the people found with his literature killed. I also find it far too soft a critique."

"Even propaganda must be entertaining," Rose said, looking around. "This would just depress people."

"It's a depressing place," Regina said. "How did you convince the Jarls to be come here? Surely, it was conspicuous taking some of the richest and most powerful nobles in Winterholme to the slums."

"I have my ways," Rose said cheerfully. He then frowned. "Not that they're particularly happy about their present circumstances. Another day in this place and I imagine they'd start going home."

"Then your plan was ill conceived," I said, staring at him and wondering about his loyalties. "You had no way of knowing I'd be here."

Rose frowned. "You'll have to bring it up with Gewain. It was his plan. He was going to handle the negotiations."

Something about all of this wasn't adding up. For all my talk about not attributing malice to what simple ignorance could cause, it seemed there was a set of invisible hands at work. But whose hands were they and what was their owner's agenda?

"Now we will," Regina said. "We will force them to obey."

Kana smiled. "That, I would like to see."

We passed through a second set of stone walls and entered the original Fire District. In a contrast from night and day, we were suddenly surrounded by beautiful gray stone buildings in pleasing, if simple, square shapes. The Fir Bolg *hidab* were stone buildings passed down on maternal lines from mother to daughter, meant to stand the test of time like the Fir Bolg themselves.

I saw many of their race wandering around in conservative heavy gray clothing that contrasted strongly to Kana and Captain Vass's wardrobe. The six-foot-tall crackling Great Fire was burning heavily in the center of the district with more than a few Fir Bolg working on converting kitchen utensils and tools into weapons.

Whoever had been armed in this city was not the Fir Bolg it seemed.

Rose gestured to one of the larger stone buildings, which had a beautiful flower decor in the stone work. "The Jarls are there. They're anxious to see you."

"Good," I muttered. "I'll enjoy a chance to do some negotiating until we have to go storm the castle…"

That was when I collapsed to one knee.

Screaming in my head was a presence, a terrible malignant horrifying presence, one that felt like an animal driving its claws into my brain. The very reality around shimmered and twisted as an unnatural unearthly color not found in nature began to appear. I felt sick to my stomach, a sensation I hadn't experienced in two and a half centuries followed by a terrible sense of *wrongness* to the universe. Regina, immediately, drew her sword. Serah started casting the strongest barrier she could. The others looked confused, but they couldn't know the reason why. They weren't gods.

The Great Fire froze over in an instance, the chemical reaction becoming a collection of icy crystals before it slowly began to produce a hideous miasma of darkness forming into the shape of a huge lumbering man-shaped thing. All around, the citizens of the old Fire District panicked and began running in all directions, the sense of unnaturalness now so powerful all could feel it. I recognized the energy as well, coming from one of the most terrible things I had encountered in my centuries of life.

Hellsword had summoned an Ice Demon.

One of the most powerful servants of the King Below.

A horror capable of killing even me.

Crap.

CHAPTER TWENTY-TWO

I was well and truly fucked.

If you are wondering what can make the God of Evil quake in his boots then one had to look no further than my present situation. The Ice Demons once numbered in the thousands before the First Great Shadow War when the sidhe had sacrificed nine out of ten to prevent them from spreading their evil across the universe. It had broken the sidhe race forever, but had ended the Ice Demons' threat.

Until now.

Describing the true form of a greater demon like it was, in simple terms, impossible. They are not of this world, being made from magic and otherworldly matter that exists in multiple spheres simultaneously. The human eye cannot perceive them in their natural form, any more than it can see the various spectra of color available to the sidhe. When you look upon them, your mind fills in the blanks from your darkest nightmares.

For the sake of clarity, though, I shall attempt to describe something like what onlookers might have seen. It is not what I saw since I could perceive things mortals could not (and how I wish that were otherwise), but it is close enough for storytelling. In my mind's eye, I perceived the creature standing twenty feet tall. It was composed of ice and shadow, absorbing light and shadow as if a hole in the world. Two enormous wing-like shadows stretched out from its back, reaching to the sky, even as a pair of witchfire pinpricks glowed from the endless void where its head should be. In the left of the creature's hands was a demonsteel blade twice the size of a man, shaped like a cross between a broadsword and a scimitar. It resembled an oversized version of *Chill's Fury*, though I recognized it to be an inferior copy created by Forgedemons. The runes inscribed to it, however, contained the souls of great warriors adding their strength to the Ice Demon's power. In the Ice Demon's right hand was a whip composed of horrific spiked tentacles, each slithering and writhing with an unholy life of its own. Chaos Whips were forged from the primal stuff of pre-universe, having no place in this reality but to warp and unmake it.

The Ice Demon's demonic form formed a mouth and breathed out a tidal wave of living death down upon us, embodying all the killing power of the Hundred Hells. It washed over us, striking us with enough entropic energy to kill a small army. It continued breathing out this horror for almost a minute. Seconds later, the storm cleared, and the six of us stood there.

Unharmed.

Ketra stared up as if this was some sort of nightmare she might wake from, Kana struggled to find her strength, and Rose looked like he'd somehow wandered into the kind of stories he wrote. Regina and Serah, however, prepared for battle.

"One would think you would be wise enough not to attack the World Below's ruler with his own realm's substance," I said, surprised it had done so.

The Ice Demon let out a low rumbling chuckle. "I had not intended to harm you. Instead, I'd intended to kill your companions so that you might suffer. I am surprised they yet live."

"I gave them a portion of my strength," I said, unimpressed. "Regina and Serah are gods as well."

"Then you are a fool. Only madmen share power." The Ice Demon's tone was mocking and I wondered if it was truly here on Hellsword's behalf. It was possible Ethinu had sent it instead. If so, then I would have to have a long talk with her before figuring out what sort of torture-cage to throw her in.

"Only fools do not seek allies," Regina said, raising her blade. "Depart this land, foul lord of carrion and leave the people here in peace and you may yet survive this. We have exterminated all those who do not bow before the Three Thrones of Everfrost. Join us, renounce evil, and pledge yourself to our cause, then you may yet find millennia of life to come. Fail and I will smite thee, scatter thy soul's essence, and leave you but half a shade across a million worlds."

The Ice Demon let forth a hideous roar that sounded, vaguely, like a laugh.

"I don't think you're persuading it, cousin," Ketra said, the sound of fear in her voice but tempered with strength of will. My estimation of the young woman went up significantly for countless seasoned warriors would have fled in terror at the sight before such a beast.

"I am Drol-Bethir, Lord of Serpents, spawn of Balor and grandspawn of Caorthannach. I was the hammer that broke Tiarnanon and ended Annwn. My name is accursed on a thousand worlds. Your party contains petty gods but I am the lord of ten thousand demons. You do not frighten me."

"I fear no monster," Regina said, still addressing it. "Merely for those around us. Can we not move this battle to less populated territories?"

"It is not you I am here to kill."

That was an interesting revelation. "We do not speak with the puppet but the hand that pulls its strings," I said, my voice low. Guessing at who was its summoner, I said, "Hellsword, know we are coming for you. Serah, erect a barrier, I suspect we'll be getting company soon—we can deal with this pathetic thing easily enough."

Serah pulled back and deprived us of one of our chief advantages, even as Drol-Bethir howled and attacked.

Which is what I'd been counting on.

Drol-Bethir brought around his sword to cut me in half only for me to draw *Chill's Fury* and block it. The actual difference in our strengths was immaterial as he was not attacking me with his physical body but his mind, which was potent enough. Pushing up with my blade against the massive sword held inches away from the top of my head, I lifted my left hand up and aimed it at his face before whispering a spell. The words were in high celestial rather than demonspeak, which caught Drol-Bethir off-guard, if his sudden jerking motion back was any indictaion.

A ball of golden flame burst from my gauntlet and sailed forth into the Ice Demon's face. Drol-Bethir roared back in surprise, stepping back, and I didn't blame him. I'd altered my gloves to be able to summon energy from the World Below and purify it the same way as Regina's sword could, despite both of us being the avowed enemies of it.

"You dare!?" Drol-Bethir screamed, only to let forth another roar as Starlight was stabbed into his back repeatedly. Regina had used this opportunity to fly up behind the Ice Demon with Kana's wind sprites. She slashed, cut, and stabbed like a madwoman, channeling the power of light magic repeatedly into each blow.

There was a suicidal fury, a berserk rage, in her blows that struck ten times harder than a normal woman in her position and twice as fast. It was not like her, even as I charged at the Ice Demon's legs, slashing with *Chill's Fury*. The god-killing sword's runes of Hope and Redemption glowed as I struck the monster again and again. Even so, I was doing far less damage than our battle plan had depended on.

Drol-Bethir lashed back with his Chaos Whip, forcing Regina to block them with her shield. The shield shattered when struck, the Chaos Whip's thorned tentacles wrapping around her armor and biting deeply. If not for the fact her platemail was composed of star metal, she would have been sliced to pieces. Instead, the tendrils wrapped tighter and attempted to squeeze her body into paste.

Regina let out a cry and a brilliant white energy flew out from her, causing the Chaos Whip to explode and her body to fall to the ground. *Starlight* was still buried in the back of the hideous monster, burning away its extra-dimensional substance even as Drol-Bethir cast aside its useless thorned weapon and reached for Regina's blade.

Above our heads, storm clouds passed over as Kana chanted, a bolt of lightning striking down from them into *Starlight* as the weapon enhanced and blessed the electricity. The shamaness's lightning sent ripples throughout the Ice Demon's body as a second bolt struck it, then a third, then finally a fourth. The Gods Between were dead, for a hundred ages at the least, but it seemed their ghosts had favored the terrorist beside us with great power.

Ketra, who had been silent during much of this battle, finished her own spell that produced an incandescent bow of light. Around Regina, the light magic enhanced to a level a dozen times stronger as Ketra pulled forth a shaft of living flame and fired it forth into the side of the Ice Demon. It struck with the force of a dozen master magicians, even as the creature's mighty barrier might as well have been hit by raindrops. Ketra did not hesitate to pour every bit of her mortal's strength and life into her magic, though, and she immediately crafted another bolt then another, despite the fact that a single one would exhaust most mages. She fought for family and had no fear of death. There was no sign of Rose.

I continued striking at Drol-Bethir's thick demonic flesh, cutting away at the body of a being that was probably the size of a small town occupying the space of large building. That was when Drol-Bethir's giant foot kicked me in the chest and sent me skidding thirty feet across the ground. A few brave but foolish Fir Bolg souls took their own blessed weapons and sought to strike at the creature but were killed almost instantly by the intense cold aura that passed over them. One heroic soul, however, managed to live long enough to jam a silver ceremonial sword for the sacrifice of animals into the monstrous beast's foot.

Drol-Bethir seemed to feel that attack keenest of all, yowling in pain before crushing the man and unleashing yet another blast of his hideous icy breath onto a collection of nearby buildings. Their roof collapsed, their inhabitants died, be they adult or child, and terrible witchfire flames emerged from its end. I could hear Hellsword chuckling and knew his presence had necessitated the act.

"Murderer!" Regina screamed at the top of her lungs, charging. She conjured forth a shield made of light, which blocked a bolt of blackish lightning that shot from the creature's eyes then slammed herself into the chest of the Ice Demon. The monster fell backwards, smashing into the Great Fire's altar and crushing it. This, as much as the massacre just performed, caused a wailing of grief and horror from the onlookers.

"Is all of our time together going to be like this?" Kana shouted, diverting herself from attacking the Ice Demon to conjure forth a storm of purifying rain that put out the witchfire beside us, preventing it from spreading to other houses.

Perhaps a costly mistake in battle.

But which made me think there was perhaps something redeemable in the revolutionary after all.

"Yes," I said, drawing back to strike again. "Almost certainly."

"Good!" Kana said. "I had forgotten what it was like to battle opponents who could fight back!"

Before I could comment, the skies above our heads darkened and I heard the roar of a dozen dragons. The sounds of trumpets and war horns signaled the arrival of the Empress's Rapine at the gates behind us. The second part of Hellsword's attack had begun. The Ice Demon looked annoyed and its movements slowed ever so slightly as if it was preparing to die after it killed us.

The realization of what was going on struck me all at once and if not for the dire nature of our circumstances, I would have let out a gallows laugh. The Ice Demon wasn't here for us as it had said. Hells, it was here to kill the people in the Fire District and then be slain by the forces coming inside. Like idiots, we'd stumbled into a false-flag operation designed to make Redhand's insane charges of black magic and demon-worship look credulous.

"I understand what is going on now," I whispered.

"Fools, you have missed the avalanche for the rocks," Drol-Bethir said, somehow hearing me. It was entering a more cautious combat stance as Regina drew her sword to her with a beam of glowing light. "Each death this day shall feed the horrors to come. You, who imagined yourselves as masters of creation, are merely like me, creatures created to be targets and slain by the Lawgiver's champions. Trophy beasts that shall be mounted and stuffed as well as serving as fodder for ballads in taverns."

I did not have time to contemplate its words before an explosion of mystical power washed over me. I felt a terrible number of deaths, a hundred or more in an instant then, just as a shadowy dome began to form above our heads, blocking out all sunlight and leaving the Fire District as dark as midnight. The night held no mysteries to my undead eyes and I knew what the dome meant: Serah had created a barrier with blood magic.

The darkest of arts worked for a desperate cause. Perhaps too late. I had no idea how many dragons had managed to get underneath the barrier first but even a few would be enough to kill the entire population. We had, perhaps, thwarted the Ice Demon, but if the army did not destroy it then they would certainly do the same to the people inside the Fire Districts. The Usurpers were not going to let the nonhumans of this region live no matter what. We needed to separate their forces from this place and deal with them one at a time. Serah's magic, however black its origins, was what we needed right now.

"I am no man's trophy," Regina said, soaked in sweat, her eyes blazing with a murderous, almost sexual fury. "But you will be mine."

"Know loss and ruin," Drol Bethir said, spreading out its wings and holding its tiny hands up to the sky as witchfire poured from the dome's bottom, landing indiscriminately on the crowds and houses around us, exploding against my own erected shields and blowing up the ground beneath me. Regina was thrown to the side. Kana and Ketra, as well. It was possible the latter two were dead.

"Ketra!" Regina shouted, running to her side and abandoning her position in battle. I, stupidly, joined her in a defensive position.

Which gave the monster a moment to begin conjuring a spell I knew all too well. The Doom of Karnath, a forbidden spell and one of the Terrible Weapons I'd unleashed during the Fourth Great War. It would kill everyone in the Fire Districts.

Myself, Regina, and Serah included.

The Ice Demons as well.

But it was not in command of itself, Hellsword was.

He had outplayed us all.

Not quite, the Trickster said. *It seems your allies are a greater advantage than I would have given them credit for.*

What?

That when the final member of our party returned, taking advantage of the distraction we'd provided. Riding on Smoke, Serah struck at our foe. The dragon breathed down a torrent of golden flame a thousand times hotter than normal flame and additionally blessed by the same spells woven into my glove.

The fiery assault wrapped itself around the Ice Demon, burning it horrifically. Drol-Bethir's magic aura struggled to suppress the flames with its own aura of supernatural cold, the two powerful magics battling for existence. The Doom of Karnath dissipated, its energy gathered failing under the assault. All the while, Serah cast words of demonspeak that invoked powers even I had no knowledge of. I, myself, joined the attack to make sure he could not regain control of the spell. At the end, just as the flames died out, black light poured from Serah's staff and enveloped Drol-Bethir. It was a spell I did not recognize but seemed to warp the entire fabric of reality around us.

Setting it aright.

Drol-Bethir fell to its knees and screamed out a cry no Between World creature could make. It raised up its now-useless wings in an expression of agony, shaking with outrage. The hellish aura surrounding Drol-Bethir, its near-infinite source of power, was gone now. Hellsword's presence was equally absent, the evil wizard banished along with whatever aid he'd been lending the Ice Demon. The monster was isolated now, and little more than a blight on the face of Creation.

Like so many more we'd destroyed.

Drol-Bethir shouted, "What have you done?"

I chuckled. "She has sealed you away from the World Below. Your magic is no longer accessible, which means you are a fish flopping on land."

"No such magic exists."

"Not until last month," Serah said, smiling like a cat having just eaten a bird. "I created the spell in case we ever ran into one of your kind.

Serah settled down her dragon in front of us, joining our war party in facing down the Ice Demon.

"Thank you, Serah," I said, grimacing as I knew Ketra was probably dead.

"Anything for my husband and wife."

"Let us see where demons go when they die." Regina stood up from Ketra's side, holding *Starlight* in one hand and a shield of light in the other. Serah slid off the back of Smoke as Regina climbed into her place instead, being a far better dragon rider than all of us.

Drol-Bethir seemed to contemplate surrender, at least that was what I guessed it was doing. Severing him from the World Below seemed to have freed him from Hellsword's control and had it chosen to swear allegiance to me, I might have recruited it as a weapon against my enemies. Pride is a dangerous thing, though, and Drol-Bethir was a proud being. Roaring, the Ice Demon threw back its useless wings and charged. The remainder of the battle lasted six minutes but was never in doubt. For all the injuries we'd had to heal, barrier fields we'd had to erect, and killing strokes we'd had to avoid—Drol-Bethir was nothing without with his magic.

While we were warriors.

The final blow was struck by Regina who, leaping from the dragon's back onto Drol-Bethir's neck, cut through it and sent its head rolling away. The rest of its body dissolved into abyssal energy that imploded into a shimmering ball of crackling dark magic.

And then it was gone.

Dissolved like the mists before the sum.

And we were left with broken bodies, widowed spouses, and dying children.

CHAPTER TWENTY-THREE

I needed a few moments to come down from my battle fury. The environment around us was chaotic, maddening even. Victory is always described by poets in terms of exaltation, triumph, and arête. For me, it has always been disingenuous to say victory ever actually exists save in hindsight. The Ice Demon, Drol-Bethir, was destroyed, but there was no magical cure to the horrors that surrounded me. Nothing that said, *Yes, we have won and all is right with the world.*

I was in my full wraith form, the Ice Demon having torn out my guts and left them splattered on the ground during our battle. Because I was dead, not a living man, I could conjure a new body with no more effort than changing a suit of clothes. It was an eternal reminder, though, that I was not alive nor never could be again. Like the Gods Between, I was a ghost of a god who had as much to do with the living world as a memory or a fireside tale.

Being in wraith form, I was spared the worst of the after-effects that came to battle. I did not have to smell the shit and half-digested food smell that came with the demise of the mortals all round me. I did not have to hear anything but the distant echo of weeping women and screaming fathers as they cradled their dead children.

As a hooded specter, I did nothing but drain away the life force of those who couldn't be healed, sparing my victims hours of painful death, and funneled the majority back into those who might survive. I kept enough that I might generate another body, even this far from Everfrost, but it would still take hours to craft. I would not be able to work light magic until then and the majority of those who needed such would be crippled or dead by then.

And people still called me a god.

Serah, at least, was a woman who knew how to take advantage of such things and continued using the Heart of Midnight to control the dragon she'd enspelled and sent it forward to the outer edges of the now-barrier-covered Fire District. My senses were keen enough in this form, I could feel the lives ending one by one. Unique, vibrant, living souls suddenly surrounded by nimbus of flames followed by screams and panic before their flesh melted off their bodies then that uniqueness passing away to charred meat.

I wasn't in a good position to know what was going on outside my immediate area but I wagered the Burning Blades had sent in many of their soldiers, perhaps as many as six or seven hundred, only to find themselves trapped without support. There was little such men could do against a dragon and witch of Serah's skill and I suspected their lives had gone to reinforce the barrier surrounding us. They had come to commit a war crime, but I spared them some sympathy. Rare was the soldier who was completely evil, and those that were often had witnessed so many atrocities that their minds were broken rather than bent.

Nearby, I saw Regina was holding the broken and battered form of Ketra. Half of Ketra's body was covered in burns and her right eye was busted wide open. There were also places where parts of her were leaking out and were only held in by the cauterized nature of her wounds. It was a miracle she was still alive but, perhaps, not one that should have been lauded. Regina was not trained in the arts of healing and there was precious little she could do to alleviate the majority of these wounds. Yet she kept pouring divine energy into the body of her cousin, hoping for a miracle.

Refusing to give an inch.

I placed my hand on Regina's shoulder and spoke with a voice that sounded like it came from the grave. "Let her go."

"No," Regina whispered, her eyes soaked with tears. "I won't lose her again."

I had no eyes to close. "You know you—"

Regina's response was to unleash some of the foulest profanity I had ever heard in my life, and I was no stranger to vulgarity.

"I want her to live!" Regina hissed. "Help me!"

"So be it." Closing my eyes, I reached out and felt a dozen surrendering soldiers. I took the lives of men with husbands, wives, families, and those who had been conscripted into this war. I sucked the life force from their chests and caused them to fall over, choking on their own blood. I poured that energy into Ketra, the foulest of necromancy, and watched as her scar tissue sealed over in an instant. Her interior organs stitched over, her lungs emptied of fluid, and her right eye regenerated. None of the scar tissue vanished, though, and it led to the rather disgusting image of her vomiting up blood on the side of the street.

"Thank you," Regina said, looking up at me. "Thank you so very much."

"I told you I would burn the world for you."

"And I you," Regina said, stroking the still-ruined side of Ketra's face. ""What about the scars?"

"They're black magic of the highest order. Why it took so much energy to heal. The Ice Demons were designed to kill those who had access to the mightiest healers. Your magic is aligned to the light and can cleanse the wounds but it will take weeks. We should probably wait until we're back at Everfrost—"

"No." Ketra spat, wiping away a disgusting pink white residue from her mouth. "I will keep the scars."

"Ketra…" Regina said.

"I am more than a pretty ornament my family wanted to marry," Ketra said, climbing to her feet. "I am a warrior of the Army of Free Peasants. Let people look upon me and know what I am willing to sacrifice."

"You shouldn't have to sacrifice anything," Regina whispered.

Ketra gave a bitter laugh and looked around at the carnage around us. "We don't live in that kind of world."

"Some men like scars."

"Some women too," Regina said, rising herself. "As you wish, cousin."

Ketra gave her sister a hug then suddenly hugged me as well. "You are true warriors of the World to Come, both of you. I must go see if I can help organize the resistance here for the next round of the attacks."

"What a strange woman." I took a deep breath, even though I had no lungs. "Regina, we should—"

"Don't," Regina interrupted, picking up Starlight off the ground.

"There is nothing you can say to keep me from now marching on the Governor's Palace and turning every single person who stands in my way into a greasy red smear. The Nine Usurpers have reminded me as to why they have to be annihilated along with all of their supporters."

Under normal circumstances, I would have simply said I'd be offended she'd think I would try to stop her. That there was nothing she could say to keep me from walking beside her to murder, torment, and slaughter the Imperials who guarded this town. There was something dark and unholy in my spirit, perhaps inborn, perhaps cultivated like a gardener's flowers.

Two hundred years of being the King Below's mind-controlled Dark Lord of Despair did not go away with the return of my free will, nor did the prior decade of serving as the most ruthless Shadowguard in an age.

I loved combat. It was a shameful thing because I'd grown up amongst pacifists who wanted nothing more than to live in peace with their fellow man. I was an aberration, though, a wolf amongst sheep. I tried my best to make myself a tame wolf, a sheepdog, but it wasn't always easy.

Right now, I wanted nothing more than to take the fight to Hellsword and Redhand, slaughter all their minions, and then piss on the ashes. I wanted to punish them for this atrocity, though. I knew that was not the way, though. Not yet, not now. I saw the bleakness in her eyes. It was the same pain and suffering I'd seen in a hundred other soldiers, my brothers and sisters in war. Even the greatest soldiers could be killed when they were running on the heat of grief than the coolness of logic. We needed a plan if we were to destroy Hellsword and Redhand, even in the face of all this.

So, instead, I said, "There are children dying around you." It was a cruel thing to say, doubly so because I couldn't bring myself to care about their suffering now over my wife's safety.

Regina turned to look at me, looking betrayed. She opened her mouth to speak an angry retort, stifled it, looked down, and then sighed. Walking to the nearest injured Fir Bolg, she said, "You bastard."

"Indeed," I said, starting to walk with her.

"No," Regina said, stopping in mid-step. "You need to organize… this."

"I'm not sure that's possible." I doubted the people wanted to be organized by a bodiless embodiment of death and despair.

"I need some time alone," Regina said, closing her eyes. "Please."

I nodded. "As you wish."

Walking over to where Kana's still form lay, I reached down to turn her over only to find her shifting and shaking. "I'm alive, Black Sun."

I loomed over her. I suspected, looking like nothing so much as the embodiment of Death. In my true form, I only had demonsteel armor, a cloak, shadows to make up my form. They were almost indestructible, embodiments of the old King Below's power, but they were a poor substitute for the basic ability to give comfort.

"Are you injured?" I asked, not offering my hand. I did not like the Golden Arrow and couldn't help but wonder how badly they had injured the empire in the region to bring down this sort of massacre on their heads. The fact that the elders of that organization had been hoping to spark a purge and Kana knew made me want to plunge my sword into her chest before she got up. I doubted any of the locals would object.

"Nothing I cannot heal. I was able to get my barrier up in time." Kana looked over to the many dead Fir Bolg around us. "How is Ketra?"

"Injured," I said, my voice echoing. "Badly. Do you feel anything at all?"

"For her?" Kana looked up to me, blinking. "Versus everyone else here?"

"Yes." I wondered if Ketra knew just how much contempt Kana and the Golden Arrow had for her.

Probably not.

"No, I'm sorry. I don't." Kana rose to her feet and crossed her arms around her stomach. "When Gewain and Ketra came to the forest, many Golden Arrow soldiers saw nothing but a pair of spoiled nobles, the kind who had been killing my kind for centuries. I assumed they wanted to use us to kill more of their kind and, honestly, I was fine with that. It became...harder...when I realized she genuinely believed not only were we friends but that one day we would liberate my people."

"Were you the one who taught her to be Rainfire? Two nobles

don't become seasoned guerillas and revolutionaries without training. I know the Golden Arrow has allied with peasant revolts in the past, even if they're all *anass* to you."

"Yes," Kana said, looking up at me. "I showed her the mass graves, the whipped bodies, the forced labor, and I made the wizardess studying to be a healer into a weapon. I also was the one who encouraged Gewain to seek your aid. I was hoping to either gain a powerful ally or spark an invasion of the Southern Kingdoms. The elders believe another war between the North and the South can only benefit us."

I stared at her. "Never mind how many burn."

"Yes," Kana said. "I would burn every an—"

"Don't," I said calmly. "Make your choice."

"My choice?" Kana asked.

"Look around you at the face of your people. The ones who choose to live amongst humans, boggans, and other races. The ones you were ready to sacrifice to gain more recruits and know you are their enemy. I give you a choice: fight for them and fight for me. I will give you back your homeland and it will be a place we can all try to live together in peace in. You can also choose the Golden Arrow and continue to fight for the ancient world you know only of in distant memories."

"You would have me become a traitor."

"I consider you a traitor to your race already. How many Fir Bolg have you killed because they did not follow the Golden Arrow's ways or spoke against them?"

"Dozens," Kana said. "If I choose the Golden Arrow, you will kill me. Do you think I am afraid to die?"

I stared at her. "No. However, if you choose the Golden Arrow I will do something you would regret."

"Which is?"

I sheathed the sword. "I will rule your people."

Kana blinked. "What?"

"I have saved this region from destruction and healed the sick. Your people know me as a hero now; a legendary slayer of monsters and archdemons. Word will spread until all know me as a friend of your race. I will go forth to each Fire District in the land and offer them a new homeland in the North. I will shower them magitech wonders and riches. I will give them everything they could possibly want and make my price only that they worship my wives and me exclusively. I will obliterate the old ways and make mockery of the Gods Between so that they will be forgotten within six generation. It will work, too, because most Fir Bolg prefer children with full bellies to dusty old rituals. They also hate the Golden Arrow almost as much as they hate the Anessian Empire. Choose peace or I will assimilate your race. Do you understand?"

Kana's eyes widened and I knew in that moment she believed. "I…understand. I…will choose peace."

"You will work against your superiors for me. Report on them and I will sponsor you and others like you to higher positions. We will eliminate the others. If you do not, know I am entirely capable of fulfilling my promise."

Kana nodded. "I am yours, Black Sun."

"Good. I must go find Rose."

"He is a traitor, you know. The spirits whisper of meetings and messages. He is the only one who could have betrayed Gewain to the Imperials. Ketra's meeting as well. This entire meeting was a trap for the Imperial's enemies."

"I will ascertain the truth of your claims." I turned to walk away. At this point, I wasn't going to be surprised by anything.

"Black Sun—"

"Yes?"

Kana then made me uncomfortable by adding something else. "Thank you for saving these people. I was born *R'Tosh*, a country Fir Bolg who lived in a village built on the most godsforsaken swamp land humans would allow us. I did not think these were my people. The *Y'Tang* are believed to have sold themselves to the anass for riches. I….changed my mind when I got to know them."

I turned to walk away. "I am not doing this for your people."

"No, but you're doing it for all. Gods' blessings upon you."

I didn't respond to that. Instead, I helped several people trapped under rubble, gave the gift of death to a man who could live for hours more but in great pain, and eventually succeeded in tracking down Rose. He was in the corner of a half-collapsed building's cellar, having gotten himself half drunk on a collection of wine bottles down there. The poet had spilled as much as he'd drunk and looked like he'd taken a long look in a filthy mirror.

The cellar was surprisingly pleasant-looking with numerous bottles of wine, fine furniture, and several boxes of clothing that would have fetched a high price on the market. The Fir Bolg hadn't been impoverished in Kerifas, at least this one hadn't, which was yet another sign of the toxic influence the Nine were exerting on the land.

"You ran," I said, walking up to him.

"Yes," Rose said, looking down. "But not because I was afraid."

I walked up to him and waved my hand. The spell I cast would not have worked had he been in his right mind, but I suspected it would now. He looked as if he was in need of a confessor. "Tell me the truth."

"About?"

"Your allegiances."

"And if I lie?"

"I will tear the truth from your mind. I don't think you're going to, though. You were sickened by the realization they were going to kill all the people here, not just the Golden Arrow and rebel Jarls."

"Yes. I was." Rose said, simply. "As for my allegiances, you're right, I'm a spy."

"How long?"

"Since I passed out my stupid pamphlets and got my entire family arrested. An operative of the Mysterium, perhaps it was Hellsword himself, ordered my release if I agreed to serve as a spy. The propaganda I make is used to track the movements of traders and informants amongst those who would conspire against the empire."

"And Gewain?"

"He was a special job. I was sent to infiltrate the Army of Free Peasants and help bring them low. Gewain's tastes were well known and I never much minded who I lay with as long as they were comely." Rose took another drink from his wine bottle. "I was ill suited for undercover duty, but knowing I'd be flayed alive if I revealed my allegiances, I managed to stay on the straight and crooked path of spying on them."

I nodded. "Are there any actual noblemen in the inn?"

"Yes. Yes, there are. Quite a lot of them. Hellsword had the plan to gather all our enemies together and wipe them out in one go. I thought he was going to arrest them. Not..."

"Summon demons and start a purge?"

"That was Redhand's doing," Rose hissed, his speech slurred. He took another drink of his wine bottle. "He's the monster."

I didn't feel like telling him that it was Hellsword's magic that had summoned the Ice Demon. "Many Fir Bolg are dead."

Rose looked down at his bottle, now almost empty. "Many I knew. I've been working out of here for months. Some of which I knew as friends, lovers, and compatriots. Gewain has always been open about our relationship."

"A quality common in his family." I stared at him. "Why continue to serve the empire, though? Is it because of your family being threatened?"

"No, they were released. They never shared my politics anyway. All a bunch of Codex-thumping empress-worshipers." Rose snorted. "I served for my own reasons after the first few months—at least until Gewain."

"For curiosity's sake, would you tell me what you see in the Nine?"

"Or you'll kill me?"

"That's likely to happen either way."

"I understand," Rose said, taking one last drink before throwing the bottle against wall across from him. "To answer your question, the Isle of Gibborim. That's the argument my superiors in the Mysterium gave me and it's stuck with me to this day. Even now, having seen all the horrors there, I think the Nine probably have the right of it."

I knew of the isle. "It was a useless lump of rock in my time."

"It's a useless hunk of rock in my time." Rose sighed. "Ten years ago, three years before the Fifth Great Shadow War, was subject of a war that killed fifty-five thousand men and women. Soldiers and peasants both."

"A terrible war."

"One of seven fought that year and that was a normal year. There has never been a single time when the Southern Kingdoms have not been at conflict. For ten ages, war has been our favorite pastime, sport, and luxury."

"I know better than most."

"Do you?" Rose asked. "Then you should know that Empress Morwen is a tyrant. She murders men, women, and children by the thousands. Great structures have been torn down, libraries burned, and draconian punishments have been instituted continent-wide."

"I sense a 'but' coming."

"No, buts. However, many believe it is *worth it* to bring an end to the fighting. No matter how many are killed, it is a drop in the bucket to the sorrows brought about by the stupidity of previous rulers. The Old World is falling and I wish to see the New World rise—united, advanced, and peaceful. I believe Empress Morwen can do that."

That I understood. "Did you have your lover arrested?"

"No," Rose said, looking down. "Gewain was someone that I argued would be better to subdue the discontent. He was going to be offered a vast amount of wealth, land, title, and more if he would turn the rabble against itself."

"Despite the fact they murdered his family."

Rose looked down. "I could have persuaded him."

"I doubt it. Not if he's anything like Regina. You also betrayed his sister to death. If not for my arrival, Hellsword would have slaughtered Ketra and her dragon before they reached the shores of the North."

Rose looked like he was going throw up. "Redhand made me talk. He was panicked about the fool's errand to the North." Rose snorted. "To be honest, I didn't even think you really existed until you showed up at the docks. I'm glad Ketra survived, though, no matter how many she's killed. Funny, that."

"Not really."

"I'm ready...or at least good and drunk." Rose closed his eyes and waited for death.

I made a choice. "I'm not going to kill you."

Rose opened his eyes. "Why?"

"Because I, too, know something about doing terrible things for the greater good. Leave this place and never return. Tell, also, that I am merciful to those who surrender."

"And to those who don't?"

"Sometimes I am merciful to those, too."

Chapter Twenty-Four

Serah was waiting for me at the top of the cellar stairs. She was soaked with sweat, her hair hanging down loosely over her shoulders, and leaning heavily on the Heart of Midnight. There was soot on her face and side of her robes was torn by an arrow, though the wound had been healed over with magic.

My wife had dropped the illusions around herself that rendered her inhumanly beautiful and now was slightly above plain, at least, to those who did not see her passionate determination to make the world better.

The sounds of people organizing underneath the barrier as well as the attacks against it were in the distance but most of the chaos and grief had died down. I could feel the anger and rage in the air, though.

It was palpable.

"Is Rose dead?" Serah asked.

"Yes," I lied, my voice still sounding like an echo of hell. I should have told her the truth but Serah would have called it sentimentality and killed him. I wanted Rose to live, despite everything. Perhaps because every little bit of mercy I showed was another piece of my soul I could hang on to. "He admitted to being one of the empire's agents."

"Best to keep that a secret," Serah said, taking a deep breath. "Morale would not be improved in this group to know Gewain's second was setting all of the people up here to die."

"I don't think he knew the full lengths the local rulers were willing to go. I'm not quite sure I understand it myself. What is going on here?"

Serah held out her hand in front of me and waved it, creating an illusion of a human form around me. I suspected she knew my true form would do little but terrify the locals. Reformed or not, the Dark Lords had been figures of evil in the Southern Kingdom's scare stories for millennia.

"That I can provide some answers for," Serah said, pausing. "They bother me in their implications."

"Your reaction to meeting me, the Lord of Despair, was to seduce me and join in my quest to gain godlike power. If something is bothering you, it must be terrible." The illusion changed my voice as well, causing the raspy hiss of a wraith to translate into something a little less terrifying.

Serah gave a half-smile. "Your sense of wit is one of the only things that gets me out of bed some days, Jacob."

"That and the prospect of ruling the world."

"Don't forget unlimited knowledge and power," Serah added, now fully smiling. It quickly turned pained. "I've figured out what they're doing here. When the battle was joined, almost all of the deaths diverted the energy somewhere else."

"You're saying they're working blood magic here?" I shouldn't have been surprised. Jassamine had been a master of it and passed it along to all of her apprentices. Forbidden Sorcery was now increasingly common.

Not that I was one to talk anymore.

Serah nodded. "I was originally of the mind they'd turned the Fire Districts into one gigantic sacrificial altar. Then I sent a sending out and I've found glyphs and runes carved into the stone throughout the city."

There were few things that shocked but this did. "The entire city?"

Serah looked up at me. "Yes. They're collecting the energies of the dead and funneling them to a geomancy point somewhere in the Palace District. It's not as good as if it had been done with the proper rituals but quantity has a quality of its own. That's why they've got all their troops prepared to attack the city. The rebels and Fir Bolg look like they're summoning demons and are slaughtered along with all the people inside the Fire Districts before the soldiers clean up the mess. Thousands upon thousands of dead, their life-energy funneled to Hellsword and Redhand."

The implications were staggering. "What could the want with that much power?"

Serah snorted. "You are a very poor God of Evil if you cannot think of possible uses."

"I have never maintained otherwise."

Blood magic wasn't the most powerful form of magic, that was the manipulation of names, but it was the easiest and most plentiful in terms of results. Every human being contained mystical life-force that could be harvested at the moment of death for great power. It was a forbidden form of sorcery, everywhere but Natariss, but the Nine Heroes made ample use of it in outfitting both the Shadowguard as well as their proxies.

Jassamine, in particular, was considered the most powerful Blood Magus who ever lived. Serah dabbled in the art, despite my encouragement for her to abandon it, and I had no real leg to stand on since I often used the life force of my enemies to heal the wounded of my allies. Still, even the most ruthless kings and queens I'd known would have balked at murdering one of the oldest cities in the world for magical power.

It was madness.

"Stretch out with your feelings. You'll sense the complicated wards and rituals throughout the city."

"All right."

Following her advice, I felt around the city to see if there truly was such a network of enchantments woven into the city's stonework. What I found was a complex network of interlocking symbols that were designed to maximize the amount of energy collected in artificial ley-lines centered around the Palace District. The pool of mystical energy was a lake of magical energy, gathered in an amount that I had never seen outside of the supply underneath Everfrost. It put Ethinu's astral mansion to shame and I couldn't help but imagine several terrifying scenarios where they harvested such a collection of magical energy to lay waste to the North. "They could be planning to use it to destroy Everfrost with a volcano, tear open a rift to the World Above, summon the Lawgiver fully into this reality, devastate the Northern Wastelands with earthquakes, conjure a host of engel minions, bring forth the ancient Typhon war-beasts from the bottom of the ocean, re-animate the Guardians of Kerifas, become gods themselves—"

Serah raised a hand to silence me. "Yes. We can't invade the city now. Any battle runs the risk of them turning that wellspring upon our forces and annihilating them outright."

I processed this new bit of military information and thought of the old saying that described a situation fucked up beyond salvation. "We are fucked."

"Yes, yes, we are," Serah repeated.

I smirked. "At least until we kill Hellsword and Redhand then confiscate the wellspring for ourselves."

Serah blinked. "That's...a straightforward plan."

"Imagine what we could do with such power."

Serah beamed, the possibilities whirling behind her eyes. "We could bring an end to this war before it begins. Though, whatever they're doing is going to require the death of the city and I doubt we're going to let that happen." She paused. "Unless—"

"No, Serah."

"Thought not."

"Can they use it to break down the barrier you've erected?"

Serah didn't hesitate. "Yes. It would require sacrificing large amounts of power, though. The barrier I erected around the Fire District isn't fueled by the sacrifices I made. I'm powering it directly from Everfrost's link to the World Below."

In laymen's terms, she'd killed a bunch of people to open a link to Hell and it was going to take all of Hellsword's blood magic to break it down.

"But they *can* break it down."

Serah nodded. "Yes, if they want to sacrifice all the energy they've gathered so far. Which, strategically, they should. Killing us would prevent massive bloodshed. The fact they don't means they've got something bigger planned than our deaths."

That did not bode well. "We should rejoin Regina and see if we can salvage this whole Jarl thing as well as recruit the local resistance. None of that is going to matter in the short term, though, and we need to begin plotting taking Hellsword and Redhand out now."

"Agreed."

I started to walk past her when she grabbed my arm. A brief

look of nausea passed over her and I wondered how gods felt when they physically touched a Wraith Knight. Taking her hand away, she said, "We need to discuss something first."

"Oh?"

Serah looked over toward the center of the Fire District. "I cannot help but think Regina will never forgive me for my role in endangering her sister, especially given her injuries."

"She will not hold Hellsword against you."

"She does." Serah sighed. "Not necessarily that I was lovers with one of the Usurpers, though that's a slap in the face to her, but that I lied about it for so long. Regina didn't know I was Hellsword's lover before today. I told you about the Oghma and my membership before her too. This is a side of me I've never shown her and I managed to keep hidden from her for close to a decade. It is a side I've only ever been comfortable showing you."

I wanted to point out she hadn't been all that comfortable showing me that side of her either. I had already forgiven her for those past associations, though. One could not be the God of Evil and cast stones. "Regina is a woman capable of great forgiveness and mercy. Not to the Nine Usurpers or the Anessian Empire, this is true. She is a woman who will hold an everlasting loathing toward them for as long as the sun shines in the sky. Nor to the Lawgiver, for being the party responsible for them and Jassamine. Not for—"

"You're not helping, Jacob."

"But she forgave me," I said, staring at her. "I was the Dark Lord of Despair. I was a Wraith Knight, a monster of immeasurable evil mothers told their children about to scare them into good behavior. I was the horror that lived in the bed and in the closet. Regina grew up with these stories the same as every other girl and boy in the empire. Yet, she looked past them to see the person beneath."

Indeed, I believed Regina saw more good in me than I did myself.

"That is what I'm afraid of," Serah said, sighing. "I fear forgiveness more than condemnation."

"You are a good person, Serah."

"I'm not. I gave up on being a good person long ago, Jacob. I embraced the evil in my heart when I decided to be the monster everyone thought I was. Regina reminded me I could be otherwise, so I pretended. It was always a lie, though, an illusion. You, you live with the darkness in your heart every day and deny it—or try to, at least. Now I've potentially led Regina to ruin and the rest of the continent with her."

"Ruin?" I asked, looking up at the dome above our heads. "We're trapped in a bubble and surrounded by enemies who can destroy us outright on a whim, but that's not the worst situation we've ever found ourselves in."

"I can't stop thinking about Morrigan's prophecy."

"So that's it." I shook my head. "I do not believe in Morrigan's prophecy. I believe the only reason it is relevant is because other people do."

"Yet, you saw the destruction of the World Between in your visions."

"I see a lot of things," I said, placing my hand over my heart. "I believe victory is possible, though."

"And if it's not?"

"I believe death is preferable to being the Lawgiver's slaves. There are some things worse than death and countless generations brainwashed into believing nothing but his lies is worse than extinction."

"Do you believe that, truly?"

I searched my heart. "Yes."

It was a lie. Morrigan's prophecy nagged at me and I couldn't help but wonder if there was something to it. I had seen the destruction of the world if Regina and the Lawgiver fought but it was only one of many potential futures. Had Morrigan truly seen so clearly into the myriad possibilities? If so, was it possible to avert her predictions? If not, then why put them down in the first place? It made no sense.

Only the Trickster and the Lawgiver knew the truth.

Oh, how right you are, the Trickster said. *The answer is in front of your face but invisible to those who cannot see past their own prejudices.*

Could you be any less helpful?

Not for lack of trying.

Serah looked down. "I wish I shared your certainty."

"Regina loves you and that is not easily broken. I believe in you. I believe in us. That is enough."

"For you, maybe. For others? Not so much."

In truth, I wasn't sure how Regina would react. She did believe what we were doing was righteous and just, that there was no moral equivalence between us and the Nine Usurpers. At the end of the day, we were good and they were evil. I was, honestly, surprised that she was as comfortable with the Golden Arrow as she was.

Then again, perhaps Ketra was closer to her cousin than I'd given her credit for. Regina might well believe their search for a homeland was justified, no matter their vile measures. Regina believed in a good and an evil with the measures to destroy the latter broad and uncompromising. It was not the kind of worldview that contained much room for compromise and forgiveness, though.

Not even of one's spouse.

"Blame Hellsword for everything," I said, deciding on what to tell Serah. "He was the poison in your ear that turned you to the darkness. A darkness that you have now rejected. Say that it is his darkness which led you astray and you have rejected him. Beg for forgiveness and say that you merely feared her reaction. Let her know you were young, naïve, and easily manipulated by those above you."

"You know that is not true."

"I do. But, I do not ask you to lie to Regina about it. I ask you to lie to yourself."

"What?"

"Blame him so you can forgive yourself. I do it every day with Jassamine, the Lawgiver, the Trickster, and others. If you repeat it often enough, you can pretend you're a good person and perhaps become one."

Serah stared at me, opened her mouth then closed it. The look on her face was confused then resigned them almost happy. "Yes, I suppose that does have a certain appeal. Would you lie to me, Jacob?"

"About?"

"Anything."

"Regina has already forgiven you," I whispered, my illusion-covered voice reassuring. "Hellsword and Redhand will be defeated today and Gewain freed. The Nine will fall without difficulty and the peasants will love us for liberating them. The Lawgiver will be cast down and better gods raised who are noble and kind. The suffering will be minimal and songs will be sung about our heroism. No one will curse our name and they will name a cookie after you."

"A cookie?"

"Serahs. They're delicious."

I wrapped my arms around her and she buried her head in my shoulders.

"All right. Thank you." Serah pulled away and straighted herself. "We need to find Regina."

"Yes."

CHAPTER TWENTY-FIVE

Outside of the barrier, trumpets blared, which signaled the forces of Hellsword and Redhand were pulling back from their assault. Thanks to Serah's actions, the Burning Blades had lost a third of their host. It wasn't much of a victory, despite far less casualties on our side than should have been possible, because we were now trapped like a butterfly in bottle.

Walking with Serah at my side, I saw the Fir Bolg citizens look to me with a mixture of awe, fear, and hate. My unnaturally keen senses picked up the whispers of conversation that spoke things like, "Black Sun", "God of Evil", "The Fallen One", and "Savior." I had protected them from the Ice Demon, but many knew me only as a figure of wickedness. It was leading to considerable confusion.

I had that effect on people.

I couldn't help but wonder how our situation was being interpreted by the people outside who, after Redhand's grand speech, were now the middle of a war in the heart of their city. Some would blame the nonhumans inside, certainly, but others still would start to wonder if their masters were as strong as they claimed. Either way, we had more people to kill before we could escape.

An ash-covered woman, her long white hair full of the dust of a collapsed building, walked in front of us holding her three-year-old's shattered body before speaking in the Old Tongue, "Please, Old One, return her to me. I don't care about the Gods Between, I just want my Satale back."

I looked down at the child.

I could restore a semblance of life to him. Make him an undead thing or a ghost or something akin to myself. But no magic beyond the Lawgiver and Great Mother's own, perhaps, could restore the dead to true life. It was one of the rules of magic the Old Humans had set down upon us, something only the gods could reverse.

And I was not divine enough to help.

"You will be reunited with your son just as all of the dead will be with their loved ones when we have triumphed over the Lawgiver," Serah said, waving her hand in front of her. "Such is the word."

I did a double-take at the monumental nature of the lie. Worse, realizing she'd added her magic to plant the idea deep in the woman's subconscious.

"Thank you," the woman said, tears falling from her eyes.

"Go," Serah said, waving her away. She then projected an aura outward that caused the others to shy away from approaching.

"That was monstrous," I whispered.

"Those who do not believe in the gods do not do so because they wish to," Serah said, striding forward. "They do so because the world has not given them sufficient cause to believe in their existence, let alone mercy. It does not matter what we are or what we can do, Jacob; our existence provides them comfort, and that is enough."

I considered pointing out that was a lie but I wasn't quite ready to live down the Trickster's accusations of hypocrisy just yet.

"Your benevolence is more real than most deity's," Serah said, continuing to reassure me what she'd done was the right thing to do. "Do you know what happens to souls that once went to the World Below?"

I remembered the vast empty halls of the thousand hells. The palaces of iron, ice, and stone that had no inhabitants but the rare wandering demon. The dungeons of endless torture, lakes of fire, and oubliettes of eternal starvation were empty as well. Whereas once a hundred million or more souls had dwelled there, not more than ten thousand remained. They had simply vanished when I'd arisen to my position and decided not to continue holding spirits against their will. An irrational part of me wondered if they'd always been an illusion the Trickster generated to convince people to worship him.

Would I do that? the Trickster asked. *Would you believe me if I said yes? How about no?*

"No," I whispered. "I do not. Some souls still come there, especially amongst our worshipers, but the rest move on."

"To where?" Serah asked.

"I don't know."

"Such is the cruelest mystery of all," Serah said, her voice low. "Better to believe my brother was amongst the damned being tormented knowing I might see I see him again than believing he is forever beyond my reach."

"Death comes to us all, even gods."

"It's not death I fear but what's after."

I saw Regina moments later, standing next to Kana, in front of the Wild Goat Inn. The building had sustained some minor damage to one of the upper floors, bashing out a few windows, but otherwise looked intact. There was a selection of the Fire District's elders as well as several well-dressed individuals of boggan and Bauchan descent around her plus three individuals who could not be mistaken for anything but Winterholme nobility.

Winterholme's rulers were all brown-skinned with a few possessing lighter skin than the others but still more so than the majority of the nation's inhabitants. They preserved the old High Human bloodlines here, more so than in other nations, with spouses often chosen by how much they resembled the old Terralan Dominion ideal. Personally, I found the whole idea ridiculous since I was a fair shade swarthier than the majority of people and that was because of my mother's line, which descended from a long string of cobblers. Hells, Serah was the most High Human-looking woman I'd ever met and until I'd met Ketra, I'd never encountered a person more disdainful of the nobility.

Their clothes weren't exactly concealing their identity either. Of the three, two were men wearing robes of office and enough gold to rival Captain Vass. The third was a woman a head taller than the others in full plate-mail forged a century ago, expensive modernized glyphs added to it, making her look more like a golem than a person.

The female Jarl was a severe-looking middle-aged woman who reminded me of Miranda ni Bathas, the Traitor Queen. She had betrayed the Southern Kingdoms to ally with the King Below during the Fourth War only to be captured days before my death on the fields of its final battle.

That would Miras ni Bathas, the Trickster informed me. *Her descendant and ruler of the largest Jarldom in the North.*

You're joking, I said, horrified. *Her ancestor should have been stripped of her rank and sentenced to death by torment.*

I never joke, the Trickster said. *That would require humanity to be more of one than it already is.*

How—

Prince Alfreid the Unsteady overpromised his supporters amongst Winterholme's nobility and foreign monarchs. By supporting her instead, a candidate no one liked, he forced her to rely on Imperial largesse to remain in power. Three civil wars and four succession crises later meant Winterholme never rose up as a rival to the empire as some believed possible. Of course, the prince never could have come up with such a clever plan by himself.

I growled, "Jassamine."

Serah shot me a strange look.

I just shook my head.

Be grateful, the Trickster said. *If she's anything like her ancestor then you have a delightfully self-interested parasite of an ally.*

Is she anything like her ancestor?

She's a noble, isn't she?

"Hello, Jacob," Regina said, turning to me. "I was conversing with our new allies about recent events."

"Allies?" one of the richly appointed men said. He was a stout, overweight, and bald but still-strong-looking. "That remains to be seen."

"Perhaps you should have chosen to hedge your bets more clearly before committing treason, Jarl Borgas," Jarl Miras said, her voice low and husky. "I do not think the Empress's Rapine will be so understanding if you decide not to ally with us after this."

"King Borgas," the man corrected. "The Winter Throne has sat empty since the royal family was slaughtered during the last war. Since none of you had the balls"— he emphasized the latter while addressing the taller woman—"to stand against Empress Morwen adding it to her honorifics, I see no reason not to claim that title with my own."

"Despite having no claim to the throne whatsoever," the other man said. He was taller than Borgas, if not Miras, but looked every inch the proper king. I also guessed from the delicate nature of his hands and face that he'd never been out of comfortable environs a day in his life.

"Fine answer, Jarl Stephens," Jarl Borgas said, "from a man who has his title from marriage. Has your wife grown tired of having a pretty but useless ornament to decorate her court? Is that why she sent you? To die so she can marry someone half as young as her again?"

"I have Jarl Wynessa's full—" Jarl Stephens started to say.

Regina gave me a look of exasperation as the three degenerated into arguing. I sympathized. One thing that had clearly not changed in the past two and a half centuries was the disposition of the nobility. All of them seemed pathologically incapable of looking beyond anything but their own interests.

All except Regina.

"The district elders have agreed to assist us in stopping the governor," Kana said, her voice as polite and calm as it first was on the docks.

"What do we care about the feelings of Stagmen?" Borgas said, growling. "We should be not meeting here in the first place."

I forced down my initial response and spoke diplomatically. "The situation has rapidly evolved, *Jarl* Borgas, which I've managed to take advantage of to do damage to the enemy. Our forces are arriving soon to take the city and then you will be able to see what we're capable of as well as how we treat our citizens. All of our citizens."

One of the elders cast me a vile look.

But held their silence.

"I take it you are forwarding the idea of Kerifas as your territory, Your Highness?" Miras asked, perhaps feeling out what my intentions were.

In truth, I hadn't had time to think about what sort of agenda I should have for this situation as I was happy enough to break up the empire to its pre-war state. Indeed, I would have been happy to break up the empire to its pre-Fourth War state. Unfortunately, Serah's warning about Regina left me wondering if Regina truly did intend to rule over a united southern and northern continent. There was also Rose's words on the subject and my own memories of the countless wars fought between the bickering nobility had consumed uncounted thousands of lives.

Could I, indeed, end it? Or would the action just create more chaos? It said volumes about my character that the chief objection I had to such a monstrous idea was I wasn't sure it would work. How far had I fallen? Oh, right, I was the God of Evil now.

I needed to remember that.

"The negotiations for this meeting are things we shall handle in the full company of the other members of this organization. The subject of Kerifas and its administration will, naturally, fall to me and my brides, however, given the strategic significance."

I had never been very good at negotiation, and it would have been better to let Regina have it but I knew we needed to establish a beachhead here. I wanted to be the one to set them in their place, though. Which, when I thought about it, meant this was all just an issue of pride.

"I think you will find the other members of the party less than amenable to dealing with anything but changing their underclothes," Miras said, laughing. "They screamed and ran to the basement when the Ice Demon appeared. One of them ran out to beg forgiveness from Lord Hellsword but was buried beneath a shower of stone."

"A fitting fate for that fool," Borgas said.

"Fitting or not," Stephens said, frowning, "Lord Karlyle was rich and influential. That is one less ally to face down against the empress's retaliation."

"More for us," Borgas said, snorting.

"Is it us now, make up your mind," Miras snapped, clearly as irritated with the pompous windbag as I was. "Also, before you start talking about balls, look to your genealogy. You are Jarl of Northkeep and the green forests of Valleyheart because of your grandmother."

Borgas started to say something that would, undoubtedly, trigger a fresh round of bickering and naysaying.

Regina spoke instead. Her voice was incredibly soft and melodic. Almost mesmerizing. "Gentlemen, milady, we must decide our next course of action under advisement from those here on the ground. You are all invited to participate in the discussions and we shall work towards a mutually satisfactory arrangement. To start with, of course, we must remain in charge of all territories seized from the empire but you'll, of course, agree this is the wisest course of action. You will, instead, administrate in our name."

"I see," Borgas said, nodding.

"Wise," Miras said.

The Holy Ones exchanged a glance before nodding.

Even Kana seemed enraptured. "Yes, that sounds like the best idea."

Serah, by contrast, looked horrified. So did I. Because it wasn't almost mesmerizing, it *was* mesmerizing.

I grabbed Regina by the arm and pulled her away. She promptly pushed me away and growled. "Jacob, what are you doing?!"

"What are *you* doing?" I asked, my voice low.

"I am helping them decide on the right course of action," Regina said, looking over at them. "They would have us carve up Winterholme like a cake then each try to take the biggest slice for themselves. You're always complaining about the poor treatment of the peasantry, Jacob, and we can fix that. They just have to do their damned jobs properly. Make them listen the way they should and behave the way proper nobles should."

"You are the most improper noble I have ever met," Serah said. "You would mentally enslave all of the others to be like you?"

Serah surprised me by not coming to Regina's defense. Perhaps she saw a difference between helping a mother come to terms with her child's death and mind-controlling all our followers into our service.

"No...I just..." Regina was obviously flush with the magic she'd channeled healing Ketra. It seemed her gift at healing had opened others, mind-control being one of the ones now at her disposal. One of the most dangerous and seductive of all gifts—as well as one of the evillest.

"And the Fir Bolg?" I asked. "Are they to give up their dreams of a homeland because of the desire of you to outdo Morwen?"

Regina looked more like she was slapped than from the actual slap. Her eyes narrowed and her voice became fierce. "How dare you!"

"We are not the Lawgiver," I said. "We are not the Trickster, either. Neither of those gods believes in free will. The latter enslaved all the Shadowkind races to his will and used them as puppets for millennia. The Lawgiver allows people the option of free will but attempts to control all choices. We have to be better than that."

Regina looked between us. "Is condemning the people underneath them to endless war better? The conflicts between the nobility, ideology, races, and...it's all insane!"

"We can't fix everything," I said, sighing. "Perhaps that is the best lesson we can learn as gods."

Regina's shoulders slumped. "What if this costs us everything? What if we can't defeat Morwen? You see all around us what they're willing to do to achieve victory. How many lives will be lost if we fail?"

"All of them, possibly," I said. "But do you want to do this, truly? How would you feel is Jassamine had made you...like her?"

Regina stared at me then stared out over at Ketra, who was returning on horseback. "I would not be alive. I would be a puppet with her hand up my ass and squeezing my lungs to make noises."

I blinked. "A rather vivid but apt analogy."

"I will not become the tyrant my cousins fight against," Regina said, biting her lip. "You realize, though, that we will have to force them to submit another way. Right? We can't let them walk away from her as enemies or even neutral parties. We need the rebel lords united behind us if we're to win."

"Yes," Serah said.

"You're right, of course," I said, feeling disgusted with myself. No matter which way we acted, war was still evil and it was merely a choice of how brutal it was going to be. "We need allies to defeat the empire. More so, we need subordinates. We must bring these Jarls underneath us as conquered subjects as well as collaborators. We just need to make them do it of their own free will."

Regina rubbed the side of her forehead "I want to bring peace to the land and kill my enemies. Must it be so hard to do both?"

"Yes, or everyone would be doing it."

Serah placed her hand on Regina's shoulder. "We can set the groundwork for our empire the old-fashioned way, without mind-control."

"How?" Regina asked.

"We start by lying," Serah said, smiling.

Serah's glib response distracted me from my next question: where had Regina learned how to bend men's minds?

CHAPTER TWENTY-SIX

The Wild Goat Inn was a large structure with a central tap room converted into our impromptu place of negotiation. I sat at the far end of the chamber, in front of the roaring hearth, keeping my presence human but cloaked in shadows so as to be vaguely ominous. Serah stood beside me, doing her best to look appropriately wizardly but mostly focusing her attention on keeping the barrier around the Fire District up. Regina, by contrast, was standing in the center in order to maximize the amount of attention she commanded.

Everyone was enjoying a meal as well as the inn's homemade mushroom ale. The taste of brew had long been ashes in my mouth, a pleasure denied to me whereas others were not, but I didn't have a body anyway, so it didn't matter. The others seemed to enjoy the Fir Bolg's brew, however, which was about the only thing going right tonight. Negations were, as expected, a complete clusterfuck.

Even with lying.

With *copious* lying.

The nobility gathered by Gewain and Rose came in roughly three types: those who were secret worshipers of the old King Below, those who didn't mind allying with the new King Below if it meant expanding their power base, and those genuinely offended by the abuses perpetuated by the empress. One could guess which of the three were most troubled by my presence. Also which ones I really wished we could win over.

Ketra had made it seem it would be easy to convince the nobility to lend their armies to us as well as political support. Indeed, that they were all ready to acknowledge us as their overlord. The truth was, of course, more complex. Some of them were, indeed, all ready to crown the three of us rulers of both the northern and southern continent with Winterholme as our first new domicile. Most, however, wanted what Kana had wanted: guarantees. They desired help in putting down their ancestral enemies, promises of territory they had claim on (or no claim at all), and copious payments in gold as well as silver.

Even those who were willing to work with as subordinates were difficult. Was Winterholme to be a feudal territory answering directly to Everfrost or a principality? Would it have its own monarch? Would they answer to the King Below directly or simply pay homage? What was the answer to issues of religion? Would everyone be expected to convert to worshiping the Iron Order's Triumvirate or would there be freedom of religion? Those who suggested reviving slavery were, at least, thankfully shouted down. Unfortunately, this just meant they rephrased themselves as requesting the right to reinstitute serfdom. I would never, ever, argue for mind-control. But, an hour in, it was sorely tempting to revisit Regina's original plan.

"Worship of the Lawgiver and Great Mother would be permitted along with the Gods Between amongst other deities both real as well as fictional," I said, clarifying the seventy-second point of tonight's discussion. "Those caught engaged in conspiracy against the Crown or nobility as well as colluding with the Grand Temple would be considered guilty of treason, however. Until the Grand Temple acknowledges the right of the Iron Order to continue to exist, it should be considered an enemy organization."

"Nothing incites the population quite like a martyr," Jarl Borgas said, taking a sip of wine from a goblet. "If we do need to execute them all, we should do in private rather than public. Priests are all fuckers of boys and girls anyway. Not a single one of them hasn't got his hand in the poor box."

This incited a fresh round of arguing which was, thankfully, paused by a round of spells detonating against the barrier over our heads. The Burning Blades' wizards were trying to breach the barrier again. The sound was dulled by Serah's magic, but still loud enough to be heard over the shouting. I imagined them probing Serah's barrier for weaknesses, plotting some way to break through to kill us all as we laid our own plans.

We will not resolve this issue tonight, Serah projected her thoughts to me. *These fools cannot agree on their own weight.*

We were never supposed to succeed in convincing any of these to join our cause. This was a trap for them. Gewain seemed to have a plan for dealing with them, but he's not present and rescuing him isn't feasible just yet.

So is there any point to negotiating at all? Serah said, shrugging her bare shoulders. She had changed into black dress that was just this side of daring compared to modern Imperial sensibilities. *Shouldn't we be focused on slaying Hellsword and Redhand?*

Aren't you? I teased.

Indeed, I am, Serah said, giving a half-smirk. *I was just wondering if you were contributing anything.*

I have ordered the gathering of every Burning Blade corpse and have had them dumped in a specific spot in the sewers. I have also gathered all the armaments present and returned them. With necromancy, we can raise a proper army to send to distract the forces gathered outside the barrier. You can weaken the barrier in the spot around them, allowing Regina and me to slip through.

Not me? Serah asked.

We can't abandon the Fire District to destruction. You need to stay behind and hold the barrier up for as long as you can. Are you prepared for that?

Yes.

Good. I sighed and gave her a further explanation. *We need to establish a precedent here at the table. Something the nobles here can bring to their fellows or demonstrate we can be negotiated with. If we appear reasonable, don't engage in the monstrous behavior of the old King Below, more people are likely to surrender and even defect. What saves lives also weakens our enemy's will to fight.*

I know how war works, Jacob. Every friend you make is one less enemy.

Sorry. I just wish there was some miracle we could pull off to get these bastards to go with us. One not involving mind-control.

That is already taken care of.

What?

Watch.

Lord Grost, a tall, bearded man in shining armor, almost drew his sword before instead slamming his fist on the table in front of him. "I grow sick of this constant back-and-forth. The Nine Usurpers are a pestilence on our lands, destroying our ancient traditions and ways, which you fools seek to prevent by inviting a greater evil! I, for one, refuse to be part of any further negotiations with this…monster!"

I looked at Serah. "Do you think he's talking about me?"

Serah rolled her eyes.

"A fine one to speak of monsters, Grost," Miras said, banging her mug against the table. "Or do you deny murdering your own brother to become baron?"

"He was mad! Unable to distinguish between fantasy and reality! He believed chairs talked to him! It was a mercy killing!" Lord Grost said, holding his hands on his chest.

"In my land, we lock mad kin up rather than kill them," a Jarl I hadn't caught the name of said in between bites of roast chicken.

This started a fresh round of arguing.

Regina rose from her seat in the center and addressed them all. "I grow weary of your constant aspersions to my husband's character. You knew Jacob Riverson as the Dark Lord of Despair, yes, but it was your ancestors who were enslaved by the King Below. The Wraith Knights are no more, and the Wraith Lord before you is one who is once more a great hero of man."

Regina was rather exaggerating there.

"Listen—" Grost began to say.

"Silence!" Regina shouted. The entire room seemed to darken as she absorbed every bit of light but what illuminated her. "You bicker here like children when Hellsword and Redhand's plan was to catch you like fish in a net before destroying this ancient hallowed city. The Usurpers do not merely come for your wealth and position but to beat and smelt your people until they are is nothing more than the whipped dogs of the empire! I have witnessed the dawning of the new and terrible age that is to come. One brought about by a Lawgiver who is not what he promised us. It is an age of flame and horror where only ashen earth remains where vibrant fields once were. I would do anything to prevent this from coming to pass and the only way to do so is unified. One sword, one shield, horse, and knight directing it."

"And you shall be that knight?" Jarl Borgas said, skeptical of her impassioned plea.

"Yes," Regina said simply. "I am the Empress of the North and South by right of blood, marriage, deed, and divine right. You will each have a chance to see a Winterholme rise to the glory equal to that of the Easternlands if you choose to fight under me. Those who do not shall not leave this city alive."

"What?" Jarl Borgas said, standing up. "How dare you?!"

Others joined him.

Regina shouted them down. "None of you can choose to agree on the terms here because you fear treachery from the others. Today we shall swear a blood oath before the Triumvirate, a binding geas that shall keep us all to our purpose! None shall turn from our cause and live. Those who fulfill their purpose shall know everlasting glory. Those who do not shall be turned out now to face Hellsword's inquisitors and Redhand's torturers." It was an outrageous demand and I expected all of them to refuse.

None did. Not even Borgas.

The threat, of course, was partially the reason. I had no doubt Regina would kill each and every individual who refused to abide by the covenant she drew up in the next ten minutes. There was more, though, much to my surprise. For all my talk of planting seeds, I had forgotten what it was like to believe in something. I had once been willing to destroy whole nations in the name of reforming the Grand Temple and ending slavery. Immortality had robbed me of my idealism, but it had not done so with these. Instead, Regina's words had cut through their anger life a knife and not even my presence here had undone it.

I see your point, I projected at Serah.

Do not be overly moved, Serah said. *Gewain promised many of these individuals' hefty bribes even before they arrived. I found out when I scanned their minds at the beginning of the meeting. Since then, I've been telepathically confirming we will pay them in Iron Order gold, land, and more. Most of them were willing to abandon their larger demands when I told them their neighbors had been willing to take up the burdens they were unwilling to shoulder—in exchange for smaller rewards. The terms I've negotiated are quite reasonable, and that's assuming we honor any of them.*

We will, I said. *Provided they behave in an honorable fashion during the war.*

The terms are quite reasonable, she repeated, *assuming we honor any of them.*

I chuckled. *Why didn't you tell me any of this?*

You've been very understanding of my secrecy so I didn't think you'd mind. Besides, I love my games.

Mine are usually less cerebral and more sweaty.

Serah snorted then smiled. *Believe me. I know. To think I used to think Fisherfolk of your time were reserved.*

I actually meant blacksmithing and war, but that works too. Does Regina know you and Gewain rigged everything?

I decided to let her do her speech uninformed. It's more passionate that way and believable.

Well played.

Regina in the next ten minutes presented a compact for each of them to sign and an oath that bore a suspicious similarity to the one the King Below had forced upon his followers. The fanatics amongst the King Above's worshipers were not present, today, while those who believed in the Gods Between had already left. The document was a little too erudite for something to have been created spontaneously and I couldn't help but wonder if Ketra had helped her sister with it. Either way, we were all in agreement in the end.

Regina stepped to the top of the centermost table and pulled forth *Starlight* above her head, beginning the binding oath. It was powerful magic that would take the mightiest archmage a year to learn but she'd done through divine will alone. Amongst the three of us, she believed in it the most, and that seemed to make it flow the swiftest and most powerful.

"We shall conquer the Southern Kingdoms and raise a United Empire of the North and South between us!" Regina shouted.

"For Winterholme!"

"For the Triumvirate!"

"For honor!"

Every one of the people here was now ready to lead their followers to the death. I felt, in that moment, very much like the Nuckelavee.

But I swore the oath too.

Only a single person merely mouthed the words and stumbled over them, unable to finish it.

Ketra.

If Regina noticed her cousin's reticence, she didn't mention it and then stepped down off the table. "We must make haste to deal with Hellsword and Redhand. Kerifas is the first city that will fall of the Southern Kingdoms and shall be a preview for every other nation to what we can do for them. We shall bring forth Gewain and the other prisoners before raising the flag of the people over this land—a land that will shine forever more as a symbol of what gods and men can do working in together."

There was an epic cheer.

They were committed now.

Gods help them.

It took all of my effort to avoid saying, *So it would be wise to avoid everyone in the city being killed in a massive blood magic sacrifice.*

Instead, I just bowed my head.

Serah, are you ready to let the next part of our plan go forth?

I will hold the Fire District. I promise you. Whenever you're ready.

I nodded. *I need an hour or so more to gather my strength. The day has been…taxing…and I do not wish to overextend myself before the fight with Hellsword.*

Do not underestimate Redhand. My old lover is formidable, but Redhand has killed armies. You cannot slay him, only slow him down.

We shall see.

Gewain's room is empty. Go there. Regina has some more hands to shake and babies to kiss.

I looked over to Ketra alone, who, despite her burns, seemed to be both excited and troubled by the directions things had took. Unfortunately, I could not bring myself to speak with her.

Walking up a set of stairs to the side, I sought Gewain's bedroom on the top floor and pushed open the door to take a moment to rest and regenerate.

Standing on the other side was Fel Hellsword.

Smiling.

CHAPTER TWENTY-SEVEN

I took in Fel Hellsword's appearance in the half-second it took for me to react to his presence. He was an impossibly beautiful chalk-white-skinned man with a single noticeable flaw: the left side of his face around his eye was covered in a thick, red splotchy birthmark that could have easily been corrected with magic, but had been left alone.

Hellsword had the thin, sharp features of Natariss's ruling caste with cheekbones so sharp one could cut a finger on them. His hair was long, stringy, and black, hanging over his shoulders with little care or attention. His complete lack of care toward his appearance only added to his attractiveness, though, given there was a sense of utter confidence as well as power radiating from the man. Hellsword was wearing a custom-tailored silk and shimmer-cloth long coat, pants, and doublet that invoked the appearance of a wizard's robes while being practical for long-term military expeditions.

Every one of his long, delicate fingers had a magical ring on it with his ears pierced with a half-dozen more. Amulets, necklaces, and charms of power hung around his neck even as I saw the top of blood wards tattooed on his chest up to his neck's base. Both his arms bore caste writing that marked his lineage in intricate, beautiful tattoos that listed an impressive array of mystical as well as political accomplishments. His sword, *Plaguebringer*, was attached to the side of his belt in a heavily warded dragon-bone sheath and seemed to whisper pleas for mercy and writhe with the screams of the damned.

I responded to his presence by drawing *Chill's Fury* and plunging it forward through his chest before he had a chance to say anything.

It went through his chest and out the other side to no effect, as if stabbing smoke.

Hellsword looked annoyed. "I'm not an idiot. I'm not actually going to show up in your room for you to kill me."

"A pity," I said, twisting my sword hilt for good measure. "An astral projection?"

"Something like that," Hellsword said, taking a step back off my blade. "I've been trying to work my way around Serah's barrier for the past few hours and only just now have succeeded. Even so, it's not exactly letting me do much."

The astral projection flickered a bit.

"Serah's improved a great deal since her apprenticeship," Hellsword said, cheerfully. "I assume that's the doing of having unfettered access to the King Below's library. Millennia of necromancers' research, the secrets of the gods, and notes reflecting experiments conducted without concern to morality or law. It must be glorious."

I sheathed my sword and closed the door behind me. "Hardly. Serah spends more of her time correcting the poor mathematics of the books than actually making progress with them. I do, however, fund her research to the limits it can be pressed. She and her assistants are the real geniuses."

"Of course," Hellsword said, smiling. "I understand you are quite the magical engineer yourself, almost as good as Tharadon the Black and Co'Fannon. A pity you murdered those two before they could lead us to an age of unparalleled technological and mystical wonder."

"Yes, well, I was young and foolish. Sorry to deprive you of the opportunity to burn their books and persecute them for heresy."

Hellsword's smile disappeared. "Witty."

"I have the suspicion you're used to being the only one allowed to be an obnoxious ass in the room. But if you'll excuse me, I have to banish your presence from this place."

I started chanting an exorcism and moving my fingers to invoke the energies necessary to drive out his spirit.

"I'm curious if there's anything I can do to make peace between our two nations."

I stopped my enchantment. "You must be joking."

"I never joke about peace. Just because it's always temporary doesn't mean it's not worth pursuing."

"You intended to massacre everyone in the Fire District."

"*Redhand* intended to massacre everyone in the Fire District. I was going to lead to an uprising by the city's nobility and criminals with a giant demon in the center to kill just as many people."

"You'll have to explain the distinction."

"Mine was more directed. Either way, it was all for the greater good."

"I find that hard to believe."

"I'm not in the habit of giving away state secrets but it relates to blood magic as you've no doubt determined. A single city in the Northern Wasteland dies, or at least a large portion of it does, to guarantee millions live."

"By killing us."

"You think highly of yourself," Hellsword said, chuckling. "You and your little nation up north will be wiped out, yes, but the efforts of my experiments here will bring peace to the entirety of the Southern Kingdoms."

"All because of a damned prophecy."

Hellsword walked over to what was certainly a chair in the room he was projecting from and sat down on it. It had the appearance of making him look like he was sitting in midair. He leaned back and waved his hands dismissively. "Morrigan's prophecy is Ethinu's concern, not mine. It may be true, it may not be, but it's proven a useful rallying point. The Oghma obsesses over things like fate and free will, never perhaps suspecting that the reason they're unable to avert it is because individuals like the Lawgiver and his minions are working to make it happen."

I raised an eyebrow. "Jassmaine."

"Amongst others. It has made the Oghma stupid and predictable, which is as good as controlling them outright. A few less players to complicate the Lawgiver's long-term plans for creation. The Trickster's as well."

Guilty, the Trickster said.

I tried not to grit my teeth at that statement. "So the Prophecy of the Black Sun isn't true."

Hellsword pointed at me. "It doesn't matter if it's true. What matters is that it has allowed both of us to become obscenely powerful and direct the course of nations."

"Not all men crave power. Some simply want to help the world."

Hellsword laughed. "Beautiful, Jacob, just beautiful. I think we would have been friends if we'd met under other circumstances."

"I doubt that."

I walked into the middle of the room and looked around. It was a pleasant chamber with a richly appointed bed, flowers in a nearby vase, a table for writing, and a window for looking out onto the streets below. There was a pleasant Fir Bolg minimalism to everything that I would have enjoyed under different circumstances but felt defiled by Hellsword's presence.

"What is your goal, really?" I said, not looking at him but aware of his presence at all times.

"To bring peace to the world. To feed the peasantry. To end war. To have justice not just an indulgence of the rich. We could work together to that end."

I struggled with both my revulsion for him and my desire to believe his sincerity. "You'll forgive me if I doubt your intentions."

"You attacked us first. Or have you forgotten Jon Bloodthorn's murder and the destruction of House Rogers?"

The subject of House Rogers was painful to remember, but didn't convince me either. "You have a generous definition of who attacked whom."

"Do I?" Hellsword said, cocking his head to one side. "You were enslaved for two hundred years and upon awakening, you've butted yourself into every conflict we've been trying to resolve. No one asked you to play the hero. You could have tottered along off to some castle somewhere in the middle of nowhere and been happy but you've been plotting our demise ever since."

"I *did* totter off to a castle in the middle of nowhere. Others have tried to kill me and mine since."

"Have they?" Hellsword narrowed his eyes. "I'm simply saying we know Regina is the one agitating for war. Serah has always been tractable in the past—"

I snorted at his description.

Hellsword paused. "All right, that was stupid of me to say. Reasonable, then. I'm just saying give us a chance. Step back, let us finish our work here, and I can sell the empress a peace treaty between the empire and the Iron Order."

"Despite Bloodthorn's death." Morwen and he had been lovers according to some accounts, close friends to all others.

"Despite. Enough blood has been spilled on both sides."

"Like House Whitetremor."

"Plotting treason against the nation."

"Regina says otherwise."

"Regina was in the Shadowguard a thousand miles away. She had no idea what her uncle was up to."

"Despite the thousands of people you have killed in your labor camps."

"Sacrifices necessary to modernize the primitive disease and famine-ridden lands of less-developed nations. Besides, we aren't working them to death, the majority died because of the summerpox and dysentery. We can't be blamed for outbreaks in lands where those diseases haven't been cured."

"So the poor working conditions are the fault of the people you've conquered."

Hellsword shrugged. "If the armor fits."

I was not persuaded by any of Hellsword's arguments. His glib responses to the massive numbers of atrocities that had occurred underneath Empress Morwen's reign did not reassure me of his good intentions. There was also the fact the Ice Demon had been located in the center of the Fire District for all of his pretensions of having another, more politically motivated, set of targets. There was also the fact—and I had to admit this was a poor excuse for disregarding diplomacy—that I didn't like him. Hellsword oozed smugness. Yet, could I really turn my back on this opportunity?

It was everything I'd hoped for.

"Tell me why you care," I said, deciding to give him a chance to convince me.

"Hmm?"

"You carry a sword containing tortured souls, you murder people by the thousands for your magic, and you are, quite frankly, an evil sonofabitch, so tell me why you care. Why do you claim to fight for peace?" I turned around to look at him, square in the face.

Hellsword looked away. "That is a difficult question."

"Is it?"

Hellsword was silent for a moment then pressed his fingertips together. "Curiosity."

"Excuse me?"

"Evil does not exist. It is a value judgment that varies from person to person. Even the Trickster was only a monster and tormentor of mankind because the Lawgiver asked him to be. Just because I am ruthless, amoral, and prejudiced does not mean I am incapable of feeling or feel some need to go kick random peasants. Even Redhand, who does enjoy peasant-kicking, does so only because of a need to gratify himself via other people's suffering."

"Lovely companion you have."

"Tremendous sense of humor, though," Hellsword said, pinching the bridge of his nose as if he had a headache. "But I said curiosity and I meant it. In Natariss, I was born a prince and was second only to the magistar in social position. However, I never stopped questioning the assumptions of our society. Why did only five percent of our citizens know how to read? Why were we using two hundred-year-old spells when the other kingdoms' magicians were constantly innovating? Why were only magic-users fit to rule and only those of the mage caste allowed to study the mystic arts? Why were the casteless considered vermin unfit for even slave labor? Why were our palaces ruins and why did we retreat closer to our capital every year?"

"Because the Natariss ruling class are a bunch of inbred parasites hated by their subjects?"

"I figured that out fairly early." Hellsword let go of his face and gave a dismissive wave. "I sought the answer to fixing these problems in other nations out of a misguided sense of nationalism. I soon realized that the problems with my nation were its people and there was no point in trying. I sought to become the greatest wizard in history, gain immortality, indulge myself, and other petty goals for decades thereafter. It was during this time Serah became my lover—"

I clenched my right fist.

Hellsword noticed and leered. "But Serah was nothing more than a plaything. An amusement I convinced to fall in love with me before I discarded her. I intended to bring her back only when I felt she might be useful in the Oghma. That all changed, though, when

I met Morwen. She was the one, not Jassamine, who assembled the Nine. Morwen provided the true answer to my questions. Questions I thought had been answered long ago but, in fact, were mere reflections of my own flaws."

"And what were her answers?"

"That, we, the people, weren't fixing the problems. That, we, the Nine, could, ourselves, save the world."

It was a shocking statement, because I believed he was being sincere. I had some experience with being a frustrated idealist who had sought someone to pledge his loyalty to someone worth following, someone who had a vision of how to make the world a better place. That Hellsword might have been the same way was not so strange an idea to me.

It meant the Nine Heroes might not be so different from us. After all, we had done questionable things in the pursuit of a greater good. But then I thought about Whitehall and the massacre here. Those were not the actions of men and women motivated by the greater good. They were the actions of sadists and bigots looking to justify their crimes.

"I have seen your way of fixing things. It does not impress."

Hellsword made a dismissive gesture with his hand. "We are building aqueducts, reservoirs, dams, steel mills, and weather towers to help the people. Many of those who have died building them are the very nobility I once called my brethren. We have beggared the empire to make the changes necessary to build a better tomorrow. There is no caste system in Natariss anymore and I was hoping you, of all people, would understand that such change requires sacrifice."

"What you would call sacrifice, I would call tyranny."

"Says the man who has wiped out traditional Formor culture and forced them all to follow his own path. No more clans, no more wars, no more genocides, or honor killings. Or would you like to know the numbers killed in your wars of conquest?"

"Fourteen thousand, six hundred and twelve. Being a god, I make sure I know *everyone* who dies because of my actions."

"And you dare judge us."

"Yes," I hissed, taking a step forward and drawing my sword again. I held it in front of his astral projection. "*I do.*"

"So there is no chance of peace between us?" Hellsword sounded genuinely remorseful. Was he or was he not trying to play me like a lyre?

I had wanted this or something very much like it for a long time. Since taking over the mantle of the King Below I had hoped for an opportunity to prevent the war between us. A peace envoy from Hellsword after his attempted massacre of the nonhumans here (or Redhand's—it didn't matter which) was terribly convenient but such things were usually made under duress. Regina had said she would accept peace with her enemies if it meant the world was better for it, but could the Nine be trusted? Could Hellsword? I knew the answer. At least enough to give mine.

"I want to believe you. I want to believe we could end this. That you are sincere and this is not just buying for time. But the man who would sacrifice all the men, women, and children in the Nonhuman District—those most desperately in need of protection from the strong—is not a man building a better tomorrow for him. I do not believe your offer Hellsword and tell you to leave my presence and know I am coming for you."

"So be it," Hellsword said, shaking his head. "You know the funny thing, Jacob?"

"What?"

"You're not the Black Sun the prophecy speaks of. Regina is. She is the one destined to destroy the world. Think on the fall of House Rogers. Think of the vengeance she wrought and ask yourself if your wife is the world's savior or its end."

With that, Hellsword vanished.

I spent the next few minutes casting a spell to prevent him from astrally projecting through the barrier again.

I wasn't sure it would work.

But it helped keep me from thinking about Hellsword's words.

I sat on the bed.

And thought of the fall of House Rogers.

CHAPTER TWENTY-EIGHT

The fall of House Rogers was a turning point for us. It all began with the first assassination attempt by Queen Morwen's minions. Three years into our reign in Everfrost, that event conjured powerful images and smells to my mind.

Blood.

Saltwater.

Foulness.

Scented oils.

The profane and sublime together in an unpleasant confusing mixture that assaulted the senses. Walking through the doors to the royal baths past two frightened Formor guards, I took stock of Regina's favorite location in the tower. The baths were a ninety-foot-long chamber with ionic columns decorated in succubi, lascivious damned souls, and satyrs. The walls contained various lewd pornography that, apparently, was the current style of art in the Imperial city, but which was very popular with guests.

A sixty-foot-long heated pool with fountain-mouthed gargoyles was the centerpiece of the room but smaller chambers were all to the sides with their own private baths—often used for debauchery during the days of the old King Below.

Bathing was a popular pastime with Imperials, both in this century and my own, with lewdness and spouse-swapping a common activity during them. This was in addition to their social function as a place for gossip, family bonding, and negotiations. Regina, as a child of the empire, considered all of that perfectly natural and was often surprised by what she considered my 'Fishfolk prudishness.' Oftentimes, she would spend hours up here with her attendants reading over reports and soaking in the waters pumped from the River of Souls below. It was her sanctuary, as the forge was mine, a place to escape the hardships of ruling a nation.

Today, the chamber was an abattoir.

A house of horrors.

Though I had seen worse during wartime, it was still a sight that shocked me. In a way, I was lucky to be in my wraith form, as I otherwise would have become ill. Waving away the two guards who had utterly failed their duties, I looked at the nightmare that greeted me.

Spread throughout the chamber were thirty black-clad bodies that had their necks broken, holes punched through their chests, bisected bodies, and shattered spines. Members of the Elder School, men and women trained from infancy in the arts of murder, they'd been tossed about the place like broken toys. Their blood and what had excreted from their bowels upon death fouled the water, even as the spells designed to keep the pool clean were slowly erasing the worst of it.

There were three other figures in the room: a headless naked woman with bright-red hair lying in two pieces on the stone walkway beside the sixty-foot-long pool, white-skinned man with long black hair and a broken neck lying naked under the heated fouled waters, and Regina still alive at the other end.

Regina was lying in a pool of blood, ichor and gore covering her naked flesh from her head down to the top of her breasts. The expression on her face was blank and unreadable, though I had seen it many times before on soldiers who had endured truly nightmarish circumstances.

In such circumstances, it was wise not to show too much affection, but give them breathing room. Stepping on the hard cobblestones, I looked away from the wide eyes of the deceased red-haired girl and went to the towel closet. Retrieving a pair of white robes, I put one over the decapitated woman's body before returning to Regina and offering her the other robe.

Regina only seemed to notice my presence then. Blinking several times, she rose out of the water, her beautiful body dripping with watery blood, and stepped into the robe before tying it around herself. She ran her fingers through her hair, letting chunks of gore and a severed finger fall to the ground.

I kicked the finger into the pool before she noticed it.

"*I'm sorry*," I whispered, my voice an unearthly rasp.

"Argh!" Regina screamed, spinning around and punching one of the ionic columns. It gave way underneath her newly divine strength, collapsing and causing a chunk of the roof above it to fall. Regina looked at her fist, then down at the thirty bodies, then laughed. It was a bitter, joyless thing.

I kept silent.

Regina walked over to a nearby stone table and sat down on the edge, taking a moment to breathe out. "They tried to kill me. Those bastards tried to kill me."

"Yes," I said, having come here from across half the country using methods I would not recommend.

Serah, by contrast, was busy dealing with an outbreak of the Red Cough and couldn't be brought back. It showed how much she had grown as a person that she chose to stay with the dead and dying wild men than rush back here.

"How?" Regina said.

I slowly took human form, believing she needed the semblance of a living man rather than a dead one. I was used to the pain of the transformation now. "Midori thinks they were brought here by cloaked airship. They bribed some of the Loyalists to the old King Below to let them up here. The garments they wear were enchanted to make them appear as whatever the onlookers expected to see. She is still building a network of informants but recommend we bind elementals and demons to watch the place."

"I want them found," Regina said.

"It is already done. They will die tomorrow."

"I want to swing the sword that cuts off their heads," Regina said, almost shaking with rage...or was it remorse? I couldn't tell.

I nodded.

Regina felt her face then looked over at the body I'd placed a white robe over. "I don't even know her name. One of my attendants for months and yet she was just another face amongst many."

"Nerissa," I said, looking over at her. "A Merrow woman. She liked...painting."

Regina did a double-take. "You knew her?"

"Yes," I said flatly.

I knew half of Regina's attendants and many more of the servants besides. Nerissa had come to serve us after being enslaved by wild men fishermen who gave her to their chief. He'd promptly sent her to us as a gift. I'd been tempted to wipe their village out for it but Nerissa had found that palace life suited her. I wish, instead, she'd gone home back to her family in the oceans. Nerissa had been a dreadful painter, a fabulous singer, and a gentle but kind spirit.

Now she was nothing.

"Did you know her...well?" Regina asked, her implication clear. There was no reproach, but I resented the implications.

"Not very well." I got her implications and wondered at her jealousy. I had only loved two other women in my life and would never love another. "I did, however, like spending time with her. Friendship is a gold coin in a sea of bronze when everyone believes you to be a god king or a monster."

Nerissa had been distressingly normal in a sea of monsters and madman. Albeit, not so normal to run screaming from this place. Her loss was not so great amongst the hundreds I'd experienced in my lifetime.

But it still stung.

"I see." Regina looked away. "They killed them both while I was here, silencing witnesses to their dirty work. Do you know the other one?"

I looked down to the drowned man with white skin. "No."

"We'll find out," Regina said. "Make sure his family, if he has any, want for nothing."

"Of course." I doubted he had any. Everfrost had become a home for those who had no other place to go. It was a kingdom for the lost, damned, and forgotten.

Not so forgotten today, the Trickster said. *Or did you really think you could hide at the Eyes of the World and no one would ever come looking for you?*

No, but I'd hoped.

"Was it Morwen or Jassamine?" Regina asked.

"House Rogers," I said, surprised by that information itself. "Though, truth be told, there was no way it was done without the Nine's approval. It did not take much to get the guards to talk. They always assume I'm going to torture them. They aren't prepared for other methods. Each of them turned on the other when I indicated they'd already been betrayed by a compatriot."

Regina closed her eyes, looking close to tears. "I once admired House Rogers. They were everything a Great House of the Empire should be: stalwart, militant, honorable, and brave. Every one of their sons and daughters served in the Imperial Army or Shadowguard. Their piety was legendary, too, creating three saints in the entirety of its four-age history."

"They also purged all the Fir Bolg in their duchy."

"Yes." Regina growled. "I don't even remember the reason. I think they just needed the money. They used the Golden Arrow's attacks to justify it, even though none had launched any assaults in their territory for a century."

"Perhaps they hoped to curry favor with the empress."

"It doesn't matter, does it?"

"No."

House Rogers had been one of the greats in my time, a collection of shining knights and mighty sorcerers just like Regina described them. The truth was, though, they had also been selfish egotistical bastards who treated their peasantry like fodder. Percivus Rogers had been dubbed by historians as the Shining Sword of Heaven for his role during the Fourth War, and I knew him to be a man who regularly took slave girls from conquered territories before giving them to his men after he was done with them. His sister had been worse. Monster and hero. How many figures of legend were both?

Some? All? I couldn't say.

Regina stood up and stared at the wall of pornography then sighed. "I've been overlooking my duty."

I did not like the tone of her voice. There was resoluteness there that should not be made in this sort of situation. The kind of anger that led to poor decisions. I had made many under similar circumstances. "Your duty is to rule here."

"Our duty is to stop evil," Regina said, looking back. "We've been lax here. Lazy and indulgent."

I shook my head. "I think the word you're looking for is happy."

Regina squeezed her right hand into a fist. "I want to build an army, one capable of destroying the empire and liberating its territories from the empress'scontrol."

"We have an army."

"We have a good-sized one, yes, but there are countless holdouts and loyalists. People who don't acknowledge you as the King Below or me as your equal. Or Serah, for that matter. We must crush them all, make examples of their false faith, and incorporate them as well as their territories into our domiciles."

"That seems an extreme reaction."

Regina's eyes blazed with fire. "There have been attacks, banditry, and even killing of emissaries. Our reprisals have been soft. They are evil. We are good. We must destroy them."

"How will that impact the empire?"

"The empire is *mine*."

I softened my voice, aware being confrontational now was foolhardy. "I understand but we still don't know where Jassamine is or what her plots are. We've thwarted many of the lesser ones and her agents, but do not yet have the forces ready to defeat the empire."

"Then work on them, Great Engineer. Build us an infrastructure of war the likes the Lawgiver and Trickster have never seen."

I should have known reason would not work. "I will go back to my plans and see whether we have created enough new factories to start large-scale production of my modular designs."

"If that means making a host of weapons, armor, and ships, then do so."

"And House Rogers?"

Regina's eyes narrowed and the anger became something cold and unforgiving. In that moment, she'd never looked more like me. "They came to me in my baths and killed my attendants. I didn't know their names, but they trusted us. They trusted us to keep them safe. They were ours, Jacob. Ours. It's just like Whitehall. They took the people we were—"

"Owners of?" I said, uncomfortable with her phraseology.

She shot me a terrible glare.

"Protectors of," Regina corrected. "House Rogers cannot be allowed to get away with this, to believe they can strike at us with impunity. They are a pestilence on the people and a blight on the empire. The house will suffer and suffer well for thinking they can harm the divine."

"We will find out who ordered the attack and they will be killed."

"No," Regina said.

"No?"

"They are a great house with hundreds of members. Cousins, uncles, aunts, brothers, and cadet branches of the house. Just killing a few will not send a message that this"—Regina gestured to Nerissa's fallen form—"will not be tolerated."

I blinked. "You want me to exterminate them."

I would not do that.

I was not a killer of children.

Regina walked up and placed her hand on my chest and gave me a kiss on the lips. Her expression softened and became sympathetic, even sad. "No, Jacob, I would never ask you to do that. You are a gentle heart and I will not see you further drawn into my vengeance than you already are."

I looked at her, confused.

"*I* will do it," Regina said.

She raised her hand to silence me before I could speak.

"Trust me."

And I did.

Arming herself with weapons, armor, and magical devices created in my forge, Regina mounted a winged unicorn and took it on a lone mission into the empire's territory. I did not like leaving her alone to that business, but kept to my promise. She returned a week later, wounded and troubled. She was unwilling to say much more than a few words for a week. One night, though, she broke down crying in my arms and I held her for the rest of the night.

House Rogers was destroyed. Most of the family perishing in one hellish night called the Conflagration where a terrible firestorm wiped out their palace during a great banquet along with dozens of servants. I did not know the details but I suspected Regina had confronted them with their crimes and they'd sought to destroy her. They were, however, a warrior house with many wizards, but a moth might have had a better chance of destroying the sun. Whatever the case, the collateral damage had been terrible, and where once had stood a castle was nothing more than a smoking ruin.

Morwen retaliated by destroying several cults to the King Below I'd never even heard of and launching a lightning raid on

Everfrost. Regina sent its men's heads back in pieces, except for two left unharmed because they'd surrendered. Those we returned.

Morwen had them tortured to death.

Was it any wonder they'd begun their twisted plot in Kerifas against us? Ethinu had said the Lawgiver and Jassamine would never be willing to tolerate us and would gleefully destroy the world to see us dead. However, had the Nine Usurpers always been so committed? Or had the death of Jon Bloodthorn and the destruction of House Rogers, one of Morwen's greatest supporters, set them on the path to a strike against us? Had House Rogers acted alone? Hellsword's words indicated this was the case, but the man lied like other people breathed. That didn't mean there wasn't a kernel of truth to his rebuttal, though, and the Nine were not quite the black-hearted rogues I'd taken them to be.

Then I thought of the children put to the sword in Whitehall at Bloodthorn's orders.

Of Nerissa.

Of Accadia.

Of the dead children here in Kerifas.

And decided I didn't care. If every way was nebulous and black then there was no point in choosing any path but the one I wanted to.

And I wanted to stop them. To make them pay.

Gods help me.

That was when Serah knocked on the door of my room. "Jacob, it's time."

Chapter Twenty-Nine

"You look like you've been raked over the coals," Serah said, walking into my room. "Which is unfortunate since my illusion reflects your emotions."

I looked over at where Hellsword had been sitting. "I've trained for two hundred and fifty years in the arts of war, craftsmanship, engineering, tactics—"

"And a thousand other arts," Serah said, sighing. "You're still a rotten card player, though."

I shot her a dirty look. "You cheat."

"Yes, and the fact you can't catch me is disgraceful. What's really going on?"

There was no point in hiding it. "Hellsword decided to drop by for a visit."

Serah immediately walked back to the door and closed it. She then locked it and returned to stand in front of me. "Gods Above and Below. What did he say?"

I thought back to our meeting, banishing all thoughts of House Rogers. "He wanted to offer us a peace treaty."

Serah sat down beside me on the bed. "What did you say?"

"No."

Serah was silent for a long time. "All right then."

"Is that you have to say?"

Serah took a deep breath. "Is there anything else you want me to say?"

"No, I suppose not. He did reveal he didn't believe in Morrigan's prophecy any more than I did, however, and all the forced labor the empire is using is designed to do the same thing I've been doing in the empire—modernize the infrastructure. It's not part of some secret plot against us or in preparation for the prophecy."

"Unfortunate."

"Unfortunate?" I asked.

"Our centralized economy and industrialization of the North was our biggest advantage. We'll never be able to keep up with a modernized South. The King Below was a genius at strategy but his grasp of logistics was abyssal."

"That's actually the opposite of being a genius at strategy."

I never wanted to win, the Trickster said, *just fight.*

I didn't disagree with Serah's assessment of the situation, though. I'd learned quite a bit of magic from Serah, sharpening my knowledge of the subject even though I had centuries on her in practice, while she'd learned a great deal about matters of war. Neither of us were as good as Regina, though, who was a master of the subject.

All three of us knew we were badly outmatched in any war against the South. Time favored the Nine Usurpers rather than us. Our advantage was never likely to be greater than now, with the infrastructure I'd erected, another reason why Serah had probably advised me to attack immediately. The discovery that the Nine had been prepping themselves removed one of our chief advantages.

"It still means a conventional war will be unwinnable," Serah said, shaking her head. "Even if we manage to take Winterholme."

"I'm not so sure it would be a conventional war."

"What do you mean?"

I remembered my terrible vision and coupled it together with Hellsword's allusions. "During the Fourth War, I used Tharadon and Co'Fannon's notes to create the Terrible Weapons with the empire's other best mages. They laid waste to much of the King Below's forces, but also inflicted unimaginable collateral damage."

"Those were destroyed after the war."

"Good."

"But it may be they hope to repeat your triumph here."

I followed her meaning. "Using a mass human sacrifice to destroy our followers…"

It made sense now what they were hoping to accomplish here in Kerifas. During the Fourth War, I had managed to bring the King Below's forces to their knees with my devices. The aftermath of their use had been horrific—sickness, famine, devastation, and worse. They had been effective, though, and the King Below's forces had never truly recovered.

So much so that when the Fifth War was launched, the Nine Heroes had been able to rally the Southern Kingdoms to defeat the King Below within a single year. If they believed I had learned from the old god's mistakes, it was understandable they might want to create their own Terrible Weapons.

Or revive some of the lost ones of old.

"It has a twisted sort of genius."

I didn't disagree with either part of her statement. "Certainly it changes the nature of our conflict. Which is exactly what you do when you can't win a conventional war. The empire could defeat us with a modernized army invading the North, even if the weather was against them, though it would cost them horribly. That would divide the empire, though, if they do not sufficient cause to attack us. If they lose too many soldiers, they'd lose their fragile peace and their empire quickly."

It was all starting to make sense now. There was no need for a prophecy or the hidden hand of the Lawgiver when common politics and economics were every bit the explanation for most of the the Nine's actions.

Serah nodded. "They need to defeat us quickly. If it can annihilate us in a suitably public manner, all the lands comprising the empire will be cowed and their position would be secured. The empress would have absolute dominion over all of the Southern Kingdoms and no one to challenge her reforms."

I now understood why Hellsword had come to visit me. Even he did not want to unleash the kind of power we were discussing. I had foolishly missed that implication. "We can't let Hellsword finish whatever he's doing here. We need to find out whatever project he's working on and destroy it. We also need to make sure he and whoever he's collaborated with can't replicate it. Otherwise, a new and terrible age of warfare will begin."

"And if we have the opportunity to turn it against our enemies? To eradicate them outright?"

I stared down at my hands. "I swore I would never use the Terrible Weapons again. Also, if we deploy such devices, we might win the war, but we'd be forced to fight the rest of the world until we either conquered them or were destroyed."

"The option to leave this world is still on the table."

"No it's not."

Serah was silent.

"Did I ever tell you the story of how I ended up with Warmaster Kalian?"

"Some of it. You glossed over a lot of details."

I paused, thinking back to that time. It had been the springtime and I could still smell the fresh flowers growing on the side of the riverbank. My hometown of Joy had been built on the banks of the River Sandu like so many others of our kind, each home built upon stilts so they would not be flooded during high rain. Each and every man, woman, and even child wore only black in honor of the Great Mother. Each member of the Fisherfolk followed the Path in such a way as to abstain from violence as well as personal gain.

We worked together for the benefit of the group, owned no property, and made decisions without the benefit of a king through mutual acclaim. We were not a subdued people, the mouth of every Fisherfolk was as filthy as a pig sty, but we were peaceful and happy with rare exceptions. I could have lost myself in those memories but forced them down. "A conflict was brewing between a fort erected by an exiled Tyrash nobleman and the Indras, who were doing their best to build a colony nearby."

"Back then you were still part of the Borderlands, weren't you?"

"Do those still exist?"

"A hundred and more petty kingdoms and principalities between G'Tay, the Southern Kingdoms, and Indras. Yes, not even the empire has decided to annex the entirety of the Easterlands yet."

I made a note of that. "Either way, the baron recruited a host of Rolant mercenaries to aid him in protecting his pitiful attempt at building his own demesne. He quartered them in our village rather than trying to feed them himself."

"A band of drunken murderous mercenaries in a village of pacifists? That...must have been unfortunate."

I thought back to that time. "Not as bad as it could have been, honestly. The Rolent are an honorable group of people. Everything the empire knows of chivalry comes from their influence. They were disciplined and it helped that while we didn't have harlots or bedmen, we had plenty of alcohol and food that we shared eagerly. Incidents were few. They were more annoyed that no one wanted to join their band, I think."

I'd hated them despite it. I'd dreamed of finding a life outside the Riverfords, but I'd despised the soldiers who took everything while giving nothing in return.

"You killed one of these soldiers didn't you?" Serah asked.

"Yes," I said. "It wasn't an act of self-defense or justice. He was a deserter because there was a battle coming up between the baron and a group of Indras mercenaries. A battle the perfumed scum thought was beneath a minor lord's bastard. I found him in the barn stealing food and he said he wanted to ask my sister Chastity to run away with him in exchange for getting her out of the dunghole of our home."

"To be his wife?"

"Considerably less romantic."

"Ah."

"They might have been lovers but I ended up sticking him." I remembered the blood, the look of sickness in his eyes, and the fact that he emptied his bowels before falling over. I hadn't intended to kill him, but I'd just been so angry and stabbing him with the pitchfork had been so easy.

"I'm afraid I don't see how this relates."

"Sometimes we think our enemies are evil when they're really just people we hate."

"What about the Nine?"

"I don't know but either way, I'm going to kill those bastards. I'm not letting them get away."

Serah nodded. "That I understand."

I sensed Ketra's presence behind the door, her life force both vibrant as well as troubled. I was still developing my ability to distinguish different kinds of emotions based on one's energy but Ketra's was similar enough to Regina that I recognized she needed to talk. "Where am I supposed to go to make our army of monsters?"

"There's a smuggling tunnel to the inn's cellar here for goods forbidden to the Fir Bolg or taxed heavily. We've knocked out a wall to make the entrance larger in case we need to evacuate. Regina is already down there."

"I'll meet you there."

Serah narrowed her eyes, opened her mouth to speak, then closed it. "As you wish." Serah proceeded to the door, opened it, saw Ketra standing there about to knock, then walked past her without a word.

Ketra as rubbing the side of her face, perhaps wondering if it was such a good thing to keep her scars. I knew that was only a symbol of her disquiet, though. The actual source was far deeper, something I couldn't put words to because I didn't know her. I knew her from Regina's descriptions but there was no worse person to get an accurate description of a person from than a relative. My own interactions with her had been sporadic at best.

Does anyone truly know anyone else or do we just deal with the masks people wear? the Trickster asked. It was a surprisingly insightful statement.

I'm always insightful. It's because I expect the worst from everyone.

"Hello, Ketra. Please come in."

The young woman walked in and took a seat on the bed. "I was curious if I could talk to you, Your Majesty."

"Jacob is fine."

Ketra was using a term of respect to speak with me, which surprised me given how ardently anti-noble she was.

"I wanted to get some, uh, spiritual advice."

"First, Ketra, you're an atheist. Second, I'm the God of Evil. Third, I was a terrible person in life."

"Regina said you always tried to do the right thing in life." Ketra, pointedly, ignored the first two points.

"That was what made me a terrible person. If I had been a bit greedier and less determined to make the world a better place, I would have done far less damage to the world in the long run."

I tried not to think of the endless field of corpses that had followed the unleashing of the Killing Cloud. How the gas turned every plant it touched into a brittle white thing that crumbled at a touch.

"You ended slavery," Ketra said, her voice almost pleading. "Is there no point to wanting to change the world for a better?"

"Slavery still exists." I looked down. "But I think, yes, there is a point to wanting to change the world. However, I believe you should always be mindful of the consequences of your actions. It is easy to look to the sky and the banners of the righteous flying above to disguise the corpses at your feet. To forget those who disagree with your paradise are not evil."

"You are a very wise man."

"No, a very stupid one since I know this and am still stumbling forward to fight the Nine and their minions." I sat down beside Ketra. "What brought about this spiritual crisis?"

Ketra looked ill. "I saw the battle with the Ice Demon, a creature straight out of mythology battling against three heroes who banished it to protect the innocent. I listened to Regina's words down at the inn and how they spoke to me. You really are Jacob Riverson and the King Below. I...don't know how to deal with that."

"God is just a title mortals bestow upon those who are more powerful than themselves or those whom they wish to revere. We do not like to talk about it but there are many gods worshiped in other lands, places we call heathen but speak of fire gods, ocean goddesses, and beings that live in all objects. Others revere dead saints and philosophers."

"Are you saying you're a god or not?"

I looked up. "The King Below and the King Above are both men of a long-dead planet called Earth. The Trickster's journals speak of such things in Everfrost's libraries. The men of Earth created this world and many others to amuse themselves after they developed the power to alter reality with thought. They made heaven, hell, and many other planes. The fact that they were born of technology makes them no less gods, nor does the fact that they ruled over afterlives make them more so. In the end, the choice is yours, not mine."

Ketra looked at me. "I think you're the kind of god I would worship if I did worship anything, but I'd rather everyone become a god than have one ruling over us forever."

"Sounds like a good faith. Better than the aforementioned stupid god out to pick a fight."

"They picked it first."

"It doesn't matter in the long run. Still, I'm going to try to finish it."

"Good." Ketra sighed. "I don't know what to do now."

"Was your cause so tied up in the fact the gods were false?"

"I grew up being told the nobility ruled by divine right and that the Lawgiver wanted the world to be this way. That everything had a place and every event was part of his plan."

I snorted. "That part, at least, I can assure you is bullshit."

"Again, good." Ketra smiled. "I can deal with the world being a terrible and awful place but I can't deal with it all being that because the King Above said it should be."

"It might be true. He's a real ass."

Ketra laughed, unaware I was speaking literally.

That was when I figured out the secret of the Prophecy of the Black Sun.

Son of a bitch! I gave Ketra a hug and a kiss then headed down to the sewers to talk with Serah.

You should take Kana and Ketra as concubines, the Trickster said. *They'll give you strong children.*

Silence. I do not have time for your lunacy.

There's always time for lunacy!

CHAPTER THIRTY

The smuggler's tunnel under the inn connected with the city's sewer system, having large eight-foot-tall tunnels that stretched under the entirety of Kerifas. They were the perfect means for invading during low tide, as it was now, but we'd managed to place our barrier spells down here as well as above.

It was here Serah was standing. She was wearing a pair of rubber boots up to her thighs and had tied her robe around her waist with belts. She had a light cloth mask tied around her face to hold back the worst of the smell. It was a ridiculous look for an archmage but prevented her from having to endure the worst of the slime and the muck, which reached up to my ankles.

I'd endured worse, though.

Regina was present in the room, wearing her armor of light and unperturbed by the disgusting mire about us. There were several crates of goods the Fir Bolg had been trying to smuggle in today, but they were of little import compared to the hundreds of corpses stretched out beyond Serah and Regina. The Fir Bolg, boggans, dryads, and other residents of the Nonhuman Quarter were absent, but almost all the Burning Blade soldiers killed in the battle were present.

Fodder for reanimation.

I couldn't help but wonder what the people thought of our plan or whether Serah had kept that part of the plan hidden. Necromancy was forbidden as the vilest sort of magic across the Southern Kingdoms, but still managed to find footholds in lands desperate to save themselves from destruction or places where the clergy was more flexible like Natariss. I, myself, hated doing it, but bringing the dead back to life as weapons was one of the singularly most effective tools I had in my arsenal. I, who believed the dead should rest in peace, was the grandmaster of creating monsters.

But none of that was important now.

Climbing down the ladder from the inn storeroom and jumping down into the muck, I said, "The Prophecy of the Black Sun is bullshit."

I had no idea why the prophecy's truth weighed chiefly in my thoughts despite the fact we were in the middle of a siege yet weighed it did. In the back of my mind, it gnawed at my confidence and left me wondering if the war we were waging had been doomed from the start. Talking to Ketra, though, it had been like someone lighting a torch in the darkness. Everything was clear now and I felt more pissed off than anything else. I had been played like a fool and needed to share my revelation with those I cherished most.

Not that Regina had any idea what I was talking about. "Excuse me? What prophecy?"

Serah frowned at me. "This is hardly the time, Jacob."

I stood in front of them, clasping my hands together. "There is a thousand-year-old prophecy preserved by the most powerful wizards in the world—Serah is one of them—that predicts the death of the King Below and the rise of a new god who will destroy the world."

Regina's eyes widened. "You…what now?"

"Jacob," Serah sighed, feeling her face. "What are you doing? We need you to focus on the mission."

"We need to focus on this. The Prophecy of the Black Sun doesn't work like any other divination I know. All of those merely predict most likely events and possible outcomes. It's the equivalent of staring up at the sky and saying the sun will most likely rise tomorrow. It's a matter of probabilities and analysis rather than anything else. This prophecy doesn't work like that, though, and seems infallible."

"Gods Above," Regina said, accidentally invoking our enemy. "We're doomed by fate?"

"No," I said, shaking a fist. "It is a trick."

Serah sighed. "We've considered that, Jacob, but there's no way anyone could fake all the events the prophecy successfully predicted. It would require the King Above and the King Below to be working together."

"But that's just it, *they were all along.*"

Serah's eyes widened. "By the gods, how did I not see."

I shook my head and continued. "The two have continually set mortals against each other. The Lawgiver and the Trickster abandoned the other gods to make this world. They murdered the Gods Between. They marshalled the Lightborn and the Shadowborn races against each other repeatedly. Why not create a prophecy that predicts the end of the world to keep the most powerful wizards and minds occupied for millennia. It's another level of control, depending on the idea some people will question everything unless they feel like they have secret knowledge. Ethinu and the Oghma are puppets to the will of the two gods."

"You kept this from me?" Regina said, turning to Serah. "More secrets."

Serah looked down.

"Forgive her. She has been tormented with her knowledge of this for years," I said, defending her. "Serah came to me just yesterday in hopes of revealing the truth."

"You should have told me," Regina snapped. "The Oghma's secrets should have been revealed the first day of our marriage."

Serah didn't deny it. "You're right."

That left Regina deflated. Looking around, she shook her head. "This is not the time for arguments. Even if what you're saying is true, how could you prove it?"

"It would also require the Trickster to be complicit in his own death."

"I'm not sure he's dead, to be honest."

That revelation went over like a hog tossed into a ballroom. Both Serah and Regina looked at me like I was mad. Of course, they had only the barest inklings the Trickster had tormented my mind with taunts, jibs, and gibes for the better part of five years. That the Trickster had been the one to release his control on my mind only near Regina was a sign I'd been his pawn all along—even my falling in love with her. The Trickster, notably, was silent during this conversation.

Serah stared at me as if I was talking gibberish and I could understand her feelings. After all, this was a theory with no evidence. Yet, I knew the Trickster from his constant torments and taunts. I knew the Lawgiver from the way Jassamine behaved and acted. I understood these two gods, perhaps better than any mortal, and how everything fit together.

"For the love of all things holy, why?" Serah said, finally getting to why I believed my theory to be true. "Why set up all these conflicts? Why kill the King Below to the public just to raise up another?"

"Meaning," I explained, "they want to give mortals' lives meaning."

"Meaning," Regina said, her voice carrying a hint she was starting to understand my point. She, as a woman who had crusaded her entire life for the righteous, would comprehend my next words better than Serah.

Words escaped from my mouth as soon I thought them. "The original Earth that the Old Humans evolved on has been cinders for eons, its sun having long since gone through its helium flash. Humans had discovered how to turn thought into reality long before then, though. We had learned to live forever and forge our own worlds via will."

"Magic," Regina said.

"If you like. For those individuals who could satisfy every desire with a snap of their fingers, it became an eternity of boredom and listlessness. They created worlds from their imaginations to serve as reflections to ourselves, gaining joy and bitterness through our feelings."

"We're fucking *pets*?" Regina practically choked on the last word.

"Or game pieces or children or, simply put, subjects. Each god treats his followers differently. For me, I felt the responsibility I had to my creations was an immense one so I had to give them the greatest gift I could possibly give, which ties back to my original statement."

"Meaning," Regina said. "Meaning is the gift you gave them."

"How do you know this?" Serah asked. "I admit, there's a certain appeal."

"You haven't had the Trickster in your head for five years."

You're right, the Trickster said. *Though not entirely.*

Dammit, I cursed. *You are alive.*

No, the Trickster said. *I am as dead as a god can be. I chose to merge with you, Jacob. My consciousness is replaced with yours, but my unconscious is still managing all the wonderful subroutines and programs that manage the World Below as well as my countless avatars. When you're an immortal, you learn the awakened mind is really just one part of a larger identity and easily replaced. Your grandfather's axe that has had its handle replaced and its blade is still the same axe.*

I have no idea what you're saying.

You will. I had a billion years to get used to being a god. You're still new at this. To make it simple, I am you and you are me and we are altogether one.

What is your game now? Explain. I want the truth now.

As if my telling you now is any more likely to give you the answers you seek. Still, you have earned an explanation, even if it is not the explanation.

Tell me.

Every human being, or elf, or dwarf—

I had no idea what a dwarf was. Did he mean boggans?

—should be able to enjoy the security of being able to fight for a cause they believe in. To have the comfort of having struggled against true evil and the satisfaction of knowing you have not fallen prey to it. That is why I had my brother play the role of the King Above and made my assortment of monsters to torment his followers.

I was sickened by these facts. *And what of the Formor and others who play the role of the villain in your grand design?*

The Trickster showed no remorse. *They have the satisfaction of being doomed moral victors. They know they are persecuted, hated, and loathed for no reason other than being hideous to be behold. They suffer and draw strength from their martyrdom as well as each blow they strike at what seems to be an invincible enemy. I ruled them absolutely and gave them nothing but the satisfaction of strength in the face of adversity.*

Anger replaced my horror. *How awful it must have been for you when I liberated the Shadowkind and offered them a new way.*

I could feel the Trickster smile in the back of my head. *I already knew what you were going to do, Jacob. You were chosen to replace me precisely because I had grown weary of the endless struggle. It did not take a genius to figure out you would attempt to save the Shadowkind. You have a fondness for lost causes, sad and broken things. It's why I picked you. Now my creations rally behind you and your wives.*

"Gods Above and Below," Regina said.

"You can hear him?" I didn't bother to disguise my shock.

They could always hear me, the Trickster said. *Just not when I was speaking to you, or did you just assume I was only in your mind?*

I wanted to reach into my skull and rip out the cursed spirit before strangling him. We'd been played for fools this entire time and had danced to a waltz designed by our enemies step-by-step. "I do not understand why they have set us up this final battle between good and evil, but I have my suspicions. For whatever reason, they no longer desire the Shadowkind and the Lightborn to wage war. So, this will be the final struggle between them."

Serah's eyes widened as she covered her mouth. "The Nine Heroes will gather together all of the nations under a single throne and make progress using tyrannical methods. We, however, will gather all their enemies together under our banner. Whoever wins the war will have completely destroyed their enemies and have total dominion over the world with no one to oppose them."

Close, not quite, but close, the Trickster whispered. *Philosophers of Old Earth called it the Philosophical Dialectic. Two opposite and antagonistic viewpoints smash together to form something newer and stronger. The White Sun, Morwen, on one side, and the Black Sun, Regina, on the other. No matter which side prevails, there will be an idealistic warrior queen to guide the world into a new tomorrow.*

"Why now?" Serah asked.

"We could ask whys forever," Regina said, shaking her head. "Perhaps they simply got bored. It doesn't matter, though."

"It doesn't?" Serah said.

"Jacob's habit of questioning everything and rebelling against authority has revealed one more layer of control to the Lawgiver and his minions. We must break the gameboard and seek a true freedom for ourselves as well as that of mankind—but it does not change that, right now, every man, woman, and child in Kerifas is counting on us. If we do not defeat Hellsword and Redhand, then they will sacrifice the city to perform some ritual to destroy us all." Regina withdrew her sword and gestured with it down the tunnels to our enemy.

"Ironically, bringing the Prophecy of the Black Sun to truth, at least in part." I understood Regina's reasoning but I didn't like it.

It was to the credit of the Lawgiver and Trickster that they'd chosen such doggedly independent as well as foolishly bull-headed champions. I could try and share this information with Hellsword and Redhand but I doubted either of them would believe me. They were as set on their course for conflict as I was with them—both of us seeing an oncoming carriage crash but unable to do the slightest thing about it.

I did have to admire the fact the Lawgiver predicted the two sides would annihilate one another with advanced magical weapons. I had used the Terrible Weapons during the Fourth Great Shadow War to great effect but the human cost of such things was beyond belief. By giving a warning of the consequences, the Lawgiver had potentially curtailed development or set his puppets into sabotaging their use. That, at least, was one area he'd failed to control adequately. Hellsword and Redhand's ritual was every bit as terrible as the weapons I'd used and then some.

It's a good thing we have you, then, the Trickster said. *Enjoy your newfound wisdom, Jacob. If you, Regina, and Serah die here then the Nine Heroes will reign a thousand years over a land of paradise and order. Take comfort from that.*

"So we just go along with our pre-ordained roles?" Serah said, crossing her arms. I noticed her staff was leaning up against the wall, half submerged in gunk. "I cannot be the only one who has a problem with this."

I stared down at the corpses and thought about my answer. "Good and evil are just directions. One man's hero is another man's villain. Yet, if I cannot protect everyone, then I will surely attempt to protect those I love. I will oppose all those who seek to harm them, be they gods in the sky, kings of the Earth, or thugs on the street. I no longer care whether this makes me right or wrong, I only care that it works. The Nine are pawns in this, but we're going to be making our own moves from now on."

I stretched out my hand and drew on all the accumulated necromantic energy spread throughout the city. It was a large amount, perhaps as much as the reservoir Hellsword had gathered, but old and difficult to access. People had died here for thousands of years, often in terrible ways during the Five Great Shadow Wars.

Drawing on that power, I mentally reached into each of the corpses and awakened them. I funneled into their bodies my anger, despair, malice, and hope for a tomorrow where they would not be necessary. The bodies rose up, hundreds and eventually thousands strong, each of them carrying only the barest whisper of who they were.

I was no petty cultist or blood magician, though. Each of the soldiers re-attached missing limbs, repaired battle damage to their bodies, and retained a full working knowledge of both tactics as well as weapons knowledge.

They just lacked souls.

Turning to me, I saw each of them stare with cold, dead eyes.

I pointed down the sewers. "Make a distraction for us. Kill as many of the army above as you can."

"Gods help us," Regina said.

"We're the only gods providing help," Serah said, getting her staff. "I'll make sure the Nonhuman Quarter survives until you return."

If you return, the Trickster said. *Hellsword is ready to use his weapon against you.*

Chapter Thirty-One

Regina and I traveled through the dark, cold, and filthy tunnels of Kerifas. The ocean tides washed away the majority of the foulness every morning but new filth was always flowing in. Hellsword and Redhand's agents were pounding against the barrier down here as well as above but they were swiftly overwhelmed by the horde of undead I sent ahead of us. Above our heads, I could feel the monsters rising through maintenance holes and toilets to attack the Imperial forces en masse.

There was no hope for the undead army to defeat our foes. A single dragon could eradicate the whole of them but they would hopefully hesitate to roast their own troopers alive long enough to avoid such a measure. The fact it would also potentially start a fire throughout Kerifas was something I hoped would also deter them, but they'd been willing to turn the city into an abattoir, so I wasn't betting on it.

Regina lifted a glowing *Starlight* ahead of her as we pressed forward to the Palace District. It provided slightly more light than a torch and gave us a good view of the tunnels' maze-like interior. *Starlight*'s illumination was also visible only to Regina and those she willed to see it.

Regina needn't have bothered on my behalf; the darkness was as clear as day to my undead eyes. Regina had also cast a minor spell that resulted in our voices not carrying beyond our immediate vicinity, another wise precaution to preserve our stealthy approach. Her skill with sorcery had been abyssal when I'd first married her, practically nonexistent except for the few cantrips all Shadowguard knew for surviving in the wilderness, but she'd shown a remarked improvement in recent months. Almost unnaturally so.

"I'm glad you came to a decision about this fight, Jacob."

"I have something worth fighting for, I always did. I just had to come to terms with that fact." We would figure out a way to liberate the world from the Lawgiver and Trickster's tyranny. That was worth going to war for—I had to believe that.

Just keep lying to yourself, the Trickster said. *You're good at it.*

That I am.

"I'm not sure whether or not to be insulted you didn't think you had something worth fighting for before."

I snorted. "That's not what I meant. You were always worth fighting for, you and Serah. I just have seen enough of war to last a lifetime."

Regina stared forward. "You know, whenever you talk about war, I feel like a fraud."

"What?"

"I was born in the Northern Wasteland, like so many of the Shadowkind I was raised to kill. Joining the Shadowguard was considered the last, best opportunity for young noblemen seeking adventure and my father was one of them. My mother had been a crofter's daughter but she was a low sidhe and that made her worthy as a spouse for a nobleman."

"I will never understand the fascination rich humans have with elves."

"They live for centuries, look beautiful, and have an inborn facility with magic?"

"Well, put in those terms—"

Regina sighed. "I grew up in a drafty fortress not too dissimilar to Caer Callig. Thugs, murderers, rapists, thieves, pickpockets, and every single one of them would have defended me with their life. You'd think a child would have been vulnerable in such company, but they were my family."

"This doesn't make me think you're a fraud, Regina."

"I wasn't...then. My father raised me with the values of Whitetremor. Honor, pride, and sacrifice. We were the descendants of Eric the Great's second son and a lineage of heroes who protected the weak as well as defended the poor."

I grimaced. "I—"

"You knew Eric personally as a complete fool who was nothing more than Jassamine's puppet. He also crushed Fireforge's kings and converted them by the sword, which makes him a fool, puppet, and monster. It sickens me to know I have his blood."

"He had an excellent singing voice," I offered. "So there's that."

Regina snorted. "When my parents were killed and the castle overwhelmed, the Formor let us retreat back to the empire. There, I joined my uncle's family in Whitehall and I was exposed to the grandeur of what being a noble was really like. Singing, dancing, embroidery, gossip, music, and learning to use what fork with which plate."

"You start with the one on the end and work your way in."

Regina rolled her eyes. "You could have saved me so much trouble telling me that as a child. I hated learning things like that. Gewain and Ketra made life just barely tolerable, but this wasn't the life the stories promised. We were a line of heroes, and yet we spent our time resolving petty disputes of peasants as well as hosting balls."

"Which is the life of the noble, last time I checked."

"Yeah," Regina said. "I rejoined the Shadowguard when I was twenty-one. They assigned me to administration."

"Administration?"

"My home, Caer Tythol, had been the last castle in the North. The Shadowguard was now as much an ornament as anything else. I wanted to be a hero and I ended up being just another painted noble with delusions of grandeur. When the Nine destroyed the King Below, it was like fate had cheated me out of the destiny I felt was mine. The Fifth Great Shadow War and I didn't even get anywhere near the front lines. Then…Whitehall fell and you came into my life, a legendary hero and a soldier and…I wanted to be you."

"Gods," I said, faking horror. "What is wrong with you?"

"Stop it, don't make me laugh. The thing is, I was not a soldier and I don't know what starting a war is like—but I knew I wanted to stop the Nine. I just worry, sometimes, that I'm pretending to be a hero instead of actually trying to be one."

"Oh Regina, that's all any of us can do."

"I know that now." Regina stared, all mirth gone from her face. "I'm not playing at war anymore."

There was nothing more to say.

Regina and I continued onward into the darkness. I could feel the magic running through the tunnels of the city, capturing all the death and destruction above our heads. I saw several glyphs carved into the walls and briefly considered destroying them.

That would do little to affect the larger spell, though, and I suspected thousands of them were carved throughout the city. Instead, I memorized each of the glyphs I encountered and pondered how the magic worked. It was being prepared for something, I could tell that, which meant we were running out of time.

Whether we had hours or minutes, though, I couldn't tell.

"Do you ever wonder about the other gods, Jacob?"

"Other gods?"

"The Trickster was the only God Below and all of the others were just masks for him, but what about the Gods Above? In addition to the Lawgiver, there was the Great Mother, the Weaver, and the Peacebringer. We haven't heard anything about them."

"What brings this up?"

"Just trying to figure out a way to win this without fighting."

"Now you sound like a leader."

"Not yet, but I'm trying. I also know we've got plenty of fighting left. The Great Mother was one of the Gods Between, wasn't she?"

"Yes. She helped the Lawgiver destroy her fellow gods and took place as the Lawgiver's consort." At least according to the Codex. I was starting to consider that book as trustworthy as the official Imperial histories that depicted the emperors as an unbroken line of civilized champions of justice.

"Do you think we should try and talk with them?" Regina asked, shaking me from my thoughts.

"The other Gods Above?" I paused, contemplating that. "That's... an odd suggestion."

"Is it? Perhaps the Gods Between can be restored to life too."

"How do you figure?" I asked.

"The Trickster isn't exactly leaving us alone either. The enemy of my enemy is my friend."

"And I thought you were the idealistic one."

"I'm still a strategist. Anyway, I was thinking about this because of our own family issues. You shouldn't have kept the prophecy from me."

"You're right, I shouldn't have," I admitted.

Regina shook her head. "But despite this, I want to have a family with you and Serah after this is over. I think…I think the only reason we couldn't was because I wasn't ready. I wanted to get my revenge on the Nine Heroes first."

That was a too-easy-sounding solution. "And now?"

"Now I have more people to hate and kill. Which is no excuse to stop living."

"I suppose that is the case." I paused. "Do you still hate the Nine?"

"I don't want to, but I saw a lot of dead children above."

"Children die in war no matter how much you don't want them to."

"Kill me if I become someone who does that."

"I could never harm you but you aren't that kind of person."

"And you are?"

"Not as long as you're there for me."

Regina paused again and turned around to embrace me, putting her sword up against my back as she pressed her lips against mine.

I kissed her back.

"I love you," Regina whispered.

"I love you too."

Our embrace was interrupted by a man clearing his throat. "Ahem."

"What the hells?" I said, pulling away from Regina.

Down the tunnel, coming from an intersection was, of all people, Rose. He was holding a lantern in one hand and behind him was a small collection of nonhuman children, husbands, and wives.

"You!" I said, stunned.

"Uh, hello, Lord Jacob," Rose said, looking somewhat embarrassed. "Queen Regina."

Regina turned around and looked surprised. "Hello, Rose, I'm glad to see you're still alive. I thought you'd died battling the Ice Demon."

"No, he survived." I glared at Rose. "But I thought you'd decided *to do something else.*"

Rose looked back to the civilians behind him. "Well, after our conversation, I thought about my situation and the merits of a good cause."

"Good cause," I repeated.

"Is there an echo here? Yeah," Rose said, smiling.

I frowned.

His smile disappeared. "If a man isn't doing something good with his life, then he isn't doing anything worthwhile at all. So I decided to use my skills at spycraft to see if I could smuggle as many children from the Nonhuman Quarter as possible."

"And Serah let you do this?"

Rose frowned. "She seemed more annoyed with you than anything else."

I felt my face. "I see."

I was going to catch hells for that.

"You didn't think to smuggle everyone?" Regina asked, surprising me with her priorities.

"The others have faith in you," Rose said. "Both of you. More than they ever had in Gewain. They don't want to risk their children, though."

I stared at Rose, trying to gauge his sincerity. I was surprised to realize I believed him. Not only was he simply attempting to do something to help the helpless but he was doing so because I'd inspired him to do so. It had been such a long time since I'd seen something done unambiguously good that I was momentarily at a loss for words.

"We are venturing to the Palace District to defeat Hellsword and Redhand as well as liberate the city," Regina said without a trace of irony. "Your actions to preserve the lives of the innocent are not necessary but I appreciate the thought. It's men like you who are going to help build a better tomorrow."

Rose looked at her then me then back at her. "You remind me a lot of Gewain. He talked that way too."

"We're getting him back," Regina said confidently.

Rose paused, a look of deep regret passing across his face. "When you catch up with him, please pass along my regrets and my hopes for the future."

"I will," Regina said. "Gods' blessings upon you."

"You would know."

Rose and his ramshackle crew walked away from us and I soon found the tunnel system that led directly to the Palace District.

There were guards posted around the entrances and several places containing grates but none of them were difficult to deal with. Regina even showed considerable foresight by letting me check for alarm wards and barriers to keep intruders from passing underneath. Either way, we were soon in front of a wall that I believed would take us directly into the Governor's Palace basement.

I was about to smash through the wall when Regina put her hand on my shoulder. "So you spared Rose's life?"

I looked up. "What?"

"He's a spy for the Imperials," Regina said.

"You figured that out, huh?"

"It wasn't that hard. The whole planned uprising required them to have an insider, and the lover of the leader is a traditional one." Regina chewed her lip. "I noticed all the discrepancies in his story as well. I figured only he could have arranged for the trap for not only Ketra but the nobility we met with."

I nodded. It was much the same as the way I'd figured out the truth. "I went to confront him after the Ice Demon. He admitted to all the actions you just mentioned and more. He wanted to die, I think. The sight of what his masters were capable of broke something inside him."

"You did the right thing."

"I did?" I hadn't expected Regina to agree, given Rose's betrayal of her cousins.

"The only people who need to die are Hellsword and Redhand."

I wasn't sure it would be that easy. "Let's hope."

"Now let's say hello to the bastards."

Regina sheathed her sword before stepping in front of a large, plain brick wall. Clenching a fist, she took a deep breath and slammed it against the stone. The stone crumbled before her like a child's building blocks.

CHAPTER THIRTY-TWO

Regina punched through the side of the stone masonry separating the sewers from the cellar of the Governor's Palace. It required a couple of kicks to create a hole large enough to pass through, but her strikes were stronger than the hardest hammer blows.

"I'm still getting used to that," I said, passing through into an expansive ninety-foot-long chamber filled with casks of wine, mead, and other spirits. If nothing else, the governor and his masters were well stocked for parties. "The powers of a god are amazing. I don't have that kind of strength, not even with magic."

"I'm still not sure why you don't have it," Regina said, stepping in after me. "Shouldn't we be able to, I dunno, snap our fingers and change reality? That's what being a god means, isn't it?"

"The Old Humans altered the nature of reality to bend to their will like a child finger-painting. We don't possess that kind of power."

"Yet," Regina said, smiling.

"Yet."

The wine cellar was absent any servants and there were no signs it had seen much use the past few months. I was surprised by this, since one would think Hellsword and Redhand would have been enjoying the fruits of such an expansive collection of spirits. Then again, that was a quality of the Nine Heroes that mystified me. They were dedicated, resourceful, and utterly without the ability to enjoy their conquests. Parties and feasts were the pleasures of other conquerors while only the next triumph awaited our foe. I wondered if that was part of the reason they were such bastards. The sober, clear-thinking monster was a far more insidious threat than the drunken, lecherous one.

Interesting thought.

Looking around for the exit, I found a staircase leading up to the main floor quickly enough. "I think the study of magic is the key. Magic uses the same principles as the gods' own abilities. It's just they tap into the power directly while magic uses some form of system as an intermediary."

"I've never had a head for magic," Regina said, sighing. "Too much philosophy and not enough practical application. I'm fine with the mathematics and science, always had a head for both, but I never quite understood the symbolism and other rot."

"Yet, you used healing magic and mind-control magic today."

Regina shrugged. "I have been getting...help."

I knew who she was referring to. "The Trickster."

"Yes."

"I am horrified and yet not so hypocritical to condemn you for it."

"I keep my wits about me, Jacob. He is a lying, scheming, and evil snake, but he cannot control me any more than he can control you. We need power to be able to defeat the Nine Heroes and the Lawgiver, which he is able to provide."

"At a price."

"No price yet."

"The price of accepting his help. We are deeply embedded in his and his brother's web, fighting a war of their design."

"It will be the last one."

"Let us hope." I paused. "The one thing that confuses me is, if my theory is right, then why can't the Lawgiver just...will us away? If he can alter the universe with, as you say, a snap of his fingers, why not make us disappear?"

"Unless he can't," Regina said, "and he's less of a god and more of a magician."

"Perhaps," I said. "We don't know what's going on."

"You think it's because we're still following his plan."

"Defiance may not be possible."

"I refuse to believe that. We'll stop the Nine then the Gods Above. We are not the Lawgiver's slaves."

The Trickster chuckled.

The pair of us reached the door at the top of the cellar stairs. It was a heavy wooden square with a large golden hoop, an old style of architecture versus the empire's elaborate knockers and handles.

Regina gripped her sword pommel. "Are you ready?"

"Yes." Truth be told, I would have been a lot more confident if Serah was present but if wishes were fishes then the Merrow would rule the world. It would be a tragic end to our story if we both ended up dying here.

But an epic conclusion to Hellsword and Redhand's story, the Trickster said. *Everyone is the hero in their own tale.*

And death is the ending to all, I rebutted. *Even you.*

Perhaps.

I couldn't help but ask the question that was weighing on my mind, though. "Which is our priority, though, killing Hellsword and Redhand or rescuing your cousin?"

Regina was silent.

"Regina..."

She closed her eyes. "My head says that killing them should take priority and Gewain would agree. My heart says he is my family and I would let them go to get him back. It's foolish of me."

I made a—perhaps foolish—decision. "He should take priority."

Regina stared at me. "Truly?"

"Jealous as I may be, I am comfortable sacrificing military advantage for your peace of mind." Besides, the earlier channeling I'd felt around the magical reservoir was absent now. Whatever they'd been planning, they'd stopped.

Or were already done.

Perhaps Serah is dead, the Trickster said, *and you've already lost.*

I refuse to believe that.

As you wish.

"Thank you." Regina walked past me up to the door, keeping a lookout for any wayward servants of guards that might be about. "Are your sure our cloaking spells will hold against someone like Hellsword?"

"No."

"You are a *terrible* partner-in-crime."

"I know."

Regina paused. "You know, you have no reason to be jealous of me and Gewain. I had a silly infatuation—"

I placed my hand on her shoulder. "Another time."

Regina nodded. She then closed her eyes and reached for the door handle. "We will kill Hellsword and Redhand unless my cousin is in grave peril."

"Agreed."

The two of us headed through the boggan-run kitchens, the four-foot-tall pudgy-faced workers working in complete silence. They did not notice us but they did not act in a natural manner either and a quick look at their auras confirmed they'd all been ensorcelled. I couldn't help but wonder if this was the future envisioned by Hellsword, an entire world of slaves not only in body but in mind.

Of course, it was also possible this was a recent development, too, with the lords of the palace not trusting the boggans not to poison their food with their families being presently under siege by the army. That, of course, just called into question why they didn't fire the nonhuman staff before they began their persecution.

Have you tried boggan cooking? the Trickster asked. *It's to die for.*

Eventually, we passed out of the unsettling servants' ward into the great hall of the palace. A relic of the ancient Terralan Dominion, the great hall possessed a grandeur that humanity was only now returning to. Its cathedral-like interior was four stories tall with grand staircases and gilded glass elevators leading to much-smaller rooms where the hundreds of bureaucrats that managed the city operated from.

Two grand statues, twenty feet high each, of Empress Anessia and her daughter, Empress Tianne, were present with the former looking every inch the great warrior in her scale-armor while the latter wore a robe and held a book. Like all such statues in the empire, I knew it to be a permanent illusion with two nameless Terralan celebrated underneath.

A great fountain in the center of the chamber was original, though, with a statue of a beautiful platinum-haired woman holding a spear riding on the back of a gryphon in battle pose. The illusion around this statue was tremendously detailed, showing pure-white skin, crystal-blue eyes, the hint of elf blood around the face, and a determination matched only by her will. She, honestly, bore more than a passing resemblance to Regina.

"Empress Morwen," Regina muttered, taking a moment to bite her thumb at the statue.

I raised an eyebrow. That was an incredibly rude gesture. "Really?"

Regina bit both her thumbs simultaneously at the statue. It was an extremely rude gesture and slightly immature. Regina then turned to me and gave me a big smile

"Point taken." I smiled back. It was times like this when I forgot just how much younger Regina was than me.

And that, sometimes, it was good to take a little humor from life. That was when I sensed a presence. It was powerful and furious. It made me sick just to be in its vicinity.

"Redhand," I whispered.

Redhand's presence was like a torch held to the chest, burning and gnashing at my very existence. If there was any doubt in my mind he was the child of the Lawgiver, anthetical to my nature, it was resolved as I approached him. Less powerful, but no less formidable, was that of Hellsword. I prayed our cloaking magic was enough to keep our presence secret from them. We needed to kill them but I wasn't about to sacrifice surprise when faced with either. We needed every advantage we could get.

My dear Jacob, are you scared? the Trickster asked.

Terribly. I am scared of losing Regina, of losing Serah, of perishing so I can't spend more time with them, and of failing all of the people counting on me.

Shameful, the Trickster said.

I disagree. Those who have nothing to lose have nothing to fight for.

The Trickster, curiously, fell silent.

"The entrance to the dungeon is this way," Regina said, staring at several of the perfumed Imperial city-born bureaucrats we passed by unnoticed. They were dressed in various shades of soft blue and white, the colors of the empress, and it was kind of dissonant to know those colors had become feared throughout the nation.

"How do you know?" I asked, wondering if she'd picked up on something I'd missed.

"I just do," Regina said. "There's no sewer entrance and it's in the middle of the palace rather than below it."

"A curious design choice."

"Everything about this place is curious."

She had a point.

"Redhand and Hellsword are between us and the dungeon," Regina said, her voice still betraying uncertainty. "It looks like fate has decided who our primary objective would be."

"I don't believe in fate."

"I do. Something not even the Lawgiver can defy."

"On that we agree."

We came closer and closer to our targets, moving from the entrance hall to a series of large, luxurious chambers full of uniformed officers, rich merchants, and bureaucrats. Listening into their conversations talked of the northern continent's richness and bounty—timber, gold, iron, tin, and more. I found myself surprised they were speaking of dividing it up given Hellsword's earlier conversations about a peace treaty between us but perhaps shouldn't have been. The Nine had come to power on the backs of military victories, advantageous marriages, gross bribery, and the sudden deaths of many powerful noblemen. They needed a war to unite their followers.

A short victorious one.

They wouldn't get it.

My enhanced senses picked up the sound of Hellsword's voice trailing down from the end of a hallway that led to a metal doorway that I suspected was the entrance to the palace dungeons. The voice wasn't coming beyond, though, but the next door over in a series of them. Hellsword and Redhand were right by us now, just waiting to be assassinated.

We just had to pick the right moment to attack.

"I am growing sick of you, Thermic, and things I grow sick of have a way of suffering for it," a voice, elegant but forceful, said from a nearby room.

"I am immortal, Hellsword," the guttural voice of Redhand echoed out to my ears. "You are not the first popinjay full of piss and vinegar to threaten me. The rest of them are all lying in the grave now, raped, skinned, beaten, or worse."

I looked to Regina, who looked ready to draw her sword and charge into the next room to begin stabbing everyone inside. I shook my head and gestured to the room immediately beside it.

We needed to know what sort of defenses they had, if any. Regina, reluctantly, nodded, and we headed in behind me. Inside there was a boggan maid straightening a portrait inside but she didn't see us and departed almost immediately. After closing the door behind her, I locked it.

The room was some kind of operations chamber with stacks and stacks of maps spread about the room. Nothing was of particular strategic significance but there were markings and notations that indicated they were keeping track of my armies' movements in the Northern Wastelands. Also, that the Imperial Army was spread thin across the continent and many units were engaged in constant movement with little strategic reserve.

"I am not limited in killing you," Hellsword said. "Imagine, for instance, me bestowing upon you a conscience and a bit of good sense! What were you thinking trying to incite a massacre against the Fir Bolg? We had a plan!"

Gone was Hellsword's cool, calculating nature from our earlier conversation. He sounded desperate and worried now.

An attitude I rejoiced in.

"A plan I decided to alter," Redhand said. "You and the others are too soft hearted. It comes from believing your own propaganda. Nine Heroes? Bah! Morwen truly believes you can unite the twelve nations into a single Imperial state without spilling oceans of blood. Bloodthorn, at least, understood you needed to make examples. His death has left you all weak. What were you thinking, talking to Riverson?"

"I was thinking of peace," Hellsword said.

Redhand snorted. "While we prepare to annihilate him."

"Yes," Hellsword said. "Convincing him we meant no harm would have bought us valuable time to finish our plans."

I gritted my teeth at that revelation.

"Ha!" Redhand said. "Now I remember why I like you."

"I might have agreed to a truce, actually, but Morwen would never consent. She mourns Bloodthorn more than she ever did her husband," Hellsword said. "Her father was of House Rogers and their deaths left her with a rage that threatens to consume the empire. The only way the Triumvirate could piss her off more would be to harm her sons."

"With good reason," Redhand replied. "I'm genuinely surprised those children are the old emperor's, though I thought he was terrified of sex because it imperiled his soul or something."

"They're Emperor Stephen's," Hellsword said. "Though I doubt they ever shared each other's bed again after the second child was born. Stephen's death was fortuitous and I sense the hidden hand of Jassamine at work. She wants these fools destroyed every bit as much as Morwen."

"And yet you argue for peace and half-measures here," Redhand said.

I exchanged a look with Regina, we needed to know more. It wasn't every day your enemies talked about their plans in front of you. I waved my hand over the tapestry-decorated marble walls with air slits to reveal the contents of the room beyond. Before a roaring fire, Redhand was standing across from Hellsword and the two were looking decidedly irritated with one another. Hellsword looked much the same from my earlier encounter with him, holding a golden goblet filled to the brim with a black-colored wine. However, he was nervous looking and entirely absent of the confidence he'd earlier possessed.

Also half drunk from the looks of things.

"Once this is done, you need to disband your forces," Hellsword said. "We can't let the race hatred and horrors you planted here infect other lands—however effective they were in getting things done."

"I'll do what I must," Redhand said, smiling. "Always play your enemies off against one another. The blade stuck in your foe's throat by another is two less aimed at you. If we make the nonhumans and humans hate each other enough, both sides will beg for us to intervene."

"That is not our cause," Hellsword said.

Redhand looked at him with disdain. "Our cause is victory and I'm the hammer bringing it about. You're just the man who sweeps up after me."

"I am a surgeon's blade, you are a cudgel." Hellsword took a long drink from his goblet. "We've been doing just fine uniting the provinces without your games. You and your fucking thugs create more trouble than you put down!"

Redhand shrugged. "Jassamine wants a single united faith, a single united culture, and a single united law. All of which means change and change means blood. Do you think the King Below and his whores—"

Regina had her sword half drawn before I gestured for her to put it away.

"—will be put down by soft words? Is that why you are planning to animate those great statues? No, you need blood magic to power those machines and that requires lives. Just not a few dozen sacrifices here and there but an entire half of a city to burn. I am giving you it. Quicker, faster, and without the need to arm traitors."

"We could have ferreted out the traitors in the city," Hellsword said. "This will simply be a massacre."

Thermic grabbed Hellsword's goblet and drank its contents down in one gulp. "Tell me, how many millions will be killed by your magic statues? Was it not our instructions to wipe out all of Everfrost and its provinces? To destroy a nation? You condemn me for a little Stagmen and Treekiller murder but plan the end of nations."

Millions? What?

Regina's eyes widened.

"Three million, seven hundred thousand, and sixty-three to destroy the Gods Below's Iron Order as the minumum amount of dead necessary to win," Hellsword said, knocking away the goblet from Thermic's hands. "I've done the math. Someone...someone reminded me I should do so."

They were going to use the reservoir to wipe us out.

All of us.

I hated being right.

Regina whispered, "*Now* can we take them?"

"What would you do to save the world?" Hellsword said, his voice low. "I have done many terrible things in my life, but this? This? This is good. It is what is necessary and righteous so that there shall be a future for us all. To avert the prophecy, I will do what has to be done."

"There is no prophecy," I muttered.

"Says you," Redhand pulled out a cigarra from a pouch at his side and lit it with a flame he conjured in the palm of his free hand.

He took a deep puff and blew a cloud of smoke in Hellsword's face. "My father believes. I'm a cudgel, like you say. A monster. I kill, rape, and pillage because it's all I know how to do and it's all I want to do. The thing is, when you're good at something, you should learn to master your talent at it. To direct it. There will always need to be people who do awful things for the rest of society to go on. One's other people point to say are monsters even as they sleep better at night because said monsters are there to get rid of troublemakers and force people to behave. The problem is, Fel, you think you're not that guy. That there's a parade waiting for you at the end of this. There isn't. We're the bad guys—we're just the ones the world needs."

Regina took my arm.

I nodded. We needed to kill them both now.

"How lovely it must be to have the moral superiority of being a murderer while not being a hypocrite. You have opened my eyes to a new way of thinking with your ancient wisdom." Hellsword sighed and took a step back from the smoke. "Whatever the case, the Triumvirate is here. I want you to finish your purge and either kill them or distract them long enough for me to get the guardians working. I must take my leave of you, Thermic, to go speak with our most important prisoner. Perhaps he might still be of some use in leverage against the Unicorn. Gewain still might serve as leverage, even if our plan to send him back as a Traitor's Goat is now impossible."

Redhand chuckled. "I don't think you'll be able to get much out of him. My boys and I got a little…excessive…with him. He won't be lasting much longer. I had him dragged to your lab to see if your apprentices could fix him. From the way he was looking when I left him, I don't think they'll be able to do much."

Hellsword looked like he wanted to strangle his associate.

Turning around, I saw Regina was already rushing to the door and out of it in the second after that.

She wasn't going after Hellsword and Redhand, though, but running to the dungeons.

Chapter Thirty-Three

Regina rushed down the halls, slammed through the door of Hellsword's lab, and drew her sword without any thought to the consequences. I followed, aware our situation was about to go to hell but unwilling to stop her trying to rescue her cousin.

Regina stopped three feet past the door and when I caught up to her, so did I. Hellsword's laboratory was magnificent.

Terrible but magnificent.

Formerly the Governor's Palace ballroom, Hellsword had cleared out the three-story chamber and filled it to the rim with alchemical and electrical equipment. Much of it was from Lakeland, that advanced nation of thinkers and merchants, but I recognized as other parts as cribbed from both Tharadon's workshop and my own inventions in Everfrost.

Twelve gigantic generators were connected around the chamber, mystical dynamos that seemed tapped into the floor where I saw all the reservoir's energy was designed to be accumulated by complicated sigils carved into the floor and walls. The eldritch machines hummed even as green lightning was exchanged between pylons on their top.

The chamber was more than just the focus of all the blood magic sacrifices being worked in the city but also a place of experimentation. Seven-foot-tall glass tubes were scattered about the chamber, each filled with horrifically mutated test subjects free-floating in an orange-gold liquid. There were several tables with bodies on them, their remains having been dissected and jars of organs spread around them. All the bodies were covered in tumors, strange growths, and signs of severe magical mutation. The kind brought about by exposure to the Terrible Weapons. There were workers all around, Hellsword's apprentices, carrying out various labors, scientific as well as custodial.

I wish I could say the sight horrified me but I was too overwhelmed by the sheer breadth of science on display. I had been working for years on adapting the magitech of the King Below with that of the Southern Kingdoms, but it seemed Hellsword had one-upped me and then some. Even more so, he'd taken the still-underdeveloped science of blood magic to a level that was equal to or better than what current alchemists could achieve with the most well trodden disciplines.

Regina, of course, was less impressed. "Murderers! Scum! Brigands! I come to bring justice for your crimes! This monstrous abomination against the gods must be torn down stone by stone! Tool by tool!"

So much for surprise.

Close to a dozen apprentices, all dressed in a less-ornate version of Hellsword's attire, turned to look at us. They were a mixture of sidhe- and human-descent with the majority of the latter being Natariss of various caste marks. There was also an eight-foot-tall steel golem forged in the image of a Imperial centurion with a set of magitech arms that seemed to carry a variety of advanced built-in weapons. Its arms transformed into a pair of cannons outfitted with glowing runes on its sides.

"Down!" I shouted, grabbing Regina and throwing myself on her. The blasts that shot out of the cannons were pure eldritch energy and exploded against the back of the wall, causing a good portion of it to collapse.

A hideous screeching noise blared throughout the chamber, which would have caused my ears to bleed if they weren't magically generated. Hellsword had covered his laboratory with alarm wards and we'd somehow triggered them. It wouldn't be long before Hellsword, Redhand, and whatever reinforcements decided to show up arrived.

"You keep Hellsword and Redhand away!" Regina said, getting up. "I'll take care of these fools!"

"Any ideas how I'm supposed to do that?"

"You're the God of Evil! Figure something out!"

I sighed, wondering how this always ended up falling on

me. Then I saw Regina knock away a blast of the golem with her sword and then another before swinging her blade and releasing a galestorm of flame that consumed five of the apprentices at once. If she could pull that off, then I almost certainly could do something similar.

Stumbling back to the damaged entrance, I dodged out of the way of a series of fireballs and bolts of lightning hurled by the apprentices from wands. They were ill practiced in the use of such things and the enchantments woven into my armor gave me the strength to move quicker than them as well redirect the closest of attacks. Each packed quite a punch, though, and I could feel my defenses weakening.

Reaching the still-standing door next to a large collection of rubble beside it, I sensed dozens of powerful spells woven into the defenses of the laboratory. Hellsword had made it virtually impregnable but had made the simple mistake of assuming he'd have the opportunity to lock it. The spells were set to only be utilized by Hellsword or his apprentices and I didn't have time to work around it.

Holding out my right hand, I telekinetically dragged one of the dead apprentices at Regina's feet, re-animated his corpse, and had the creature cough up a disgusting command word that caused the laboratory's glowstones to emit a bright shade of red.

"Garrhhhh!" the undead burnt face of the apprentice yowled beneath me. I snapped its neck and got up.

By the time I got up, almost all the apprentices were dead, a good portion of the lab equipment was destroyed, the scent of formaldehyde was everywhere, and Regina was in a battle with the steel golem. The creature wielded two electrified swords that moved faster and with more force than any human was capable of. The machine was also significantly more graceful than it should have been, more like a dancer than a gigantic lumbering hunk of metal. Regina conjured a glowing shield to block two of its blows then stabbed it in the chest with her blade.

"Shatter," Regina commanded.

The steel golem promptly exploded into a dozen pieces across the ground. The scent of formaldehyde was joined by one of oil and smoke. Tiny mechanisms were everywhere and a few of the parts continued to move despite the machine's destruction.

I sighed. "I liked these things better before they were made from clockwork."

"Clockwork? Where have you been for the past two centuries?" Regina asked, looking back.

"Enslaved."

One of the apprentices, who had been playing dead, lifted a wand behind her. Regina spun around to block the lightning with her shield then brought down her foot on the woman's face. What ensued was not pleasant.

"How much time do we have?" Regina called over.

I could already hear Hellsword tearing down the spells outside of the door. Looking at the complicated series of wards and glyphs, I drew *Chill's Fury* and slammed it into one of the connecting runes. That would prevent Hellsword from simply invoking his power to bring down the barrier, in effect 'breaking' the spell by leaving it up.

"Not long," I said, looking up. "Still, we're benefiting from the fact that the more complex the spell, the easier it is to ruin."

"I sense my cousin's presence here," Regina said, looking around the chamber. "Gods Above and Below..."

"Allow me to help."

"No," Regina said, shaking her head. "I don't know enough about any of this to know what Hellsword has been doing. I can sense it's the heart of his plan. Go...smash it up or something."

I stared at her, wondering if she wanted me to literally do that or just needed to do this alone. "As you wish."

Walking over to one of the corpses, I leaned down and placed my hand on their foreheads before drawing as much knowledge as I could from the deceased apprentice. It was only a flash of insight here and there but told me the machines around me were channels for the resevoir of energy beneath me. Hellsword and Redhand had all but confessed to their plan to re-animate the ancient Guardians of Kerifas to destroy Everfrost—my necromancy merely confirmed it.

It was an audacious plan, truly, making use of the relics of a culture that had been millennia more advanced in magic as well as science. It was a testament to Hellsword's ingenuity that I believed he very likely could do it. Smashing the machines wouldn't do anything from my limited understanding of our situation since they were designed to simply process the energy into the guardians.

This had been in the works for months.

Imagine the juggernauts sitting in the bay at your command, the Trickster whispered, his voice now seductive and powerful. *The hundreds-foot-tall statues would intimidate any army in the world into surrender or retreat. They are immune to magic, weapons forged in this age, and all but the power of a god. Each of them can bring down death and destruction on an unprecedented scale with eyes that rain down flames as hot as the sun. You could defeat the empire in an hour and then move to G'Tay and Indras. Other worlds...*

You mock me.

Do I?

You want there to be a protracted war between the Nine and me.

No, dear Jacob. My brother and I want one of you to conquer the other completely. There are worse things out there than us, and it is time to end our squabble and prepare for them.

Liar.

Believe as you will.

I found an old leatherbound book next to one of the overturned tables and flipped through it, finding a good deal of the research being done on how to re-animate the guardians. The original guardians had been animated and controlled through the use of Name magic, which was impossible to replicate since the names of the ancient statues had been lost to time. Hellsword was attempting to compensate through sheer brute force application of magic, planning to massacre thousands within the city to provide the necessary power to permanently restore them. Flipping to the final entries, I noticed they had only enough power to animate the statues for a few minutes.

Which gave me an idea.

Walking to the side of one of the humming machines, which I knew now to be called Eldritch Transference Devices, I pulled open a panel and saw the myriad pattern of copper wires and runes within. I adjusted several of the runes as well as created a few of my own before carefully replacing the panel. This device was the one that would carry the orders of the individual who activated the machinery. My idea would, theoretically, sabotage their efforts to control the guardians.

I had no idea if Hellsword had any redundancies in place, though, or even if my idea would work. I just didn't have the time to properly analyze all the material around me. The best solution would be to keep Hellsword and Redhand from activating the machines or destroying them outright but even that would do little to stop them as there was nothing that would prevent them from starting this project anew in another city or here again should we fail to take Kerifas.

"Jacob!" Regina called.

Rushing over to her side, I saw she'd shattered one of the tubes containing a body and dumped its contents onto the ground. I was stunned to see the still-living form of what I presumed to be Gewain ap Whitetremor. The sight of him was enough to make me recoil, despite all the terrible and horrible things I'd already seen in this lab.

He'd been flayed.

I could tell he'd been subject to other tortures, what kind I couldn't say, but the front of his chest had been sliced away to reveal the muscle beneath. Mystic runes were branded into the gory mess. It was flesh-magic designed to keep him from dying even as they did nothing to help with the healing or pain.

Gewain's face, which must have once been one of the most beautiful sights in Creation, was all but destroyed. They'd removed his teeth and used a brand to destroy the right side of his face as well as gouging out both of his eyes. His long white hair hung in stringy patches from his head, most of it having fallen out from whatever tortures they'd used on him. His right arm, made of bronze clockwork, was hanging uselessly at his side, having been damaged with hammers. Gewain was dying now, the tube's contents having been preserving his life. There was nothing we could do for him now.

"You monstrous bastards," Regina muttered, cursing under her breath. "We're going to help you Gewain, I promise."

"Regina?" Gewain said, somehow miraculously speaking despite his condition.

"I am here. With my husband, the King Below. We have come to rescue you."

Gewain actually managed to give an anguished last laugh through struggled breaths. "Save the people of this city instead... Save...."

Death was not dignified like it was in stories, and he babbled on for several more agonizing minutes as Regina tried but failed to heal him. There was no life force to steal, though, not even from the mutated twisted wretches around us. In the end, I sucked away the last of his life to give him the peaceful death he deserved.

"I'm sorry."

Regina closed Gewain's eyes with her fingers, then stood up. "This is not your doing, Jacob, but our enemies'. Did you find out what you needed to?"

"I think so."

"Think so or know so?"

"Yes."

Regina nodded and drew *Starlight* from its sheath. "Then let us show them how we in the North deal with our enemies."

"Yes. Let's."

I lowered the barrier.

CHAPTER THIRTY-FOUR

Much to my surprise, only Hellsword and Redhand entered. A group of Imperial soldiers were behind them, but after a swift look from Redhand, they exited down the hall. The reason for such was heard soon after: there were the sounds of fire and spells within the Governor's Palace. Neither of the two Usurpers looked concerned but the attack didn't sound like a small incident but a full-scale assault.

"Trouble?" I asked, keeping *Chill's Fury* in a ready position.

"It would seem the death of the last dragons at the hand of your witch, aided by some of the dragon riders taking bribes from an unknown source. This has resulted in a uprising against our regime. Some idiot bard left rumors that I had taken to animating the dead to kill the citizens who revolted and it coincided with a massive attack of your creatures." Hellsword drew *Plaguebringer* and held it before him. "It seems I'm going to have to have a talk with Rose."

"You're not going to be able to talk with anyone ever again," Regina said, the fury in her voice almost palpable.

"If you say so." Redhand gripped his great-axe tightly. "I will say it's going to be a bloody good time putting this revolt down. It's going to be weeks of fun before we whip this city back into shape. Well played."

Hellsword shot Redhand a look that could have melted steel. "Remember whose side you're on."

"The Lawgiver's," Redhand said, smiling. "Someday I'm going to share with you what that means and why it doesn't matter who wins today."

I was tempted just to attack, to use my knowledge of the guardians to turn them against the Usurpers, or toss off a spell. Seeing what they'd done to Gewain and how it was affecting Regina made me want to kill the pair. But knowing what I knew about the prophecy? Knowing how this was all a sick, twisted, joke? I had to try. Try to keep this from escalating.

Foolish, the Trickster said. *Admirable, but foolish.*

"The conflict between us was pre-arranged by both the Lawgiver and the Trickster," I said, keeping my eyes squarely focused on the two warriors. "The Prophecy of the Black Sun, the Great Shadow Wars, gods know how many other conflicts, they're all frauds worked to keep the Lightborn and Shadowkind at each other's throats."

Regina shot me a glance that made me wonder if she was about to attack them anyway. The look on her face was one of anger, grief, betrayal, and then, surprisingly, resignation. Regina held her attack, but I could tell it was killing her not to cut down the two individuals where they stood and avenge Gewain's torture and murder.

Hellsword stared at me, ignoring Regina and processing my words. A second later, he looked over at Redhand, who just chuckled, as if my figuring his father's plans out was the most amusing thing he'd heard all day.

"Is this true, Thermic?" Hellsword asked. "You alone know the Lawgiver's will."

"Not so funny when it's you who is being moved like a game piece, is it?" Redhand said, not even bothering to look at him. "The Old Humans became bored when they achieved omnipotence. They needed games to divert themselves. Our wars are what they do to pass the time. Good, evil, law, chaos—they're all just colors for the players to tell each other apart."

"It's to provide purpose for our lives," I said, half wondering why I was even bothering to do this.

"If you say so," Redhand said. "I find the people on the ground often make up reasons for why the guy above them wipes his shit on them."

I could *feel* Regina's hatred radiating off of her. My wife stood there, looking like she could pounce at any minute against those who were part of the group that had stalked her for her entire adult life. Yet, muscles taut and the body of her cousin and first love on the ground, she did not attack.

I was proud of her for that.

Sad but proud.

"I know what your plan is," I said, still stunned by the sheer monstrousness of it. "I know you want to animate the Guardians of Kerifas and unleash them unto Everfrost. I know every single horrible deed you were willing to commit in order to prevent us from becoming a threat. I even know your offer of peace was a lie, *but we can end this.* We do not have to follow the paths set out before us."

Redhand snorted.

Hellsword, however, looked thoughtful. "You would make that offer, even now?"

"I could have unleashed the guardians upon your forces. They're not powerful enough to operate for long but they could wipe out every Imperial in this city before they're done. I know how. I'm willing to kill you and the rest of the Nine. I'm willing to bring war to your shores and march my forces all the way to the Imperial city and shove your vile empress's head on a spike. I won't let you threaten my people and I am prepared to do what it takes to eradicate you. I'm not going to if I don't have to, though."

"That's your mistake," Redhand said. "War is written by the winners, no matter how vile."

"But peace is lived by the survivors," I replied. "Let us make a lasting one."

"And you?" Hellsword asked Regina.

"You're the refuse of humanity," Regina said. "I won't sacrifice my people for my revenge, though."

Hellsword looked down and Redhand looked over to him, questioning. "Tell me you're not listening to this shit."

"I am." Hellsword gazed up. "But she should have abandoned her revenge earlier!"

Hellsword swung at Regina's head only for me to block his blade thrust. *Plaguebringer* and *Chill's Fury* sent forth sparks of witchfire from where the two swords met. The two of us throwing each other's strength against one another's while testing our magic in a contest of wills.

Redhand, meanwhile, lifted his left hand and unleashed a hellish torrent of flame that Regina blocked with her shield before the energy construct dissipated and she was forced to flee to the side. Redhand swung around his axe, burying it in the ground even as Regina just barely managed to duck out of the way in time. Redhand had millennia of experience killing, not dueling but killing, and I doubted there was anyone in the Three Worlds who could match him blow for blow.

My gold was on my wife, though.

Hellsword brought his blade against mine and struck again and again, each of his blows sending me a step back only for me to rally and strike anew. *Plaguebringer* and *Chill's Fury* were identical in make, both constructed by the King Below as weapons for his Wraith Knights, but Hellsword had empowered his weapon with countless imprisoned souls. Against any other opponent, they would have allowed him an insurmountable edge but my godhood allowed me to hold my own.

Albeit, just barely.

It was a contest of skill now, as well as sorcery. Hellsword's movements were enhanced with spells and he moved three times faster than a normal man as well as four times as strong. I focused my own spells on divination, ironically enough, giving me knowledge of where he would strike and enhancing my aura. Each of his attacks was thwarted by my blade, his amazing dance of movements and stunning array of assaults all knocked backward before they could ever get at my armored frame.

"I am the greatest swordsman of this age," Hellsword said, hoping to demoralize me. "I am a great wizard. You think your godhood gives you an advantage? I have slain dozens of lesser gods, messengers, and demons. Beings more powerful than you. You were nothing when you were alive, just Jassamine's catspaw in the Shadowguard. A deluded mutt she decided to take pity on and left to die when you were no longer of any value."

He moved like a swarm of bees buzzing around me, but nothing seemed capable of penetrating my defenses. In a way, he reminded me of the waves crashing against shoreline. The fact he managed to make several glancing blows meant nothing as my enhanced demonsteel held against his strikes. "It must be terribly frustrating knowing the limits of your greatness. I was never the kind of great wizards you and Serah are or even the kind of warrior Regina is.

However, I do possess one thing you don't, Hellsword, and that is time. I have had two hundred years to practice and train. You fight like a mad genius, an artist throwing paint at a canvas and declaring it inspiration from the gods."

I left an opening in my defenses, which he brought *Plaguebringer* down to strike at. I grabbed his wrist in midair and he found himself unable to bring it down further.

"Impossible," Hellsword proclaimed.

It was ironic he thought this contest was evenly matched as I was holding back most of my power. If I'd wanted, I could have reached out to Everfrost and drew on the necromantic energy of a million ghosts. The entire World Below was at my command and I was a god, not a mortal. He assumed he was fighting a Wraith Knight and he was but only because I willed it. Not even Regina and Serah suspected just how much I chose not to wield against our enemies. Because every time I unleashed my full power, I felt myself becoming more like the King Below and less like Jacob. Besides, I didn't need that kind of power to defeat Hellsword. Even as Jacob Riverson, not the God of Evil, I was still a bloody killer.

"I fight like a blacksmith," I said, knowing it was time to end this charade. "I know how things are made."

I then contacted every soul in *Plaguebringer* and offered them their freedom. With a push of necromancy, the thousands of imprisoned spirits rebelled at once and caused the sword to shatter in Hellsword's hands. The entire room was bathed in light for a brief moment, blinding the Namtariss wizard. Which let me slug him across the face with the back of my hand, sending him to the ground.

Hellsword was dazed on the ground and confused, which gave me the opportunity to strike. Lifting my sword for the killing blow, I was struck by two bolts of glowing light from his hand. They were painful beyond belief, bolts designed to kill Wraith Knights, and sent me down to my knees. Hellsword's next spell threw a bolt of green eldritch energy into my wrist, knocking *Chill's Fury* from my hand as well as destroying the fingers that held it.

"Blacksmith? As if that was something to be proud of!" Hellsword said, spitting on the ground a part of a tooth. From his hands a series of translucent white chains shot forth and began wrapping themselves around my arms, legs, and throat. "This world has lived under the tyranny of petty short-sighted nobles, mad wizards, and gods for too long. You act as if you are the solution? Fool, you are part of the problem, and if I have been played as a game piece then know I am taking control of the board!"

The last of the chains merged together and began squeezing me. It was not damage to the body but the soul. The Chains of Aibon were a spell designed for the purposes of imprisoning the greatest of spirits and required unimaginable power from the wizards involved. The fact Hellsword was able to conjure it alone, with no preparation, was a sign I was out of my league. I had gotten lucky, it seemed, when I faced Ethinu.

Regina and Redhand were playing a game of cat and mouse throughout the machines beside us. Regina had struck numerous blows against the demigod but each of them had healed almost instantly. Regina's armor had managed to absorb a similar number of blows from Redhand's axe but it looked like she was favoring one arm over the other. There was also a burn on the right side of her face where she'd only managed to barely deflect one of the monster's flame strikes. She conjured yet another shield for yet another attack, but was in no position to come to my aid.

"Farewell, Jacob!" Hellsword said, rushing to one of the machine's controls. "Your rebellion will be stopped now along with all of your ambitions. The number of dead in the city will animate the guardians and give us an empire that will last ten thousand years!"

I struggled against the chains, summoning as much strength as I could (at least without drawing on the power of my godhood). I knew the intimate workings of the spells and that its form as a chain was more than just a visual metaphor but an actual symbol of its existence. Concentrating on a single link, I focused all my remaining energy to cause it to shatter and dissipate.

I failed to scratch it.

Hellsword finished throwing several switches and turning dials. This caused the machines around us to rumble. The resevoir of blood magic energy drained away and there was a terrible sense of power that grew from miles off. A look of jubilation and triumph passed across Hellsword's face. It faded when the sense of power began to diminish within moments, and then disappeared entirely within a minute.

Hellsword's face fell. "What?"

"I altered the symbols in the controls," I said, sighing. "Like I said, I fight as a blacksmith. The guardians are presently smashing each other to pieces. No one should wield that kind of power, even for the greater good."

Truth be told, I had sabotaged the guardians as much for myself as any real higher purpose. If I used them here, I would almost certainly use them everywhere and justify my actions through arithmatic. The guardians could only be used as weapons of subjugation. I wasn't so confident of my ability to lead morally that I would let them be unleashed. It was the same reason I didn't simply animate every corpse in the Southern Kingdoms and begin the end of the world. I wasn't sure I could do that but I wasn't sure I *couldn't* either. The power I wielded was all-consuming. It changed me every time I usedit. Better to win by cunning. As long as I won.

Hellsword spun around and stared at me before actually giving a short laugh. "I really should have seen that coming."

"Yes, you should have."

Hellsword seemed almost relieved and I suspected, no matter how many atrocities he'd committed over the past decade, he'd developed enough of a conscience not to want to destroy Everfrost. We were not so different in that respect. That wasn't going to keep him from killing me, though, and all my efforts had done little more than give me access to my minor spells like telekinesis and witchfire. Not exactly the sort of stuff that could defeat an archwizard and master swordsman like Hellsword. I could draw on deeper magics, the kind only gods had access too, but the consequences of such could wipe this city off the map. No, I would fight on a lesser front even if it disadvantaged me.

"Say hello to the King Below for me when you reach wherever gods go when they die," Hellsword said, conjuring a spirit blade of glowing light magic. It trembled with power and I knew it was infused with all the wizard's power in the same way I had tried to strike at my chains with mine.

"You assume he's dead."

Hellsword charged, aiming the blade's tip at my skull.

I closed my eyes and concentrated on a piece of glass, sending it skidding against the side of Hellsword's femoral artery. Without a barrier, he was left unprotected and blood began to pour out of the wound profusely. Falling to the ground, his sword dissipating to nothingness, the wizard covered the wound and struggled to heal it.

That gave me time to grip *Chill's Fury* with my mind and send it spinning at Hellsword's throat. His eyes widened in the split-second before his head went flying off. I collapsed to one side, that action having left me exhausted and bereft of strength.

Some god I was.

Turning over despite my efforts and the excruciating pain the Chains of Aibon inflicted, I struggled to see the battle between Regina and Redhand. I dreaded the possibility that millennia of fighting, immortality, and his absolute utter disregard for life would give the monster an advantage over my spouse. That she was like Hellsword, gifted, but lacking the experience to defeat the horror.

I should have gone with my gut instinct.

"Have you ever fought someone who could fight back?" Regina said, holding the decapitated head of Redhand before her by its hair. She was addressing the immortal with a look of utter contempt on her face.

The head's mouth moved up and down but no sound escaped its lips. The immortal's body was chopped into five pieces on the ground, each appendage having been kicked away as well as set on fire. Already I could see the head starting to form a new spine and sinew, though.

"Jacob, I need you to freeze the head of our good friend here," Regina said. "We will then bury it in concrete at the base of Everfrost or toss it in the deepest hell we can find. Redhand is immortal, but I doubt that will mean much if he's locked in demonsteel chains in a place where even the air in one's lungs freezes."

I was impressed and appalled by Regina's ruthlessness. "I would gladly do so, but I'm a trifle...bound."

Regina lifted her sword at my chains. "Dispel."

The chains shattered like they were nothing.

I then froze Redhand's regenerating head, dumped it in the closest container I could find, and filled the container with the same noxious substance as the few remaining unshattered tubes around us. I promptly froze it as well, leaving the immortal trapped in a state of outrage, shock, and horror. I suspected that would keep him until we were back at Everfrost and could find suitable accommodations in the dungeon.

We did not have to be savages after all.

However tempting that might be.

Regina looked around the corpse-strewn and bloody ruins of the lab. "So this is what victory over your mortal foes feels like."

"Regina—"

I didn't get a chance to say more before half of the ceiling collapsed due to a runestone smashing the floor above us.

The revolution was bringing the Governor's Palace down around our heads.

CHAPTER THIRTY-FIVE

The Governor's Palace was in chaos.

The spells that kept all the servants subdued had faded with the deaths of Hellsword and Redhand. As a result, the hundreds of nonhumans were in a state of panic as well as outrage. The guards were trying to maintain order as the Imperial staff were trying to escape with as many of their possessions as possible.

Runestones launched from cannons had caused the collapse of floors above even as the assault was intermittent, perhaps because the enemy had pierced the very walls of the building itself. Several times, we came across groups of dead bodies of either citizens wielding magic weapons or members of the staff.

Regina and I moved through the palace, both of us still at a fraction of our former strength. I had wrapped my destroyed hand in gauze even if it would have been better to simply let it dissipate. The pain was a reminder of what it was to be alive and helped me solidfy my connection to this world. Redhand's head was carried in a burlap sack over my shoulder, a morbid trophy that was sadly not the strangest thing I had ever acquired from an assassination mission.

Regina held *Starlight* in front of her even with her right hand even as she held her ribs with her left. It was an irony we were able to heal almost any other wounds but the ones we needed most.

Moving into a ruined office as the sounds of shouting and detonations moved closer, Regina took a moment to catch her breath. "Can you do another of those obscurement spells?"

I shook my head. "I drained an elixer's worth of life force from Redhand's thrashing limbs, but even that isn't enough to do much more than divert attention for a few seconds. I am well and truly spent."

Regina nodded, her voice hoarse and cold. "Is magic supposed to be this exhausting?"

"War is this exhausting. Have you never reached your limit before?"

"The battles fought against the Formor were usually over as soon as they began." Regina stared forward. "I always felt it best to make sure any time my troops engaged in battle, the odds were so heavily stacked in their favor that it was a foregone conclusion they should win."

"We called that being a good general in my time," I said, chuckling. I decided to risk what little bit of power I had left to mentally contact Serah. *Are you there, my wife?*

You live, Jacob. Does Regina?

Yes.

Thank…well, us. I am leading the assault, as much as such can be said, on the Palace District. It is more like a riot with looting, rape, and murder.

Can you control the masses? We should try and prevent any atrocities we can.

You or Reginas would be better at that, though I've kept it from degenerating into the wholesale mass murder of every Imperial in the city.

How did you manage this? I asked, speaking more about the fact the uprising Gewain planned had transformed from an Imperial trap into a successful revolution.

You can blame your friend Rose, whom we will discuss later. When he returned to help evacuate the Fir Bolg's children, he let it be known the Burning Fists' dragon riders were subceptible to bribery and not as loyal to their commander as they seemed. He also let it be known the garrison's marshall had no great love of the Usurpers. Most of the Imperial forces withdrew once it became clear the entire city was against them. How is Gewain?

I closed my eyes. *Gewain is dead.*

Serah was silent. *I'm sorry to hear that. I knew him. He was every bit the good and wonderful leader Regina aspires to be.*

There wasn't much to say to that. Good and wonderful people died in war all the time. *We need to get control over the situation until the actual forces from Everfrost arrive. Can you conjure illusions of dragons and our forces? We also need soldiers capable of maintaining order.*

I can do the former but you'll have to ask Kana about the latter. She has since arrested all the leaders of the Golden Arrow outside the city and seized power in your name.

She...what?

Kana has pledged herself to the gods of the Triumvirate and claimed herself as your priestess. That you offered to not only restore Fireforge but also equal rights for all nonhumans as well as land for them in the North. Did you do this, Jacob?

Uh, yes, it was meant to be a threat. This was embarrassing,

Well, as threats go, it's done wonders for morale. You're going to have to get control over her.

I nodded. *We'll handle her when the time comes.*

Probably not the handling she wants. She adores you both. Serah mentally sighed. *Stay safe and come home. Tell Regina I love her.*

I will.

Regina glanced over to me. "How's the situation?"

"Chaotic. Also, we may have accidentally laid the groundwork for a massive migration of nonhumans to our lands."

Regina nodded. "Good. The empire's loss is our gain."

I sighed, trying to figure out how to comfort her despite our situation. Putting the sack containing Redhand's head on the ground, I said, "Regina, I'm—"

"You don't need to comfort me, Jacob. I know you would do anything for me."

"I...see. That still doesn't mean I shouldn't try."

"There is a time and a place for everything."

There was a hard edge to her voice as well as a distance. It was something I wasn't used to hearing from her. Regina was a woman who wore her emotions on her tabard, rage and love both. She was a woman of extreme passions and great honesty. I'd rarely seen her try to hide her feelings but it was clearly what she was trying to do now.

"I'm sorry about Gewain."

Regina's expression didn't change. "I do not blame you for his death, Jacob. I do not think he would have survived if we'd gone sooner, and even if he did, it would have been questionable if he would have been the same man. The Imperials have proven again and again their ruthlessness and the only question is whether we can be as ruthless in return."

"Meeting power for power is a..." I trailed off. I was going to give her a platitude about how one should not degenerate as low as one's enemies but it would be monstrously hypocritical. Also, sometimes, the ends did justify the means. It was just when that was your justification for everything, as with the Nine Heroes, that it became evil.

Yes, evil.

It was strange that I finally accepted that word. There might not be a cosmic definition of what was good or evil, the gods certainly couldn't agree on it, but I believed in it now. I saw a cracked reflection in the Nine Heroes but did not confuse myself with the idea we were the same. Jassamine and I had started similarly, but we had taken very different paths. I was now comfortable with saying, even if I was not good, I would try to be better than her.

"Jacob?" Regina asked, noting my silence.

"I have no answer for you. I would love to mention there is some secret wisdom or truth. That peace and good will shall win the day or winning the conflict against them is guaranteed. The truth is, I have no idea. We are facing formidable foes and even our victory today is merely opening the way for a much larger war."

Seizing Kerifas was a major first step to taking the southern continent as would be recruiting the many allies we had at the Wild Goat Inn. It would not win us the war, though, and was no different a strategy than had been tried and failed by the King Below numerous times before. We had numbers, comparable technology, and if we could convince the Southern nobility and peasantry to sit beside us then we could fight them. The fact the Oghma were sitting this one out was a powerful win and the Nine Heroes had just lost two more of their members.

I wasn't sure we could beat them, though.

We would try, though.

For humanity's freedom.

Easy to hide behind that when you're still in charge, the Trickster said.

Silence, spirit.

As you wish.

Regina gathered her strength, her wounds starting to heal before my eyes and, in a few moments, she was all but healed. Another power of hers I didn't possess. "The stories of war are much more entertaining. They don't mention the rapes, the starvation, the famine, dysentery, or pointlessness of it all."

"No one wants to think their loved ones died for nothing. Yet every war has a loser and that will sting the pride of those on the other side. I sometimes wonder if every war is a result of the previous one, spinning out into eternity."

"Can the cycle be broken?"

"No, war...is eternal. Men and women killing each other for reasons relating to wealth, pride, or because they want to be something more than merely alive. It doesn't change. That doesn't mean it shouldn't be fought, both in terms of cause and to end it."

"That does go in the book."

I chuckled. "Yeah, I think that actually might be worth writing down."

Regina stared upward at the ceiling as we heard another runestone explode. "I will end war on the Three Continents."

I stared at her. "Regina..."

"You made your choice to be willing to fight for those you loved and those you cared for, Jacob, and I respect that. Now do the same and respect mine. I cannot end the conflict with the Usurpers peacefully but I will unite the empire with the Iron Order. I will enforce a peace if I cannot negotiate one. It will be a bloody, nasty, and ignoble business, but maybe we'll actually be able to change things."

"You think you can change human nature?"

"I can damn well try."

I paused and thought about that. "So many of our enemies believe everything they do is in the name of righteousness. The Usurpers believe the killings, slavery, and torture is all done to make the world a better place. The Trickster and Lawgiver believe they can do the same through giving people distractions. Now we join their ranks. In the end, I suppose that's the lesson from it. Everyone wants a better world, but everyone disagrees about what constitutes one. Our vision is perhaps no worse than anyone else's."

"Thank you, Jacob."

"Don't thank me just yet. We've still got a war to win."

"We will."

"Why?"

"Because we're the heroes." Regina smiled.

I chuckled. "I suppose we are."

Regina drew *Starlight* and we headed out into the ruins of the governor's palace, fighting guards and helping the servants escape. We passed by the fallen form of Prince Alfreid along the way, just another casualty of the carnage.

The Sixth Great Shadow War had begun.

To be continued in:

WRAITH KING

Book Three of the Wraith Knight Series

ABOUT THE AUTHOR

C.T. Phipps is a lifelong student of horror, science fiction, and fantasy. An avid tabletop gamer, he discovered this passion led him to write and turned him into a lifelong geek. He is a regular blogger and also a reviewer for The Bookie Monster.

BIBLIOGRAPHY

The Rules of Supervillainy (Supervillainy Saga #1)
The Games of Supervillainy (Supervillainy Saga #2)
The Secrets of Supervillainy (Supervillainy Saga #3)
The Science of Supervillainy (Supervillainy Saga #4)
The Tournament of Supervillainy (Supervillainy #5)

Esoterrorism (Red Room Vol. 1)
Lucifer's Star
Straight Outta Fangton

Cthulhu Armageddon (Cthulhu Armageddon Series #1)
The Tower of Zhaal (Cthulhu Armageddon Series #2)

Wraith Knight (Wraith Knight Series #1)
Wraith Lord (Wraith Knight Series #2)

I Was a Teenage Weredeer (Bright Falls Mysteries #1)
A Teenage Weredeer in Michigan (Bright Falls Mysteries #2

Straight Outta Fanton (Straight Outta Fangton #1)
100 Miles and Still Vampin' (Straight Outta Fangton #2)

Curious about other Crossroad Press books?
Stop by our site:
http://store.crossroadpress.com
We offer quality writing
in digital, audio, and print formats.

Enter the code FIRSTBOOK
to get 20% off your first order from our store!
Stop by today!

Made in the USA
Coppell, TX
12 May 2020